Praise for
CITY UNDER THE MOON

"The best werewolf novel I've ever read."
– **Richard Hatem**, writer/producer of *Grimm*,
The Mothman Prophecies, *Supernatural* and *The Lost Room*

"Fast-paced, action-packed and terrifying."
– **Mila Kunis**

"The rabid love child of Stephen King and Michael
Crichton… a propulsive page-turner… I cannot
recommend this book enough."
– **Robin Taylor**, Amazon.com reader review

"The story moved along at a breathtaking pace. The
characters were well crafted and the amount of detail
and research that went into this story is amazing. I
truly felt like I was on a rollercoaster ride."
– **Mike Pickerington** on Goodreads

"Suspenseful and horrifying… a ride unlike
anything you'll find on bookshelves today.
If you like Brad Meltzer or Michael Crichton or
James Patterson or Daniel Silva or Thomas Harris,
you NEED to read this book."
– **Bob Taylor**, Amazon.com reader review

Praise for
FRESHMEN by Hugh Sterbakov

CITY UNDER THE MOON

HUGH STERBAKOV

CITY UNDER THE MOON
Copyright © 2012 Hugh Sterbakov

Lon's quote from Ovid's Metamorphoses: Ovid, *Metamorphoses*, Bk I:199-243. (A.S. Kline, translator). Ann Arbor, MI: Borders Classics, 2004.

Cover Art: Rob Prior
Cover and Book Design: Katrin Auch

Published by Ben & Derek Ink Inc.
Print Version - ISBN: 978-0985245610
eBook ISBN: 978-0985245603
Facebook.com/CityUnderTheMoon
On Twitter: #CityUnderTheMoon
Contact: Info@CityUnderTheMoon.com
Please visit CityUnderTheMoon.com for supplemental material.

Even a man who is pure in heart
and says his prayers by night
may become a wolf
when the wolfbane blooms
and the autumn moon is bright.
   —The Wolf Man *screenplay by Curt Siodmak*

Awwwooooooo
   — Michael Jackson

PART ONE

One

Greenwich Village
Manhattan
December 30
8:29 a.m.

Brianna Tildascow was shocked awake by a bass-heavy club beat pinballing through her skull. Her eyes came to focus on a framed poster of a silicone-infused woman lounging on a Lamborghini.

They still made those posters? They still made guys who hung them?

Yep. And that guy had a bass-heavy club beat as his ringtone.

She fell back onto her pillow. There were her mother's soft features, shiny blond curls and big blue eyes. So perfect, so delicate, so *her mother*…

…staring back from a sex mirror over the bed.

At age 33.

This was going to be an epic walk of shame.

"Absolutely. Of course, sir," said Mister Right Now into his phone as he fretted over a mark on his silk sheets.

She'd gone home with *this guy?* Was the club *that* desolate last night? And was he really flexing his biceps while holding his phone?

"Yes sir, right away." He ended the call and whipped his eyebrows into a dramatic frenzy. "I have to go."

"Okay." First good news of the morning. Now to start the esteem-choking process of gathering clothes. But that was gonna require the world to stand still.

"It's a national emergency."

"Alright," she muttered. She'd faked enough last night.

"The thing about working for the CIA is that your job never stops, day or night. So the vigilance can never stop."

"What do you do for the CIA?" she asked. *Of course* she'd snagged the zipper of her *open for business* miniskirt.

"I'm a courier."

"So you drive things around?"

"It can be very dangerous work."

"It can be very dangerous work," she repeated. Just to hear it again.

"I never know when I'll be able to come out from under cover. Leave your number and I'll call if I can. You'll have to show yourself out."

Wow! But the place was almost the size of a double-wide shoebox! How would she ever find the door through the haze of Kenneth Cole Black?

Another ringtone on the attack: *Bang your head! Metal Health will drive you mad!* Tildascow found her BlackBerry on the night table, next to the— ugh, the K-Y jelly. Caller ID read "Mr. Snuffleupagus."

"This is Tildascow," she answered. The minister of cologne listened while fastening his two-pound watch. "Yes sir, Mister Director. I'll be there in 15 minutes. Thank you, sir."

She ended the call and sighed. No time to whip her mother's blond curls into some semblance of professionalism, and her jacket was too flimsy to cover the slutty nonsense she'd worn last night. She needed to have a serious conversation with herself.

"Who was that?" asked the courier.

"The Director of the FBI, with an assignment from the Attorney General's Office," she said while retrieving her gun from under the bed. "I have to go."

"You work for the FBI?"

"Yes. Where are my shoes—" Yep. She'd worn her strappy stiletto fuckpumps.

"What do you do?"

"I hunt people. And usually kill them. It can be very dangerous work."

"Can I get your number?" he asked.

"Watch out for potholes."

Two
First Avenue at 44ᵗʰ Street
December 30
9:04 a.m.

The morning glare felt like a punch in the eyes as Tildascow stepped out of the taxi. First Avenue was the last of New York proper before United Nations Plaza at the very eastern edge of the island. There were no skyscrapers left to shield her from the cruelty of unfettered sunlight.

The scene was on the south side of 44ᵗʰ Street, a dozen yards from First Avenue. NYPD had blocked off the courtyard next to the UNICEF Building, Number Three UN Plaza. The crowd had spilled outward and was choking the entrance to the Millennium United Nations Hotel on the other side of the street. Law-enforcement officers were shooing looky-loos; the news crews had already been kicked to First, where they were congesting southbound traffic.

Tildascow pushed her way through the pedestrians, loving the odor of New Yorkers in their natural habitat. Her badge got her under the police tape and into the dense crowd of law enforcement officers: UN Peacekeepers, NYPD uniformed and plainclothes, and reps from the Department of State. No better way to screw up an investigation than to add another clownpack of law enforcement officers. Best news of the morning was that she didn't have to deal with any of them; her briefing had been delivered to her BlackBerry.

The victim was Holly Cooke, *née* Deneen, Caucasian, age 52. Her husband, Archibald "Archie" Cooke, had overcome his unfortunate name to become the US Ambassador to Italy and San Marino.

Holly Cooke was a world-class socialite, on the job at black-tie fundraisers, international balls and state dinners. She was naturally gorgeous—a stunning brunette who'd had the sense to let herself age gracefully. But Cooke was no trophy wife; she had a PhD from Harvard in Political Economy and Government. She was also a cousin of the First Lady.

Archie Cooke had recently retired at age 61. He was in the process of wrapping up his affairs in Italy in preparation for a transition to New York, where he would assist the Department of State when his diplomat friends visited the UN. The Cookes had recently adopted a child in Italy, where the process was much smoother than in the US. This was their late shot at a "normal" family.

Holly Cooke had arrived ahead of Archie and begun shopping for a home in the City, according to the briefing. And then something happened.

The courtyard that Tildascow saw was littered with bloodstains. Most were ancillary footprints that came in the aftermath of the attack. The major pooling occurred near the ivy-covered back wall, where they'd found Holly Cooke. A child's stroller lay toppled a few feet away, in the shadow of a Littleleaf Linden tree.

Last night around ten, Cooke had taken her son for a walk. Odd timing, Tildascow thought, but Cooke might've been jetlagged. She'd emerged from the General Assembly Building on UN Plaza, crossed First Avenue, and proceeded west on 44th. She was attacked less than twenty yards down the street, and now she clung to life at Bellevue. Prognosis was grim. And the child was missing.

Tildascow took a moment to figure out how to squat without Sharon Stone-ing the crowd of predominantly male LEOs. Settling on the path of least comfort, she put her knees on the freezing concrete and sat in *Vajrasana*, her meditation position.

The crime scene photographers' dual flashbulbs strobed off the UNICEF Building's wall. Forensics were documenting a backspatter stain that looked like it'd come from the backswing of the assailant's weapon. A spatter guy wielding a tape measure worked to determine the angle of impact.

But it was the stroller that told Tildascow most of the tale.

A forward spatter across the canopy marked the first impact, which had sent Cooke reeling toward that back wall. An expiration pattern on the handle's crossbar suggested that the stroller had remained upright during the melee.

But something wasn't right.

Tildascow peeked over her shoulder, keeping her eyes below any conversation-sparking contact with the other officials.

The attacker had come from the direction of the hotel and swept up on Holly Cooke from a low position. The weapon cut into her, but it also had a blunt component that pushed her backward. A cast-off stain on a pillar a few feet away indicated that the first swing had had some serious velocity.

Cooke had landed on her back, close to the base of the ivy-covered wall—about eight feet from where she was initially struck. The assailant then stood over her and attacked again. It was the backswing from this second assault that had cast that spray on the UNICEF Building.

The backspatter had landed in three streaks, suggesting a pronged weapon. The angle wasn't right for a rake or a pitchfork. And the hospital report said the wounds were too ragged to be the result of a cutting instrument.

It was an animal's claw.

Tildascow scanned the various reddish-black footprints: shoes, in looping patterns to and from Holly Cooke's final position. No animal tracks, not even among the dimmest prints on the outer rim of the scene.

The stroller was another puzzle. The bloodstain patterns indicated that the child had been removed from the carriage after Cooke was neutralized, but the marks on the shoulder straps were…

Tildascow stood up and shook her head. "Excuse me," she called to a police officer, holding her ID in front of her cleavage. "Has the stroller been tampered with?"

"First arrivers said that's how they found it."

Right. What reason would anyone have had to put their hands on the shoulder straps if the kid was already gone?

She reexamined the straps. Blood was smeared on the shoulder guards and plastic clasps, but the lock had been unlatched, not broken. So the child had been taken in a delicate manner.

Too many unanswered questions here. How could a man inflict these wounds? How could an animal unlatch those clasps? Either way, where did they go afterward?

She scanned the perimeter of the blood spill.

And then her eyes crept up that back wall.

Three

Bellevue Hospital Center
First Avenue at 26th Street
December 30
5:12 p.m.

Tildascow watched the sky darken over the East River as her taxi inched south toward Bellevue. She'd spent two hours at the scene only to learn that she wouldn't be able to talk to anyone from the UN, and it'd taken another four hours and her breast assets to gain access to the Millennium Hotel's thoroughly worthless surveillance cameras.

She'd also called the Cookes' adoption agency in Italy. The kid was an orphan and the agency worker who spearheaded the adoption had since retired. They said they'd track her down for a statement, and they'd reassess the paperwork, which had at least been filed correctly.

It'd been a long time since Tildascow had operated far enough aboveground to get caught in red tape, but she hadn't forgotten the bitter taste. Still, as far outside her anti-terror wheelhouse as this case might have been, the Director's office had assigned her as per a priority request from at least the Attorney General, maybe higher. If it took a little brushing up on her people skills, so be it.

So far so good: She'd only made one person cry during her first round of interviews.

Cooke had been discovered at 10:15 p.m. by a passing jogger, who immediately alerted one of the Millennium Hotel's bellhops. The hotel's manager called 911, and an ambulance arrived ten minutes later. The jogger, the bellhop, and the manager each gave exhaustive statements to various LEOs, never wavering on details.

The jogger was the one she'd made cry, when she asked him to slowly and clearly describe the specifics of Cooke's grizzly injuries. Maybe she'd pushed the guy a bit far, but she was trying to gauge the likelihood of Cooke's survival.

The answer to that question didn't come until close to 5 p.m., when she received word that Cooke was not only alive, but awake. Apparently she'd made a miraculous recovery after intensive surgery.

Tildascow couldn't get to Bellevue fast enough. She abandoned her taxi, hoofing the last couple of blocks faster than rush-hour traffic was moving.

Bellevue Hospital Center was established as a six-bed convalescent shelter in 1736, and grew into a cluster of buildings now accommodating more than half a million visitors per year. At some point they'd tacked a glass atrium onto the main entrance's forlorn limestone façade, probably so folks could tell they had that new electricity stuff.

Tildascow's casework had taken her into Bellevue's infamous maximum-security psychiatric ward in the past, but that was guarded by the Department of Corrections. She'd never dealt with the actual hospital police, so she had to ask for directions to their office, a glorified closet just off the lobby.

Her badge earned her an escort to Cooke's room: a petite lad sporting guyliner. He gave her eveningwear a sneering nod of disapproval, so she mentally counterattacked by pegging him as a wannabe female impersonator. Their silent war carried through the first-floor hallway and into the elevator, where Tildascow removed her shoes to give her blisters some air.

The lad hated her stilettos just as much as she did.

Finally, they reached the fourth floor and Barbra Streisman sang goodbye with a ringing "THANK YOU." It would have been unprofessional for Tildascow to draw her weapon, and she could think of no other response.

The elevator opened to a picture window overlooking First Avenue.

The sun was fully gone; this clawed magician had almost a full day's lead.

Two plainclothes NYPD detectives were in Holly Cooke's room, which meant the UN blind-closers hadn't yet arrived. Tildascow knew she'd lose access to Cooke the moment they did, so she couldn't afford to politely wait for the cops to finish their business. The FBI and NYPD had a decent relationship, but nobody liked to be sent to the locker room early.

She showed her ID at the nurse's desk across from 424. "I need to talk to the doctor who saw Holly Cooke last night."

"Oh God, another?" the half-asleep nurse whined at her badge.

"It's been a long day," Tildascow responded. In other words, *Shut the fuck up and do your job.*

"That would be Dr. Kenzie," the nurse said, nodding toward a petite brunette in a white coat.

Kenzie was already fielding questions from a uniformed cop. She looked unkempt and pale: no make-up, no hair product, and dry hands with no nail polish. Like an old woman trying to burst out of her young skin.

As Tildascow approached, she pulled frizzy blond strands from her ponytail. FBI Interrogation 101: "Familiarity mirroring." Agents are taught to mimic their subjects' disposition and intonation, creating the illusion of a fundamental bond. *Hey, man, I'm the same as you.*

"… I don't know what else to say," Kenzie hissed at the cop. "I've already answered the other officers—"

"I understand, ma'am, but we all have our jobs, and I can't let you leave until I personally get these details—"

"Excuse me," Tildascow interrupted. Kenzie was set to boil, and then she'd be totally uncooperative. Tildascow had no choice but to immediately sack the cop. "FBI Special Agent Brianna Tildascow. Officer…?"

"Dougherty," sighed the cop.

"If you don't mind, I'll take it from here."

"Have a good day, ma'am," he muttered on his way off.

"I'm sorry for this," Tildascow said to Kenzie. "We're all frantic because Ms. Cooke is a VIP of sorts. Look at the clothes I'm wearing…"

Kenzie's face soured further. Tildascow picked up the read and swerved to follow. "I didn't even have a chance to change from undercover work. I mean, *look* at this."

Kenzie's eyebrows rose, and Tildascow knew she'd scored a point. "Are you supposed to be a prostitute?"

Tildascow paused, and then decided against self-defense. *Yeah, I'm gonna have to have that conversation with myself.*

She walked Kenzie back toward the picture window, distancing her from the frustrating conversation with the cop. "You see, law enforcement officers have this method of interrogation where they'll ask a suspect to tell their story over and over again."

"But I'm not a suspect—"

"No, of course not. It's just that they have their ways of rooting out the truth, and they think this works." She hit *they* hard—suggesting to Kenzie that *she* wasn't one of *them*. "They'll look for inconsistencies each time you tell the story, to see if it holds up. Sometimes they'll repeat it back with little mistakes, just to see if you correct them."

"Well it's exhausting. I've given police statements hundreds of times, and it's never been like this."

"I understand," she said, "and I'm really sorry. But they're trying extra hard here. And so are we. Mrs. Cooke's child has been abducted." She noticed that Kenzie was wearing the medal of St. Benedict on a necklace, so she tossed in, "May God watch over him."

"It's a terrible sin."

Ding! "With God's help, we're trying to find the man who took him."

"I don't think it was a man," Kenzie replied. "Her wounds were the result of an animal attack."

"An *animal?*" Tildascow feigned surprise.

"No question. Probably a large dog. She had a bite mark on her torso, just below her rib cage." With a conspiratorial whisper, she added: "I hate to say it, but I think it's possible that the animal…" She shook her head, unable to speak the words.

Yeah, there was a good chance that the kid was currently working his way into something's lower intestines. Tildascow had considered that, but she liked her read on those blood patterns—the kid had been taken with care. And there would've been some evidence if an animal had eaten the kid, even if it took him somewhere else for a quiet snack: a shoe, a sock, maybe a drumstick.

After a moment of silence, Tildascow whispered, "God forbid."

"God forbid," Kenzie agreed, waving her medal in the sign of the cross.

And then a colossal *crash* shot through the ward.

It had come from an open room further down the hall. A woman's shriek followed, and then a wet, heavy *thunk*.

Officer Dougherty was the first to head toward the commotion. Kenzie followed, her white coat billowing like a superhero's cape.

A heart monitor launched from the doorway crashed through the plasterboard on the opposite wall. It must have hit the power line, because it ignited a fire and took out the breakers.

The overhead lights went out. Alarms blared. Confusion and fear spread through the crowd.

And then someone leaned out from that doorway.

He was large, hunched over, and moving deliberately, a shadowy wraith in the dim, flickering light. His eyes sparkled orange as they reflected the flames.

The emergency lights kicked in, dropping a sickly blue tint on the hallway. The man in the doorway was gone.

Dr. Kenzie continued toward his room. Tildascow caught her by the arm. "Stay here!"

"There's a patient in there!"

And then a *howl* echoed through the hallway.

Everyone froze, listening intently, as it diminished in slow, melancholy waves and finally drowned beneath the alarm.

Kenzie backed away.

Tildascow drew her Springfield M1911A, the FBI's standard .45. Fuck the wimpy Glock they dumped on female agents at Quantico.

Officer Dougherty approached the doorway, motioning for her to cover him. She nodded and crept in his tracks.

Behind them, the plainclothes detectives had emerged from Cooke's room. One of them yelled, "Everyone get into a room and close the door!"

Tildascow threw her back to the wall next to the doorway and dropped to one knee. Dougherty took the door, weapon ready.

He fired with no hesitation.

At the same moment, something large and pink whizzed past Tildascow's head, hammering Dougherty backward into the electrical fire.

Keeping clear of the doorway's line of sight, Tildascow pulled Dougherty free of the jagged machinery. Shards of glass and metal had embedded in his back, but he'd escaped serious burning.

The pink projectile fell off and rolled across the floor, and then Tildascow realized it was a body—a mangled, decapitated torso in nurse's scrubs. Blood sputtered from the severed throat.

What. The. Hell?

The door slammed shut with enough force to dislodge the metal frame. A bellowing roar emanated from behind it.

Was it a fucking *bear?*

Through the thickening haze, Tildascow realized another commotion was brewing at the far end of the hall. Most of the hospital workers and patients had already fled, but something was happening in Holly Cooke's room. One of the detectives rushed back inside.

But Tildascow had to focus on the room in front of her. She threw her back next to the doorframe. The handle turned. The latch clicked.

Now wild screams from Cooke's room, followed by gunfire. Crashes and clangs throughout the dark hallway. Blinding smoke.

Glass shattering behind this door. The window?

She threw the door open and took the turn.

The room was clear. And devastated. The window had been

shattered. One remaining fluorescent flickered off shards of glass clinging to the pretzeled frame. The other light fixtures dangled wires and plastic, and the heavy bed frame had been twisted silly. Blood everywhere. Syringes, swabs and tongue depressors floated in the red pond on the floor.

And yet, it was oddly still.

Tildascow raced to the window, shuddering as her bare feet splashed in the muck. The night air pricked her face as she scanned First Avenue four stories below. Traffic had stopped; motorists were out of their cars.

But the *whatever-the-fuck* was gone.

More screams from the hallway—there was still another crisis.

On her way out, she saw the nurse's severed head sitting lopsided in the sink. The poor woman's blank eyes were still popped in shock.

The hallway was a chaotic jumble of gore. Near Cooke's room, a—

a dog?

—had Kenzie pinned down, with its massive paws on her shoulders. As it bit into her chest, Tildascow fired five shots from her 1911.

The beast jerked from the impacts, taking all five before rolling off. Maintaining momentum, it sprang up to—

to its hind legs?

—and turned to Tildascow.

The smoke was thick, but this thing was only twenty feet away, looking right at her, and she still couldn't figure out what the fuck it was.

It roared, and she answered with three more shots: good, upper-body hits, knocking the thing back down to its knees. But it was still plenty vital.

Clip empty, she dropped her spent mag, stocked her spare, slid the rack—

But the animal had had enough. It pounced at the picture window and smashed through the reinforced glass.

She raced after it, stepping over bodies and limbs to reach the window. Leaning out over First Avenue, she searched now for a second animal.

Gone. The gathering crowd was still reacting in its wake.

She retreated from the window, and the magnitude of the carnage inside hit her. A doctor had been broken backward over the nurses' desk, a nurse impaled on the metal guts of an overturned gurney. One of the plainclothes cops sat slumped with his ground-meat face in his lap.

In the middle of it all, Dr. Kenzie lay on her back, gaping at the ceiling like a dying fish. "She needs attention!" Tildascow yelled.

Officer Dougherty staggered to her side, dazed and bleeding himself. Kenzie looked like a goner, but at least she had the presence of mind to keep pressure on her chest wound.

Heads emerged. Screams followed. Two hospital cops arrived from the stairs. Their faces went pale as they surveyed the floor.

"Don't touch *anything*," she yelled. "Nobody touch anything!"

She looked into Holly Cooke's room, searching for a bandage— gauze—*something* to dress Kenzie's wounds.

One of the plainclothes detectives who'd been questioning Cooke was face-down in a bed of his own guts. The other was slumped in the corner.

The only sign of Holly Cooke was the imprint she'd left on the bedsheets.

Four

Bellevue Hospital Center
December 30
9:23 p.m.

Tildascow spent the better part of the next four hours giving statements to various law enforcement officers. But no matter how many times she recounted the events, the police were never going to be able to make sense of it. *She* couldn't make sense of it. Scenario after scenario played through her mind, and the only conclusion she'd come to…

Well… There had to be *another* conclusion.

The NYPD had cordoned off the intensive care ward and moved witnesses to a nearby cardiology department for interviews. She'd stuck around and jumped through hoops to hear some of the other witnesses' statements, but it was time to get back on the move.

Ostensibly looking for the rest room, she slipped through the throng of UN, CDC, hospital, state, city, and federal investigators on her way out of cardiology. Passing one door, she caught a glimpse of Dougherty gesticulating wildly with bandaged hands.

As she took the turn toward the restroom and elevator cluster, she altered her persona from witness to investigator, resetting her ponytail, throwing her shoulders back and moving with purpose, and kept going until she reached the IC Ward, where CDC Epidemic Intelligence Service Officers—the "Disease Detectives"—had taken over for the shell-shocked NYPD officers.

From the smashed window at the elevators to the scorch marks from the fire, the carnage stretched thirty feet. At least half a dozen mangled bodies lay scattered in the hall, and left far too much blood to distinguish individual patterns. The closest corpse was the plainclothes detective with the mangled face. As Tildascow passed, an EIS forensic scientist swabbed its shredded flesh and peered at the sample for some kind of clue.

Hey, honey—I think we know the cause of death.

She scanned the crowd, looking for the hospital official—he'd be the thunderstruck guy thinking *"What is all of this going to mean?"* When she found him, a short man in a K-mart suit, the only word he said was "Christian"—no indication whether that was his first name, his last name, or his brand of God. When she asked to see the surveillance tapes, he nodded emptily and escorted her back toward the elevator.

As they passed the second floor, he cleared his throat and muttered, "We have a no-animal policy."

She failed to cover her giggle with a half-assed cough.

The little guy sulked, like she was laughing at the end of his career.

They arrived at the first floor and she followed Shorty to the security office, a nondescript alcove barely worthy of a broom closet. A couple of NYPD plainclothes were waiting outside, their badges hanging from their necks. Their emasculated frowns meant the feds already had the room. She flashed her own badge and left them with a sympathetic nod.

The "command center" was a suffocating room with loud fluorescent lights and no windows. It stunk of stale coffee and lunchmeat belches.

Four agents were huddled in front of the monitors. They'd boxed out a hospital HR guy, who was trapped between a coat rack and a water cooler.

"Special Agent Tildascow?" asked one agent. "It's an honor to meet you. I'm Anderson. Matt Anderson. I'm a fan."

Respect was nice. His brown suit was not. "Nice to meet you, Anderson."

"You want to see it from surveillance?"

"Please."

The hospital still used industrial three-quarter inch video tapes for surveillance, resulting in low-rez images that suffered even further on their tiny black and white monitors. A hospital cop at the controls reversed the jog wheel and the image rolled back, undoing all of the gore the animal created.

The tape began with a view of Doctor Kenzie shouldering her way between the uniformed cops to reach a chart on the wall next to a patient's room.

"That's 424, Holly Cooke's room," Anderson said.

"Do we have another angle on this?" asked Tildascow. This camera's giraffe's-eye view only covered the lower quarter of 424's door; the dark window in the walkway corridor dominated most of the frame. And the whole thing blurred here and there as the camera tried to focus on an exit sign. "And any sound?"

Anderson shook his head.

On the tape, a nurse approaches Kenzie from the observation walkway. The woman seems unsteady on her feet, maybe feverish. They speak for a moment before Kenzie directs her down the hall.

"Who is that?" Tildascow asked.

"Another nurse, a Nancy Laurio," Anderson said, reading his notes. A confirming nod came from the HR guy. "This is the last we see of her. Looks like she's sick or something. Kenzie sends her to lay down."

"Back it up," Tildascow requested.

The hospital cop zipped the video back to the moment when Laurio first approached Dr. Kenzie. She did appear ill, but she wasn't coming to Kenzie for medical advice.

"See how she approaches?" Tildascow said, studying Laurio's body language. "She'd wanted to look at Cooke's chart."

Kenzie points Laurio down the hall, maybe to that back room where it all started.

"Was Laurio on duty when they brought in Holly Cooke?"

The HR guy nodded.

On the screen, Laurio walks out of the frame a moment before Officer Dougherty approaches Kenzie. Their conversation quickly escalates into a spat. In the foreground, a nurse rises from the desk, looks toward that room at the end of the hall, and then goes off in that direction.

That, thought Tildascow, was probably the nurse who lost her head.

Another minute of heated pantomime between Kenzie and Dougherty follows, and then Tildascow herself enters the scene and steps between them. She moves Kenzie back toward the observation window, they speak for a moment, and then the commotion begins. Dougherty, Kenzie and Tildascow leave the frame, and the screen goes black.

The hospital cop fast-forwarded until the picture returned, dimmer now under the emergency lights.

"Here's where it gets crazy," Anderson said.

A plainclothes detective emerges from 424 to investigate what's going on down the hall. He spins back toward Cooke's room, where he apparently sees something that scares the hell out of him. He draws his weapon and fires twice, and then he's struck and stumbles out of frame.

A nurse and a doctor rush toward the fallen detective—and then a dark blur surges out of 424, ramming the doctor with such force that he breaks backward on the desk. The nurse tries to flee, but the creature rakes her back. She spins, hosing the walls red. And then the animal stands on its hind legs.

They could only see it from the elbows down. "This is the best angle we have?" Tildascow asked.

"It's the *only* angle."

The creature pounces onto Kenzie and they fall out of frame, leaving only her quivering arm to indicate the moment when it bites into her chest.

Tildascow's shots come and the creature quakes from their impact, rolls past the camera, and lands on its feet in the bottom left-hand corner of the frame. More shots, and then it smashes through the window.

"Did the doctor die?" Tildascow asked.

"No," muttered the HR guy. "She's in surgery."

Two rooms. Two incidents. Two women, thought Tildascow. *Assuming they never met before the hospital, they had to have had contact before it all began.*

She asked, "Did Laurio work Cooke's arrival at the ER last night?"

The HR guy nodded.

"And do we have that tape?"

They'd already pulled the previous night's video. The tech selected the new deck for the monitor's feed and zipped backward.

At 22:34 on the time code, two emergency medical technicians burst through the back door of the Emergency Department, pushing Holly Cooke on a gurney.

"Let me take over," Tildascow said. The hospital cop slid out of the way and she advanced the video frame by frame, making a mental recording of the details.

In the counterterrorism business, a hand grenade won't do when you need a horseshoe. Tracking is about details, and details are about recollection. Outside of spy novels and TV shows, the concept of "photographic memory" is nothing more than hyperbolic bullshit. Sure, a couple of people in the world can remember details from every day of their life, but some of them can't even memorize their times tables. Even the savants, those with so-called "eidetic memory," are hit or miss when it comes to immediate and comprehensive recollection. No one can make flawless, on-the-spot mental recordings.

No one except Brianna Tildascow.

In the mad scramble to *do something* after 9/11, the Department of Defense ramped up their super-soldier programs with more aggressive leaps into theoretical science. They recruited elite test subjects from federal law enforcement and the military for their "Prime Program," next-next-generation therapies running the gamut from chemical and surgical enhancements of the mind and body to speculative prep for futuretech.

Tildascow graduated from the FBI Academy at Quantico in the spring of 2002. For the first time in her life, she'd been in the right place at the right time.

The program unfolded as a series of escalating "educated experiments." They began with brain stimulant cocktails, which resulted in a lot of quasi-profound philosophical introspection—and the munchies. Soon the docs introduced advanced meditation techniques, which enabled her to pull off some psychophysiological circus tricks like suppressing pain or slowing her heartbeat. Neato stuff, but nothing that martial artists hadn't perfected centuries ago.

The real breakthrough came when she underwent a procedure called *repetitive transcranial magnetic stimulation* (RTMS). The doctors bombarded her brain's left frontotemporal lobe with low-frequency pulses, dismantling some of its subconscious processes. This allowed her to shift into a mental manual drive called *hyper-systemizing.*

In order to minimize its workload, your mind makes use of reliable patterns to enable quick recognition. In a bowl of fruit, you'll immediately understand that an orange is an orange—you've seen oranges before and you know this one won't transform into a robot or spontaneously explode. That process is called *systemizing.*

RTMS short-circuited Tildascow's mind's automatic systemizing, enabling her to shift her perception into hyper-systemizing, absorbing and storing an unprecedented amount of visuospatial detail. Hyper-systemizing mimics the characteristics of Savant Syndrome, but her ability to shift in and out keeps her from being crushed by the onslaught of details that frequently paralyzes savants.

The Prime Program provided excellent tools, but it didn't give her a hotline to God, a key to the universe, or an understanding of why people liked jazz. But once she learned how to really use it, all became clear—especially jazz.

Patterns. Mathematics, music, astronomy, sociology… Everything relies on patterns. Especially human behavior.

And Tildascow's primary interest: hunting.

Even post-RTMS, today's hunting philosophy isn't any different from what it was in the stone age:

You start with your prey's footprints. These days they're found in biometric passport chips, DNA analysis, SIM card and IP tracing, and telescopic, wall-penetrating satellite surveillance. Marry the technology with the simple psychology of human beings—ego feeding, comfort in repetition, and the distracting necessities of biology—and you find patterns.

Men always fall into patterns.

But Holly Cooke wasn't attacked by a man.

The surveillance camera in the Emergency Department had a much more useful angle than the one in the recovery ward. The shot had been framed to cover three resuscitation rooms and the ramp leading to the ambulance entrance.

The double doors swung open at 10:34 p.m. on December 29. Holly Cooke's shredded body arrived on a gurney pushed by two EMTs. They were greeted by Dr. Melissa Kenzie and escorted to resuscitation room number two.

Tildascow's memorization technique was known as the *method of loci*. Her prime subject, or master locus, was Holly Cooke's body. She traced its path from ER's ambulance entrance, through a turn into the second resuscitation room, and into its final position on the room's bed. Every other person or object would be recorded according to their spatial relationship to the master locus. Nonessential information—a fire extinguisher, an exit sign, the motion of the swinging doors, a janitor standing next to them—fit into pockets divided by "key frames," which marked the major spatial transitions of the master locus.

Before Cooke arrived, Nurse Laurio had been prepping the resuscitation room. "There's Laurio," Tildascow said, and the HR guy confirmed her identity with a hum.

On the tape, the EMTs lift Cooke onto the bed. Her gurney and body board are soaked in blood. Laurio attaches a pulse oximeter monitor and readies an IV.

When Laurio sticks her, Cooke bolts upright and throws out her hands. Kenzie gets an arm under her chest to keep her from toppling over the foot of the bed. The EMTs restrain her arms and legs.

Laurio moves into a corner of the room that's obstructed from the camera's view, and then she crosses in front of the bed and washes up in the sink near the door. She seems to specifically examine her arm.

Tildascow jogged the tape backward, shifting her master locus to Laurio for a second pass. She was a good nurse, moving with the speed and confidence of an ER veteran. Cooke had shown no signs of struggle, and the IV insertion was routine. She had no reason to expect—

There.

When Cooke lunges forward on the bed, the doorframe obstructs her hands as they reach full extension. But Laurio recoils, grabbing her arm—

"Cooke scratched Laurio when she was brought in." Tildascow said, turning to the HR guy. "Did she report it?"

"I'll have to check."

"We'll find out," promised Anderson, who seemed startled when she turned around. All of the men's eyes had gravitated toward her ass.

She quietly thanked no one in particular and made her escape. Crossing the hospital's atrium, she kept her eyes on the floor and quickly re-ran the ER video in her mind, combining the passes for each master loci.

"Tildascow!" Anderson called out.

She quickly shushed him: If the UN guys realized an eyewitness was escaping, they'd retain her for more questioning—and if the EIS decided to lock the place down, she might be quarantined.

He gave her a manila envelope. "All the witness statements. And more."

"Nice. Good work, Anderson." She quickly surveyed the contents. The bonus material included files on Cooke, employment records for Laurio and Kenzie, and some photos and video stills. "NYPD just handed this over?"

"Came from way up. They wanted it in your hands. I guess Cooke's a V-I-VIP."

"She is now."

Five

First and 26ᵗʰ
December 30
10:03 p.m.

Some two hundred people were clogging Bellevue's main entrance. The area was awash in noise and lights. Traffic jams, dueling helicopters, police and fire vehicles, and an endless sea of reporters.

Tildascow jostled through the crowd and walked north on First. The crisp air was refreshing after so long in the hospital. It was a clear night. Bright. The moon loomed heavy in the sky, just a sliver shy of full.

She smiled at the dumb idea that had crept into her head, and walked faster. The cold was starting to set in. She never wanted to see this damn outfit again.

As she crossed 29ᵗʰ, something shifted behind a parked car. She heard animal nails skittering across the cement. She made out a glimpse of fur just before it moved into her blind spot.

She whipped out her 1911 and took position behind the vehicle.

Only the one spare mag; what ammo she had left might not be enough to take down one of those animals. But she couldn't just let it go. And no time to call the police.

Deep breath, and she shifted around the car, looking down the barrel—

—at a possum scrounging in the gutter.

Perfect bookend to this day. She kept walking, chuckling at herself. It bloomed into flat-out laughter when she heard her stiletto footsteps.

But still, she stretched her neck around every corner. Those creatures were out there. Had Holly Cooke been attacked by one of them? And then there were two in the hospital.

Had the one infected two?

And if so...how many tomorrow night?

She looked up at the moon again. This time she didn't smile.

A taxi almost hit her at the intersection of First and 30th. At least the driver had the decency to stop. Getting out of the cold was preferable to giving him a piece of her mind, so she pulled her hemline below her ovaries and climbed inside. The cab was a modest four out of ten on the stench chart, a significant victory for the long drive across town.

"Chelsea," she said. The office in Chelsea was the unofficial HQ for the FBI's counter-terrorism squad. And, essentially, it was Tildascow's home. She kept an apartment in Hoboken for her off-season clothes, tax records and stale condiments, but she often went weeks between visits.

The cabbie nodded and turned up the yodeling on his radio. She settled in for the ride, looking forward to a hot drink and a warm blanket—but not the phone call she planned to make afterward.

The file Anderson had collected from the NYPD contained 23 eyewitness accounts. Somehow this was the one spot in the city where no one had a cellphone camera handy.

The first statement came from a hippie performance artist who had been on the other side of First while, in his words, "impersonating a tree."

The windows shattered up there, his statement read. *I think like the sixth floor. A gorilla jump out and lands on top the car. The windshield busted and it was all this noise, people was screaming, and it ran across the street over there. And then another gorilla jump out that other window and go the other way.*

Other eyewitnesses described the animals as hyenas, dogs, cheetahs, or "panthros." One guy, a "clothing designer who blogs on the side," insisted he'd seen a similar event staged by a spontaneous performance troupe in a San Francisco mall.

The best description of the animals had come from a man who'd been escorting his pregnant wife to the hospital. Just as he stepped out of his taxi, the first animal crashed down on its roof.

It was shaped like a human, his statement read, *but it was really hairy and big. It snarled at me and ran away on its hands and feet. And the second one was identical. I've never seen anyone move like that. I don't think they were in costumes. I know it sounds ridiculous, but I think they were werewolves.*

Six

FBI Counter-Terrorism Squad Offices
Chelsea
December 30
11:22 p.m.

Tildascow hadn't scored a proper office until she got her second Director's Award, the FBI's equivalent of the Oscars. Her investigation into an Al Qaeda plot on New York's water supply had revealed a loose thread that unraveled a billion-dollar international electronic banking scheme. It was pure serendipity, but she had no qualms about parlaying the glory into a real office. The couch had come out of her own pocket, but at least she got to pick the color.

She stretched out on the black leather in her cozy jeans and Quantico hoodie, sipping hot chocolate and fiddling with a stupid sleeved blanket. She checked her email, well aware that she was looking for an excuse to procrastinate.

Anderson had sent a couple of updates: three animal attacks reported within the first hour; now the number had grown to seven. More were sure to come. The police were on alert, but it was a big city and those things were crazy quick.

She scrolled to "L" on her BlackBerry and picked up her landline. Shitty cell service; they said we'd have a flying car by now, but it took two phones to make a call.

Tildascow had never before dialed this phone number. She'd gotten it in an email, which she'd never answered.

By design, she had no connections to her old life. No relatives, no relics, no old friends to call and reminisce. No one who knew that little girl with the curly blond hair and the bright blue eyes, the one who looked just like her mom. They'd all fallen into the chasm between the girl Brianna and the Special Agent Tildascow.

Except one, who stubbornly refused to go.

When little Brianna turned seven, her mother had enrolled her in the Brownies, the minor-league Girl Scouts. It was important to make new friends, Mom said. This was supposed to be accomplished at bimonthly troop meetings, which would be held at the home of a girl named Kelly.

The moment Brianna arrived at Kelly's house was precisely when she discovered that there were rich people and there were poor people—and the Tildascows were not rich people.

Their Brownies Troop Leader was Kelly's mother. She was a sharp, well-spoken woman with a no-nonsense aura, which must have served her well in her day job as a big-shot attorney-turned-government-gunslinger. She would arrive for their meetings with an assistant in tow (always a sharply-dressed young woman), and dismiss her with work orders precisely at 5 p.m. Then she'd immerse herself in the girls' baking and papier-mâché follies for two solid hours.

She always made sure to personally engage each of her Brownie mini-monsters during the course of the evening. She'd inquire about whatever little dramas they were facing, and offer uplifting advice in a warm, dignified tone. Soon Brianna felt like she'd found a secret best friend. Most likely, all of the girls felt that way. It was honest mutual respect from an adult they admired, and it positively lit them up.

At 7 p.m., the assistant would reappear with updates from the office. Kelly's mom would vanish for a few minutes while the live-in cook (*the live-in cook!*) served s'mores. She'd make an encore at 7:30, offering cookies to the parents arriving for pickup, and leave the girls with sticker books, fun assignments, and hugs with encouraging whispers.

She was just too damned good to be true. And the girls of Troop 60421 weren't the only ones who noticed. Kelly's mom soared up the ranks until she had nowhere to go but Washington. First it was Attorney General. A year ago she'd become the National Security Advisor.

Brianna knew her as "Mrs. Luft," but her name was Rebekkah.

After what happened to seal that little girl in her past, she had tried like hell to shake Rebekkah Luft. Something about the way she offered affection made Tildascow angry. Or maybe scared. Whatever it was, she'd needed everything gone, and that relationship was part of everything. She did enjoy hearing about her former friend's remarkable ascent, but she kept her eyes averted when she appeared on TV.

Still, she'd often wondered if a few turns in her career weren't the result of Rebekkah Luft's silent machinations. Why hadn't the incidents in her past kept her out of Quantico? Or the DoD's Prime Program? Luck, skill, or Luft?

They'd crossed paths here and there, sometimes in ways that felt arranged. Like the time Luft—then Attorney General—spoke at Tildascow's graduation from Quantico. She'd never done that before, and never did again.

Every time they met, Luft would put a hand on her shoulder, look deep into her eyes, and ask, "How are you?"

She'd never realized how much that question could hurt. Not until it was asked by someone who knew the answer.

The phone rang. She braced for impact.

"Hello?" Luft's sleepy voice made Tildascow feel like she was going to get in trouble.

"Mrs. Luft? It's…" She hesitated too long, feeling stupid, and finally blurted, "Tildascow."

"Brianna? Brianna, how are you?"

"Listen," she snapped, spiking the lump in her throat. "Um… Mrs. Luft, I… I've got… Something happened that I think I need to bring to your attention."

"Okay, but don't you dare call me Mrs. Luft again."

PART TWO

One

Akron, Ohio
December 31
12:58 a.m.

"I swear to God, I'm gonna wolf out!"

That wasn't the most prudent thing Lon had ever said to a roomful of people, but he simply refused to tolerate mockery by inferior intellects.

He'd been dominating the *Magic: The Gathering* tournament—as usual. And this was the big one, the regional qualifier for the Pro Tour. He was just three wins away from a free trip to Las Vegas, and his "weenie-meanie white and greenie" deck had proven unstoppable. He hadn't lost a game, let alone a match (except one to mana screw), when the stupid judge misunderstood the stack rules of his *Tarmogoyf*.

And it was a staple card! Everyone knew it!

The other players laughed at him. Bitter bitches got to feel like big king shits because he got cheated out of a win.

Lon's therapist said that he put other people down in order to feel better about himself. And that, pseudo-philisopho-theoretically, was what kept him from having friends.

The way Lon saw it, he just hadn't met anyone worthy of being his friend.

Well… maybe there was one. But first he'd have to get up the courage to meet her in person.

Lon walked home in misery, kicking every rock he could find along the two-mile dirt road from the comic shop. His hands were buried in the pockets of his ever-present black overcoat, which was more a statement than a practical shelter from the wind. He may have been freezing, but it was too late to call his mom without incurring the wrath of his stepfucker, Frank.

He was a puffy eighteen, maybe the last kid at school who couldn't

33

even grow peach fuzz. Not that it wouldn't look ridiculous on his always-blushing fatboy cheeks, especially if it matched his flaming-red Chia Pet 'fro.

Honestly, he couldn't blame the people who found him distasteful. Hell—Given the choice, even *he* wouldn't want to be his friend. But what can you do about that? Body swapping only happened in bad eighties movies and secret government laboratories.

Life was so much easier on the computer. In his forums, video games, and chat rooms, he was respected for his expertise, his authority, and his mentoring skills. That world seemed less arbitrary. And also, he didn't have to struggle to look people in the eye.

He turned onto the long, lonely road to Frank's farm, and that familiar dread crept into his throat. Even if he didn't get to Las Vegas for the *Magic* Pro Tour, he was going to find a way out of his stepfather's house, and he was going to do it on his own terms. Most of the kids at school were still in emotional diapers, but Lon felt certain he had the clarity to live on his own. He just needed the money.

He snuck through the back door into the kitchen. It was a good bet that Frank was already passed out, but he didn't want to risk an encounter. He'd memorized all of the kitchen floor's creaks. It only took three well-placed steps to reach his sanctuary in the—

"How'd it go, Lon? You win your card game?"

Fuck.

Frank's disingenuous sing-song tone meant that Lon's mother was nearby—and even still it carried an undercurrent of threat. Fucker never failed to turn into a monster as soon as Mom strayed far enough.

"No," Lon muttered as he hurried into the basement. That was where he lived, literally and figuratively. His beloved cave, ten feet by six, containing everything he had in this world.

A black light threw its glow on his vintage velvet posters: Siouxsie and the Banshees, The Cure, Nick Cave. His unfurled futon bed filled the narrow gap between the wall and the card table he used for a desk.

The computer was his Fortress of Solitude, and its layout was supremely specific. His side-by-side widescreen monitors cycled a montage of artwork inspired by the writings of H.P. Lovecraft. An open notepad next to his trackball contained a list of the in-game materials he'd been collecting to level up his *World of WarCraft* character's crafting skills once the new expansion arrived. Against the far wall, two iron bookshelves were overstuffed with his vast library of occult reference material—all except for the eye-level shelves, which boldly displayed the room's *pièce de résistance:* his collection of miniature pewter statues (all hand-painted by the arch-mage himself).

Lon hadn't taken the time to fold up his futon, so there was no room to pull his chair from the computer table. Instead, he took his wireless keyboard and mouse to the bed and bumped up the font size on his Opera web browser.

He was currently administrating six websites. One of them wasn't live yet; he'd been hard at work creating content to launch modernwitchcraftandmagick.com by February first. Another, truthabouttheblairwitch.com, he'd all but abandoned. He usually only got about ten messages a day from his Lovecraft shrine, but his *Magic: The Gathering* site's forum could get up to a thousand posts per day. The others fell somewhere in between. Tonight there had been a little spike on one of his less-traveled pages, ofwolvesandmen.com.

Of Wolves and Men was his master's thesis on *lycanthropy*, the transformation of man into wolf. Unlike his other sites, it was distinctly non-interactive. There were no forums, no feedback button; his contact information was listed only for solicitors of his web design services. He didn't want to hear from the *Twilight* girls who kept pictures of Jacob on their hope chests (although it was a blessing that they'd finally stolen the thunder from the *Buffy* fans who claimed to be wiccans because they knew how to light candles). He'd spent time in the faux-werewolf "community" and become familiar with the "scene," which existed primarily in competing forums and YouTube videos. He'd played their "misunderstood by society" game for a while, even commissioning his own dentures from a well-respected fangsmith. But at the end of the day, those people weren't interested in the truth; they'd just latched onto a clique that'd given them an opportunity to shun society back for their own perceived social excommunication. Lon wasn't looking to lycanthropy for something precious to call his own.

Not that he'd deny his passions. He was a fan of many things: collectible card games, vintage sci-fi, massively multiplayer role-playing games, the women of seventies-era sci-fi television; the fantasy writings of Neil Gaiman, George R. R. Martin, Robert Jordan, and master J.R.R. Tolkien; the artworks of Bernie Wrightson, Frank Frazetta, and H.R. Giger; music of articulated spite; all things *Lord of the Rings;* and much more. He lived to indulge in fandom, and unlike the pussies at school, he wasn't afraid to let his passions show.

But his interest in the occult—in lycanthropy specifically—wasn't a matter of fandom. Even a modicum of research would result in far too much evidence for any educated mind to deny the truth.

No, the *truth* (if such a concept could be removed from abstracts and primal fears) is that preternatural lurkers are all around us. Hiding in the mist, scratching in the dark, flirting with our subconscious... But their dark magicks became hidden eons ago. Those "in the know"—interesting that they called themselves *Illuminati*—forged a dark pact with the Devil (*perhaps,* but not necessarily *specifically,* the Biblical interpretation of such a beast), shrouding corporeal manifestations of evil in alternate planes of existence, thus obscuring the truth so that normal folk might sleep peacefully. But, alas, the human imagination would not be thoroughly repressed, and so our creative minds had invented bastardized versions of the demons persisting in our nightmares, and proliferated them throughout popular culture.

Every society in the history of the world has concocted its own legend of a human shapeshifter! Coincidence? *Please!*

But everything was about to change. The Internet was a new tool, one that could never have been imagined by the silent monks, banished priests, and outcast lepers—those purged from society in order to keep the secret of the dark pact. Righteous warriors, speakers of the dark truths, would band together through new information networks, sharing their intelligence in virtual secret cabals, restoring to mankind the lost knowledge we so desperately need.

Diddle-eee! Diddle-iddle-dee-dee-do-dee-dee!

Diddle-eee! Doo-dee-doo-due-do-eee…

Lon's Instant Message ringtone was the opening bars to *Toccata und Fugue in D minor* by Johann Sebastian Bach, the ubiquitous aural introduction to horror radio plays, B-movies and TV commercials for haunted houses. Pedestrian, he knew. But his head wasn't too bloated for irony.

He reclined on his futon, smiling at its charming creak, and resumed play in iTunes, thus spilling the ballet suite from *Swan Lake* through his wall-mounted speakers. The melancholy theme never failed to remind him of *Dracula*, director Tod Browning's 1931 masterpiece starring Bela Lugosi.

Lon cracked his knuckles as he eagerly read the IM, a beckon from the screen name *GothkGrl*. "Are you there, my dark prince?" was scrawled in purple zombified font.

'Twas the fair Elizabeth, the love of Lon's life. Their affair had begun with flirtatious missives on sundry occult forums and blossomed into six months of heated IMs.

He was working up the nerve to call her, but never mind about that.

"Good evening, my grotesque beauty," Lon typed with a mischievous grin.

As he awaited her response, curiosity led him to open his Internet Protocol tracing program. The surge to his *Of Wolves and Men* website had come from the northeastern United States. New York and DC. Maybe *An American Werewolf in London* had run on cable.

"Evening, hardly," Elizabeth responded. "I'm five hours hence from slumber. And my harridan host womb woke me at an unconscionable hour this very morn, blasting her loathsome radio."

He loved it when she got bitchy.

Lon began typing an in-depth description of the travesty he'd suffered at the *Magic* tournament, but he froze when he heard the cellar door open. It could only be one of two people, and the heavy footfalls suggested the greater of the two evils. He quickly shut his monitors and speakers, leaving his lady love in mid-sentence, rolled under his covers, faced the wall, and feigned sleep.

The bottom of the stairs always took Frank by surprise. The oaf caught a bookcase and paused for a moment, probably ogling one of Lon's *Lord of the Rings* action figures. Several of them had hackjob superglue repairs from Thanksgiving, when Frank had stomped on them during a drunken rant. Great night that was. Lots to give thanks for.

Frank came closer and stood next to the futon, looking down on Lon. "You ain't a-sleepin'," he said in a questioning tone.

Lon wished he could cough up his hatred like some kind of diseased sputum and spit it right in Frank's face. He was also coming to despise his mother for bringing him into this hell, no matter how damn lonely she'd gotten. And for being so stupid that she didn't see Frank for what he really was.

"Maybe I'll just take one of these here action dolls if you ain't awake."

If Frank was going to take one of his collectibles, Lon wouldn't be able to stop him. He'd learned that lesson on the ass end of more than one beating.

His stepfather stood over him for a good, long while, breathing unevenly through his drunkenness. Was he going to pass out, or did he fall asleep on his feet? Or was he imagining something disgusting?

Time passed—seconds felt like minutes.

Could Frank tell he was awake? How long had it been?

Lon felt himself slipping into helpless despair. What was this creep going to do? Why wouldn't he just leave?

Lon's mind always wandered back to the same hole: What had he done to deserve his life? He couldn't convince anyone to like him. Not the kids at school, not Frank, not even himself.

Maybe he deserved these beatings.

The wait was maddening.

Finally, Frank shifted. His leather boot creaked out one final threat. After another moment, he turned and plodded up the stairs.

Lon fought as hard as he could, but still the tears came.

Two
Akron, Ohio
December 31
6:14 a.m.

"Lon, could I see you up here?"

Lon stirred to consciousness, hoping he'd dreamed that voice.

"Lon, could I see you up here?" Frank asked again. The first request had been three-dollar-bill polite. This was an ultimatum.

Mom would have left for work by ten after six. The dust probably hadn't settled in the tracks of her Isuzu Rodeo.

"Up here. Now."

Lon sighed and fumbled for his glasses. What a way to start a day. He looked around for some pants—

Frank started down the stairs.

Lon bolted to intercept him, meeting him midway. If he couldn't avoid a fight, it might as well be upstairs where his collectibles weren't within reach.

"What?" he asked, mustering as much nonchalance as possible while quivering in his tightie-whities.

"You get up here when I tell you to."

He followed Frank up to the kitchen, wondering which flavor of bullshit—

"I wanted to have a conva'sation with you 'bout them cards you play with," Frank said, nodding in agreement with himself as he spoke. His face was a twisted collision of beady eyes, droopy ears, furry eyebrows and a snaggletooth that protruded from the right corner of his mouth. How could anyone have sex with such a man? "How much you spend on them things?"

Lon sighed. They'd had this talk before and it always went back to this: "It's my money, Frank. I earned it myself."

"Yeah, but it's family money. Y'see, I earned the money for the food that goes into your mouth, but I don't see none of that back, you unda'stand?"

Lon kept his eyes on the floor. "Yes."

"Now I don't care what your mom says, you're gonna start givin' back for all's that you's takin' from this family, you unda'stand?"

"I..." Lon sputtered. Agreeing would probably lock him into forking over most of his savings. But he couldn't take a stand now, not without his mom's protection.

Frank threw one of his massive hands at Lon's neck and slammed him against the refrigerator, which clanged in alarm.

Lon couldn't get any air. He clawed at Frank's hand, but there was no competing with the strength of a lifelong farmer.

"Do. You. Unda'stand?" His breath was putrid.

Lon couldn't respond, couldn't nod, couldn't even look Frank in the eye.

"Little pissy fag. You like to fuck boys? Or maybe you think about fucking your mom, hmm? Wish I wasn't in the picture?" Every word fueled his own anger. This was when he was the most dangerous, when he got himself going. Lon had often wondered if Frank might kill him some day. Maybe this was it. No warning. No reason. No pants.

The world grew cloudy, the cold against his back faded, and Frank's taunts warbled away as if they were leaving through a tunnel. He'd felt this sensation before; it meant he was about to pass out. All he could do was hope that he'd wake up, and that Frank wouldn't break any of his things.

Then he heard a new, unfamiliar noise: a rhythmic pounding, whirling in his chest. Maybe the washing machine had come on. Or maybe he was having a heart attack. Then it got bigger, enveloping the room. The rickety house began to shake and Frank gawked at the walls. So it wasn't just his imagination.

Finally, Frank dropped him.

Lon crumpled, and his lungs raged with saliva-filled drags and honks. Each gasp was more humiliating than the last. He couldn't help but cry, even though he knew Frank reveled in his suffering.

That whirling was still pounding at the walls.

WHUPWHUPWHUP.

Two men in black suits knocked at the screen door. They'd just arrived by helicopter.

"I didn't touch him!" Frank wailed, shooting his guilty hands into the air.

The men let themselves in. In perfect David Caruso fashion, they removed their sunglasses and assessed the scene for a long, silent moment.

"I didn't touch him," Frank repeated with more conviction.

The men were looking down on a purple-faced eighteen-year-old lying on his kitchen floor in soiled tightie-whities, and their faces bore no expression.

"Are you Boris Toller?" one of them asked.

Lon rasped, "I am."

Three
The White House
Washington, DC
December 31
8:12 a.m.

Lon couldn't make his legs stop shaking.

The White House.

He was waiting to speak with someone very important, maybe even the President of the United States. And wondering *why.*

Signs pointed to something bad. He must've done something wrong. Something *very* wrong. If it was what he thought it was, Frank was finally going to snap his neck once and for all.

Six years prior, Lon had sent the previous administration a stern letter warning that lycanthropy was a present threat to America. Furthermore, he'd demanded that they send an expedition of scientists and commandos to investigate unsolved murders in Romania. *(Um, and maybe he'd offered to lead it.)*

He should've known better. The government may be slow to react, but they do take that kind of shit seriously.

But come on! It wasn't like he'd threatened the president. Or, at least, he *hoped* he hadn't. Could he have worded something badly?

Oh man, had it sounded like a threat?

Still, though… helicopters? *Really?*

"Can I get you something to drink, Mister Toller?" the secretary asked with a smile. "Something decaffeinated, maybe?"

Lon shook his head. What was *that* about? What did she know?

When he was in third grade, Lon accidentally tripped the sweetest girl in school, Caroleigh Combe. She fell on a curb and broke her two front teeth. As they carried the cutie patootie away—screaming, bleeding, and disfigured from her encounter with Lon the Horrendous

Monstrosity—the playground official told him to wait on Mister Harris' bench. That was where all the bad kids went, where your stomach turned knots as you imagined the cruel fate awaiting you within that office. Nobody knew what went on in there. Or even what Mister Harris' job title was. But that fucker was scary and *Holy Frak, if this chair didn't feel exactly like that bench...*

The open door to the hallway read "National Security Advisor's Office."

They hadn't arrested him. But does the government even have to arrest you? Couldn't they just lock you up and, like, waterboard you?

If something didn't happen soon, he was going to have to go to the bathroom, and it was going to be the kind of visit where he needed to be home. Like when he ate something with lactose, he'd need to spray "Poo-Pourii" to nullify the—

One of the doors opened and Lon stood (well, maybe he jumped, maybe like an alarm had gone off inside his ear). Then he immediately sat back down. *Be cool. The Fonz cool. Sam Jackson quoting The Fonz cool.*

An important-looking man in a distinguished suit emerged from one of the offices behind the secretaries. He said some words, none of which Lon was able to process, and then he squished Lon's hand like an earthworm. The guy was at least six inches taller than Lon, and his slick hair and tailor-cut suit made him look like one of Ocean's howevermany.

Lon felt underdressed and unworthy, like a hobbit in the Matrix. He just wanted to leave.

"Mr. Toller?"

Lon swallowed air and followed the man into his office. It was tight and cluttered and not at all what he expected. He was grateful when he found the nameplate on his desk. *Derek Freese, Assistant to the National Security Advisor.*

"So...Boris. You're probably wondering why we have you here today."

"Lon."

"I'm sorry?"

"My father was… ah…" Lon hated having to explain this. "Well, a week before I was born, Boris Yeltsin announced that Russia was going to stop targeting the United States with nuclear weapons."

"So 'Boris'… happened to you."

"That's why I go by Lon."

"Why Lon?"

"I just do." This had gotten embarrassing enough. "Sir."

"Derek will be fine. And I'll call you Lon. That's a great name," he said, as if it were a malignant tumor. "So, Lon, they tell me you're the foremost authority on werewolves."

What what?

"Lon? Do we have the wrong person? Werewolves?"

"Lycanthropy," Lon blurted. Habit.

"Is that… that's a werewolf, right?"

"Lycanthropy. From the Greek *lykoi*, 'wolf,' and *anthropos*, 'man.' It's commonly misrepresented as a psychotic state in which a person believes he or she is a wolf. Which is to say, of course, this is a misnomer, because mainstream medicine hasn't yet accepted the truth of the—"

"Lon," the deputy whatever interrupted, "I'm sorry, but we're in a hurry. In five minutes, Secret Service agents are going to escort you to the National Archives Building, where you'll be exposed to every shred of information the government has collected in regard to werewolves. At some point later today, you're going to report back to us, *in as succinct a manner as possible,* and reconcile what you find against popular lore. We need to separate fact from fiction."

Lon wanted to say something profound—

Deputy guy leaned forward. "Lon. Do you understand?"

"Can I ask why?"

"Yes. But I won't answer."

Four

Arlen Specter Headquarters and Operations Center,
Centers for Disease Control and Prevention
Atlanta, Georgia
December 31
8:31 a.m.

Jessica Tanner gripped her desk as a new wave of cramps rippled through her abdomen. She focused on the soothing light shelves at the far end of her office and tempered her breathing until the pain ebbed.

This was her third attempt at in-vitro fertilization. The process had begun with a ten-day regimen of self-administered needles and pills: hormones to hyper-stimulate the ovaries into producing extra eggs. Earlier that morning, the doctor had used a needle—a *big* needle— to extract the eggs, which would be fertilized in a lab somewhere. Meanwhile, the punctured ovaries filled with fluid, swelling to—

She gritted her teeth for the next wave. This was always the worst part of it. Once the local wears off, the cramps hit like a bowling ball shot from a cannon.

Maybe the pain should be a warning sign. A pregnancy at 47? Why go through it? She would've been fine with adoption. It was Richard who wanted his own child, and she just couldn't disappoint him.

No. It wasn't him; it was her. It was the paranoia. Was she getting too old? Too boring? Not smart enough, or willing enough, or sexy enough? Now she was treating herself like a pincushion to keep him happy.

Ow. She bent over and groaned at the floor.

But Richard was her lifeline, not only to the rest of the world, but to herself. She hadn't existed before she met Richard.

Pathetic, but true.

Her childhood had been arduous. With intelligence came premature confidence and rapid alienation. She'd had no interest in entertaining uninspired minds simply to sate the immature need for companionship.

By her teenage years, she'd given up on a social life and focused on work, where discourses were limited to intellectual debates. The effort took her to Harvard, to UCLA, and to the CDC.

Dating? Never. No askers, no takers. There were compliments, particularly on her red hair, but no contemplations. She'd had her desires like everyone else, but how to make sex happen? And they said it was supposed to be easy for a woman. Eventually she abandoned the idea as hypothesis disproven. Most evenings, her CDC colleagues flirted over dinners and drinks while Jessica remained behind her microscope.

Research and dissertation. Research and dissertation.

Consequently, she leapfrogged her counterparts to become Director of the CDC. Gone was the safety of the lab; now she'd been thrust into the dirty world of politics. She'd become the administrator of hundreds of scientists, but she couldn't negotiate a personal conversation with any one of them.

That all had ended when she met Richard Tanner.

"My love," he said as he kissed her cheek. "Feeling any better?"

She hadn't even noticed his entrance. And no, she wasn't feeling better, but his touch and his cologne were comforting. "Yeah, better."

"We'll have a quiet night in tonight. Get some sushi; watch the ball drop. There might be a foot rub in it for you."

He was a handsome fireball of curiosity, ambition, and charisma. Five years her junior, and so beyond her stratum that his initial interest seemed preposterous. It took him three long years to convince her that he was serious; that he saw something in her that she'd never seen in herself. What had she done to attract him, or even to deserve him?

Someday you're going to have to believe in me, Jess, he'd say.

Her abdomen wanted to burst. She gripped Richard's hand on her shoulder and held her breath until the cramp subsided.

A knock came at the door, exactly the distraction she was looking for. "Come in," she hollered, rather than risk standing.

Leilei entered. She was Jessica's assistant, rocket-fueled as always and armed with the day's itinerary. "Good morning, Dr. Tanner. And Dr. Tanner." She was well short of five feet, so their eyes were level with Jessica seated.

Richard's hand slipped from her grasp. "I'll meet you there. I have to check on something." He was out the door before Jessica managed to stand.

"Are you ready for this?" Leilei asked.

Jessica nodded. She took the only file on her desk and they slowly left her office, starting out on their routine morning walk.

"Possible E. Coli in Topeka. We've got a team on it. Bill Mariani from Cincinnati is the lead and Amy Neely is awaiting his report. Seven sick in Baker City, Oregon, waiting on cultures. They suspect it's from a batch of eggs shipped from Idaho. The farm is organizing for a recall."

Jessica's title, "Director of the Centers for Disease Control and Prevention and Administrator of the Agency for Toxic Substances and Disease Registry," was as thankless as it was exhausting to say. It was a presidential appointment—a tremendous honor—but in politics, the spotlight only ever shined on failure or fear. The list of complaints was long and ineradicable. The CDC wasn't prepared for H1N1; they hadn't jumped on AIDS fast enough; maintaining their live virus samples was too dangerous. And where were this year's flu shots already?

"Nick Ross is talking with Pfizer about…" something something something. Leilei had learned to regulate Jessica's attention with her tone of voice. Unimportant updates—which staff member was negotiating with which pharmaceutical company in which country to get flu shots to which region—were delivered in a *you can ignore this* melody.

They made their way to the high-security conference room. It was a spacious improvement from the safe room in the old CDC headquarters, but it was also a long walk from Jessica's office. The brand-new CDC building was designed to discourage the use of elevators in favor of exercise and energy conservation. Not exactly accommodating for her next wave of cramps.

They took the stairs to the twelfth floor and proceeded along the curved perimeter corridor, looking out over a panoramic view of Emory University. It was a bright morning. People and trees shivering in the wind.

Leilei raised her voice to *pay attention now:* "You're okay for the call with USAMRIID? I tried to reschedule, but they shut me down."

"It's okay. Dr. Tanner has the lead. The other Dr. Tanner."

"That's good. Take it easy. Don't forget, I won't be able to listen in on this one," Leilei reminded her, meaning Jessica would have to take her own notes.

"Of course," she said, relieved that they'd reached the end of their walk.

"Buzz me if you need anything," Leilei said, off on her merry way.

The conference room was known as a Sensitive Compartmented Information Facility; it was a steel trap designed according to the government's TEMPEST standards for classified information. Jessica turned the door's combination lock and took a seat at the long conference table. The decor was thoroughly utilitarian: simple chairs, empty walls, and one lonely speakerphone designed by the best techies in the country. Other than bizarre acoustics, it didn't feel special at all.

She opened the thick envelope she'd taken from the security filing cabinet that had been installed in her office by the US General Services Administration. The envelope was white, with a thick orange border, and labeled TOP SECRET at the top and bottom. The file inside had a matching cover and, again, it was labeled TOP SECRET at the top and bottom, with a caveat that always made Jessica laugh: "This cover sheet is unclassified."

(U) Project BLUSHBED (TS-codeword)

The title was standard government jargon. The (U), or unclassified title, *Blushbed*, followed by the indication that the material is (TS) Top Secret and known by another codeword (the codeword itself being classified).

This is what happens when you put men in charge of the world.

The classified codeword, the title of the project, and the baddest-ass bioweapon Jessica had ever seen, was SORCERER.

Sorcerer, a bacterium the military initially labeled "M7949," had (apparently) been found in an abandoned laboratory in the Sar-e Pol province of Afghanistan. These things never made their way straight to the CDC; they'd take a long detour through the US Army Medical Research Institute of Infectious Diseases Special Operations, in Fort Detrick, Maryland. The biodefense guys at USAMRIID always had home-field advantage on so-called *select agents.* The scary ones.

And Sorcerer was very scary.

"Staphylococcus 241," as it was known within the CDC, was a multidrug-resistant bacterium causing rapid, deadly flesh-eating disease. It could be delivered as an aerosol, and it would disperse quickly after exhausting any harvestable flesh—which meant it was a perfect biological flash bomb. Wipe out a town, a city, or a country and move in on top of them a few days later. Just sweep the bones out of the way and take up shop.

The problem (or the solution, depending on how you looked at it) was that Sorcerer was impossible to transport unless it was frozen. The bacteria were dying if they weren't eating, and no growth medium could keep up with their appetite.

Since USAMRIID had delivered Sorcerer to the CDC, accompanied by comically redacted documentation, they'd found every which way to ask questions without asking *the* question.

Can it be turned into an effective weapon?

The CDC was running out of ways to give answers without giving *the* answer.

Once again, her knight in shining lab coat would sweep in to save the day. Richard's short route to the acting head of the CDC's Special Pathogens Branch began when he was a wunderkind at USAMRIID, where he was known as Lt. Col. Richard Tanner, Ph.D., of the Center for Aerobiological Sciences. He'd retired from the service, but he could speak the government's language and still maintain the renegade mirth of private sector scientists.

Richard blew in, kissed her on the cheek, sat down, checked his watch, and opened his own Sorcerer file.

"They'll call any second," he said. "Don't hesitate if you need to leave."

"I'll be okay."

"Doctor Tanner?" Leilei's voice came through the triangular speakerphone at the center of the glass table. "Should I put them through?"

They steeled each other with deep breaths. "Go ahead, Leilei."

"You have Col. Stefan Massey, Lt. Col. Oliver Osman, and Dr. Lynn Bailey from USAMRIID, and Adam Henston from the Department of Defense." Jessica consulted a buck slip in her file to remind her who these people were. Massey was the top dog, the Chief of the Biological Agent Identification and Counterterrorism Division.

A click was followed by a scruffy, white-haired-sounding voice. "Hello?"

"Stefan!" Richard exclaimed. "You alcoholic son of a bitch! How's that miserable wench you never should've married?"

They all dissolved into frat-house laughter.

But Jessica wasn't laughing. Richard's familiarity with these men always made her nervous. It reminded her of something once said to her by Alan Hoxie, Richard's predecessor as head of Special Pathogens. Literally on his way out the door, he warned her that Richard was a plant by the military. His advancement through USAMRIID had been too quick, no matter his skills or his charm, and he had oddly close relationships with men who should have been his superior officers. She thanked Alan, an old (but still undeniably sharp) man, and promised him she'd watch Richard closely. She didn't tell him they'd already begun a relationship.

But she trusted Richard. *Wanted* to trust him. And whenever her conviction waivered, he was there with his charming smile.

Someday you're going to have to believe in me, Jess.

Nausea boiled in her stomach again. Suddenly she had to get out of there. Between his rapid-fire jokes, Richard nodded goodbye.

Head floating, she stumbled across the hallway, crashed into the women's room, collapsed onto a toilet and dropped her head between her knees. She couldn't even muster energy to kick the stall door closed. By the grace of Galileo, the bathroom was empty.

Her consciousness faded, as if someone had pulled the plug on her heart. Scary as it was, she'd been here before. Literally, on this very toilet. She knew it would pass in a few minutes.

They'd scheduled this procedure for the 31st, expecting to have the day off. But this call *had* to be today, the government guys insisted.

Why, though? Why today?

Not so she'd be distracted, right? If Richard were going to conduct espionage, would he—*Oh, what are you even thinking?*

Her phone buzzed: text message.

Christ, don't tell me they need me back in there.

She patted at her lab coat pocket, found her iPhone and let it sit on her thigh. The text was from Leilei: "Call me. 911."

Oh God no.

Deep breath. She returned the call.

"Doctor Tanner," Leilei sounded flustered. "I'm sorry to interrupt your call, but they told me I had to."

"Who?"

"The office of the National Security Advisor."

"Who?"

"Rebekkah Luft is requesting a videoconference immediately."

***

Jessica wiped her face with a wet rag as Leilei prepared her computer. They so rarely used her office's encrypted videoconferencing that she'd never bothered to learn how to work it herself.

She scanned Rebekkah Luft's Wikipedia entry via her iPhone. She'd never spoken with the woman. Communications with the White House traditionally went through the Secretary of Health and Human Services.

The White House logo appeared on her monitor. There had been days when Jessica sat in front of that image for more than an hour, waiting for—

"Good morning, Dr. Tanner." Luft appeared in mid-sentence. She was a well-dressed black woman with an authoritative voice. Her Wikipedia entry said she was 61, but she looked good for early 50s. "It's a pleasure to meet you. I'm going to get right into it, if you don't mind."

"Of cour—"

"Last night there were over a dozen reported incidents of violent animal attacks in Manhattan. We have videotape of the first one, from Bellevue Hospital, which we're about to show you."

Luft nodded to an off-camera assistant and the image switched to grainy, silent security-camera footage. It was a wide, overhead angle of a hospital corridor, with a patient's room in the center, situated across from a nurses' desk and next to a long picture window.

After a moment of normal hospital traffic, everyone on the tape reacts to something off-frame to their left. They all move in that direction. A minute later, something else happens in that center room. There's confusion, and then a man stumbles out of—

It looked like his face had been ripped off.

A doctor rushes to his aid, but he's knocked down.

Jessica grimaced, but forced herself to keep watching.

The doctor is sent hurtling backward, so hard that his spine breaks backward over the nurses' desk. A nurse appears from off-screen, spinning around as a geyser of blood erupts from her back.

Whatever caused it steps forward into the shot… a man. A *large* man. Is he… wearing something black, or is he covered in hair?

And then he moves, and it's not right. Not human.

"Is that a baboon?" Jessica asked.

"We don't think so."

He—*it*—pounces on another doctor, a woman. The creature lunges downward, delivering a fearsome bite. And then it recoils—gunshots. Several gunshots. But they hardly slow it down. It rolls over, charges the window, and cannonballs right through the reinforced glass.

And then Luft's face reappeared on the screen.

"What was it?" Jessica asked.

Luft's response seemed guarded. "It seems to have been a patient. She was brought into the ER the previous night, after she herself was the victim of a severe animal attack. She scratched a nurse while they were tending to her wounds. The next night—last night—both of them became these things."

"Became?"

"That video is in your personal FTP folder now," Luft said, taking a cue from someone else in the room. "This sounds as absurd to me as it does to you, Doctor Tanner, but these animals were responsible for attacks all over the city last night."

"You're saying the patient and the nurse… transformed? In… to…?" Luft dealt with the other in her office, letting Jessica sputter until she finally reached, "…werewolves?"

Luft nodded, validating both her conclusion and her incredulity. "More than a million people will be in Times Square tonight. Drop everything else."

"Of course."

"We're bringing a victim to you, the lady doctor you saw bitten in the video. You need to determine if she has an infection. This is a 14c."

Section 14c was a Top Secret clause in the United States' Biological

Threat Assessment Protocol, a drastic measure giving clearance to conduct extreme tests on a human subject. It meant they could kill this doctor if necessary.

"Also, Doctor Tanner, you should know that the first victim, on the night of December 29, was a diplomat's wife. She did a lot of traveling. That may not be relevant, since she was the victim of an attack herself, but I'll have her file sent over to you."

"Where is she?"

"She's still missing."

"I understand," Jessica said, not really understanding. "We should quarantine the hospital and anyone exposed. At least until we know what we're dealing with."

"That's just it, Doctor Tanner. I need you to tell me what we're dealing with. Godspeed."

And then she was gone. Maddening that she didn't respond to the request for quarantine.

Jessica paged Leilei via her intercom.

"Yes, Doctor Tanner?"

"I need the heads of staff in here immediately."

Five
CDC Headquarters
Atlanta, Georgia
December 31
8:50 a.m.

The red and white EMS helicopter glimmered in the morning sun as it came to a soft landing on the CDC's rooftop helipad. Richard Tanner led the nurses and techs against the pulverizing wind as they met the in-flight EMTs.

Jessica waited by the door, eagerly anticipating a look at this patient. When the gurney hit the roof, Jessica felt the impact in the lump in her throat, as if it were some kind of physical assault on her trained scientist's skepticism.

The patient was wearing a muzzle.

Werewolves?

When she was a kid, Jessica frequently watched the Sunday creature double features on the UHF stations. It was against her parents' strict orders, but her mother was always in the garden and father on the golf course. In the daytime safety of their wood-paneled living room, the monsters were as exciting as the mad science creating them.

Nighttime was different, though—that was when the monsters came out. Her father had said night terrors were the hallmark of an active imagination, a sure sign of superior intelligence. But that was hardly consoling when even Michael Jackson conspired to fill her mind with werewolves and zombies.

But those sleepless nights were forever ago, and there were real things to fear nowadays. A bacterium like Sorcerer, for example. IVF treatments. A mortgage taken before the bubble burst. And yet, Jessica realized, nothing quite stings like the irrational dread of childhood nightmares.

They wheeled the patient closer.

What to expect…? Fangs? Fur?

Not at all. Jessica exhaled with the same sensation she got from the false alarm stingers in those silly horror movies.

Even muzzled, this petite, shriveled woman couldn't suggest less of a threat. Her thin skin, already Irish pale, looked chalky from blood loss. Her brown hair was trapped beneath a surgeon's cap, and her body was practically mummified in bandages.

Jessica held the door for the gurney train. The patient's silver necklace glimmered just before it slipped from beneath the sunlight.

***

"Dr. Kenzie, my name is Richard Tanner. I'm the head of the CDC's biochem team. This is my wife, Jessica Tanner, Director of the CDC. You're here with us in Atlanta. And you're okay. We're just going to run some tests on you."

Kenzie nodded, her eyes still coming to focus.

Richard reached for the muzzle on her face.

"What are you doing?" Jessica snapped.

"Relax," he said, undoing the clasps.

"Thank you," Kenzie said, closing her eyes as the air reached her cheeks.

"Dr. Kenzie, can I call you Melissa?" Richard asked.

"Yes, of course." Her tongue was thick. Richard held a cup of water to her lips. "Oh praise the Lord, thank you."

Kenzie winced as a nurse stuck her arm, filling the first of a half-dozen empty vials with her blood. The techs moved silently, making no eye contact as they clipped her fingernails and scraped her feet. All the while, Richard kept her focused and calm.

"That's nothing to worry about," he said. "It's all precautionary. Can you tell us what you remember about your accident?"

"I was in the hospital. It was crowded. We had a VIP. The police were interfering. They were rude. There was a woman officer. We were talking. And then... I can't remember." Her eyes went distant, as if there were other memories, ones she didn't want to speak of, and then she whispered, "Nightmares."

"Yes, well, you were injured, but you're going to be okay. We're taking care of you," Richard gently answered. "Can you tell us what the nightmares were about?"

"I... It was dark. I was in a forest, I think. I was chasing something."

"What where you chasing, Melissa?"

"I don't know. I can't remember. I think I was hungry."

The nurse pulled the first vial off her syringe. Richard's curious eyes followed as a tech took the blood sample and beelined out of the room. Jessica nudged him to return his attention to their patient—she knew Kenzie was a doctor herself, and dangerously privy to the Tanners' unspoken communications.

"Dissociative amnesia?" Kenzie asked, self-diagnosing. "Fugue state?"

"May be, Melissa," Richard reassured her with his prescription wink. "You're a good doctor, but let *us* take care of *you* now. Your only job is to relax while we run some tests."

"Why tests?"

"Nothing to worry about. We'll take good care of you, I promise."

"I have to call my mother," Kenzie pleaded. "She lives by herself—"

"We've contacted your mother; she knows you're okay," Richard said, so adept with a casual lie. "More water?" Richard held the cup toward Kenzie's lips.

She winced as she tilted forward. "Neck. My neck."

A massive blister sat in the pit of her left collarbone. It was immediately clear to Jessica that it wasn't an infected laceration. This was a contact reaction, perhaps dermatitis or urticaria. Richard shifted

Kenzie's necklace aside and prodded the wound through his rubber gloves.

"You have some inflammation here, nothing to be concerned about."

"It burns," she rasped.

And the lesion was spreading. A new patch of red grew before their eyes. Richard moved the necklace again, to examine the new—

The necklace.

"This is silver?" Jessica asked as she pulled it over Kenzie's head.

"Please don't. It was a gift from my mother."

"I'll put it right here, Melissa. It'll be safe," Jessica said, laying the necklace on the bedside tray. The pendant rattled on the metal, calling everyone's attention to her shaking hands. "This is sterling silver, right?"

"Yes."

Jessica tilted Kenzie's head for a better look. The spread had stopped.

Any child knew that werewolves were supposed to be allergic to silver—at least, any child who watched their creature double features. But in the real world, silver is antimicrobial. We use it as a disinfectant. We eat off of it.

Silver should not cause lesions.

Richard's eyes silently warned her to stay calm.

Six

United Nations Plaza
New York
December 31
8:58 a.m.

FBI Special Agent Brianna Tildascow was deep in the spellbinding throes of a perfect meatball sandwich: silken ground beef cut with a perfect balance of bread crumbs and Parmesan, dripping with spicy meat-infused tomato gravy, draped in thick mozzarella and nestled in a crispy, chewy Italian roll. The masterpiece steamed off a robust bouquet in the twelve-degree morning air.

The vendor had just plugged in his street cart when she arrived. He was the kind of Italian who'd bleed tomato gravy if you cut him, and Tildascow was contemplating doing just that if he hadn't canned it with the breakfast talk and made her a meatball special. His eyebrows furrowed with dirty thoughts as she demanded extra extra cheese.

Most women—especially young ones—felt uncomfortable when they sensed a man sizing them up. Tildascow took it as a compliment. Hell, she took pleasure in it. The way she saw it, men always got the ass end of society's sexual hang-ups. If it was a crime for a middle-aged man to see a 14 year-old pop starlet as a sex object, why was it okay for those girls to dress like whores? What, exactly, did they expect?

She was careful not to lead anyone on, of course. And she knew how to handle herself if a guy took it too far. But when handled properly, the art of flirting was the same as interrogation: Read your target, give them as much as they need, take as much as you want, and hope you were graceful enough to improve their day. A little validation could go a very long way.

She bit into the sandwich and cooed heartily for the vendor's delight. *Yummmmm.* A hundred percent in the tip jar, and then she headed east across First Avenue.

"Happy new year!" he called with a wave.

"You too," she replied. It sounded like "oofoo" through her stuffed mouth, but what the guy really wanted was the wink and the toss of her curly blond hair. Better than the tip, and it cost her nothing. *Leverage everywhere.*

Tildascow climbed the wide concrete stairs to the elevated promenade of the United Nations Headquarters, which was just across the street from the scene of Holly Cooke's attack. Dealing with the UN was always a pain in the—

A series of honks turned her attention back toward First Avenue.

Cars had swerved to avoid a woman who'd stumbled into the heavy morning traffic. She was soaked head to toe in blood, her tattered hospital gown exposing all the bits and pieces.

Tildascow drew her weapon and raced back down the stairs and into the street, holding up a hand to traffic. "FBI!" she called out to the woman. "Put your hands in the air and move to the sidewalk!"

But the woman didn't acknowledge her. She continued across First Avenue, heading west toward 44th, shambling like some kind of zombie, oblivious to the growing shouts, honks, and camera phones. Tildascow stayed with her, keeping her 1911 trained. "Ma'am. Can you hear me?"

The Jane Doe was in her late 50's. Face coated in bloody grime and raked with tear streaks. Her right eye had been beaten glassy; right shoulder hung at the wrong angle from a broken collarbone. More injuries beneath the gown, but nothing inhibiting mobility. With each step, her bloodstained feet peeled from the asphalt.

"Get out of the way!" Tildascow yelled at the clustering onlookers. She kept pace with the woman as they crossed onto 44th Street, moving west and away from UN Plaza.

Sirens blared in the distance. As long as this woman remained calm, Tildascow would wait for the police and their stun guns. She wasn't posing any kind of threat.

"My... my..." she mumbled deliriously. "Where... where is my..."

"What's your name, ma'am?" Tildascow yelled.

No acknowledgment. More onlookers crossed the street, pacing in front of the two of them, laughing and taking pictures. Fucking idiots. "FBI. Step across the street and get out of the way!"

It was about to get worse: A news crew had been reporting from in front of the Millennium Hotel. Probably an update on—

Ohmigod.

"Where is he?" the woman whimpered, her drained eyes wandering in every direction. "Where is he?"

The woman was Holly Cooke.

"Where's my baby?"

Seven

CDC Headquarters
Diagnostic Study Laboratory
Atlanta, Georgia
December 31
9:42 a.m.

"She definitely has *something*," Jessica Tanner said.

"But what is it?" Richard mumbled.

Sure enough, an unidentified virus had been located in Melissa Kenzie's blood. Jessica examined an analytical presentation of the pathogen, spread across several flat-screen monitors, as Richard and half a dozen members of his virology team peered over her shoulders. It was as if they were waiting for her to conjure some kind of magical diagnosis.

The raw data from the pan-viral microarray analysis of RNA-Kenzie01 displayed as thousands of colored dots across a black matrix, each representing *oligonucleotides*, or features of the virus' DNA. It resembled a nighttime cityscape, with all of its beauty and mystery.

Data analysis suggested the pathogen was related to several disparate viruses at once. When the comparison fields were narrowed, the computer offered no codification whatsoever.

"No homology," Richard grumbled.

She turned to the others: dumb faces across the board. "Can I see it?" she asked.

The microarray analysis was replaced by an image of the virus itself, as seen on a low-temperature micrograph at 65,000 times magnification.

"Look at the shape of the capsid," Richard said. "So bizarre."

The *capsid* is the protein core containing the virus' genetic material. They were usually shaped like helixes or twenty-sided polygons called icosahedrons. Variations weren't unprecedented, but this particular shape had never been recorded. It looked like two flat pentagrams had been used to make a sandwich, and they'd been twisted to scrunch the filling.

"It's a pentagrammic crossed-antiprism," explained one of the virologists.

On its side, the capsid's bookends resembled five-pointed stars. "Pentagrammic crossed-antiprism," Jessica repeated.

"It's RNA-based, and enveloped," said another of the virologists. Some viruses have protective envelopes, which are often created from stolen portions of the host cell's membranes and used as disguise to facilitate further infiltration. Enveloped viruses tend to be fragile, so they don't live on doorknobs or toilet seats, and they can't spread through the air. Good news.

And that was where the good news stopped.

After her bizarre conversation with Rebekkah Luft, Jessica had assembled a team of physicists to match the spectral qualities of last night's moonlight over New York. Using diffraction gratings and spectrophotometers (and guesswork to account for atmospheric scattering and other variables), her team adjusted the light's frequency, polarity and phase to create a "moon lamp."

Werewolf, meet moon.

The effect was… humbling.

Photocatalytic reactions in the virus caused a cascade of effects, many of which they couldn't yet track. The result, however, was profound: rapid shifts in the host's DNA.

The alterations were located in sequences known as "junk DNA," so-called because they had no apparent function. Junk DNA were thought to be evolutionary artifacts, scars on the human genome caused by millions of factors over thousands of generations.

Junk DNA sequences weren't implicitly benign, however. Any of them might contain undiscovered *homeoboxes*, the master switches used by cells as instruction manuals to build the body. Flipping one of these switches might result in mutagenesis, or the creation of genetic mutations.

Mutations could materialize as subtle inter-species discrepancies, like height, weight or skin color. Or, in theory, they could manifest major organism transformations. Applied mutagenesis might someday replace human parts with those of a bird or a plant… or even take leaps through the evolutionary chain. One team in Canada was attempting to devolve chickens into "Chickenosaursus Rex."

"I can't wait to see what happens when the virus catalyzes inside her body," Richard said.

Jessica was at a loss for words. "This is—"

"We don't know *what* this is."

But at the same moment, someone behind him had a different answer: "Dangerous."

Eight

FBI New York Division Headquarters
Jacob K. Javits Federal Office Building
26 Federal Plaza, Manhattan
December 31
10:42 a.m.

TV crews had set up camp in front of 26 Fed. Turned out that a half-naked woman photobombing the morning news had caught the media's attention.

Tildascow hopped out of her taxi a block away from the office. Counterterrorism work necessitated anonymity, so media attention wouldn't do.

A couple of male reporters took notice as she approached an unmarked entrance. The blond curls tended to draw the eyes of men. But she was forgotten like a deflowered prom queen when an FDNY ambulance turned the corner, siren and lights blazing. The red and white truck slogged through the congregation and into the underground parking structure. Security staved off the press as they strained for a peek at the mystery passenger.

That would be Tildascow's appointment.

She took the discretionary stairs to the lobby, where flustered NYPD plainclothes were grousing at a liaison. The Holly Cooke case had a stratospheric profile after it was advertised on live TV, so politically, the cops had to fight for access even if they knew it wouldn't come. Tildascow would've liked to include them, but she had no time for diplomacy.

She ignored the escalating argument and swiped her access card at an unmarked door. It unlocked with a buzz, letting her into a sterile hallway that served as an access point to sensitive facilities. On her left was "the cage," where confiscated materials were catalogued and stored. Across the hall was the server station, a massive temperature-regulated facility housing backups for the regional government virtual private network servers. She'd spent a week in this room reconstructing the tracks of a deft Taliban hacker. Farther down the hall was a vault containing the most substantial armory in Manhattan.

A door with a keypad lock led to a security portal granting access to the holding cells. She descended into the humid sub-basement, taupe tile under sickly seventies-era lights, and arrived at an iron-on-brick gate where she displayed her badge to a camera.

Beyond the bars, she could see a flurry of CDC EIS officers in banana-colored biohazard suits. Seemed like overkill, but that was probably smarter than underkill. She was greeted at the gate by a guard and a banana, who insisted she wear one herself.

Arguing would just slow things down. The alcohol-and-plastic stench of the thing wasn't as bad as the fact that it weighed a ton.

An EIS Officer escorted her onto the medical wing of the cell block, where all six infirmary cells were occupied by victims of last night's animal attacks. A few were up, alert and scared. Others lay in gurneys, mummified in bandages.

Tildascow's escort directed her to the last cell on the left, where CDC techs were hurriedly prepping monitors around their star patient.

Holly Cooke was strapped to an upright gurney. Thin-skinned, anemic, and covered in bruises, her 52 years had finally caught up with her.

EIS had cleaned her up and documented her contusions, breaks, and sprains. They found eight gunshot wounds matching the shots Tildascow had put into that animal last night, but they looked like they'd undergone a month's worth of healing. She also had a nasty fracture to her right orbital socket, which could have happened when she (it?) hit the window.

When Cooke saw her in the suit, one more faceless stormtrooper, she dropped her head and continued sobbing. Tildascow fought the gasmask until she was free of its plastic choke. The hall's stench of bleach made her eyes water.

"Holly," she called through the cell bars. "Holly Cooke?"

Cooke's eyes flickered, but she didn't have the strength to respond.

"My name is Brianna Tildascow. I'm with the FBI. I know this is scary, but these people are going to take good care of you. You're going to be okay, your husband is flying in."

"My son," she rasped.

"That's what I'm here for. I'm going to find him. I need your help."

Cooke winced as an EIS guy pricked her arm with a ferocious needle.

"Could you hold off on that for a second?" Tildascow asked him.

He searched for a word to summarize his incredulity, finally settling on a venomous "No."

Game, set and match to that guy.

"I just want my son," Cooke whimpered. "Please." Her head wobbled as she tried to see Tildascow through her good left eye.

"We'll find him, I promise. I just have to understand what happened to you. Do you remember the attack, or anything from the hospital last night?"

"I…" She took a deep, sobbing breath. "I want to go home."

"We'll get you home as soon as possible, Holly. I promise. But I need you to help me try to find your son. Can you remember the attack at all? Or anything from last night?"

"I don't know," she whispered. "I want to go home."

Her words lingered as Tildascow squinted.

Boy, she dropped the concern for her son pretty quick. Now she's focused on going home?

"Do you remember what happened last night, Holly? At the hospital?"

"I… don't."

Cooke didn't look like she was stumped. Not if Tildascow's read was good. She looked like she'd been shut up, like a lawyer had covered her mic and whispered into her ear.

"Try, Holly. It's very important."

Cooke gazed down and to the right. Her profile said she was right-handed, so casting her eyes in that direction suggested internal dialogue. But Tildascow's interrogation training was hardly necessary to read this sham.

Cooke was inventing a story.

"I was taking a walk... We were walking on the street... and we were attacked by something... some kind of dog. It pushed me down, and... and it got on top of me. And then I woke up in the hospital." Her tone suggested recitation, like a kid fed a lie by a guilty sibling.

"Holly, this will take longer if we can't figure out what happened to you. It will take longer to find your son. And you may not be able to go home for a long time." *Long.*

Tears dripped from her eyes. "I know."

"Holly, what happened at the hospital last night?"

She shook her head and silently sobbed, mouth open, saliva dripping. This part was honest: "I don't know... I just blacked out. It... it hurt so bad, I thought I was dying... and then..."

She cried in great heaves, and then the EIS officers stepped in to work her upper body, cutting her off from Tildascow.

Holly Cooke, a soft-skinned socialite, had suffered a sudden and savage physical assault. Her son was stolen. And then she'd transformed into some kind of monster and woke up half-naked on the streets.

And after all this, she was hiding something.

Protecting something?

Some... *one?*

Nine

National Archives Building
Sensitive Compartmented Information Facility
Washington, DC
December 31
9:52 a.m.

Lon had never been more disappointed in his life, and that included the full-scale shit-flinging assault on cinematic posterity commonly referred to as the 2010 remake of *The Wolfman* (they didn't even get the name right).

The government's "complete" and "official" aggregate of data on the subject of lycanthropy was, in a word, pathetic. In fact, the most insightful piece was a lengthy (and startlingly well-written) manifesto written by Lon himself and sent to Congress some eight years ago as part of a school project.

Even the rest of the occult section was unacceptably sparse. There were some pamphlets he recognized as issues of *The Necromantic Gauntlet;* that would please their author, Donnie Tuttle, Lon's internet forum nemesis. Bah. There were also a few grimoires of the A∴A∴ (*Arcanum Arcanorum)*, a magical fraternity that Lon was, frankly, desperate to join. But these spell books had been unearthed decades prior, and their veracity was under deep contention.

The jewel in the government's collection? A wretched interpretation of the *Necronomicon*, Master Lovecraft's legendary tome described by him as the "image of the law of the dead." This was a flimsy 1988 prestige format graphic novel, defaced with faux post-it notes by some daft "expert." They even misspelled the name of the author, referring to Abdul *Alhazred* as "Abdul *Alhazered!"*

How embarrassing.

All of the government's werewolf photos were already available on the Internet, all of their "sightings" previously documented by the lycanthropy community. Their knowledge base was chiefly informed by commercial propaganda… and they didn't have a *single mention* of the countless alleged incidents in Transylvania!

The emperor had no clothes. There wasn't an old man behind the curtain. The Matrix didn't explicitly revolve. *Fuck!*

A wave of depression hit Lon and he sat back in the squeaky chair. He was at a mahogany desk in a sparse room, some kind of man-sized safe in the basement of this *supposedly* important government library. The air was musty with the depressing smell of dying paper. Dust was snowing underneath his lamp. Where the hell had his tax dollars gone? Well, not *his*, but his mother's?

He'd been working with his therapist to dissociate professional affronts from personal insults, but this was too much to bear. Why had they brought him here, anyway? To show him that the occult wasn't a concern to the government? To put him in his place? To…

Wait a minute!

Maybe they'd enlisted him to organize and enhance their files! Maybe he was to become the first official United States Inspector of Lycanthropy!

His therapist constantly warned him about his swelled head. But how would women react when they saw his *government badge*—question mark and exclamation point!? This was the greater destiny he'd always imagined!

Perhaps he could assemble an FBI team to investigate the occult! Like *The X-Files,* but with enthusiastic sanctioning, an informed crew, and more than a fleeting modicum of veracity!

If the government was searching for the right man to preside over the truth seekers, they had found him in Lon Toller.

The door to the safe room opened to the two stiff Secret Service agents who'd escorted him from the White House. "It's time, Mr. Toller. Bring whatever you need." The archivist guy who'd prepared the documents wanted to protest, but a glare from one of the agents made him swallow his words.

Lon brought the puny folder, hoping they'd let him keep it for his website, but his *mind* was all they'd need. He couldn't wait for the debriefing. Surely they'd see that his expertise was indispensible. Maybe they'd take him out for a drink. He'd always wanted to go out for a drink.

It occurred to Lon that this might be a time when his head was getting too big. People found it off-putting when he lectured. At the behest of his therapist, he was tracking this phenomenon in his introspective writing.

He determined to keep his ego in check and make everyone part of the discovery. It would be more of a discussion than a lecture.

This was gonna be great!

Ten
White House Conference Room
December 31
11:04 a.m.

"Well then, I'm glad to see the government has finally decided to wisen up to matters of the occult. Who will be asking me questions today?"

Lon sat at the head of a mile-long conference table in the most modern room he'd yet seen in the White House. Flat-screen panels and cameras lined the walls, and a badass touchscreen map of the world was mounted behind him. He thought he might put that to use while discussing the eighteenth-century lycanthropic infestation of Transylvania.

Nine other people were seated at the table, and not one of them answered his question. One senior military guy scowled so hard that his white nose hairs spread like fangs.

"It's understandable, though, right? The modern world doesn't have the balls to admit that the things that go bump in the night are real."

Still no reaction.

The door opened behind him. Everyone stood expectantly, so Lon followed suit.

A black woman glided in and waved the room back to their seats with a curt smile. She was attractive for her age and exuded importance. Her graying kinky hair was pushed behind a black headband, and she smelled of citrus. He'd seen her before, maybe on TV. But he didn't follow politics. It all seemed too futile, since he knew there were more malevolent powers puppeteering society.

She approached Lon, and a gofer dude standing at the door introduced them. "This is our werewolf expert," he said. "Mr. Boris Toller."

"Mister Toller," said the black woman as she extended her hand.

"Rebekkah Luft. Nice to meet you."

"Hi," he muttered. His hand squished in her grip. He was going to have to learn how to do something about that.

"*National Security Advisor of the United States of America,*" said the gofer dude, picking up on Lon's obliviousness. Very helpful.

"I appreciate your coming on such short notice." She directed him to his seat. "We're here to talk about werewolves."

"Of course," Lon smiled, tossing the archive file on the desk for the sake of drama. "But they're nasty little buggers then, aren't they?"

Luft exchanged a weary glance with the gofer dude.

"You see ma'am, obviously I don't know what this is about." *Although I hope I'm guessing right!* "But there was very little in your files that isn't already available on the Internet. The personal accounts, the hazy photographs—I've had the whole bloody lot of them on my website for years now—"

"Have you spent time in England, young man?" the nose-haired general interrupted. His scowl was back.

"Er, no. Why?" But Lon realized he'd slipped into his English accent. His stepfather hated that too. But the royal vernacular sounded far more elegant when it came to educating.

"Keep going," urged Luft.

"Well, quite honestly," he said, easing back into Ohio commonspeak, "I've found far more convincing testimonials in European texts, particularly those from seventeenth- and eighteenth-century Romania. If you'd like, I could translate—"

Luft suddenly diverted her gaze. "Where are we with the patch-throughs?" she asked the gopher. What a brazen interruption!

"They're on stand-by."

"Put them through."

Two side-by-side flat-panel screens came to life on the far end of the room, both displaying women's faces. The one on the right looked like an overworked schoolmarm. Lon remembered her face from his contact list: She was the head of the CDC; he'd sent her information about lycanthropes as well. But he didn't recognize the other woman, a younger, more attractive blonde.

"Brianna," said Luft. "Always wonderful to see you."

Eleven
Jacob K. Javits Federal Office Building
26 Federal Plaza, Manhattan

Tildascow sat alone at the center of a long table in the conference room. The Chelsea building was nearly empty; everyone was in the field, prepping for NYE or off for the evening. If she weren't a grown-up, the place might've seemed creepy. Or maybe the anticipation had gotten to her. The CDC apparently had something, but she couldn't squeeze out any more details before—

The video screen in front of her flashed from the White House seal to a conference room packed with advisors. Rebekkah Luft was seated at the head of the table.

"Brianna," said Luft. "Always wonderful to see you."

"Good morning..." she sputtered, unsure how to address her. "Mrs. Luft."

"Oh please, Brianna," Luft chuckled. Her diamond-studded watch jangled as she waved off the formality. "I've known her since she was in the second grade," she informed the others at her table.

Tildascow smiled hollowly as the officials nodded her way.

"We're connecting you to a feed from the CDC."

The video switched to a QuickTime interface. A black screen with white text.

New York Lycanthropy Unclassified-Group VI.

Twelve
White House Conference Room
December 31
11:04 am

Lon read the screen again. And again.

New York. *Lycanthropy?* Unclassified? Group VI?

What could that combination of words mean?

"Ladies and gentlment, this is Dr. Jessica Tanner, Director of the CDC," said Luft, "Dr. Tanner, you have the room."

"Good afternoon, everyone," said Jessica's voice over the video. "I'm afraid we haven't had very much luck with this."

The video began with a flat, grayscale image that was reminiscent of the microscopic photographs Lon had seen in science textbooks. Moving, roundish blobs appeared to be blood cells.

The image jerked as the video's speed adjusted, and then a new shape entered the top of the frame.

"This is the virus," said Jessica.

A highlight appeared over the virus. It looked like—Lon squinted—it looked like an Oreo, if the cookies had spikes on their edges.

"It reproduces through what we call the 'Lytic Cycle without lysis.' In the Lytic Cycle, the virus enters a cell, multiplies inside, and then bursts out an exponential number of progeny, or baby viruses, which then go on to infect more cells. The 'without lysis' part means that the initial host cell isn't destroyed. It continues to serve as an incubator, expediting the infection even further. This particular virus spreads remarkably fast. Progeny are released within an hour, and they face no resistance because they hide inside an envelope constructed from the host cell's membranes. In fact, white blood cells don't even seem to recognize the intruder's presence."

The image was replaced by a static closer shot of the virus.

Lon leaned closer.

Those weren't spikes on the edges. The sides of the virus—the cookies of the Oreo—were *pentagrams*.

Jessica continued speaking over the image. "We tested the spectral response of the virus under a lamp replicating the intensity and polarization of last night's moonlight in New York. Under very short wavelengths in the x-ray region, a photocatalyzer molecule activated the virus, which in turn catalyzed genomic alterations to sections of the cell's DNA."

Huhwha?

"We call these sections 'junk DNA,' because we don't really know what they do. But they appeared to be dormant." Jessica's voice went soft as she responded to someone off-screen. "Okay, we're ready with the lamp."

Lamp?

The video switched to a wide angle of a hospital room, where a poor, terrified woman was strapped Bride-of-Frankenstein style into a gurney and covered with electrodes and bandages and IVs.

"Kenzie, Melissa, A01" was stamped at the bottom of the screen, followed by the military time, the date, and some technical jargon about wavelengths, intensity, and polarization.

Lon couldn't swallow. Was his imagination running wild or…

…or did everyone else think they were about to see what *he* thought they were about to see?

Thirteen

CDC Headquarters, Secure Recovery Room
Atlanta, Georgia

Melissa Kenzie struggled to remember.

She was doing her rounds in the hospital. And then *something* happened. People screaming over her. Ceilings rolling past. Vehicles. A helicopter?

She'd spoken to a charming doctor. They gave her some ice and took some blood. And then she went to sleep.

Yes, that's what happened. They must've given her an anesthetic.

But why was she *here,* in a diagnostic room? This place was more elaborate than anything at Bellevue. She was strapped to a gurney *(why?)* and propped upright facing a mirror. And why was she being videotaped?

Anxiety spiked her pulse ox. The beeps pounded against her temples.

"Melissa, we're about to run a test." The woman's voice came from everywhere at once, but she couldn't see her anywhere. "Just relax. It won't hurt, and it'll be over in a minute."

"Where are you?"

With a *clack,* a new light source changed the room's color to lavender. It was quite dim…so why did it make her squint?

"What's happening?" she cried.

Who are these people? What godforsaken thing are they doing?

She pulled at the restraints, but a tearing pain across her breast reminded her there were stitches.

Why am I restrained?

"I want to call my mother!"

No response.

How long had she been here? Did they even tell her mother?

"Please! Please let me out of here!"

She stopped struggling. Suddenly it wasn't so important. She took a deep, refreshing breath. Finally, the volume of the pulse ox relented. Her muscles relaxed, her fog cleared. Her strength was returning. It felt good. So good.

She was *hungry*.

How long had it been since she'd eaten?

What was that smell?

God bless, something tasty. Salty and wet and—

"Melissa, how do you feel?" the voice thundered.

"I'm okay," she chuckled. "I'm—"

Pain in her right shoulder. Harsh, as if she'd been kicked from behind, leaving an aching throb spreading across her shoulder blades, pushing... *pushing* her collarbone into submission.

She screamed as it struck her other shoulder. Her whole body shook from the impact. And now a searing tear on her chest, those stitches—

Dear God, am I smelling my own blood?

It seeped into her bandages, creeping red swallowing the white.

What is this pain?

Her joints erupting. Her bones pulling apart.

"Help me God, help me God..."

So hot. Sweat racing with tears. Inside, too. Boiling in her lungs.

"It hurts!"

"What hurts, Melissa?"

"Everything. Please... please help me."

Her legs wrenching from her hips. Her shoulders arching forward, never mind that they were attached to her back, which was—*oh please God*—splitting apart. Her jaw ripping from her skull, *breaking*—

That smell...

Sparks shot through her limbs. Energy like she'd never felt, fueling such strength. She had to run—away from the pain, away from this light, this pounding noise—

But more than that she just *had to run*. The night called.

Her neck, her ears, her joints kept detonating, but the pain didn't matter.

Now she was angry.

And hungry. And trapped. She wanted to scream.

No, not scream but—

Fourteen
CDC Headquarters, Patient Observation Room
December 31
One Minute Earlier

Jessica took a deep breath and pressed the intercom button. "Melissa, how do you feel?"

"I'm okay," she chuckled. "I'm—"

Kenzie's shoulder jerked violently, leaving her breathless, her mouth hanging agape, as if the pain had insulted her.

In the crowded observation room, heads perked up from monitors. Shouts came from all directions: "BP 160 over 95!" "Temp 102 and rising!"

"Help me God, help me God," Kenzie whispered to herself. She regained her breath to scream: "It hurts!"

"Ask her to describe it." Richard said.

"What hurts, Melissa?"

"Everything. Please...please help me..."

Kenzie shrieked as her body contorted. Her neck flared, her eyes swelled. Veins bulged through her crimson skin. She quivered breathlessly for an agonizing moment until she finally exhaled a deep, rasping *growl*.

Jessica couldn't believe—

Kenzie's fingers stretched right before their eyes. Thick, terrible nails pushed from her fingertips.

New hair sprouted between her knuckles, spread to her wrist, and crept up her forearm. More slinked from her sideburns to cross her cheeks.

Her face darkened as fear gave way to savagery. Her eyes yellowed.

She screamed again, but it was choked by whatever was changing her. She threw her head back as her mandible stretched to create a severe underbite.

And then came the fangs.

The pain subsided and the monster became aware. It shook off the waning agony of the transformation and celebrated with a whooping *Howl*.

Fifteen
Jacob K. Javits Federal Office Building
26 Federal Plaza, Manhattan

Questions and implications and incredulity raced through Tildascow's mind, until she realized her mouth was hanging open. She'd been leaning so close to her monitor that her eyes stung.

It had seemed impossible. Now it seemed inevitable.

Kenzie had turned into a werewolf. In real life. Right before her eyes.

Tildascow's feed abruptly switched back to the White House conference room, where the suits had devolved into a paranoid mob. One white-haired guy stood up and spun in a circle, literally chasing his own tail.

But Rebekkah was Rebekkah, cool as a cuke. She looked to a pudgy, redheaded boy sitting next to her. He looked like he'd been plucked from some high school's *Dungeons & Dragons* club.

He was still locked in a slack-jawed grimace from witnessing Kenzie's physical torture. As realization crept in, his eyes grew wide behind his glasses. Suddenly, he leapt from his chair.

"Yes! Yes! I *knew* they were real! I knew it! *Yes!*"

PART THREE

One

New York City
New Year's Eve

In the embryonic days of Manhattan, the British colonists gave the name "Longacre Square" to the bustling convergence of 42nd Street, Bloomingdale Road, and Seventh Avenue. General George Washington, Commander in Chief of the Continental Army, used Longacre as a rest stop when the colonists fought for their independence in the Revolutionary War.

Longacre Square flourished as a stable and carriage district through the mid-1800s. But as the area's population boomed, seedier elements followed. Society fled, and the southern districts of Manhattan began to thrive with upscale commerce and industrialization. Abandoned Longacre decayed into a notorious Red Light district known to locals as the "Thieves Lair."

At the turn of the century, *The New York Times'* owner and publisher Adolph S. Ochs began construction of a new headquarters building located in the heart of Manhattan, the vertex of Longacre Square. Times Tower, at twenty-five stories, became the second-tallest building in the world. In honor of Ochs (or in his debt), Mayor George McClellan renamed the intersection "Times Square" on April 8, 1904.

Three weeks later, the first electric billboard appeared on the side of an adjacent bank. The age of American Gauche was born.

At midnight on January 1, 1905, Times Square celebrated the dawn of its first new year with a lavish party for some two hundred thousand revelers. The neighborhood's appeal skyrocketed along with the grand finale's fireworks. Another tradition was added two years later: a descending ball of electric lights.

Times Square transitioned into high society. Eager to escape the emotional burden of the first World War, Americans took advantage of the transportation revolution to visit mythic Manhattan. The fabulous stages, movie theaters, and hotels beneath Times Tower became celebrity hotspots and tourist magnets. Despite ever-present crime and corruption, Times Square had become the sexiest cultural hub in the world. The former "Thieves Lair" earned a new nickname: "The Tenderloin."

But the rollicking twenties came to an end and Times Square followed the rest of the country into the Great Depression. Long abandoned by the newspaper, Times Tower fell into disrepair. In the 1940s, the electric ball went dark for two years to conserve energy during World War II.

Advertising impresario Douglas Leigh recognized the world's lingering fascination with Times Square. In 1961, he purchased the iconic building solely for its value as billboard real estate; the tower's office spaces weren't even worth the cost of retrofitting the building for modern heat and air conditioning. To this day, there are no occupants above the retail floors.

It was the dawn of globalization, and Times Square's visibility and advertising potential rose to new heights. But its darkest period was about to begin. Pornographic theaters and underground brothels boomed while crime intensified. By the mid-1970s, Time Square was the most dangerous area in New York City. Legitimate businesses fled this new incarnation of the Thieves Lair.

In 1983, twenty-three hundred crimes were reported on 42nd Street between Seventh and Eighth avenues.

And yet, Times Square was to rise again. In the latter part of the 1980s, Mayors Ed Koch and David Dinkins forged new developments in the western parts of Midtown, sowing the seeds for Rudolph Giuliani's "Disneyfication" of Times Square. Quite suddenly, Times Square once again became an upscale tourist attraction. Bitter racial and cultural tensions eased and New York's reputation soared to its greatest height since the Roaring Twenties. And the city became every American's backyard on September 11, 2001.

By 2009, New York City was ranked as the safest of the 25 largest cities in the United States.

Today, over half a million people will pass through Times Square.

As the final hours of the year dwindled down on this crisp December night, the sun descended and the mercury plummeted. And fervent partygoers from every part of the globe converged on Times Square.

The AP predicted over one million visitors, *The New York Times* estimated 1.5 million, and Fox News reported two million. Internally, the NYPD special commander in charge put his calculation at "a cubic fuckton."

Preparation for New Year's Eve's mind-boggling logistics begins weeks in advance, when the NYPD begins their intimidation game with random appearances of "Hercules teams," black-clad NYPD shock troopers armed with assault rifles, and "Critical Response Vehicle Surges," in which as many as forty squad cars swarm crime scenes. These spectacles are designed for the eyes of anyone who might threaten New York. And while bystanders watch the show, the NYPD watches them back.

On New Year's Eve, Times Square is closed by 4 p.m. Entrances are accessible only at carefully monitored access points. Sniffing dogs aid police officers as they patrol on foot and bikes, in motorcycles and cars. Helicopters and hidden snipers watch from above, aided by four hundred high-speed closed-circuit cameras capable of reading a thousand license plates per second. All codes cycle through NYPD headquarters, One Police Plaza.

Emergency Medical Services, the New York City Fire Department, and Animal Care and Control assist the police, along with an invisible contingent of federal officers, including the FBI counterterrorism division. Over two hundred NYPD detectives are enrolled in the Joint Terrorism Task Force, a partnership between the FBI and the Department of Defense.

In all, nearly eight thousand law enforcement officers monitor the crowd.

Revelers are ushered into "pens," metal barricades that divide up Times Square's real estate and minimize the danger of stampeding. First arrivers secure the plum vantage point directly across from the ball at 43rd Street. The pens fill behind them, northeast through the intersection toward Central Park.

Opening festivities begin around six. This year's celebration will include a troupe of parachuting violinists; a "tweenage" all-girl pop band populated by not one but two future porn stars; a questionably-tasteful burlesque performance sponsored by an internet site; a practice New Year's Eve kiss; hourly appearances by celebrities including Dick Clark, Ryan Seacrest, Hugh Jackman, Kermit the Frog, Christina Aguilera, and Justin Bieber; a massive balloon release sponsored by Pepsi, and nearly two tons of flame-proof confetti branded with uplifting messages like "peace," "hope," "love," "happiness," and "health."

Tonight, the Thieves Lair would be prowled by a new kind of predator.

Two
The Oval Office
Washington, DC
December 31
12:24 p.m.

William Weston, a conservative Democrat from Illinois, was two weeks from completing his first year as President of the United States. He was a much younger man when he took office at the age of 48 years and 11 days (as calculated by CNN). The muscles had faded from his thin frame, the salt in his hair was drowning the pepper, and the feel of his wife had become less compelling than a few moments of precious sleep. All the while, promises were broken, approval ratings dropped, wars dragged on, and the blindly partisan vultures in Congress were more concerned with their special-interest pocket-fillers than with helping him get things fixed. He couldn't have expected anything different, but optimism was easier to muster from the other side of the podium.

One thing he knew: He had the skills for the job. He was a calm, rational, prepared man, and that was a comfort to a country that had just spent eight years as backseat passengers to an imbecilic cowboy. Just as voters put their trust in Weston, Weston learned to put his trust in himself.

Weston's trademark "move," as defined by the jokesters on *Saturday Night Live,* was a long, thoughtful breath taken at a desk with his hands steepled before his mouth. But Weston wasn't intimidated; in fact, he found himself doing it more frequently as the caricature spread. It wasn't a bad thing for the people to know that the guy in charge was taking a focused moment of consideration while they stared at their cellphones and ignored the world's crises.

Even now, his hands were steepled under his nose.

"How the hell do they show this on television?" muttered Teddy

Harrison, his Chief of Staff.

"Local news at ten in the morning," Weston sighed. "No disclaimer, no warning. I hope the FCC is on this."

They had been reviewing the Morning Book, a compilation of summaries, cables, and reports assembled by the White House Watch Team, when Press Secretary Jim Bunim brought them this clip from this morning's broadcast of Channel 9 news in New York.

The tape picked up in mid-sentence, an attractive female anchor speaking to the camera. "...Holly Cooke, first cousin to First Lady Marilyn Weston, was attacked in front of Three United Nations Plaza two nights ago. Her two year-old child was abducted, and is still missing. Cooke was supposed to be at Bellevue Hospital, recovering from her wounds. But this morning, a bystander took disturbing video of a dazed and injured Mrs. Cooke walking in the middle of busy traffic on First Avenue, right near the scene of her attack."

The picture cut to shaky cellphone footage of Holly Cooke, naked and blood-smeared, stumbling across First Avenue. At least someone at the station had had the good sense to add a digital blur to her privates.

"Help me... please God, someone help!" she screamed, spinning among unnerved onlookers. Nobody stepped up to help her.

"Mrs. Cooke was believed to be the victim of an animal, or animals, that went on a rampage through lower Manhattan last night. At least four people are dead and many more injured. Animal Care and Control are asking for tips, and police said they're checking with local zoos to see if there have been any breakouts. According to witnesses, the animals appear to be dogs or hyenas. The NYPD has released a statement saying that they're adding to the substantial security at—"

Bunim paused the video and turned to the President. "Sir, they want to hear from you."

Teddy spoke first. "Tell them we're involved with the investigation. They'll have answers when we have answers. Just remain calm, and be responsible with their reporting. We'll have people shooting their pets."

Weston's intercom lit up.

"And our hearts go out to the victims," Weston added as he checked the message from his secretary. Rebekkah Luft, his National Security Advisor, was here to see him.

"Rebekkah. Were we expecting her?" asked a surprised Weston.

Teddy shook his head no, and Bunim shrugged. This wasn't at all regular; most updates from the National Security Agency were delivered via duty officer.

"Send her in," Weston said.

As the door opened, all three men stood to greet Luft. Teddy proffered his chair and took another for himself from along the curved wall.

Luft looked distracted and pallid, far from her usual self. She sat without looking at the chair. Her mind was somewhere else.

"Good morning, Rebekkah," Weston said.

"Mister President, I have a situation I need to bring to your attention."

Three

United Nations Plaza
44th Street near First Avenue
December 31
1:22 p.m.

Brianna Tildascow's second meatball special of the day was on the house.

She tried to pay for it—these guys sure as hell couldn't afford to give their stuff away—but the vendor wouldn't take a cent. Law enforcement officers often ate free because owners liked seeing blue in their shops, and he'd seen her draw her weapon and cover Holly Cooke until the police arrived. And maybe he remembered her flirty face—a dividend paid far sooner than she could have expected.

It was the first free meal she'd ever gotten as gratitude from a civilian. And it tasted even better than this morning's breakfast, since the meatballs had marinated a few hours.

She ate while people-watching on the busy promenade of United Nations Plaza, waiting for her Department of State contact. He was predictably late. The message was both clear and trite: She'd missed her earlier appointment, and now she was paying for her disrespect.

As UN officials are always so eager to point out, the plaza isn't *technically* a part of New York, or even the United States of America. It's considered international soil. And the FBI is regarded as a hostile intelligence agency by the United Nations. Agents are forbidden from entering the international territory unless they're escorted by a liaison.

Technically, she was already in violation of that bullshit. Privately, the FBI considers the UN just as hostile. So eager to handcuff America into playing "fair" with an enemy that isn't beholden to conventions and tribunals, so pompous in their scolding when we act in our own defense—or, God forbid, out of anger. Whether the UN liked it or not, in September of 2001 the United States of America became angry.

As planned, she waited on the plaza's promenade by the *Non Violence* monument, a bronze sculpture of a .45 revolver with its barrel twisted into a knot. Reminded Tildascow of Valentine's Day: sweet sentiment, obviously impractical, easy to ignore. And, like the UN's effectiveness, it was absurdly puny. The base barely came to her shoulders.

The sculpture marked the northwestern corner of the complex, between the curved row of flags representing each of the UN's member countries and the flower-lined garden that served as the plaza's front lawn. It was the public gateway to the United Nations Headquarters, the north face of the General Assembly Building.

The GA Building's tasteless vertical stripes of marble and glass struck her as a hideous amalgam of Greek and Asshole, but that's what you get when you try to please all of the countries all of the time. Beyond it to the south, the Secretariat Building, a monolithic steel domino, blocked New York's view of the East River and beyond. Not that there was much to see in Queens.

As flocks of pedestrians crisscrossed the promenade, she read the front-page story of *The New York Times* on her BlackBerry. The headline was priceless: "Who let the dogs out?"

If only they were dogs.

After the incident at Bellevue, fourteen animal attacks had been reported. Four dead, and at least three dozen injuries.

Christ, you'd think a couple more of them would've had the decency to die.

So there would be at least three dozen werewolves tonight—and how many unaccounted for?

On New Year's Fucking —

"Special Agent… Tilda's coe?"

Here was her State Department contact, an Ivy League pimple popper in his daddy's suit, trying to look important between long hours of fetching coffee and opening mail. His shifty eyes said he'd prefer buying women to charming them.

"Til-*das*-cow," she warned him. "Like 'kill jazz now.'"

"Ah. So do you hate jazz?"

"No. I hate my name being mispronounced."

She ignored his name and used the remnants of her sandwich to avoid shaking his hand. Since he was in no rush, she led him through the makeshift security tent and into the lobby of the General Assembly Building, a cavernous, echo-filled circus populated with self-important people looking at self-important artwork. A wide marble stairwell began to their right and made a dramatic and highly impractical U-turn, becoming a swash of green that arced above the hall to crash into the lowest of three white cantilevered balconies. If that said something about diplomacy, it was over the head of this Ugly American.

Just beyond the metal detectors, where the guards made a big show of taking her gun, she and her gofer of state were greeted by a stolid member of the UN's Department of Safety & Security. He escorted them underneath the balcony and through a secure door.

They took a flight of stairs down into a nexus of underground tunnels spanning the entire United Nations complex. Among the federal government, this facility was described in nigh-mythic terms. The UN's security measures were necessarily highly secretive, but legend had it that there might not be a safer place in the world than the long-term doomsday shelter underneath the UN: If a nuclear bomb dropped right on top of the plaza, partygoers in the basement would barely feel the shake. She thought it was an absurd breach of security that they had such a facility hidden beneath American soil, but the rules weren't hers to make.

The UN security hub was a sprawling, curved theater reminiscent of the General Assembly Hall. Packed with state-of-the-art tech, this was one of the few real-life government rooms that looked the way they'd imagine it in the movies. A computer-generated map of the world occupied the focal point in place of the podium, glittering with diplomatic conditions, situations and ops data. A network of monitors on the left curved wall displayed profiles of specific diplomats, probably those staying on site. At the back of the theater, where Tildascow had entered, an electronic board detailed security schedules and shift commanders. Leave it to the UN to use an LED monitor where a white board would work better.

"Special Agent Tildascow, I'm Daniel Milano, Chief of Desk for Security Coordination." He extended a firm, no-nonsense handshake.

"Good to meet you," she said. He couldn't see it, but she was casing the dual-door weapon caches stationed between each of the room's four entrances. Handprint locks, smart stuff.

"We've been reviewing the tapes for December 29th, the night of Mrs. Cooke's attack. Nothing jumped out as overly suspicious, but we were asked to show you everything."

Tildascow followed Milano, grateful that they didn't have to slow down so he could sniff her. The tapes were queued up on sequential monitors. A media tech ran the deck for what seemed like a rehearsed presentation. The UN Security Force was solid.

Milano directed Tildascow to the first monitor, where they'd prepared various angles of Cooke emerging from her room in the Secretariat Building. The raw footage was marked with time code.

KAM5422 UNSECINT 122910 21:56:10 showed Cooke negotiating the baby carriage through her room's door. KAM5418 caught her stepping through the hallway. On, KAM5401, she pushed the stroller onto the elevator.

"She was staying here?" Tildascow asked.

"Temporarily. She was to move into the Millenium Hotel on the second of January. The hotel was booked for New Year's Eve."

Indeed, Tildascow had seen Cooke's reservation on the computer at the Millenium Hotel. Everything appeared to be on the up and up, but that's what she'd expected. Despite the suspicious interview, she'd all but eliminated Cooke as a potential perpetrator of this… whatever this was. After all, the woman had been shredded to within inches of her life.

No, Cooke was the first infected, but she wasn't the one doing the infecting. Still… her prominent standing, the brazen location, the missing kid… it all seemed too measured for a random attack. She was part of a plan.

And there had to be a trail. It started somewhere. If not from Cooke, then maybe the UN.

"Nothing out of the ordinary the whole night?"

"Nothing at all in the interiors," said Milano. "We've left a message for our nightshift custodial manager, but he hasn't returned and he has tonight off for the holiday. When we hear from him, we'll put him in touch with you. You can feel free to examine our surveillance footage at your leisure, but we've prepared a time-lapse presentation for you, with the exclusion of classified areas, of course."

"Of course."

He'd made the time-lapse video sound like a couples' massage. And sure enough, it held nothing of interest. Security patrolling, custodians cleaning, administrators administrating, and a graduate student reviewing artwork for a thesis.

"Did anything out of the ordinary happen outside?" Tildascow asked.

"Well, there's no barometer for 'ordinary' on the streets of New York. We have a constant flow of eccentrics—homeless persons, tourists, activists, drugged-up wackos and, well, New Yorkers. Nothing in particular stood out, but we do have time-lapse footage."

"Let me see the exterior of the Secretariat Building, where Cooke exited."

She watched carefully as the tech sped through the tape at high speed until he found Cooke.

"Wait—go back."

He rolled the tape back to KAM0233 UNSECEXT 122910 21:09:10, an hour before Cooke emerged through the security gate.

At that moment, a man steps in front of the camera and pauses before moving on.

"Have you ever seen that man before?"

Milano hummed as he thought. "No, not that I recall. We logged him, but I couldn't see how he might pertain to an animal attack."

Tildascow seized the image. "Play it again."

He moves with the precision of a dancer, his keen eyes staring directly into the camera.

She'd seen this man before.

As Milano droned on, she delved into her recollection of the Bellevue Hospital's security footage, recreating the images through spatial mnemonics. There was Holly Cooke, her master locus. There was Dr. Kenzie. Each detail evoked the next: Nurse Nancy Laurio, the EMTs, the IVs and the monitors, the walkway…

As she hunted him in her memory, Tildascow studied his image on the monitor. Age 38 to 45. 5' 10". Dirty and unkempt, suggesting homelessness, but with an air of confident intelligence.

Dichotomies always held interesting tales.

Rooted determination in his eyes, which were so pale they nearly glowed beneath his burly eyebrows. His beard was thick and lightly salted, but his hair was a hood of sheer black. The utility muscles on his lithe body were shaped by labor, not the gym. Americans with this man's disposition rarely did manual labor. Light skin and bright eyes suggested she should start with a European origin.

His clothing was patchwork and dark. His formal button-down shirt was heavily weathered, likely worn for weeks. But it may have been hand-made. Dark pants, dark shoes. She couldn't make the cut of the cuffs, which were usually the most useful detail in pinpointing the etymologies of clothing.

More often than not, the prime characteristic of a mark—a thick beard, bold sunglasses, a dark hat—was an intentional misdirect, a countermeasure too loud to be useful. Given this leisurely amount of time to study the still image, Tildascow preferred to examine the proverbial elephant last.

This man had a plain white tee shirt stretched tightly over his formal shirt. Something was haphazardly written on the tee, probably with a black marker. It was impossible to read in this distant, grainy shot.

And now she found him in the hospital footage.

He'd been skulking near the ambulance entrance in Bellevue's ER, observing the doctors as they worked on Holly Cooke. She had mistaken the tee shirt for scrubs and written him off as a janitor.

Again, he stared right at the security camera. In this image, the text on his shirt was far from legible.

Three stacked lines. The middle contained only one letter. The top and bottom were similar in length, each four or five letters.

That was her man.

And he had a message for her.

Four
President's Briefing Room
The White House
December 31
1:45 p.m.

President Weston took his trademark deep breath and settled into his seat. The briefing room's soft overhead lighting, blue carpets, neutral walls, and mahogany paneling were designed to calm stress. If only it worked.

Rebekkah Luft had just delivered a comprehensive summary of the security routine in Times Square, using a John Madden-style telestrator to draw circles and arrows on satellite maps. Sadly, Madden had the technology long before the government.

"Options?" Weston asked. As always, he posed the question first to his Chief of Staff, Teddy Harrison. They'd met almost 30 years ago in the bullpen of the Harvard Law Review, and their relationship spanned business ventures, politics, and family life. They were each other's best men. When they coined the phrase, "I couldn't do it without him," they were thinking of Teddy "Bear" Harrison.

"Calling the event off wouldn't deter the revelers at this point," Teddy lamented. "They're already in transit. If we restrict access to Times Square, they'll spill out all over the city in a less manageable manner."

Weston's National Security Council was seated around the long mahogany table. The dunderheaded but attractive Vice President Allison Leslie; Secretary of State Anthony Michaelson; Ronald Greenberg, Secretary of Defense; Attorney General Michael Shinick; Darryl Turner, the Director of National Intelligence; and Teddy Harrison. He also had Dr. Jessica Tanner, the Director of the CDC, via closed circuit on a monitor.

He looked to General Alan Truesdale, Chairman of the Joint Chiefs of Staff, his military advisor. "We have a sufficient military presence?"

"We'll have spec ops all ready in place for the ball drop," Truesdale said. "There isn't enough time for a Rapid Deployment Force. NORTHCOM is scrambling, but we might not make it till daybreak."

That was followed by the loudest silence Weston had ever heard.

The presidential briefing room was part of the five thousand square feet of intelligence complex beneath the West Wing, which included the Situation Room, several conference rooms and the all-important Watch Center, where round-the-clock teams monitored worldwide events.

At the moment it felt like a life raft.

Luft chimed in with some optimism: "Mister President, it's been two hours since any fresh reports of injuries. NORTHCOM, the FBI and the CDC have been working closely with the NYPD, and they feel confident they've detained everyone who might have been infected last night. It may very well be contained."

"They *hope* it's been contained," interjected Jessica Tanner. Weston had her pegged as an alarmist, but that was her job. "If not, it will spread fast. If there were two last night, there may be a dozen tonight. Tomorrow there could be hundreds."

"The *timing* of this," Weston lamented.

"Too perfect to be a coincidence," agreed Truesdale. "This is by design."

"But whose design?"

The silence returned.

Jessica jumped back in. "We have to quarantine the city, sir."

Murmurs passed across the table.

"We can't do that in time," said Leslie, the VP.

"We can prepare for a safe evacuation. The infected will be easy to identify if we have properly secure conditions—"

Leslie interjected: "That would disrupt every facet of life, not only in the city, but the entire country—"

"The disruption is already here. We can't ignore it." Jessica had come prepared with a white board behind her seat. "It will be like the Lytic Cycle, the same method of reproduction as the virus. Think of Manhattan as a blood cell."

She drew a circle on the board.

"A cell that has been penetrated by a virus."

Small stars inside the circle.

"In its incubation period, the virus replicates within the cell."

Arrows from the stars, each pointing to two new ones.

"Two become four. Four become eight. This is what our werewolves will do every night. In fact, it'll be even faster as each one leaves whatever number of infected—maybe dozens—in its wake. Once the virus is strong enough to assault the larger body…" She drew a sunburst exploding from the cell, followed by arrows spilling out in every direction. "It will become a global threat."

"Good Lord," Weston muttered. He'd been so preoccupied with security for the revelers in Times Square that he hadn't considered the bigger picture.

"It *must* be contained," Jessica implored.

"We'll make arrangements." Weston nodded to Truesdale, who silently excused himself. Teddy ducked out as well.

"Dr. Tanner," said Luft, "our werewolf expert said that only silver bullets could kill them?"

"Yes, well, our patient seems to have newly manifested a severe allergic reaction to silver and silver compounds. This morning, we witnessed a rash forming on her skin almost immediatley upon epidermal contact with her own sterling silver necklace. We tested a sample of her blood against pure silver, and the result was catastrophic to—"

"So that's a yes?" Greenberg interrupted.

"Yes. Exposure to silver kills the virus-infected cell and sends self-destruction orders to nearby infected cells. The virus begins to consume its host."

"Can we put silver in the water? Or something?" asked Leslie.

"I don't know if we could find enough silver to effectively contaminate a water supply of that size," Jessica said politely. "The level of exposure from the penetration and fragmentation of a silver bullet is more likely to result in death."

"Regular bullets won't kill them?" asked Luft.

"It's still a biological creature. If you do enough damage to any physiological system it'll shut down. But the virus pumps up the heart rate and lowers the pain threshold. It's similar to the effect of methamphetamines, but significantly stronger. It'll be like trying to stop the worst speed freak ever."

"Good work, Dr. Tanner," Weston said. "Keep going and keep us informed."

"Mister President, you *have* to quarantine—"

"We're working on it. Have your people ready. We'll be in touch soon." Weston signaled to Luft to shut the closed-circuit link.

Everyone started talking at once. Weston raised a calm hand. "I'll listen to each and every one of you in a moment."

The president nodded to Greenberg. The Defense Secretary moved toward the door while receiving his instructions.

"We need every warm body armed with silver bullets. RDFs, cadets, reserves, veterans, boy scouts with good aim."

"Yes sir," Greenberg said as he exited.

"How much time do we have?"

"The moon rises at 9:58," said Luft.

Five

The United States military didn't have enough time.

Under military command, five thousand silver bullion coins were transferred from the United States Mint facility at West Point (once known as the Fort Knox of Silver) to the Radford, Virginia manufacturing facility of Alliant Techsystems, the military's preeminent supplier of ammunition. There, silver would be added to the molten lead alloy used to produce bullet cores.

Ballistic experts were charged with determining exactly how much silver could be introduced into the lead-based, ball-point 9x19mm Parabellum round, easily-produced ammunition for the ubiquitous 9mm service pistols favored by the NYPD. There wasn't enough time to develop refined equations, so they took an educated guess.

There wasn't enough time to determine the precise quantity of silver needed to catalyze the virus's self-destructive cycle.

Wasn't enough time to safely refit the machinery of the bullet factory.

Not enough time to properly test the viability of the new ammunition cartridges.

Or to properly explain to the law officers why they were being issued last-minute ammunition reassignments.

The federal government took every possible shortcut, issuing blanket warrants and orders of dubious legality. Because the sun wouldn't stop dropping.

By quarter after four, the sky over New Jersey burned crimson and purple. NYPD began closing the 45th Street pens, securing revelers under the moving lights of the electric circus. As the mercury plummeted, the party simmered.

The president and his advisors watched the clock. The moon would rise at 9:58. That was a truth they could rely on. Everything else was speculation.

At sunset, Holly Cooke's cell in the basement of 26 Federal Plaza filled with an anesthetic gas, putting her to sleep so her restraints could be reinforced. Nine other "dog attack" victims slept in adjacent cells.

Just before 5:30, a call was issued to the two hundred NYPD members of the Joint Terrorism Task Force. Soon after, they assembled for a briefing at the Midtown South Precinct on West 35th Street, the triage station closest to Times Square. In a packed conference room, an FBI Special Agent named Elmore Cahill explained that the previous night's animal attacks were the result of a street gang's pack of fighting dogs that had broken loose. The dogs had been juiced with adrenaline and a normal shot might not put them down, so five bullets laced with "animal tranquilizers" were issued to each officer. No word on how many dogs were still out there, but Cahill said they might be rabid and should be shot on sight.

As the officers spilled out into the cold and hopped into a paddy wagon for transport to Times Square, most of the chatter was about the all-girl pop band's skimpy outfits.

A couple of the men were curious about these new bullets. Very shiny.

NYPD Officer and JTTF member Mack Meely warned them that these dogs were no joke. He'd seen them himself. Last night, he and his rookie partner had responded to a breaking & entering at the Gramercy Meat Market. One of those things was cleaning out the inventory. He took a couple shots at it, all hits, but the fucker barely flinched. Barreled right past him and took a swipe at his chest. Left him with four stitches and a helluva nightmare. He was still pissed that he couldn't get tonight off.

Most of the guys loaded the new ammo right then and there.

But these bullets were really goddamn shiny. One of the guys asked what a lot of them were thinking: "How the hell do you put tranquilizer into lead?"

"I don't care," Meely responded. "As long as it works."

And now his shoulder was aching for no damn reason. What a week.

Just before six, Dick Clark and Ryan Seacrest appeared on the large screen in front of the Disney-owned Times Square Studios, which neighbored One Times Square. They thanked the crowd for coming, but it was drowned out by the cheers.

Opening ceremonies began after six. Two Latino stars of a popular telenovela joined a representative of the Phillips Lighting Company as they flipped a giant ceremonial switch. Fireworks lit the sky and the New Year's Eve ball began its glittering ascent.

Meanwhile, FBI Special Agent Brianna Tildascow hunted.

Six

CDC Containment Room
Atlanta, GA
December 31
6:58 p.m.

Melissa Kenzie awoke to hammering in her skull. The aches wracking her body were surely the work of the Devil.

She was strapped onto a gurney, tilted upright and facing a mirror. Her fog parted to remind her of a terrible thing she had seen in there: herself, her body, transforming into a monster.

Could it really have happened?

She'd felt pain. Torment. And then fury. And hunger.

It was a terrible descent, a free fall from humanity. Despair and helplessness, as she was forced from her mind and her body, both of them seized by something else…

…and yet so… *liberating*… to embrace the cravings and shed the rest.

The transformation was torturous, every second an eternity. It fueled the beast's anger, stoking the Devil's presence and distracting her faith. It was God's will: The transformation was a test, and she had failed.

No, God said in her heart. *It is a reckoning. A penance.*

For what?

She had no way of knowing. It was someone else's sacrament.

The *other*.

In the enraged nightmare, a beast had run alongside her. Man, or wolf, or both. They hunted as a pack. *He* was her cherished leader.

The impurity in her soul yearned to protect *him*. Their love was a blasphemy, because God had forsaken *him*.

She prayed God would save her from the beast.

Or was it the other way around?

Seven
President's Secretary's Room
The White House
December 31
9:25 pm

Lon had waited in the anteroom to the Oval Office for so long that he'd started to believe what he'd seen on that CDC video.

The door to the Oval Office was angled into a nook in order to fit, well, the oval. That was the only interesting thing in this depressing waiting room. The folksy Americana furniture, grandmotherly beige curtains and yuck-brown carpet were straight out of a 1970s TV family drama.

One of the Secret Service agents had taken his cell phone before they got on the helicopter. He hadn't seen that guy again, and he was faux-politely rebuked whenever he asked for his phone back. Elizabeth was probably worried sick. He couldn't wait to tell her that he was part of an important federal investigation!

One of the president's secretaries offered to contact his parents, but Lon didn't care about them. Let his stepfucker Frank think they were going to come lock him up any minute now.

Heavy traffic flowed past during those long hours. People went into the Oval Office, but never came out. Some guy in a sweater vest brought him a turkey sandwich for dinner. A Secret Service agent escorted him to take a piss. By the end of the day, he had managed to grow bored… while he was waiting in the White House to talk about a werewolf he'd just seen.

He passed the time re-reading and re-re-reading everything in the National Archives' files on lycanthropy. His own letter to President Bush was included, scrawled in his fumbled attempt at calligraphy.

And then the door to the Oval Office opened. The freaking President of the United freaking States emerged with a freaking football in his freaking hands.

"Boris Toller?" the freaking president asked.

"Um…" Lon managed to move his chin up and down while he got his feet under him.

The president tossed the football and Lon caught it against his chest. That might've been the first time he'd ever held a swineskin (*Right?*) in his life.

"Nice to meet you, Boris, I'm William Weston," he said with an outstretched hand.

Lon put his boneless, sweaty mitt into the president's grasp.

"Want a picture?" Weston asked as he pushed Lon toward the office.

"Hi. Hi. Sure."

One guy popped out of nowhere to take the football and another guy took their picture, and then suddenly they were gone. The ritual was probably standard operating procedure, Lon thought, but it felt intensely disingenuous.

"It's a beauty, isn't it?" asked Weston, referring to the office.

Lon couldn't deny the majesty of the Oval Office. It was time to say something profound. "It's a cool…"

The president gazed at him for a moment, probably wondering if Lon was capable of making it through this. But there was no judgment in his voice when he spoke again. "How about we go watch some television, Boris?"

With a hand on Lon's shoulder, Weston led him through a door on the opposite side of the oval, into a curved junction between two hallways. Smart suits rushed to and fro, nodding respectfully to the president. Their quick looks made him feel embarrassed for his unaccomplished life.

"So you run a website?" the president asked.

Lon wasn't quite ready to speak outside of his own head.

Weston turned him so they were face to face. Something about the stance magnetically yanked Lon's eyes upward into a lock with the president's. He fought the urge to run away.

"They tell me you're the expert we need right now, Boris."

"Lon."

"I'm sorry?"

"Lon, sir. I go by the name *Lon*."

"Why?"

"Why what?"

Weston spoke slowly. "Why do they call you Lon?"

"For Lon Chaney Jr., sir. He was an actor, he played the Wolf Man."

The president raised a ponderous eyebrow. "That's better than Boris."

Lon closed his eyes and swallowed. So. Damn. *Stupid*.

And then they were moving again. Weston pushed him into an open doorway across from the Oval Office. "This is the Roosevelt Room."

Lon peeked in. He wasn't sure what he was supposed to see, or even which Roosevelt it was named after. Long table, lots of chairs, big flags, paintings, and a fireplace. He nodded that yes, this was indeed the Roosevelt Room.

They proceeded to their left and crossed a hallway with more beige and brown. Weston said "goodnight" or "happy new year" to everyone they passed.

The president pushed Lon into a right turn and Secret Service agents greeted them at an open elevator. They all got inside—wood and brass and mirrors—and one of the agents pressed a fancy security button. The combination of the men's colognes put another twist in Lon's stomach.

"Great actor, Lon Chaney," Weston said with a politician's smile.

Lon nodded, still stuck on the whole *guy is in charge of the free world and you tell him you've named yourself after an—*

"But I was always partial to Karloff the Uncanny."

Lon's heart burst with excitement! "Oh my God! No! Have you ever seen *Son of Dracula*? Chaney made a better Dracula than Lugosi!"

"Have *you* ever seen *The Black Room*?" asked the president. "Karloff in dual roles? The man had range, beyond the makeup. How about *The Comedy of Terrors?*"

Lon followed Weston off the elevator into a marble-tiled lobby. He was totally turned around, couldn't have found his way out if he was being chased by a minotaur.

"Okay, alright," Lon conceded, "but have you seen the 1939 *Of Mice and Men?*"

"I'll admit I haven't," Weston responded, gesturing Lon through a door to their immediate right, past more bland artwork. "Is it good?"

"You won't believe Chaney's performance! That's where he really stepped out of his father's shadow."

"I'll check it out," Weston said as they entered a new hallway and a decidedly different environment, one far more modern than the rest of the White House. The Na'vi carpeting, wood panels, and halogen lights were homey, but the dead room tone and cool recycled air felt oddly counterfeit, as if the walls were hiding something far more sophisticated.

They passed a pod bustling with televisions and energetic people in headsets, and the president sensed Lon's curiosity. "That's the Watch Center. Those guys monitor all the news in the world, all the time."

They reached a long conference room, with massive flat-screen televisions built into its wood-paneled walls. A high-sheen redwood table was populated by a lot of the same people he'd met earlier, including Luft, Greenberg, and Truesdale. Others were seated behind them.

Lon had seen this place in the movies! This was the White House Situation Room, where the president decides to drop nuclear bombs!

"Have a seat, Lon." Weston directed him to sit in a chair behind his place at the head of the table.

Woah… Was he going to become a cabinet member?

"Can we get some popcorn?" Weston asked a duty officer, trying to disarm the tension. "And champagne? Anybody want champagne?"

A few people shrugged or nodded. The officer hurried off.

"Mister President," said Greenberg, "We've distributed silver bullets among the New York police in the JTTF. It was the best way to single out a number of officers."

"And the quarantine scenario?" Weston was far more relaxed than the others.

"We're readying checkpoints at all of the bridges and tunnels. We'll be reinforcing all night long. We should be able to close everything down." And then he added, softly: "If necessary."

"Here's hoping it won't be necessary," said Weston. He turned his attention toward one of the TVs, where Dick Clark's New Year's Rockin' Eve had just returned from a commercial. The other screens were showing New Year's Eve programming from CNN, Fox News, the Fox network, Comedy Central, and MTV, all with closed captions.

"Thirteen minutes until moonrise," said Luft.

Wait. *What?*

Weston turned Lon's way. "Well, we've got a few minutes and popcorn is on the way, so why don't you tell us about werewolves?"

The entire Situation Room turned toward him. The taunting ring of *Under Pressure* by David Bowie and Queen danced through his head. *Ding ding ding di-di-ding ding. Ding ding ding di-di—*

"Lon?"

"Well, uh... sir, there are hundreds of different versions of the legend."

"Let's start from the beginning."

"Well, the first true werewolf story was written in the year 8 AD, by a Roman called Ovid. It was in Book One of his fifteen-volume narrative poem, *Metamorphoses.* This was a history of the world from creation to Julius Caesar, in mythological terms, of course. Ovid wrote of the notorious cannibal Lycaon, the king of Arcadia, who tested Zeus' power by serving him a meal of stewed children. In response, Zeus transformed him into a wolf. The better translation from Ovid's Latin reads as follows:

"Lycaon ran in terror, and reaching the silent fields howled aloud, frustrated

of speech. Foaming at the mouth, and greedy as ever for killing, he turned against the sheep, still delighting in blood. His clothes became bristling hair, his arms became legs. He was a wolf, but kept some vestige of his former shape. There were the same grey hairs, the same violent face, the same glittering eyes, the same savage image.

"Now, the first mention of the mortal werewolf came from *The Satyricon*, a satire novel by Petronius, from the court of Nero later in the first century. This was really the only other surviving novel from the Roman Empire, so it's interesting that they both mentioned werewolves. But *The Satyricon* is much more lighthearted, like a relationship misadventure sitcom for the bathhouse set. In chapter sixty-two of Volume Two, the narrator has attended an extravagant dinner at the lavish estate of—"

"Lon," President Weston interrupted.

That was when Lon realized that everyone was frowning at him like he was an infected pustule. Oh, how he knew that look.

"I'm sorry," Lon said.

"That's okay. I hope you'll write down all of that for us later. In the meantime, let's keep it succinct."

"Yes. I'm sorry."

"It's okay," he repeated. "Now how does one become a werewolf?"

"In pop culture—in the movies—it's usually from the bite of another werewolf. In *The Wolf Man*, Lawrence Talbot, Lon Chaney Jr.'s character, is bitten by a werewolf who turns out to be the son of a Gypsy fortuneteller. Other legends claim that you can become a lycanthrope, a person who transforms into a werewolf, by donning a belt made of wolf skin during a full moon, or drinking rainwater from the footprint of a wolf, or drinking or bathing in the blood of a werewolf. And those are just the stories indigenous to America; there are really weird ones from—"

"Which one is the truth?"

"It certainly comes from a bite. But many accounts suggest that the attacks aren't random. Very often, the lycanthrope will know their victim. It's usually someone they love. The important distinction is that lycanthropy isn't a disease; it's a curse, a metaphor for atonement, punishment for sin."

"So who does the cursing?" asked General Truesdale. "Who created the first werewolf?"

"That's up for conjecture. Modern occult writings refer to witches or warlocks or shamans or, again, Gypsy mystics. But anthropologists have tracked legends of shapeshifters through the folklore of virtually every culture in history. Native Americans had their skinwalkers, like the Navajo *yee naaldlooshii*, or 'he who runs on all fours.' If you're looking at pure shapeshifting, I mean that goes all the way back to Homer—"

"Let's stick with werewolves," Weston said. Some of the others squirmed with impatience. "Traditional werewolf legend. The moon and silver, right?"

"Yeah. The most 'traditional' version says that when there's a full moon, a man cursed with lycanthropy will transform into a werewolf."

"Tonight's not a full moon," said Luft.

"Neither was last night," added the president, gesturing at Lon to continue.

"Well, the full moon thing has been under contention forever. It probably started with Petronius, who wrote that when he first saw a man turn into a werewolf, I quote, 'the moon was bright as day.' But, I mean, if you think about it, it's really stupid—why would it only work under a full moon? It's transmogrification, not PMS." Lon paused for the proverbial rimshot, but nobody laughed, so he continued: "There's no reason to expect that a lycanthrope wouldn't transform whenever he or she is exposed to moonlight."

"Interesting," Weston said, throwing a glance toward Luft.

"And silver is the only thing that will kill them?" Luft asked.

"Some say holy water or fire will do it, but they're confusing them with vampires. And I mean, I assume with modern weapons—if you blow a werewolf up, he's probably gonna die, y'know? Also, they're repulsed by wolfsbane, like vampires with garlic."

"Wolfsbane is a flower?"

"*Aconitum napellus.* There's debate about which specific subspecies the lore refers to, but I believe it to be *Aconitum tauricum Wulfen,* simply because of its endemism to the Southern Carpathians, in and about Romania. It's a tall, romantic purple flower—"

"Why Romania?" interjected Luft.

"Oh, man, well, lycanthropy lore—all of the classic monster lore, really—is distinctly European. Horror literature reached its golden age when London was the world's capital of society, and Romania was best known for the morbid reign of Vlad the Impaler, who served as Bram Stoker's template for Count Dracula."

"But Dracula was a *vampire*," said the president.

"A lot of the fiction is tied together. See, it's all drawn from primal fears. The vampire is the violator. The werewolf is the betrayer. I've already done a first draft of my doctoral thesis on this."

"We're looking for fact, not fiction."

"Werewolves are fact. Vampires are fiction."

"You're sure?"

"Yes."

"How?"

"Because Lord George Gordon Byron essentially made vampires up for a story he created during the same writing exercise in which Mary Wollstonecraft Shelley wrote *Frankenstein: or, The Modern Prometheus,* in the volcanic summer of 1816, commonly referred to as the 'Year Without a Summer,' but he abandoned his so-called *Fragment of a Novel,* and that influenced his physician, John William Polidori, to write *The Vampyre,* which defined the creature as we know it."

Everyone in the room stared at him in silent dismay. He wondered if perhaps he should repeat that last part more clearly, but—

"Answer me this, young man," said Truesdale. "If this man becomes a wolf, and whomever he bites becomes a wolf, where does it end? Why haven't they overrun the world?"

"I…" That one gave him pause. "They just don't spread that way. People don't usually survive a werewolf attack. And some of the legends say that when you kill the originator of the bloodline—the first werewolf—everyone he infected, and everyone down the line, gets cured."

"The originator of the bloodline," repeated Weston.

"The first werewolf," Lon confirmed.

"So we have a target," said Truesdale, and people started moving. *A target?*

"We'll get our men this information, sir," said Michael Shinick, the Attorney General. Shinick's aide had already stepped into a futuristic phone booth. When he closed the curved door, its transparent glass turned milky white. So cool!

"Anything else, Lon?"

Lon shook his head, still on the phone booth thing. "If I think of something, I'll let you know."

"Anything might be valuable. Please speak up."

The president's aide returned with hot buttered popcorn. Weston grabbed a handful before it was on the table. "Thank you, Tommy. One last thing: Could you send my wife a bouquet of roses and tell her I'm sorry I had to work?"

"Yes sir."

"And get me a DVD of the 1939 *Of Mice and Men*." He winked at Lon.

"The moon rises in five minutes," Luft said.

"Let's see what happens," Weston said with a full mouth.

"What…*happens?*" Lon muttered, thoroughly confused. He followed their eyes to the television.

What *might* happen?

Eight

Jacob K. Javits Federal Office Building
26 Federal Plaza, Manhattan
23rd Floor Research Library
9:53 p.m.

Tildascow checked the clock again. No matter how hard she tried to concentrate, her eyes kept sliding back to that goddamn clock.

9:54.

The FBI's research library was so comprehensive that it defeated its own purpose. Post 9/11, they collected so much goddamn data that research was a constant fucking drowning in a "narrow this search" stupor. She never thought she'd miss the microfiche, but how could you find a needle in a haystack when the haystack kept getting bigger?

She'd commandeered twelve research assistants and assigned them to data mining in the FBI's Sentinel database. The public (and, more importantly, the *enemy*) still thought Sentinel was a broken mess, but in truth it was a nice improvement over the old Automated Case Support system. Case files, leads, suspects, forensics, and intrabureau communications, all linked for cross-referencing. Her favorite Intelligence Analyst, Charlie Frank, had all quarters reporting to him while she free-swam through the database.

They sifted local and federal criminal case files, security tapes, plane manifests, passports, and driver's licenses, trying to make a connection to a man they could barely see.

That wasn't by *his* design, though. He'd stood right in front of the cameras at the UN and at Bellevue.

This guy wanted to be seen. And he got what he wanted.

Her BlackBerry buzzed with a text message from the Assistant to the Director of the FBI: "Concentrate on Romania / Transylvania."

Nice. Had anyone thought to dig up Lon Chaney's corpse?

Tildascow rubbed her temples. She'd reminded herself a hundred times that debating the likelihood of this thing would only slow her down. She'd seen it with her baby blues. And if there were werewolves, they might as well be from Transylvania.

9:56.

"Charlie, look at inbound transportation from Europe," she called out. "Focus on Transylvania or Romania or nearby, including transfers."

"Hear ya," he hollered from one of the other cubicles in the maze. The sexiest thing about Charlie was that "hear ya" was all he ever said until he had pertinent and concise information. She didn't give a shit about anyone's family or their take on the weather.

She typed "Transylvania" into Sentinel's aggregator field and cross-referenced it against her man's image.

9:57.

The search would take a while and she'd go crazy staring at the clock. Was there somewhere around here to find a werewolf movie on DVD? Watch it in fast-forward?

Ping.

That fast?

As the data mining continued, she linked out the first hit to an adjacent monitor. It was a December 18th security tape from the Newark airport. Facial recognition scans of passengers from Lufthansa flight 412 from Munich, where several passengers had connected from Bucharest.

And there he was.

"Charlie, I need a manifest on Lufthansa flight 412 from Munich, December 18. Right now."

"Hear ya."

He was 6' 1" and a lithe 175 pounds. Salt and pepper stubble, long and unkempt black hair. She linked to surveillance footage from the flight's deplaning and spun the jog wheel to find him emerging from the jetway. Fucker glided right through the logjam of passengers, slippery slippery. His eyes—bright brown, practically yellow—carefully scanned the concourse before settling on the camera's point of view.

He looked right at her.

That tee was already stretched over his shirt. It was cleaner and clearer eleven days prior to the footage from the UN. The message was awkwardly scrawled in lower-case letters. She thought from the previous images that it was written in marker, but here it seemed like some kind of brushed ink.

Her watch's alarm buzzed.

9:58.

Nine
Moonrise
December 31

In the basement of 26 Federal Plaza, six guards and four EIS Officers looked up from their poker game.

Nobody needed an explanation for what they'd just heard.

They approached the monitors with their mouths full of half-chewed tortilla chips. An hour ago the inmates had been gassed with enough tranqs to knock them out for a couple of days. But here they were, already awake and thrashing in pain.

One by one, they began to howl.

"Ern't no two ways 'bout it," said Conor Burns, the head guard. "Them folks is werewolves."

***

Just before 10 p.m., the stars of the *Twilight* film series made a surprise appearance on the TV screen at Times Square Studios, creating an unexpected crush of screaming fans. NYPD officers were taken by surprise as stampeding began in several of the pens.

Officer Mack Meely had been feeling sick even before it happened. His joints ached like he was coming down with something. He hoped he didn't catch anything from that dog at the butcher shop last night. Fuck, coulda been rabies.

When the pushing started, one of the pen's metal barriers was lifted from its mounts and got stuck between a lamppost and a tree. A woman at the front was being crushed against the barrier. She wasn't trying to loose herself, and Meely realized that it was because she was using her arms to protect her two kids.

Meely wedged himself into the crowd and pushed against the metal crossbar to create room for the mother to escape. She followed her kids out of the crowd and breathlessly turned to thank—

Then she screamed bloody hell.

Meely tried to calm her but she stumbled to the ground, taking her kids with her. He reached to help her up and that's when he realized his hands were covered in thick grey fur.

His body seized and his joints contorted, forcing him to the cold, hard cement. Was he having a heart attack? But the fur, what the fuck was—

The mother wouldn't stop screaming. Her kids joined in, ringing aggravation on top of the pain. Everything began to spin. He was getting angrier—*angrier*. His back was breaking and he wanted to—

Roar.

***

In the park on Second and 15th, seven blocks south of Gramercy Meat Market, several NYU cinema students were filming in front of the statue of the peglegged colonial governor Peter Stuyvesant. They had no permit, and their actress would have to scream in this shot, so they only expected to get off a couple of takes before cops showed up. Hopefully the New Year's Eve stuff would distract them.

The redheaded actress had been sleeping with the director to make sure she got the lead role. He'd told her he had a lead on financing for a big-budget version, so she kept him on the hook even if he was a colossal douche.

"You stupid motherfucking asshole!" the director shouted at their fourth sound guy in four nights. His French accent made his anger sound like fear. "What does it mean to you when I say keep the mic above the statue? Does that mean you should drop it down to here, so it's in the shot?" He held his puny little hand at his eyebrows, barely five feet off the ground.

The producer and the production assistant, both also students, politely kept their eyes down, each praying they'd never have to work with this—

A howl echoed through the park, silencing the director.

The sound guy was a too-skinny hipster wearing big headphones. He turned his boom mic toward the darkness behind the statue. His eyes grew wide as he listened to something the others couldn't hear.

He dropped the mic and backed away, but his headphones were still attached to the heavy-duty digital recorder resting on its metal cart. The whole thing came down with an expensive crash.

The sound guy took off in a sprint. From near the exit of the park, he screamed back at them, "Geeyaaouuuaathere!"

"Typical American work ethic!" the director yelled after him. "You will not get credit for this!"

When he turned back, an animal was on top of his redheaded actress. Her scream was cut short as the animal ripped into her chest.

The director ran for his life, ducking branches and leaping rocks. His lungs burned as he stumbled into the street with nearly horizontal bounds.

Something hit him *hard,* and then he was in the air, flipping maybe, but he was still okay, and then the ground was rushing up toward him and he felt snaps first in his ankle and then his wrist, and then his face popped like a flashbulb.

A car had just hit him. It was okay, though, because there were lights and that had to mean safety from that beast.

"Help me!" he pleaded.

And then the animal landed on the car and slid across the hood, leading with its black claws, and he felt fire on his chest and—

***

Milena Castro was alone in a crowd of a million people. She clutched her two children as the police officer wriggled on the ground.

He had just helped them escape the crowd. Dozens of other people were trapped and crying for help. None of them noticed what was happening.

The officer had turned into some kind of monster. He was covered in black hair. His nose protruded like a dog's. His lips parted to reveal fangs and he screamed at the sky.

***

Max Cafolla hated his whole damn family.

Everyone was feeling sick from the pot roast, which his cheapskate parents had bought at a discount from Gramercy Meat Market, no matter that they'd had some kind of problem over there last night. The meat never smelled right, and the blood in the wax paper had a damn weird consistency. He told his wife not to feed it to their kids, but that nagging bitch never listened.

So all he ate was the vegetables while everyone raved about the roast. Now they were all complaining about the flu and he was shitting his guts out in a bathroom the size of a phone booth.

He gripped the sink and shivered through the latest siege of cramps. Fucking lactose. His mother said there was no milk in the creamed corn. Probably didn't even listen to what he'd asked. Nobody ever listened to him.

Best he could hope was that his miserable wife would just up and die from whatever the roast had done to her.

He flushed and forced himself to his feet. The medicine cabinet was fogged up from his gasping and sweating. He braved through another wave of cramps and then threw open the bathroom door.

"I thought you said there was no fucking milk in the corn!"

Grandma, Dad, Mom, Becca, and both of their toddlers turned to him. He only recognized them by their clothes, because they had all become—

***

Just three blocks from Times Square, newlyweds Robbie and Kaylie Johnson had started their own kind of celebration. Unable to wait for their New Year's Eve kiss, they'd stolen away from the crowd and now they were making out on a car hidden behind a tree. With hardly anybody on the street, Robbie thought he might be able to get Kaylie to hit it right there. What a story to tell at his poker game.

He was just about to slip down her panties when he heard the crash. At first he thought it was fireworks, then he realized something had hit the car.

Robbie cradled his wife in his arms, shielding her from the thing standing on the roof.

But then Kaylie screamed over his shoulder. Things (animals? people?) were jumping out of a window above. One, then another, then smaller ones. They were the shape and size of people, with faces like dogs.

They landed quietly, almost magnetically, snarling in harmony.

Robbie and Kaylie were surrounded.

***

The rush had died down, but the crowd was still packed tight. Girls were all screaming as the *Twilight* guys said some shit nobody could hear.

125

The tallest person in the crowd was a high school basketball player and aspiring poet named Joaquin. He could see to the edge of the pen, but it didn't look like anyone was in charge up there. Where were all the police?

All the way at the front, something flew up in the air and then fell back into the crowd.

Joaquin squinted. Could he have imagined that?

He waited, unsure what to do. Nobody else reacted, so...

Then it happened again. A woman shot up, face to the sky, six feet over the crowd. Blood squirted from her neck, all over the people below.

Then the crowd rippled backward.

Next a guy got launched, twice as high as the woman. By the time he landed, the sea had parted enough for Joaquin to see his head splatter like a water balloon.

And now he could see the cause of it all.

A motherfucking werewolf was ripping shit up.

Joaquin got the fuck *out*.

***

"Break break break, this is Black Heart One," yelled Grim Reaper into the radio. "Possible tango spotted in the crowd, east side of the square, on Broadway near Seventh."

Staff Sergeant Christopher "Grim Reaper" Angelone was the mission commander of this bullshit. He and his Surveillance and Target Acquisition platoon were operating under the worst possible conditions. They'd been called up on two hours' notice and forced to swap out their M40A3 sniper rifles for fucktastic close-quarter MP5Ks because some fool—probably not even military—insisted they use 9mm cartridges.

Arming snipers with close-quarter weapons was like asking a surgeon to operate with chopsticks.

Grim Reaper radioed: "Interrogative Black Heart Two and Three: Do you have eyes on possible tango? Over!" He searched the crowd through his tripod-mounted spotter's scope. Gunnery Sergeant Richard "Lunk" Hedd lay prone before him, tracking through his own MP5K's crosshairs.

"Negative, One, we do not have a visual," radioed the spotter for Team Two. "I repeat: We do not have a visual."

"Break break break! This is Black Heart Three, we have picked up possible tango, spotted in police uniform in the crowd."

"Roger, Three," Reaper responded as he adjusted his scope.

"Tango has engaged multiple civilians. Request permission to fire. Over."

"Engaged civilians how?" asked Reaper. He couldn't see a damn thing. Firing into the crowd was a tough call. "Do you see a weapon?"

"Negative, Sir. I don't think the tango is human! Looks like a—I think it's a werewolf, sir! There are bodies all over! He's killing civilians!"

"Did he say 'werewolf'?" Lunk asked.

"Permission to fire granted," radioed Reaper.

"Fuck! We lost him. Tango moved northeast on the same street. Three, can you pick him up?"

"This is Three. Negative, we do not have a visual."

"Break break break! This is Four, we have another possible Tango, approaching from southwest corner, repeat southwest corner—there may be multiple—"

"Break break break! This is Three, we have visual, there are at least two, engaging civilians—"

"All teams, fire when ready!" called Reaper.

Lunk found the commotion in front of Times Square Studios. He couldn't see the target, but civilians were flying into the air—whatever it was, it was *fucking people the fuck up.*

"I have the location, but I don't have a clear shot—"

"Stay on it," said Reaper, tracking Lunk's target through his scope.

The crowd finally shifted and they could see… *whatever* it was.

"Target acquired."
"Fire!"

***

CNN broke the story first. Anderson Cooper, bundled in a black overcoat and scarf, had been addressing viewers from a platform elevated above the street when his cameraman caught the melee in the crowd.

The east pen closest to 42nd Street had burst. The mob stampeded in every direction, pummeling anything in its way. Police were overwhelmed. Even horses were toppled in the scramble.

And then a high-pitched gunshot pierced the sky.

"Ladies and gentlemen!" Cooper ducked as he yelled at the camera, "Something is happening in Times Square! We have shots fired—"

Ten
White House Situation Room
10:11 p.m.

The president and his advisors watched silently as CNN broke the story.

The Chairman of the Joint Chiefs, General Alan Truesdale, entered the private phone booth and called the mission commander in New York. National Security Advisor Rebekkah Luft checked the status of military and CDC prep teams in place for the quarantine procedure. Chief of Staff Teddy Harrison and his team of speechwriters shifted into overdrive.

Lon turned to the president, whose expression was hidden behind his steepled fingers.

Truesdale opened the phone booth door. Everyone watched as he nodded at the president with some kind of solemn confirmation.

Weston sat back in his seat and took a long moment to say: "Go."

"We are a go for Operation Wolf's Den," confirmed Truesdale. Everyone at the table went to work. "Initiate all contingencies, tell the CDC to go. We're cutting all transportation in and out of Manhattan. Mister Secretary—"

Greenberg was on his way into another phone booth. "The RDF is en route," he said.

"Seal it up."

Eleven
Times Square

The first shot came so close to the werewolf that the snipers saw its draft ruffle the creature's fur.

They'd never seen anything of that size move with such speed. It was nearly impossible to track. Uncertain shots were risky with the crowd in flux, but that thing had to be stopped.

The werewolf loped through the crowd, caroming from body to body, leaving behind gruesome claw wounds. Another shot zipped above its head and punctured the chest of a nearby civilian.

The wolf continued west along Broadway, bounded into a tree, and pounced on an unsuspecting cop, crushing the poor guy like a bug. Never losing momentum, the wolf took off in another crazy leap, narrowly escaping the third sniper's shot.

It landed in front of mounted police officer Jason Orlandi, a member of the JTTF and five-time marksmanship award winner. Orlandi fired three silver "tranquilizer" rounds into the werewolf's chest.

The creature bucked and shrieked and clawed at the burning wounds as it collapsed. Orlandi moved his nervous horse closer and squinted at the thing. That was no dog.

In fact, the *whatever it was* was…changing.

Where a wolf fell was now a man. A cop.

"Hold on—we'll get help!" he shouted. "Dispatch, we have a ten double zero at Times Square. Request ambulance immediately!" No immediate response.

Jesus, had he just shot a cop?

"Dispatch, are you there? Request—"

Now screams from behind. He twisted in his horse's saddle to find two new creatures loping through the crowd at jungle cat velocity, mowing down civilians in their path.

And zeroing in on him.

His mount bucked, but it was too late. The creatures shot from the ground, and then Orlandi felt his horse's insides rupture from the impact as he tumbled through the air.

Dazed and numb, Orlandi stirred to sounds of ravenous chewing. He was trapped in the saddle, his leg broken underneath his horse. He pulled at its mane, got no response. But it couldn't be dead, it was trembling.

No. It *was* dead. And something was tearing at its stomach.

He couldn't get his head up to see what was happening and he couldn't find the air to call out. And none of the thousands of people around him were coming to his aid.

One of the creatures crested the horse's belly. It was smaller, squeakier than the last one, but no less threatening. Blood dripped from its teeth, splattering on the horse's ribcage. Orlandi closed his eyes as it closed in on him. He could smell its hot, salty breath—

Two cracks in the air and the monster jerked from a one-two punch. A second later, another shot sizzled and the second creature rolled from behind the horse's stomach.

The animals silently shriveled. Their fur retreated and their faces softened and they became human children. Just toddlers.

Orlandi covered his eyes and cried into his elbow.

Twelve
CDC Observation Room
10:21 p.m.

Twenty-three minutes after moonrise in New York, after the story had already broken across the major networks, the glimmering blue light of the moon dawned over the horizon of Atlanta.

Jessica Tanner watched Melissa Kenzie roar awake from a dead sleep. The fangs pushed through her gums, thick hair sprouted anew, and her hands twisted into claws as she thrashed at her bonds.

This transmutation was at odds with what they understood to be fundamental pillars of biology and virology. Or, at least, what they *thought* they understood. How could a virus hijack DNA to such an extent that it reassigned its host's *species?*

It just couldn't be possible, no matter how real it was.

There hadn't been enough time to properly interview Kenzie between the morning inducement and the moon's rise. Post-antithetical transformation, she'd remained in a feverish state, exhausted and uncommunicative. They didn't want to risk taxing her heart with methamphetamines, so their questions would have to wait until morning.

But waiting wouldn't do anymore, not with those creatures loose in Times Square. The exposure rate tonight would be astronomical.

"DNA polymerase," Richard hypothesized, whispering to himself as they watched a tape of the new transformation repeat in slow motion. "The virus catalyzes change in the DNA. It doesn't lose the original template, so moonlight must trigger it to synthesize and overlay a new strand."

Jessica stood beside him, but she wasn't watching the tape. She had a question for her husband, and she was fearful of his reaction.

He gasped as he thought of another possibility. "Or... epigenetics! Trans-species polymorphism. It just flips a switch in evolution." He smiled like he was sizing up a Playboy spread. "God, I can't wait to get under the hood of this thing."

"Richard," she began, steeling herself, "we need those SCORN files from the DHS. Can you get to anyone over there?"

Some years ago, one of Jessica's predecessors claimed to have "accidentally" seen a Top Secret file labeled as part of a database called Project SCORN. This document, which contained data on mutated strains of smallpox, was intended for the Biochem Division of Homeland Security Science and Technology, a branch of the DHS and a mysterious cousin to USAMRIID.

Theoretically, Project SCORN contained a wide variety of information about experimental biological and chemical testing that the CDC and other facilities were forbidden to pursue—everything from the obvious hot-button issues like stem cell research to absurd sci-fi surgeries and, very likely, exploratory mutagenics. The name had become legend among the CDC community and synonymous with government obfuscation.

Richard frowned. "SCORN? What are you talking about?"

"You know what SCORN is. If they have something on silver, we need to know. There's no time to waste."

There were myriad conspiracy theories about magical cure-alls suppressed by the government. The most common thread between them was silver. She'd done post-grad research on one herself: Internet crackpots had swarmed around a mythical compound called *Tetrasilver Tetroxide,* which was supposed to electrify the blood and destroy AIDS and HIV pathogens. A 1997 US patent on the process was granted to an Israeli rabbi who also claimed to have invented a nuclear submarine reactor and a battery for credit cards. Of course, an issued patent is no endorsement that a process actually works; you could patent a method for time travel using a garden rake if you submitted all of the forms properly (and if the rake's design didn't infringe on someone else's patent). Meanwhile, alt-med nuts were overdosing on silver, turning their skin Smurf blue from argyria and going on the Oprah Winfrey Show.

But there was plenty of smoke. Maybe that meant fire.

"If the DHS or USAMRIID or anyone has something helpful, they'll bring it to us," Richard assured her, running his hand through her hair. "Contrary to what you insist on believing, they're in the same fight we are."

Richard had always been notoriously quiet about SCORN and protective of the military, and the truth was it bugged the hell out of her. It reminded her of Alan Hoxie's warning that Richard had been planted in the CDC to feed information to USAMRIID.

Keeping a secret like SCORN didn't necessarily imply nefarious intent; secrecy was part of a government scientist's job. But as his wife, she found secrets frightening. And if he could keep *one*…

She backed away from his caress, trying to sound authoritative. "Were they experimenting with silver while you were at USAMRIID?"

"Of course, Jessica. They're experimenting with *everything*. That's how research works. But they don't have a magic tonic that cures everything." He smiled, trying yet again to charm away her doubt. "Someday you're going to have to believe in me, Jess."

Thirteen
26 Federal Plaza
FBI Research Library
10:24 p.m.

Tildascow had the name from the flight manifest.

And exactly nothing else.

The fuck were they doing for security in Romania? And how did this shit fly with Homeland Security? No police record, no fingerprints, no travel history. The passport was issued early in 2008, before Romania began using the new ones with biometric ID chips. The address had no street number, no zip code. Birth date listed as January 1, 1970, which screamed generic bullshit. The US Embassy said the Romanian Ministry of Interior had no records of land ownership, taxes, or utilities. No birth certificate, no hospital records.

Just a name.

Discord spread through the room. The research assistants gathered around a flat-screen television. As Tildascow approached, Charlie yanked the cord on the courtesy headphones. The audio went loud.

"—reports of gunshots, both sniper units and law enforcement officers on the street. There are dozens of bodies sprawled through Times Square. As we can see from this overhead shot—"

The reporter was shouting over a helicopter shot of mass mayhem in Times Square. Police cars, ambulances, and fire trucks were trapped amid a violent mass exodus. Cleared areas were littered with injured or dead. Dozens, maybe hundreds.

The reporter's tone changed: "This just— They're telling me we have video from the ground. We have video from the ground, and I've been told to advise you to excuse your children from the room. This is graphic footage from just moments ago in Times Square."

The overhead gave way to a haphazard point of view from the CNN platform just above the street. Revelers chaotically fleeing Times Square. Screams. Gunshots. Sirens. Trampling.

Suddenly a closer, high-pitched scream erupted off-screen, and the cameraman jolt-panned right to find a werewolf in mid-leap, claws extended and fangs glimmering—

The picture bounced and fuzzed before landing sideways, allowing them to see the cameraman's lower body jerk as the monster tore him apart.

Some of the researchers shielded their eyes. Others gasped.

But Tildascow saw something else.

As CNN cut back to Wolf Blitzer in their studio, Tildascow scoured the control board for a rewind button.

"No tape here," Charlie said, already on the move. "Downstairs."

They bolted to the stairwell.

The watch center on the eighteenth floor was Charlie's home base. His passkey granted access to a media room where small monitors ran all of the news stations and major networks. He brought up CNN on a large monitor and pointed Tildascow toward a jog wheel.

She zipped backward through in-studio reaction shots until she reached the tail end of the live footage from Times Square. There was that cameraman taking the mauling.

And there, in the last twenty frames, she found him.

He turned toward the camera, shifting in his catlike manner. Trying to get himself seen—she was sure of it—but they'd cut away. And there was his shirt, emblazoned with his message: "find a cure."

"Hello you," she muttered.

"Mm-hmm," Charlie said.

He was the only stillness in the mayhem. A leaf settled amid a hurricane.

Demetrius Valenkov.

PART FOUR

One

Brianna Tildascow understood the "normal" world, where people lived and loved and worked and played, but it wasn't a place for her. Her job was to watch from the outside, appraising the "normal" people with a wistful smile of jealousy and predation.

Could she hurt them? Sure. Possibly. *Probably.* But she suppressed those urges.

Her friends at DARPA knew that. There had to be a scope trained on her somewhere, or they were even more provincial than she'd imagined. In the meantime, they'd forged her into exactly what they wanted: an executioner's sword, stripped and sharpened until everything that remained had lethal purpose.

Brianna was born the first time on August 4, 1976, in lower-middle-class West Virginia. Her mother was a flower in full bloom, the kind of woman who struck poets speechless. Wild blond curls and eyes so blue they made you thirsty.

She was a chosen one, that Lucy Hennessy was, blessed with vigor and grace and infinitely generous love. And her voice… Her voice was a warm quilt.

She was the town's perfect child. Everyone had high expectations for her future. But she wasn't interested in college, and money wasn't important to her. When high school ended, she took up shop at a local coffee house, strumming her guitar and singing her lullabies. Her admirers multiplied and her performances grew crowded, but she turned down invitations from Nashville and LA. *No need to complicate things,* she'd say.

They always thought her unpredictable, but Lucy was never more a surprise than when she chose Mark Tildascow, a flannel-clad bear with dark scruff and a ubiquitous baseball cap. He was a *plumber* of all things—so embarrassingly out of place in Lucy's ethereal glow. How could she have chosen *him?*

It was a cold November evening, threatening to snow. Mark had been called to fix the toilet in The Hazel's Nut, a mom-and-pop coffee shop at Third and Laine (it turned into a video rental store soon after, but they always pointed it out to Brianna). Lucy had just arrived for her performance. They met by chance at the counter. They didn't have a thing in common; in fact he thought she was just being polite by laughing at his stupid jokes. She touched his hand and said goodbye. No—she *sang* goodbye. Lucy's voice always sounded like music.

Try as he might, Mark couldn't shake her laugh. He drove 25 miles before he got the courage to turn around. He pushed his rickety van (named Cindy after Ms. Crawford) past a hundred miles an hour to make sure he didn't miss her.

Not three miles from the shop, Cindy skidded out on a bend. She went sideways over the curb and got stuck in the snow.

This was the part of the story where her mother took great delight in mentioning that Mark had painted "Chilled? Has Plow!" beneath "Tildascow" on the side of his van, to let people know how to pronounce his name. And yet, he had no plow. This was an area where folks needed snow plowed a couple of times a year, so his ad in the yellow pages led to quite a few disgruntled callers. Imagine their satisfaction at seeing the "has plow guy with no plow" stuck in the snow.

So, in the middle of what was becoming a blizzard, Mark trudged half a mile and back to call a tow truck. And anyway, did he really think that girl would go out with him? She belonged with a guy in a suit. Or hell, a guy who *owned* a suit. Just when he decided that turning back was the stupidest thing he'd ever done, headlights appeared over a dip in the road. He was shivering so hard that he almost couldn't wave down the tow truck.

Except it wasn't the tow truck.

After that night, it took Mark and Lucy all of two weeks to get married at City Hall. A few years later Brianna came along and they blissfully re-discovered the world through her eyes.

Mark Tildascow and Lucy Hennessy made a perfect life together. No one they knew woulda thunk it. That Lucy was perfect, all right. And a perfect mystery.

But not to Brianna. Her mother's beauty was in her simplicity, and in Mark she saw a genuinely good heart, loyal and honest and not afraid to love. In his way, a way no one but Lucy could have seen, he was perfect too. He worked hard, played fair, and would have died for his family.

Tildascow was born again on June 10th, 1992, the humid night of her high school's sophomore dance. Her escort was Gary Holm, her boyfriend of three months. Sweet, nervous Gary was hoping with all of his teenage might that she would have sex with him afterward.

"Will we or won't we" was a big topic of conversation among all the girls, but Brianna simply hadn't made up her mind. It helped that her mother vaguely approved of Gary. She said he had "a good heart in there, but he was easily distracted."

Easily distracted. It was the best Lucy could do to muster an insult.

After the dance, Brianna and Gary joined their friends in a party limo. They ended up at a secluded overlook, where each couple left the car to find some privacy in the woods. Gary was too nervous to consummate the night, but she let him put his hand under her dress as a consolation prize. What he managed to accomplish down there wasn't altogether terrible.

The partiers ate breakfast at a decrepit Denny's before watching the sunrise from atop Wissihickon Plateau. Her friend Meg had done the deed, and all she could talk about was the mind-shattering ramifications of those forty seconds. She was so impressed that she failed to notice when her boyfriend got the Denny's waitress' phone number.

Brianna was happy with the way the evening had unfolded. She thought her mother would approve. The less her father knew, the better.

The morning dew hadn't dried when the limo dropped her off. It rolled away with a victorious beep, and she walked the gravel path toward the modest Tildascow family home, carrying her strappy shoes with their broken heels.

All the while, she wondered why the front door was open.

It was a hundred or so feet from the fence to the porch. Her father always said that someday he'd fill their massive yard with a swimming pool, but really it was a poop playground for their mutt, Chester.

She never saw Chester again.

She found footprints on the beige cement, damp and reddish, taking clearer shape as she approached the house. Leaving while she was coming. The red had collected in the etching they'd carved when the cement was laid in 1982.

Mom + Dad + Brianna '82

It was hot and damp inside, and eerily still. The room tone was mute.

"Mom?"

Blood everywhere. Splattered in every direction, ruining her mother's oil paintings and coating the windows, turning the sunlight a furious red.

How could there even be so much?

"Mom?" she cried. "Mom! Mom!"

Her eyes fell on a boot sticking out from behind the couch. Their hideous orange couch where she used to hide her extra Oreos.

"Dad?"

He was lying crooked on the floor, his arms curled under his shoulders and his cheek pressed into the blood-soaked carpet. His glazed eyes stared off into nowhere.

She screamed for her daddy, but he was never going to answer again.

Brianna turned toward the kitchen, maybe thinking about the phone, and found her mother lying on the table. Her throat had been cut. The ceiling was red from the spray of her blood. Her legs were spread, her yellow sundress ripped and stained. Her arms dangled over the edge of the table, still elegant even as they dripped the last of her life.

She looked back at her daughter with those infinitely blue eyes, mouth open like she was about to say something.

Brianna ran for the kitchen phone, squelching in the drowned carpet, and fought the rotary dial, forcing it to recoil quicker, quicker, and argued with her mother. *You'll be okay, Mom. You'll be okay.*

She begged the police to hurry. *Don't let my mother die.*

Mom's chef's knife sat on the counter, coated thick in drying blood. Brianna began to realize what it had done. It had cut their apple pies, their lasagna, their fresh watermelon—and now her parents' throats.

The police arrived, and the ambulance; but no matter how much she demanded, they wouldn't help her parents. Instead, they rushed *her* to the hospital. But she wasn't hurt. They gave her counseling, but she wasn't crazy. They brought her food, but she wasn't hungry. They asked her questions, but she had no answers.

All she knew was this: Whatever was before was now over.

She became a ward of the state. In the months that followed, she was taken from her school. She lost touch with her friends. There was some sort of underage asylum / halfway house for the first few months, then an orphanage. New people, new places, even new clothes. Every part of her old life had been cut away by Mom's chef's knife.

One day an orphanage counselor called Brianna into her office. The elderly, bug-eyed woman told her to sit down, and offered her a caramel. When it was clear that Brianna wasn't interested in pleasantries, the counselor asked her if she wanted to hear about what happened to her parents. Some West Virginia newspaper had an article wrapping up the story.

"It would be okay if you don't," the counselor said, her voice rising with selfish hope. "Sometimes these things are better left unsaid."

Brianna nodded and stayed silent while the counselor put on her glasses and silently read the opening paragraph.

"Three drug addicts broke into your house," she said, paraphrasing. "They were on a binge and they needed money."

She read ahead. When she spoke again, her voice shattered the silence.

"They tied your mother down, and one stayed with her while the other two took your father to an ATM. He withdrew cash and gave it to them, and then they returned to your home," she said, glancing over her glasses to read Brianna's empty expression. She read ahead, looking for some kind of positive thought, some sort of consolation prize that was not there.

Brianna Tildascow didn't have the edge to survive in a merciless orphanage. The curly golden hair she shared with her mother had lost its sheen in the long stretches between showers. Their milky skin grew hard and the luster of their blue eyes dimmed. Honestly, it was a relief to look in the mirror and see someone else.

Her father had a $25,000 life insurance policy, something from some plumbers' union, but she never saw a cent. There were costs for a funeral she didn't attend, reparations for debt she didn't understand, taxes for things she'd never bought.

She was alone and terrified. But she could still hear her mother as she went to sleep at night, that honey-coated voice reminding her not to be easily distracted.

And so she learned.

First it was button-pushing.

She started with the other kids in the orphanage. Sex worked, gossip less so, but their insecurities were always the sweet spot. Manipulating their emotions was like changing radio stations—she kept going till the song fit her mood. Thinking beyond surface interactions, it was easy to adjust their personalities to suit her needs, or to torpedo their spirits altogether and cast a new mold in which they were beholden to her approval. Soon she moved on to the matrons—*it couldn't be that easy, right? Not with adults?* But it was even *easier,* because their souls had been so crushed. She danced between their complexes with the same grace as her mother strummed her guitar.

Then she learned to fight.

Her strength was unreliable, so she studied methods of shutting down the human machine. She learned to analyze quickly, adjust on the fly, and use unconventional weapons. Environmental awareness. Pain tolerance. Damage control.

She shaved her mother's blond hair because it was too easy to grab. Clipped her fancy nails short and wore scuffed, sharp rings on her fingers. No earrings. No dresses; they invited rape.

She understood the intimidation game. One display of sheer brutality, and her enemies' courage would wither. But prevention wasn't interesting; she sought ignition. One night a teenage boy pushed the issue. When he bent down to unfasten her jeans, she fractured his skull with her knee.

A trail of broken victims accumulated in her wake, and so did days spent in juvie. She was on the verge of eighteen and running out of pit stops before real prison. They appointed her a special counselor for repeat offenders.

He was "Aaron Burke from upstate Michigan" (that's how he'd always introduce himself), and he was 35 years her senior. Doughy and soft and altruistic as they came, Aaron was woefully unequipped for both of his chosen professions: the army, then juvie counseling.

But, like her father, he had a good heart.

It took some time, but Aaron's awkward jokes and goofy nerves chilled her rage. He liked stupid action movies where nobody fought properly and even stupider romantic comedies where nobody thought properly. His voice was calm, his presence was relaxing, and his bed was safe.

The affair began not from a particular attraction, but because she wanted to make him feel special. His gracelessness had kept him from marriage, maybe from dating at all, and theirs might have been the affair of his life. She made the most of their relationship, even allowing a couple of her calluses to soften, but she could never convince Aaron that she loved him. Because she didn't.

In fact, she couldn't feel anything.

She *knew* things—Aaron was attracted to her; Aaron needed to be reassured; Aaron was concerned for her future—but she never *felt* anything. Not for Aaron, not for the kid whose skull she'd broken, not when that counselor told her what had happened to her parents.

It became a growing obsession with Aaron that she should enter the military. They'd turned his life around, he said, and they'd do the same for her.

This new generation of the military has wisely learned to become more accepting of women and all of their multifaceted talents, and you'll find a place to make the most of the unique skill set you've developed. He could deliver a speech to ask for a club sandwich.

It wasn't all self-sacrificing on his part. He felt guilty about their age disparity. He worried that he was keeping her from a normal life and normal family. *Normal.*

When she left for basic training, she kissed Aaron goodbye and thanked him for whatever might come. She wrote him a month later. As expected, she never heard back.

Army life came too easy. And the right people noticed.

Her drill sergeant said he'd never seen anyone—man or woman—take so readily to the physical demands of basic training. She mastered their combat methods, and taught them a thing or two of her own. Three weeks, and she beat their best in knife work. Five for advanced hand-to-hand.

The momentum fueled her studies. Her bachelor's in communications came in three years; could've been two if they'd let her take a bigger workload. She rarely finished a curriculum before she was bounced upward.

She would not be distracted.

Every step came with barrages of counseling. At the beginning, they were concerned about her past. Soon enough, her aptitude tests made them interested in her future. The CIA tried to recruit her, but she didn't want to go abroad.

She wanted to stop the enemy from coming into her home.

She thought the background checks might put the kibosh on her application to the FBI. A traumatic past made for a dicey profile. Oh, and had they noticed that she was a sociopath?

Nevertheless, because of her performance in the army and confidence from various sources—including Aaron, and maybe an angel named Rebekkah Luft—she was accepted into Quantico.

And then the Prime Program came along.

When the Department of Defense recruiter described the parameters of the job, she responded with a question.

In other words, you want me to be a killer?

No, he said. *Those are the exact words.*

There were golf pros and computer whizzes and people who could spit watermelon seeds. Tildascow was a killer. The government needed people like her, people who knew but did not feel. And she needed them, to point her in the right direction.

Two

FBI New York Headquarters
26 Federal Plaza
Watch Room
10:58 p.m.

Tildascow couldn't afford to sit still this long.

It took twenty fucking minutes to get the Situation Room on the phone, even with the FBI's pre-approved hard-wired encryption line and expedition by the Director through the Attorney General himself.

Hell, the president had personally commended her twice and passed a note through the Director a third time. The next time they met, she was going to ball up and ask for his cell number. What's the worst that could happen?

The wait was even more interminable because every bone in her body wanted to get to Times Square. She knew she wouldn't be able to get anywhere near the melee, and she didn't have any silver bullets anyway. But the helplessness burned in her chest. Maybe that was the one thing she *could* feel.

Finally, the automatic lock on the door sealed, the sound dampeners whined and the flat-panel monitor came alive with the presidential seal.

A few seconds later, the president and the harried members of the National Security Council appeared. Tildascow spoke with no introduction.

"I've found our man."

Three
Situation Room
December 31
10:48 p.m.

Lon Toller was sitting behind the President of the United States and his National Security Council as the catastrophe unfolded before their eyes.

The staff was at Warp 10: writing, whispering, strategizing. Only Lon and the president were silently glued to the surreal horror unfolding on television.

Headlines appeared on a panel screen positioned to face the National Security Advisor. *ABC has transformation on tape, broadcasting,* it read. *Rush on Penn Station, authorities struggling. All transportation frozen as per quarantine. State of Emergency declared in Manhattan.*

CBS News had grainy footage of a werewolf leaping from tree to tree, divebombing its victims like a massive falcon. Lon never imagined they'd move so fast. They sure didn't act like the classic Wolf Man.

Dead and injured lay everywhere—how many could be infected?

Manhattan must be hell on Earth on right now.

Manhattan…

"My girlfriend is in Manhattan," Lon sputtered at the same moment the thought occurred. "Elizabeth…"

"There are *two million* people in Manhattan," said Luft. She turned to a duty officer, but spoke to Lon. "We're going to ask you to leave this room right now."

"Okay, but I need my cell phone." Nobody cared. He turned to the president: "Please. I have to call to her."

"They'll take care of you, Lon."

The national something or other shouted from one of the phone booths: "The FBI has something. They say we have to see it immediately."

Lon wanted to hear what that might be, but a duty officer took him by the shoulder. Guy smelled like corn chowder.

The last thing Lon saw was a dour blond woman appearing on one of the flat-screen panels and introducing herself as FBI Special Agent Til-something. As the door swung shut, he heard her say a name.

"Demetrius Valenkov."

Waitaminutewaitaminutewaita—

"Wait!"

"Please don't fight," the duty officer said, lifting him into the elevator.

Lon threw out his leg to stop the doors.

"Mister President! I have information on Demetrius Valenkov!"

The officer threw him against the back of the elevator car, making the whole thing shake. "Stop fighting!"

"Ow, please, I'm just trying to help—"

"Bring him back!" the president shouted.

The duty officer let him go, and Lon fell forward out of the car. He righted his black overcoat as he hurried back toward the Situation Room, where he met severe expressions.

"This better be good, Lon."

"It is, I promise," Lon said, completely aware of how badass he looked right now. He picked up the National Archives' lycanthropy file and flipped through the documents and—*fuck, where was it?* His hands were starting to shake. "Please continue," he muttered to Tildascow. Ugh, cottonmouth.

Tildascow kept going: "We have security footage of Valenkov at the UN just before the first victim was attacked, and again at the hospital when she arrived. He wants to be seen."

She plugged an image onto the screen: airport security footage of passengers emerging from a skyway. Tired businessmen and grinning tourists looking for their next destination. All different and yet all the same.

And then one distinctive man emerged—a wolf among the deer.

He was a roguish devil with dark, shoulder-length hair and dense facial scruff. Dark pants. He had a tee shirt stretched over his button-down shirt, with a handwritten message scrawled on the front.

"Find a cure?" observed the president. "For the werewolf disease?"

"Found a good way to get what he wants," said Truesdale.

"Get Jessica Tanner from the CDC," Luft said to another duty officer.

"Here it is!" exclaimed Lon. He waved a handwritten letter, etched on thick parchment and sealed in an evidence bag. "It's from Demetrius Valenkov, dated April 2007, addressed to President Bush at the White House. Check it out, it's on real vellum; I think it's calfskin. This is a tradition that went back to ancient Rome—"

"What does it say?" urged Truesdale.

"It's in Romanian, uhm—"

"Can we get a translator?" asked the president.

"I can read it," Lon chirped. "I learned Romanian as a hobby."

"We have Doctor Tanner from the CDC on the line," said Luft. Jessica's face appeared on one of the flat-panel screens.

"Read it, Lon."

"Uhm… 'Mister President, I am writing to….'" Lon read ahead to summarize. "He wants help. He says, 'My father, The Right Honourable Zaharius Baron Valenkov III, has fallen under a curse which transforms him into a wolf under the light of the moon.'" Lon's voice rose with excitement.

"Keep going!"

"'Your western medicine has cured many….'" Lon struggled with his translation. "Weaknesses. He means diseases. 'I beg for your assistance.'"

Jessica spoke up: "So his father is Patient Zero. We have to find him; he'll have the purest version of the virus. From there we can deconstruct its genetic origin and hopefully develop a vaccine."

"But he's the originator of the bloodline," said Truesdale, turning to Lon. "If we kill him, everyone is cured?"

"According to the mythology," Lon said.

"That doesn't make any sense, not scientific or practical," Jessica argued. "How could a virus inside a body react to the death of another separate organism? If you kill Patient Zero, the virus will die in his system, the purest strain will be lost and so will our best chance to cure the disease. We have to separate science from fantasy."

"Fantasy just tore up Times Square!" Lon exclaimed.

"All right, young man," Truesdale said.

"Is there anything else in that letter, Lon?" the president asked.

Lon read ahead and summarized: "He greatly anticipates a response. And he says he can be reached at the Valenkov estate. And then it ends with 'God Bless America. Yours Sincerely, The Honourable Demetrius Valenkov.'"

"The Valenkov estate, that's all?" asked the FBI agent.

"It's not a modern country," Lon reminded them. "You could probably send a letter and it'd—"

"We're going to send a lot more than a letter," interjected Truesdale. "Do we have anything on these people? He's a baron?"

The Director of National Intelligence scanned notes on his aide's laptop. "Nothing, sir. We'll get the Romanian government on open-source immediately and divert our closest operatives to that region."

"We need him alive, Mister President," Jessica urged.

"We're going to get him."

"Is he the right target? Should we be trying to find the son in New York?" asked Luft.

"The son isn't a werewolf," said Tildascow. "He was in Times Square. I saw him in news footage after the others had transformed."

"We can have an Aurora team ready in an hour," said Truesdale. "There will be seats for two, and one for the father."

"I know it's not my jurisdiction, sir," said Tildascow. "But I'm the best—"

"You're on it. And good work, again, Agent Tildascow."

"She's a domestic agent," said Shinick, the Attorney General, "She's going to need an escort, someone who understands the region."

"We have operatives mobilizing," the president agreed.

"Send them, but I'll move faster on my own. I just need one person who knows about werewolves."

Eyes reluctantly fell on Lon.

Four
The Clock Strikes Twelve

The horrified eyes of the nation weren't on the clock at the turn of the new year. In fact, the glowing ball at One Times Square never even dropped.

As soon as the outbreak began, the New York Port Authority, NYC Department of Transportation, NYPD, CDC Field Ops, Army Special Forces, and ragtag Rapid Deployment Forces moved to cut off every artery from Manhattan. The operation had been initiated hours earlier as minor roadblocks in the form of DUI filters. Even the authorities grew surprised and confused as the seal intensified with the arrival of hardened military.

The quarantine of Manhattan became a reality.

The largest thoroughfares were the easiest to close. Major bridges, including the Triborough, Manhattan, and George Washington, were susceptible to bottleneck checkpoints, as well as the four subterranean vehicular traffic tunnels. The Metropolitan Transportation Authority shut down the complex web of subway tunnels connecting to the mainland, and NYPD K-9 units patrolled the tracks. Once traffic was clogged, it was a matter of keeping people calm as the CDC EIS worked their screenings.

Penn Station and other hubs halted their fleets, and incoming trains were cancelled. Authorities and volunteers tried to keep travelers calm, but everyone wanted to put distance between themselves and Manhattan.

Dead bodies were scattered throughout Times Square, and the carnage spread to the surrounding areas. Dozens killed in the initial skirmish, hundreds of car accidents in the aftermath, thousands injured, and millions at risk.

The hospitals became disastrous.

Having no way to determine infections, caregivers were forced to treat the wounded as pariahs. Some off-duty doctors chose to stay home, and many others couldn't find transportation. Morbid terrorism protocols were routinely drilled at all of Manhattan's major hospitals, but they couldn't be prepared for *this*.

By half-past eleven, the island was effectively sealed.

Tildascow was among the last to leave, via an MH-6 "Little Bird" helicopter piloted by an agent of the FBI's elite counter-terrorism Hostage Rescue Team. It didn't feel much sturdier than a soap bubble.

They cleared the restricted airspace over Manhattan at the Little Bird's maximum speed of 175 mph and followed the southwestern trajectory of I-95 through Trenton and Philadelphia before cutting across the Chesapeake Bay en route to Prince George's Country, Maryland, just a few miles from the White House. A bit more than an hour after takeoff, they arrived at Joint Base Andrews Naval Air Facility Washington, the home of Air Force One.

Back in New York, the last kernels of sirens, gunshots, and screams were still popping in midtown while NYPD SWAT snipers were in pursuit of at least two werewolves via helicopter.

The Stuyvesant Square werewolf had already taken three .300 caliber kill shots, but it kept on skipping across the trees of Central Park with astonishing speed and dexterity, crashing down on any hapless stragglers in its path. SWAT informed dispatch that their weapons were proving ineffective, and police coordinators tried to direct silver-bullet-armed officers into the werewolf's chaotic path; but the park was too dangerous to enter on foot.

Internet servers buckled as surfers worldwide sought constant updates. Government officials asked the YouTube maintenance team to suppress the most graphic footage, but soon the video-hosting site crashed with all the rest.

Instead of the glowing ball, all eyes were on Press Secretary Jim Bunim in the last moments before midnight. He arrived in the White House Briefing Room to announce that the president would be making a statement, but not taking questions simply because they didn't have answers.

The president arrived at the podium just as the clock struck midnight.

"Good evening. As you know, there has been an unprecedented and horrific event in Manhattan over the past two nights: A disease has struck that transforms men and women into wild creatures upon exposure to moonlight."

Car horns went silent in the congested Lincoln Tunnel as drivers turned up their radios.

"As fantastic as this sounds, we've all seen the evidence for ourselves. The military, along with the Centers for Disease Control and Prevention and state and local law enforcement, are acting aggressively to contain the infection."

At the East River docks, the Coast Guard's quick-scramble Deployable Operations Group were still assembling their blockade when they saw a fishing boat attempting to flee the island. The driver didn't respond to their warnings, so their Helicopter Interdiction Tactical Squadron was sent to intercept. Snipers on the muscular MH-64C Dolphin helicopter shot out the boat's engine. The driver attempted to jump overboard, leaving the officers no choice but to shoot him.

"The scientists at the CDC, with the help of the World Health Organization, are well into an understanding of the disease, which seems to be caused by a blood-borne virus transmitted through open wounds. We'll all be looking forward to a statement from the CDC as their discoveries progress, but for now our prayers are with them as they work."

At CDC Headquarters, security was reinforced by the Atlanta Police Department as reporters, onlookers, and protesters massed outside.

Inside, all eyes were on Melissa Kenzie the werewolf. Molecular biologists, virologists, physicians, veterinarians, medical techs, toxicologists, biochemists, and statisticians pored over her test results.

"If this disease were to spread unchecked, it could become an epidemic of catastrophic proportions. The CDC has requested that we quarantine Manhattan Island, the only known location of the infection at the moment. All of our resources, federal, local, and volunteer, have been deployed to halt traffic to and from the island, and airspace has been cleared except for military purposes.

"If you live in Manhattan, we ask that you stay in your homes. Keep your doors locked. Stay off the streets. Police are doing their best to accommodate stranded visitors in shelters. At this trying time, cooperation is key."

Triage and temporary placement centers were opened up in Madison Square Garden and Pennsylvania Plaza above Penn Station, in the upper floors of One Times Square, and in the concourses of Grand Central Station. With citizens frightened into cooperation, operations went smoothly. A brotherhood formed among the stranded as they listened to the president's address.

"Manhattan is the beating heart of our nation. We will not sleep until she is safe and sound. Put your faith in your scientists, your authorities, your government, and God, and together we will prevail through this, as individuals, as families, and as a nation. Good night. And God bless America."

The press corps anticipated the end of the president's speech with a flurry of raised hands and fired questions: "Where did they come from?" "Will the injured people become werewolves?" "What happens tomorrow night?" "Silver bullets?" "When will people be able to leave New York?"

The president waved them silent. "Ladies and gentlemen, I'll ask you and all of the media to cooperate with us during this trying time. Spreading panic and disorder will only make the authorities' jobs more difficult. We're all in this together. We need everyone to step up and do their part to help the good people of New York."

"What are we doing to stop it?" yelled a voice from the back of the theater. The crowd rumbled in support.

"Everything we can," replied Weston.

In Times Square, body bags littered the streets.

NYPD had begun directing the injured to triage centers. One officer barked orders over a megaphone: "If you've been injured in any way, you must register with us and be seen by an attendant. Even if it was just a scratch. We won't hurt you. You *will not* be—"

And a werewolf tackled him into a roll. When they stopped, the creature clamped down and ripped his spine from his throat.

The crowd erupted anew.

A quick-draw officer fired three silver slugs into the werewolf.

"Enough already," he yelled. "Fuck!"

Five
Joint Base Andrews
Prince George's Country, Maryland
7:55 a.m.

Lon sat on the corner of a cot, wide awake. How could he possibly sleep? He didn't know how long he'd been here, or what time it was, or even *where* he was, or what was going to happen. These people had completely subjugated him in the name of patriotism.

Some kind of barracks or something. More like out of a Ridley Scott movie than a Michael Bay movie. It smelled like old canvas and aftershave.

How do these people find the courage to do this shit? These snipers and fighter pilots and soldiers? Freaking Japanese Kamikaze pilots getting in planes when they know they're gonna die? If you die, you don't see the new *Hobbit* movies or the next release of *Magic: The Gathering* or the expansions to *World of WarCraft*. There was supposed to be a live-action *Star Wars* TV series some day! Life wasn't important to these people?

They *had* to realize he couldn't do this.

Gah! He had to *tell them* he couldn't do this!

And that should be okay, right? They have satellite phones and secret communicators, and he could see what the agents were seeing through special cameras in their glasses. He didn't want to go to fucking Transylvania with an assassin and watch her fight werewolves. No way, Fay Wray!

Wait—no. He *did* want to go to Transylvania! It'd been his wildest dream since he could remember. He wanted to go there more than anywhere else in the world. (Since Middle Earth and Azeroth were necessarily excluded.)

He just didn't want to do it *this* way.

And that should be okay. Right?

He rocked back and forth as his heart raced and his arms grew weak. And the unnerving sounds from the airfield weren't helping any. Pistons firing, "Pshhh!"; wrenches wrenching, "Vreet! Vreet!"; engines revving right through his chest.

And didn't it break one of the Bills of Rights to take away his cell phone?

But then there were all of those people in New York. And Elizabeth was one of them. He couldn't just sit by if those people needed him. Or could he?

He really missed the comfort of his basement.

And then there was this feeling that he really hated. He wanted…

Well, he wanted credit.

Yeah, it was an ugly want. Self-aggrandizing, to say the least. Brave soldiers die for their country every day. But he wished people could know about the sacrifice he might be about to make. George Washington had the entire country supporting him. Nobody was behind Lon.

If he died in Transylvania, who would even—

The door opened with a loud clack that bounced all over the walls. It was that blonde FBI agent.

"Lon Toller?"

He nodded, too worked up to talk. He didn't want to risk crying.

She dragged over a cot and sat two feet away, leaning forward with her elbows on her knees. She had an aura of confidence. And she looked like a ninja in sleek black clothes that were probably full of crazy weapons.

"My name is Brianna Tildascow. I'm a Special Agent with the FBI, a counterterrorism expert."

Lon couldn't look at her. He could feel her studying his face.

"I won't bore you with my résumé, but I'll promise you that I am the right person for this job."

Lon nodded and accidentally sniffled. Ugh. Humiliating.

"I guess you're wondering if *you're* the right person."

She slid back on the cot and crossed her legs, putting more distance between them. He was glad for the breathing room.

"They tell me you know more about them than anyone. They said you're our country's foremost expert. I read your website, and I think they're probably right. What do you think?"

"I am."

"You sure?"

"Yeah."

"Someone said there's another guy, a Donnie Tuttle?"

"Fuck Donnie Tuttle."

"Oh yeah?"

"He copies all of my stuff for his piece-of-shit blog. And he only beats my traffic because his mom pays for Facebook ads."

"So then I shouldn't ask him."

"No! Fuck him. He doesn't know a therianthrope from a jackalope."

"Then it has to be you. You're the only one."

"Well…it shouldn't be Donnie Tuttle."

"Then I need *you*."

No doubt. But still! "Couldn't I just do it by phone or something?"

"I need your eyes on," she said. "Don't forget, we're going into a civilized country, talking to regular people, moving as quickly and safely as possible. If we hit something dangerous, you'll be out of the way. I promise."

Duty to his country on the one hand… Shitting his pants on the other.

"Listen, Lon, you'd be crazy if you weren't scared. That's the right way to feel, believe me. They're fucking *werewolves,* right? That's scary."

"Aren't *you* scared?"

She smiled…but was there some sadness in her eyes? *Gah.* Hot girls always made Lon feel soggy.

"I need you, Lon. It has to be you."

Lon sighed. And nodded. And sighed.

"Here," she said, proffering two white-and-black capsules. "They'll help you stay sharp. The fear just won't feel so important."

"I don't take drugs."

"You don't have to," she said, putting the pills into his soggy hands. "It's up to you." Her grip felt like steel wool.

"Two minutes!" a voice called from the doorway.

Tildascow lowered her head, forcing a connection with his eyes. "These military guys—they remind you of the kids who give you shit in school?"

Lon nodded.

"Now they need your help. Kinda nice, right?"

"Yeah." *Yeah*. It certainly fucking was. He could inhale that perspective quite deeply.

She patted him on the shoulder and started for the door. When he didn't follow, she turned back with a "come hither" smile. He wanted to stand, but suddenly the cot felt magnetic.

"I'm… I'm not really a man of action."

"I'm not a man of action either."

And then he found himself alongside her, the two of them striding in slow motion, like the crew in *Armageddon*… or maybe like something might explode behind them like in… well, like in every action movie ever.

A military guy entered, barking in their pissed-at-everything tone.

Tildascow whispered one last encouragement: "*They* need *you*." Then she went rigid and hollered, "Buck Sergeant Brianna Tildascow, 77th RRC, United States Army, reporting for duty, sir!"

"Lon Toller, reporting for duty, sir!"

The general recoiled as if Lon had spit at him. He spoke only to Tildascow. "At ease. You're FBI?"

"Special Agent Brianna Tildascow, FBI Counterterrorism Division, Operations I, ITOS I and II. Sir."

"Special Ops training come in handy pushing papers?"

"Hunting terrorists, sir. Wetworks."

The general nodded. "Lieutenant General James Fasolo, 316th

Logistics Readiness Squadron, United States Air Force."

"Sir."

"I'm told you're quite a badass, Tildascow. Might tickle my balls to meet you if it weren't under such perverse conditions."

"The feeling is mutual, sir."

"A spec ops RDF is scrambling to support you if necessary. You've been briefed on that?"

"Fully, sir."

"All right, then. Let's get moving. There's a lot to do." He tossed a sideways glance at Lon. "A *lot* to do."

Fasolo led them out of the barracks and across a landing strip. Lots of helicopter and fighter jet activity. It reminded Lon of *Top Gun*, and Maverick yelling, "I got the need, the need for speed!"

His head was filled with the winsome electric guitar theme. Tildascow met his grin—seemed like she heard it too.

Fasolo stopped short, and Tildascow nearly plowed into his back. She shot Lon a *whew* with her flashlight eyes. He bit his tongue to keep from laughing.

"What you are about to see are Top Secret weapons of the United States Air Force," Fasolo yelled over the din. "They're not to be discussed frivolously."

"Yes, sir!" Tildascow snapped.

"Yes, sir!" Lon concurred. *Screw it,* he figured. *They need me.*

They reached an open hangar where the last of three planes was being elevated from an underground garage.

Spy planes. *Cool.*

The Auroras weren't like any aircraft Lon had ever seen, even in cartoons or movies. Not Batman showy or James Bond phallic; in fact they were simply flat and narrow triangular darts, with the subtlest of curves delineating the cockpit from the wings—like the progeny of a fighter jet and a surfboard. Tiny shark fins protruded from each of the back corners.

Three pilots came from the hangar, wearing dark flight suits. They sprung to attention in front of Fasolo.

"At ease," Fasolo said. "These are your people, Tildascow."

"Army men?" Tildascow asked.

"Yes ma'am," said the tallest one.

"Brianna Tildascow, FBI Counterterrorism Division, formerly 77th RRC."

"Earle Beatty, 199th Special Operations Aviation Regiment, United States Army. Trained in conjunction with 35th Strategic Tactical Wing, USAF, and operating with CIA Special Activities Division. Call Sign Beethoven."

"That's a mouthful," said Tildascow.

A mouthful of nothing Lon could understand.

"That's why they don't talk about what they do," Fasolo said. "They're Shadow Stalkers. Flying commandos."

"You are?" Tildascow asked the second one.

"Jaguar, ma'am." He was a sturdy black man in his late twenties. Dead serious.

"Mantle," said the third pilot. His big ginger head looked like a lollipop on his thin frame.

"These men are fully briefed and under your command," said Fasolo. "There will be a UN and Romanian attaché awaiting your arrival."

"Thank you, sir."

Tildascow and the pilots saluted, and the general left. Lon felt better immediately; he was his own worst enemy and didn't need any goddamn help.

Mantle whistled, looking Lon up and down. "Wowee," he said with a thick drawl, "the Aurora is gonna take a bite outta you." He was probably 25, the youngest of the three, and wore a perma-grin like he was always thinking of a joke at your expense.

"Shut up, Mantle," said Beethoven, the team leader. The dusting of grey in his auburn hair made him look wise.

"'S'what we call counterproductive," added Jaguar as he smacked

Mantle on the back of the head.

Lon looked up at the aircraft and his stomach tumbled.

***

The pilots helped them into "multilayer anti-G flight gear," costumes that reminded Lon of spacesuits, which would send magnetic pulses over key arteries to keep their circulation going. This was on top of painfully tight undergarments designed to keep their blood from pooling in the lower half of their bodies.

Fantastic. Lon didn't want his blood to pool.

Once he was suited up, a tech directed Lon onto a portable ramp, which shook with each step he took. It terminated above the tight, two-man cockpit of the Aurora, and Lon was suddenly struck with claustrophobia on top of everything else. He turned to flee, but the tech was blocking his escape route.

Mantle flashed his crooked smile from the front seat of the cockpit. "Come on, buddy. Seat's all warm."

And there was Tildascow, in her own spacesuit, on her own ramp, nodding at him again. Like a reassuring cult leader about to rape him.

"Whatcha got here is the SR-105 Aurora, top-secret smartplane that cost y'all about fifteen billion dollars in taxes. Polyorganic exterior is retro-engineered from spider's web to make it, oh, 'bout a thousand times stronger than steel. Ain't that cool?"

Lon jerked when the tech put his hand on his shoulder and directed him where to step. Deep breath.

"AI steers the craft using GPS," Mantle said in the nonchalant tone of a flight attendant. "So I don't have to do much, which is good because it's awfully tough not to black out at this speed. We'll be travellin' just under Mach 8 today, almost double the non-classified airspeed record. Although we'll be above the atmosphere, so technically this here is a spacecraft and you will be an astronaut."

The tech assisted Lon as he tried to negotiate the steep—

Well, he fell into the plane.

"Y'okay?" asked Mantle.

Lon hated Mantle too much to answer him.

The tech went prone to lean over and help Lon with his helmet, a two-part assembly with a breathing regulator.

Now Mantle's voice came through a speaker. "The hypersonic propulsion thrusters use nuclear pulse projection, which means tiny atomic bombs are this puppy's fuel—"

"Could we stop talking?" Lon asked.

"Give the kid a break," said Beethoven over the radio.

But Lon didn't hear Mantle's response, because his heart went into his throat when the tech produced a syringe.

"I-don't-need-that-why-would-I-need-that!"

"You need an IV. Won't hurt at all." The tech ripped open a Velcro double-flap panel on the inner elbow of Lon's flight suit. The cold swab of alcohol made him feel pukey, but his arm was trapped in the shape of the seat. An IV port with two bags of clear liquid was built into the side of the cockpit.

"No, but no—Fuck!"

But the tech stuck him anyway. None of these fucking people ever listened! Lon's legs quivered as the tech taped down the needle and closed the flap. The pulling in his skin made him burp vomit.

Mantle stood up and leaned over the back of his seat to demonstrate as he inserted his own IV. "This'll keep you hydrated and help you relax. Pressure will be *wowee* intense. We're gonna be movin' almost three times the speed of a bullet. You could lose five pounds during this here flight. "

Pills, IVs… Were these yutzes military or were they pharmacists?

Lon looked around, wondering if he could still escape from this mess. Tildascow waved at him from the cockpit of the next Aurora. Christ, it felt like she was stalking him. And he was trapped against his will, all *Clockwork Orange*—

"Hey… How old do you think I am?" Mantle asked.

"I don't know," Lon whimpered. "How old are you?"

"Almost 28. I look younger than I am, right? Youngest Shadow Stalker pilot they's ever been." He slapped the Shadow Stalkers patch on his sleeve. The emblem featured a gryphon (body of a lion, head and wings of an eagle) pointing a glowing sword toward a crescent moon. Symbological cross-pollination, Lon thought. Bizarre and uninformed.

These people have no idea what they're doing!

Mantle settled in his seat as the motorized platform wheeled away. Lon's seat jolted forward—*FUCK!*—and locked into place.

The aircraft's vibration increased, like a snake hissing before it unleashed. Well maybe he didn't want it to unleash while he was inside of it!

Oh man, oh no.

The plane lurched forward with a rising electronic hum. Cross-chatter on the headset told them various systems were ready. They were clear for taxi. Mantle gave a thumbs-up to someone on the ground.

"You ain't afraid of heights, are you?" Mantle chuckled.

"No."

"Then we'll have no problemo, jalapeño."

"I'm afraid of pain."

"Oh. Well, this *is* gonna hurt."

As the Auroras taxied to the runway, the Andrews Control Tower released a concentrated electromagnetic pulse toward the sky to interrupt satellite photography.

The nuclear pulse engines roared to life, and Lon was thrown against his seat. A series of escalating booms crashed from somewhere beyond the confines of his deafening mask. His body vibrated into numbness.

Suddenly, he felt sleepy.

The three planes launched eastward over the Atlantic, quaking the sky.

Six

Situation Room
9:25 a.m.

President Weston watched constant updates on CNN.

Cellphone cameras had the mayhem covered like the Super Bowl. His old-fashioned sensibilities wanted the media to show some restraint with the hyper-violent imagery, but wishful thinking didn't mix with politics. The broadcast networks had blown past their standards, the FCC be damned, and all but the most obscure cable channels had been pre-empted for wall-to-wall werewolves. Reporters had already been killed, but the rest just kept up the charge. The police were having as much trouble wrangling the press as they were the creatures.

Chairman of the Joint Chiefs of Staff General Alan Truesdale, National Security Advisor Rebekkah Luft, and White House Chief of Staff Teddy Harrison were at the president's side. It felt like the entire world was watching over their shoulders.

With no warning, MSNBC broadcast a stomach-churning shot of a werewolf ripping out a woman's guts as her two children shrieked in horror.

Teddy rubbed his temples. "We should consider blocking transmissions from the island," he muttered, somewhere between question and statement.

"Not yet," said Truesdale. "Let them see. The liberals can't complain if they don't want these monsters in their backyards."

Weston couldn't disagree.

"And it will justify whatever we have to do," Truesdale added. "Later."

Weston nodded. *Later* was too foreboding a concept to dwell on at the moment. "It's a step we may want to take at some point. What are we doing about the injuries from last night, the ones who may be infected?"

"Locking them up," said Truesdale. "Hospital rooms. Police stations. We're requisitioning hotel rooms. We have the upper floors of One Times Square. We're also looking at clearing some space at Riker's Island."

"Can we be sure they're all accounted for?"

Truesdale's solemn eyes turned toward him. *Of course not.*

"There are so many," Luft thought out loud. "Scared and confused, in denial, maybe injured badly or even unconscious."

"We'll be more prepared tonight," Teddy said half-heartedly.

"We have to consider worst-case scenarios," said Truesdale.

Weston diverted his gaze as more violence unfolded on TV. "Draw up some options."

Seven
CDC Observation Room
January 1
11:25 a.m.

Jessica Tanner and her expanding team had worked through the night.

Everyone but the janitors had been diverted to lycanthropy study. Experts recruited by the Department of Health and Human Services were steadily arriving by helicopter, and each of them brought their own mini-teams of colleagues and assistants: more lungs taking up air, more stray bottles of water, more shuffling papers. And their collective data was regularly being uploaded to a WHO server for the worldwide think tank. The more brains the better, but their in-house team had been siphoned into so many teleconferences that the collective was losing touch with the latest empirical data (which in the past hour had been a report on the virus' effect on certain hormones and glands). Every report brought the same conclusion: No one had ever seen anything like this, not outside of movies or nightmares.

The herd crowded into the observation room just before 11:10 a.m., officially-predicted moonset in Atlanta. As they waited, observing their captive werewolf through the two-way mirror, the stink of coffee breath grew so powerful that Jessica thought she might have to run back to the bathroom.

Within minutes, the werewolf lost consciousness. Its heart rate dropped, breathing slowed, and the lupine physical characteristics regressed. The reverse transformation lasted just over a minute, and then they were once again left with the fragile Dr. Melissa Kenzie.

"H-1 interval was six minutes, thirty seconds," Richard said, reviewing data over the shoulder of a CDC analyst. "A full minute less than we recorded during our first study cycle last night."

"Was the H-1 interval the only inconsistency?" asked Dr. Diana

Benrubi, Director for Biodefense at the University of Texas Center for Biodefense and Emerging Infectious Diseases.

"Not at all," said a CDC analyst, directing them to a monitor with side-by-side images of the Kenzie werewolf's two transformations. "Look at this."

To the naked eye, the lycanthropic effect was more pronounced during their second study of the cycle. Kenzie the werewolf's ears had grown bigger, her maxilla stretched into the beginnings of a canine snout and her fangs extended further. Her neck had also bulged wider, toward broader shoulders.

"Higher moonlight intensity, more transformation," noted an uptight female virologist from the Viral Diseases Division at the Walter Reed Army Institute of Research. Jessica had already forgotten her name twice. "Makes you wonder how far it can go."

"It doesn't make any sense," Richard sniped. He'd been steadily losing patience all night as lycanthropy evaded their diagnoses. "There's no such thing as 'moonlight.' It's sunlight reflected off the moon. Why aren't they transformed by sunlight?"

"We're working on that," replied a hotshot physicist from Yale, Timothy something-or-other. "The moon absorbs selected elements of the spectrum, so the characteristics of moonlight aren't quite the same as sunlight. We've been testing the spectral response of the virus, but we haven't been able to find the precise ratios that catalyze the transformation."

"If we find that wavelength, could we block it with sunscreen?" asked a Korean man from WRAIR's Retrovirology Division.

Thus began another lap on the track they'd circled all night long. Bright minds tossing out bright ideas, all of which fell into one of two categories: things they'd already tried or things they couldn't try.

"Solid walls can't even block it," Jessica said. "She transformed in the containment room, and those walls are reinforced with 55 millimeters of lead to block nine hundred kilovolts of x-rays."

Next they asked about polarization, or strobing another light source to interrupt the light of the moon. Good theories, but absurd in practicality. A dog whistle … of course they'd tested it, to no effect. Weiko Tsong, Richard's old friend from USAMRIID's Department of Vector Assessment, Virology Division, suggested applied lethal mutagenesis, a dangerously irresponsible technology that they couldn't begin to implement in time. Although Richard made her laugh by suggesting that might turn them into weretyrannosaurs.

Someone mentioned Ribavirin. Another asked about comparing antibodies from either phase of the transformation. Tried, useless. The woman from WRAIR suggested attaching something to the virus, a target the white blood cells could track, but the virus' rapid and massively error-prone replication would leave the WBCs chasing its fecal matter.

"My God, have we checked the host vectors?" asked Dr. Lisa Rohr, one of Richard's virologists. "What if it infects rats or mosquitoes?"

And then, as usual, the conversation devolved into trampling voices as fear conquered reason. These roundtables were just sped-up, melodramatic versions of the same Abbott and Costello routines she'd endured at her conferences. *Who's on first? What's on second? How can a virus do these things—third base!*

"It just—it does things it's not supposed to do," Rohr complained, right on schedule. "Things it *can't* do."

Having come to this conclusion herself, and observing everyone else arriving at their own pace, Jessica was left with only one explanation—one she probably wouldn't have blurted in such distinguished company had she not been so damn tired.

"It may just be what the movies say it is. Supernatural."

The word hung in the room. *Supernatural.* A sacrilege.

Richard scowled at her, as if she'd committed treason. "So, what, we should put out a call for witches and exorcists? This is not magic, this is a *virus;* a biological entity we can quantify, study and attack. It's ahead of us, but we'll catch it."

Jessica withered in her seat, wishing she'd just kept quiet. The others cast piteous glances her way. *How embarrassing for the poor woman, she's crumbled under the pressure.*

"What we need is a place to start," said Tsong.

"Patient zero," said Rohr.

"Still waiting for the cultures on Holly Cooke," said Benrubi.

"She's a secondary," said Rohr. "She was attacked before she was brought into the hospital. Whoever or whatever started this is still out there."

"That's who we need," said Richard.

Eight

Henri Coandă International Airport
Bucharest, Romania
6:30 p.m. Eastern European Time

The flight was rough.

As the Aurora crashed through the upper layer of the atmosphere, the G-forces crushed Tildascow's body like a 200-pound blanket. Meditation helped, as well as the steady flow of oxygen and the effects of her anti-G flight suit. Still, every damn second was harrowing.

From strip to strip, the 4,880-mile jaunt was just under two hours. They were traveling at less than of half the Aurora's maximum speed, because Romania wasn't far enough to safely achieve Mach 8 and decelerate—and she and Lon didn't have the training to handle that kind of speed.

When they touched down, the three Auroras taxied off an unassuming airstrip into a UN Special Ops Hangar at the Romanian Air Force 90th Airlift Base. They were just outside *Aeroportul Internaţional Henri Coandă*, the primary public airport of Bucharest, the capital of Romania.

This place occupied a black hole in Tildascow's professional interests. Institutional corruption and bickering with Hungary had kept them from the international playfield, and the region offered no geographical or political advantage for adversaries of the United States. She'd taken a cursory look at FBI intelligence, but as she looked out over snow-covered Bucharest, she might as well have been scoping Mars.

Like so many European countries, Romania was struggling through puberty into a modern globalized culture. They'd experienced an economic boom after their 1989 overthrow of communism, and symbols of their oppression, like the stadium-sized "Hunger Circus" domes once used as food distribution centers, were being repopulated with hotels and malls. Restorations of surviving medieval architecture were underway to

174

attract tourists.

The population was comprised of Vlachs, Hungarians, Saxons, Bulgarians, Armenians, Jews, and the secretive, nomadic *Ţigani*, also known as Gypsies. Werewolf lore frequently pinged on Gypsy legends of hexes and curses. In the original *Wolf Man*, the first werewolf was the son of a Gypsy fortuneteller.

That last bit of information had come from Lon, of course. He'd also said he'd know the way once they arrived. And she'd have to rely on him, because they had a wide-open map. She'd thought Transylvania was a city, but it was actually a massive plateau separated from the rest of the country by the reverse-L-shaped swath of the Eastern and Southern Carpathian Mountains. The region occupied nine counties and more than half of Romania.

Her boots crunched unspoiled snow as she stepped onto a balcony at the rear of the hangar. Fresh air and quiet were godsends after that torturous flight. The temperature was the same as in New York, but the crisp wind, clear sky, and evergreen aroma were decidedly Un-American.

So fuck nature, she thought with a smile.

And there was the moon, blazing bright on the horizon. So close to full.

"Please, I need a bathroom. Or a trash can." Lon's husky whines carried across the hangar.

Beethoven, Jaguar, and Mantle were busy securing the Auroras, making sure the UN and Romanian Air Force understood that they had to be kept out from under the prying eyes of satellites. They'd left the poor kid to fend for himself. He was bent over, hands on his knees, in position to let loose from either orifice. She decided to leave him alone for a minute, to see if he could recover on his own, and maybe spare his pride.

She'd had a few minutes to look over Lon's website during the layover at Andrews. The details were obsessive and indignant, and most of the discussions in the forum went his way or an ugly way. This identity he'd created as a werewolf expert reeked of faithless hubris and hollow vanity—both indicators of low self-esteem.

She also scanned his therapist's notes, which were well kept, insightful, and surprisingly accurate. And she wasn't surprised that Lon had suffered a major trauma during early childhood.

When Lon was five, his father developed a brain tumor. It spread quickly and mercilessly, causing memory loss, hallucinations, impaired speech and motor skills and, finally, a lonely death. Most importantly, noted the shrink, his father's personality took sudden turns, leaving baby Lon to try to understand why a stranger was in his father's body.

By the end of the father's life, Lon's mother had already suffered and dealt, and relief was all she had left. She thought Lon felt the same: He didn't cry for Daddy, he didn't get sick, he didn't even alter his preschool routine. The mother was a simple woman trying to crawl out of someone else's grave, hardly capable of recognizing the child's clinical dissociation.

His nightmares began two years later.

It was tougher to forgive her missing the connection between the father's shapeshifting identity and the werewolves running through the kid's night terrors. But she'd started a new relationship—which she was probably desperate to keep—and Lon was keeping her boyfriend awake.

Cut to the beginning of high school, and Lon has grown into a perfect instrument of self-destruction. He's convinced that people dislike him, even before they have a chance to make up their own minds. He says the nightmares are gone (he won't even acknowledge they ever existed) and his father's death is a non-issue because it happened before he can remember. The interest in werewolves is purely scientific, he insists, and his social problems come from interactions with what he describes as "untellects."

Untellects. Made her smile.

The kid was clever. And his enthusiasm was infectious… even cute. But he'd have to learn to get out of his own way. And come to terms with his awkwardness…

….she thought, as she watched him dry heave on the tarmac.

"Welcome to Romania!" came a burly voice from the far side of the hangar. It carried a thick Romanian accent.

A heavy-coated diplomat approached Lon, flanked by six Romanian soldiers in camouflage fatigues and blue berets.

Tildascow hopped the stairs to intercept this potentially sour turn in diplomatic relations.

"I am Ghin Dumitru, your legal attaché from the United States Embassy," he said, offering Lon a handshake. "Are you Special Agent Tildascow?" He pronounced it "pill's poo."

Lon vomited his greetings just as she stepped in front of him. She whipped off her hat and tossed her hair for a distraction.

"Hello, gentlemen," she said. "FBI Special Agent Brianna Til-*das*-cow, retired from the United States Army and the commanding officer on this mission. This is Mister Toller, my civilian advisor."

"Ah," muttered Dumitru. "Nice to meet you, Special Agent Tildascow. Welcome to Romania."

"Thank you," she said over Lon's next wave of retching. "I trust you've made arrangements for our transportation to Transylvania?"

"Yes, we have a helicopter. But I'm afraid we do not know where to direct you. Outdated records in Braşov mentioned a Valenkov farm quite some distance from the city, but we could find no specific address."

"Do you know where we're going, Lon?" she asked, keeping her eyes and smile on the Romanians.

"I think—*guh*—I think we'll be looking somewhere in the southeast, near the juncture of the Carpathian Mountains. Not far from Braşov."

Not the precision Tildascow was hoping for.

"No local networks?" she asked Dumitru. "No eyewitness accounts of werewolves?"

"I'm sorry. Like you, we believed such monsters to be superstition."

Dumitru was an easy read: He wasn't hiding anything, but he was also powerless and had no connections, probably because he was a grade-A dullard. No way this werewolf thing could be going on *right here* and nobody knows about it. Someone had to know *something*.

A dozen or so techs were milling about the hangar, ogling the Auroras. "How many locals are working in this facility right now?" she asked.

The question surprised Dumitru. "Perhaps fifty or a hundred?"

"Do me a favor, sir, and round up as many as you can." She directed the soldiers as well: "Spread the word, nothing official, just have them gathered outside the hangar in three minutes. And anyone else you can muster from the airport, civilians or employees. Just don't let them see our planes, please."

Dumitru spoke to the soldiers in Romanian. They went on their way before he finished speaking, leaving with no deference.

"I apologize if you feel we have not properly investigated the matter. The situation in New York is of grave concern to us all."

"I'm not questioning your integrity, Mister Dumitru. We all have our methods. Let's see if mine work."

Dumitru nodded in an unconvinced but polite manner.

Lon retched again, and Tildascow covered it with: "What time is it here?"

"Eighteen-thirty five. We're on Eastern European Time, seven hours ahead of New York."

Tildascow pretended to set her watch. "Excellent. Okay, I think that's all we need. If you wouldn't mind rounding up the locals?" Also known as: *Go do what the fuck I told you to do and stop marinating in the kid's vomit.*

"Yes, yes of course." He left, passing the Shadow Stalkers on his way.

"We're good to go," said Beethoven.

"It'll be a couple minutes. I have to do their jobs for them," she said, nodding toward Dumitru, who was wandering without direction. *No, dude, there aren't Romanian civilians in the Aurora's landing gear.*

Beethoven and Jaguar stood at ease. Mantle knelt next to Lon and rubbed his shoulders with a wicked smile. "How you doin', tough guy?"

Lon collapsed on his side, dangerously close to his own vomit.

Tildascow squatted over him. "I need you sharp, Lon. Did you take the pills I gave you?"

Lon's eyes rolled.

"Help him up," she said to Mantle. "Did you take those pills, Lon?"

"No," he said, as Mantle got him to his feet.

Tildascow bit off her gloves and reached into one of the zillion pouches on the black MOLLE vest she'd picked up at Andrews. She came out with a pillbox and jiggled out two black-and-white capsules.

"It's not your courage that's failing, Lon, it's your body. There's nothing to be ashamed of, you're just not trained for this. Does that make sense?"

His lazy head swept into a nod.

"Take these, okay? I haven't steered you wrong yet."

She put them in his mouth and he accepted a shot from her canteen. One of the pills became stuck in his throat and his eyes bulged as his throat clicked. Mantle slapped him on the back and he fell forward.

She caught him just before he landed in his own mess.

"Oh God," he muttered.

"We all have our days, Lon. It's okay."

Jaguar smacked Mantle in the head, hard enough to make him stumble. Jaguar didn't talk much, but he knew when to swat that kid. So far, Tildascow liked him the best of the three.

"Fucking hell," Mantle muttered, rubbing his scalp.

"Agent Tildascow!" Dumitru called from the edge of the hangar.

She shifted Lon into Beethoven's arms and issued orders to the guys: "Stay quiet, stay behind me, and don't do anything to draw their attention. Keep your eyes on my shoulder blades. You too, Lon."

Tildascow preceded them out of the hangar. Around the corner, a crowd of maybe fifty was gathered in a loose block formation. Most were ground crew or soldiers, but there were also assorted bus drivers, luggage handlers, clerks and civilians. Only men, for whatever reason.

"Excellent, thank you, Mr. Dumitru. Would you mind translating?"

"Of course."

"*Ladies* and gentlemen," she said pointedly, "I'm sure you've heard that something has happened in the United States of America." As Dumitru repeated her words in Romanian, she scanned the crowd's eyes. "There's been an outbreak of werewolves. We believe it originated here in Romania."

Locked on the crowd's eyes, she listened carefully to Dumitru's words. His voice struck hard on the word *vârcolacii*, which she took to mean *werewolves*.

Faces in the crowd were puzzled, frightened, bemused—

But one set of eyes sunk to the floor. A soldier in the back row. *Gotcha.*

"Do any of you have any knowledge of werewolves here in Romania?" she asked the crowd, already knowing their answers.

Dumitru translated. He only got a few negative mumbles as they gauged each other's responses. Eventually, all eyes fell back on Tildascow. The very last set to arrive belonged to that soldier in the back.

She reeled him in with a beckoning finger.

As he approached, Tildascow nodded Dumitru toward the helicopter. "Get that bird whirling."

"No, please," whined Lon, "no more flying."

Nine

CDC Headquarters - Patient Observation Room
Atlanta, Georgia
11:35 a.m.

They'd kept her bound up like an animal. Bound, muzzled and prodded. How long until they lobotomized her? Or raped her?

She wanted to strangle each and every one of them.

"I'm sorry for the discomfort, Melissa," said that woman doctor, Jessica Tanner. She stood over her, using a dental tool to pull back her lips and look at her gums. *The godforsaken thing burns,* she thought, spitting out the taste of metal. And the husband was drawing yet another vial of blood. Lord, how her arm ached from the constant pull.

"Why don't you just open my wrist?"

"I'm sorry." The husband had the nerve to feign innocence. "We just need to run some more—"

"Enough of your damn tests!"

"Okay, we'll take a break. We've got enough for now." He tossed his syringe on the table and snapped off his rubber gloves.

"Are you feeling irritable, Melissa?" the wife asked.

Stupid question. No wonder these humans couldn't cure any— "What's that on your hand?"

Tweedlestupid and Tweedlestupider looked over his hands.

"What?" he asked.

"*That,*" she repeated the obvious. "On your hand."

"What do you see?" Jessica asked, turning over his palms.

"The star! The star in the circle." The fools were oblivious. *"On his hand."*

"Can you describe it?" Jessica asked.

"It's right there!"

It was clear as day! Practically glowing! And alluring. Tickling her salivary glands. Like the firm ass on a strong young man. God in Heaven, she didn't want to look away. She wanted to be free, now more than ever. She needed to touch that star on his hand. To taste it.

"Let me out of here!" she screamed.

"Stay calm, Melissa," Jessica said with a quiver in her voice.

No, she wouldn't stay calm. She had another life now, another world far more interesting than the one where she was restrained under these *fucking* bright lights.

She'd lived in fear of God all of her damn life: praying, begging, showing penance—and for what? What had she ever gotten in return?

Now she had a new Man, alongside her and inside her always. Finally, a Father who reciprocated her faith. All she wanted now—all she would ever want, for all eternity—was to return to the dream and hunt and love with Him again.

Their love was angry and passionate, a greater *feeling* than any she'd ever experienced. The sex was brutal and animalistic, because they *were* animals. But it was also primal and honest, a mutual ravaging. None of the fumbling stupidity of human sex, the politics before and the abandonment after. When He was inside her, it was the apex of a bond eternal.

And they fed from the weaklings because they could. Not to kill, not yet. Now only to spread, as was His decree.

She longed to rejoin Him and rend these fools, especially this man with the star on his hand.

Oh, how she wished she could tear into his flesh.

They asked about the transformation, and she told them about the physical truths: the pain, the stretching, the descent into the rage dream.

They asked about the dream, and she told them about the sensations, but she protected Him. She was a faithful soul.

The hunger would wait. In her heart, He whispered that she would have that star. And she believed in Him.

Ten
CDC Conference Room
11:51 a.m.

Jessica was drowning in panic.

The pentagram. A quick Google search confirmed what she already knew, what she'd seen in those creature double features. But instead of acting, she was waiting—*waiting*—on hold while some White House operator connected them to Transylvania. Richard always got his way.

"It right here in the—"

"It's everywhere!" he shouted.

They'd been yelling across the table for 20 minutes. What started as loving concern had devolved into utter pugilism. As always during their worst arguments, her tears hadn't slowed him one bit.

"The pentagram figures in every major religion, from Neopagans to Pythagoreans," he barked. "It's the wounds of Christ, it's the *rejection* of Christ, the 'elemental spirit', the *descent* into spirit—"

"A werewolf saw it in your palm, Richard, and *there's only one explanation for that, anywhere!*"

"They're putting us through," said Rebekkah Luft over the intercom, as if to remind them she was listening. On top of it all, the disintegration of their marriage was unfolding before an audience of the country's best scientists and culminating on a conference call with the National Security Advisor of the United States.

"Hello?" Lon Toller's thick voice was barely audible above the din of a helicopter.

Richard seethed while Luft quickly explained to Lon that Melissa Kenzie had seen a pentagram in the palm of his hand.

"If a werewolf sees a pentagram in someone's palm, it means that person will be their next victim," explained Lon.

"That doesn't make any sense," Richard snapped.

"Richard—" Jessica started.

"No, Jess, you're saying the disease can see the future. It's absurd."

"I'm just telling you how the story goes," Lon said. "It's an obscure part of the mythology. Honestly, I thought it was invented by Hollywood. It didn't appear in any legitimate texts before the *Wolf Man* movie in 1941. But the virus thing looked like a pentagram too, right?"

"That's right," Jessica said pointedly. They'd gone around on that too.

"It goes back to the whole thing being a curse," Lon continued. "The werewolf usually sees a pentagram in the palm of their loved one, someone they're tragically destined to kill."

Richard's eyes narrowed as he scribbled in his file. "There *is* no curse. A curse is a sentence for a crime. This woman didn't do anything wrong. She didn't deserve to be bitten by a werewolf. And I've never even met her before today. We have no connection."

"I guess so," Lon said. "Like I said, I never really believed in the pentagram lore. But, I mean, you should get away from that werewolf, as far as you can. Better safe than sorry."

Jessica nodded at Richard, who went on simmering. "Okay, we understand. Thank you, Mr. Toller, and thank you, Ms. Luft."

"You'll keep us updated, Doctor Tanner."

"Of course. Our team will be in touch within the hour."

Richard made quickly for the door. "I have results coming in. When you're ready to get back to science, come find me."

Eleven
Transylvania
6:58 p.m. EET

The *Forţele Aeriene Române* helicopter crossed between the jagged stone peaks of the snow-capped Carpathian Mountains.

Lon recognized this valley as the convergence between the Southern and Eastern Carpathian Mountains, the bottom right corner of the triangular Transylvanian plateau. He'd seen plenty of pictures of this area, but he never imagined the real thing would live up to the glamour shots. The snow glimmered so brightly under the moon that the mountain ledges cast upside-down shadows.

He sat by Tildascow and the Shadow Stalkers in the rearmost seats of the helicopter's cabin. They'd given him a helmet that smelled like metal and aged vomit. The headset was terrible compared to the one in the Aurora; the volume kept leaping from whispers to ear-splitting and back again. Nevertheless, his headache and sour stomach were all but gone thanks to Tildascow's pills. In fact, he'd felt great until that phone call.

"They see a pentagram in the hand of their next victim?" Tildascow asked him. They'd overheard the call patched through from the States.

"Seems that way," he said. "Man, it's number three on my list of most ridiculous lycanthropy misconceptions. So embarrassing."

"Fucking nuts," said Mantle. "Right on their hands?"

"In the palm. God, they're gonna filet me on the forums. I'm an idiot."

"Lon." Tildascow turned to look him the eye. "The people on the forums weren't enlisted by the United States government to fly to Romania in an experimental plane and find the source of the werewolves."

"I know."

"Go a little easy on yourself, alright?"

Great. He'd promised his therapist he'd work on the self-criticism, and he fell right into—

"Pentagram," a tepid voice whispered through their headsets. It was *Maistru Militar* Trandafir, the soldier Tildascow had picked out of the crowd. But they didn't know Trandafir could speak English. "Mark of the werewolf."

Trandafir sat across from them in the helicopter cabin along with five other Romanian soldiers. He was a spiny man-child with a big head over a chicken neck and brown eyes bugged out by thick glasses, hardly what you'd expect from military. In fact, the other soldiers towered over him.

"You speak English?" Tildascow asked, leaning forward in an intimidating manner. "Tell me what you know about werewolves. Why are we headed to this location?"

Trandafir recoiled like she'd held a gun to his head. "My aunt marries Gypsy carpenter. They settle in village north of Braşov. It is simple place, close families, Gypsies who only stay short time. Men work in copper mine." The other soldiers whispered jokes about Trandafir. The poor boy just kept his eyes down and went on. "We visit the village when I am young. Each night, wolves' howls keep us awake. Villagers all lock doors and hang fresh—" Trandafir hesitated, searching for the English words, "flowers. On windows. *Mărul Lupului.*"

"Wolfsbane," Lon explained. "*Aconitum tauricum Wulfen*, of the buttercup family *Ranunculacea—*"

"Okay, Lon," Tildascow interrupted.

"It keeps werewolves away," he needed to add. That was the point.

"Okay. Thank you." Tildascow nodded to Trandafir to go on.

"One night there is more than howls," Trandafir continued. "Wolf was near. My uncle's goats cry all night long, very scared, and then we hear wolf kill them. It is terrible sound, they cry even after they are dead. My cousin Andrei covers his head with pillows. Soon we hear scratches at door. My uncle loads his gun and tells us stay under our beds. Andrei does as he is told, but I want to see. I peek through window—"

Trandafir shook his head. The other soldiers had grown quiet.

"Go on," said Tildascow firmly.

"It is right in front of me, terrible beast. Wolf's face on body of man. It reaches through window and grabs my neck. I am certain I am to die. But my uncle shoots creature, and it runs off." He took a long swallow and shook his head.

"Did your uncle say anything about it?"

Trandafir shook his head. "We never speak of this. I wish to believe it is dream. I refuse to return to village for many years, even for my uncle's funeral. Until one year ago, Andrei calls and says he is to be married. He begs me to come, and he says beast is killed. I had not seen my cousin in long time, so I return. We hunt deer for feast to celebrate reunion. In forest, we come across another hunter, most fearsome man I have ever seen. Seven feet tall and wide as two men. Andrei tells me this is man who kills werewolf. His name is Yannic Ilecko."

"Yannic Ilecko." Tildascow repeated.

"This is the man he told us to find," Dumitru confirmed from the front seat. "I have investigated with the SRI," he said, referring to the *Serviciul Român de Informaţii*, the Romanian Intelligence Service. Lon had also sent them a letter back when, to request a police report about a murder that Romanian Internet conspiracists had attributed to a werewolf. Dumitru continued, "There is a Yannic Ilecko employed at the Costeşti Mine. A few miles southeast of Covasna."

"Would he be at work?" asked Tildascow.

"We expect so. They operate around the clock."

"Hooah!" yelled Mantle. Jaguar and Beethoven hollered back the same.

"Hooah," agreed Tildascow. She settled into her seat.

"This was last time I speak with my cousin," Trandafir continued quietly. "This summer, everyone in his village disappears."

Twelve
Carpathian Mountains
7:12 p.m. EET

Ten minutes later, the helicopter touched down on virgin snow at the cusp of the open-pit copper mine. The Carpathian Mountains loomed high above them, pointing toward the moon. They were a few miles from Transylvania's easternmost cities.

The helicopter conjured a snowstorm as it lifted off, forcing all but the Shadow Stalkers to all fours. She thought the bite would relent once the bird was in the air, but the narrow valley created a wicked wind tunnel that kept it coming. Whistling freeze blew from every direction, kicking up intermittent whiteouts.

The helicopter's spotlight illuminated their path around the wide perimeter of the mine's basin. A hundred yards from the drop point, they reached a zigzagging vehicle path and began the steep descent into the pit. The entrance was only fifty feet below the valley's surface, but it was treacherous ground.

Three neurotic miners greeted them, human squirrels chirping in Romanian as their headlamps lit up the swirling snow. The pit's vortex carried the bitter reek of cyanide used in the copper extraction process. Tildascow could only imagine what it was like inside the mine. Poor guys were probably poisoning themselves.

Dumitru's soldiers barked threats at the miners. Weapons were up before Tildascow cleared the vehicle path.

"Whoa, whoa," she yelled at Dumitru. "What are they saying?"

"They don't take kindly to men who refuse to join the army," said Dumitru. "They say they are *dezertors,* traitors to their country."

"Shut them up," she said.

Dumitru whined in Romanian, but the soldiers ignored him and kept on riling the miners.

"Shut them up now! What kind of help are your people?"

"They are not *my* people," Dumitru exclaimed between barbs with the soldiers. "I am only a liaison!" He pleaded some more, but the soldiers had their dicks out for a swordfight.

And then something stopped them cold.

A man with a pterodactyl's span emerged from the pit, caked in soot and steaming from sweat, flanked by swollen, stonework arms. Tildascow's train of thought went way off its tracks as she… the… uh… the rest of him was barely covered by triple-patchwork pants and a canvas tunic tied with rope. His face was hidden behind a graying caveman's beard, and tangled auburn hair fell past his shoulders. But who the hell was looking at his face?

"This is him," whispered Trandafir. The pipsqueak had found his way to a coward's position in the back, even behind Lon. "Yannic Ilecko."

She hardly needed the confirmation. Carnal thoughts had never been an issue on the job. The taste of the hunt was far more intense. But this guy—she chuckled out loud when the wind blew a new chill through her warming body—this guy screamed violent fantasy. Greco-Roman wrestling or jackhammer fucking? Either would do. Both.

The giant's thin gaze narrowly escaped his pronounced brow. He lobbed one hoarse word at the crowd, something in Romanian, maybe a warning to the miners. Whatever it was, it landed with silencing devastation. The other miners moved off to the side, leaving Ilecko as a target on a firing range.

One of the soldiers stepped forward, wearing a weasel's smile.

"Tell him to back off," she said.

Dumitru yelled at the soldier in Romanian. He shot them a "what are you going to do about it?" glance and continued forward as his comrades snickered.

The soldier looked up at Ilecko's eyes for only a second and then he struck with the butt of his rifle. Ilecko never flinched as he grabbed the stock and whipped the barrel around, shattering the guy's face.

The other four Romanians raised their rifles—

Put-put-put and the Romanians dropped. Steam swirled from the barrels of the Shadow Stalkers' rifles. Jaguar spun to cover Trandafir, but he'd already dropped his rifle and fled up the path. Dumitru was right behind him.

"Hooah," she muttered, in case they had any doubt that she approved.

"Hooah," they replied steadily.

Tildascow took a cautious step toward Ilecko. His face remained rigid.

Whaddya need, big guy? A little flirt? A big threat? Some lion-with-a-splinter-in-his-paw desperation? Bargaining for a big reward? She scanned his eyes for any hint. Nothing in return, so she started with the obvious.

"We need your help."

Ilecko's eyes passed from the fallen soldiers to the Shadow Stalkers and from Lon to her. Then he turned back toward his mine.

She'd brought a flashbang in case she needed it for Valenkov, but—

"Ea este numeLon, sheea este American!" Lon yelled, in a pitiful caricature of a Romanian accent. Just in case they hadn't thoroughly infuriated this guy. *"New York a fost poknit epidemie de găini!"*

The other miners snickered. It grew into bellowing laughter.

"What did you say?" Tildascow asked.

"I told him my name, and I said we're American and New York City has been struck by an outbreak of werewolves."

"You sure that's what you said?" asked Mantle.

"I've studied Romanian for ten years. I know how to talk to this man."

Thirteen
Carpathian Mountains
9:10 p.m. EET

"She is name Lon, and she is American. New York has been punched epidemic of chickens!"

The miners buckled with laughter.

Yannic Ilecko did not find this funny, if it was true. And these soldiers had killed men to prove it so.

But why would the Americans request his help through this boy, with his pathetic grasp of *limba română?*

"Chickens are on our New York City," he cried. His face was as foolish as his words. *"Hundreds people have been killed. Thousands people maybe more tranquilizer."*

The laughter intensified. But the boy was earnest.

"Thousands chickens! They is to overfulfillment our country. She is beg for your help."

The American woman's keen eyes tried to read his thoughts. She was a clever commander. The boy quivered from humiliation, yet she ordered to him to continue.

"She must find a man yell Valenkov. Forehead of the pipeline."

The miners slapped their knees. If only he could slap their faces.

The woman spoke again and the boy paused to translate. *"The United States will pay you—"*

"Your money means nothing to me," Ilecko said in *limba română. "You will never find the man you seek."*

He cursed himself for responding to them. He did not want to engage this fool, and he certainly did not want the attention of the military, be they Romanian or American. He preferred to be left alone, make his *bani*, and tend his farm. He could not afford to lose his job, and it would not sit well that his presence had brought distraction to his co-workers.

The others made way as Ilecko retreated to the nearby lot, where his four-horse stagecoach was parked. He unhitched as the Americans argued among themselves.

"Please, you help us?" the fat boy pleaded. *"Eight million people trapped on island infested with chickens!"*

Ilecko pulled up on his four-in-hand reins, turning his horses toward the road. His coach trundled past the fallen soldiers in their puddles of reddened snow. The Americans made no indication that they would stop him by force.

He came alongside the boy, a porky redhead with thick, flushed skin and frozen glasses. He might never have worked a day in his life.

"My girlfriend she is there!" he whimpered.

"Your soldiers will protect her. They can handle this on their own."

"They do not understand the way of the chicken!"

The other Americans remained quiet. Their woman commander was confident in the boy. Was she desperate? Or stupid? Or had she actually read his thoughts?

Because there was something. *Something* made him like this boy.

"The United States of America asks for my help, and you are their emissary?"

"And you think she can handle it on our own?"

Fourteen

CDC Headquarters
Atlanta
2:15 p.m.

Jessica Tanner sat alone in her office. The others were off updating their files, barking ill-conceived theories and re-re-redefining their terminology. Of course they'd agreed with Richard that he should stay. She was just being reactionary, they thought. Intimidated by the big bad monster.

This is not magic, this is a virus, Richard had said. And they'd all agreed with him. *When you're ready to get back to science, come find me.*

Somehow she'd been branded a proselytizer.

But were they clinging to their own dogma because they'd be lost without it? Or were they braver and smarter than she?

The blinds were drawn, the lights dim and the televisions dark. She tried to take a sip of tea, but her hands wouldn't stop shaking.

Richard floated through the door in mid-sentence. "—reconfiguring the lamp to test the catalysis at various spectral intensities. You need to see this. They may have a different state every night of the month!"

She looked at him with doe eyes, praying that he would just do this for her. "Richard. You have to leave."

"Oh, come on, Jess. Not again. We settled this."

"We didn't settle it."

They stared at each other, arguing silently in the way that husbands and wives do. *Someday you're going to have to believe in me, Jess.* Around and around they went, and she kept losing.

"You have to *leave,* Richard."

"I *can't* leave, there's so much—"

"Just go!" she screamed.

Richard slowed his tone and put a hand on her shoulder. She could practically hear him cock his charm rifle. "I hear you, Jess, I do. And I care about how you're feeling. I love you. But I can't leave." He paused, searching for reasons. "Too much of the data is in my shorthand. I'd have to transcribe it all."

"You taught half the viros here. They can transcribe your notes. Go home and they'll conference you in."

"I need to see the data. I need to see *her*. Jess, she's *restrained*. Don't let your fear run wild with your emotions."

"Oh my God," she muttered. Not only had she been stripped of her professional and personal dignities, now he'd been callous enough to put his finger on it.

"Look," he said, sensing her simmer, "we'll call for more—"

"Get out. Or I'll have security throw you out."

He smacked the wall on his way.

Fifteen
White House Oval Office Dining Room
2:30 p.m.

Weston and Teddy endured long silent moments during their lunch, unable to wrench their hearts from the conversation they'd just left in the Situation Room. And they both knew Truesdale was off somewhere with his men, brewing unconscionable plans in their cauldron.

So starved were they for optimism that both men sprung from their seats when Rebekkah Luft entered with a muted smile. "I have something new in the latest CDC report, something we might be able to use to our advantage."

"Do tell," Teddy urged.

"The werewolves' transformation varies according to the lunar phase. The closer to the full moon, the more 'wolfy' they become."

"Okay."

"They won't transform at all during the night of the new moon. And it shouldn't be much worse than a bad mood for up to three days on either side."

"Seven days," said Teddy. "We can take control, get them into safe containment—"

"When does it start?" asked Weston.

"The 12th. Runs through the 19th."

"We just have to keep them contained until then."

Weston crashed into his chair as the pressure valves released in his chest. Teddy laughed at the ceiling. Luft's smile grew.

But they all knew Truesdale had to keep going.

Sixteen
Southeastern Transylvania
9:38 p.m. EET

Every known superstition in the world is gathered into the horseshoe of the Carpathians, as if it were the centre of some sort of imaginative whirlpool.
   —Bram Stoker, *Dracula*
   —Lon Toller, opening quote, *Of Wolves and Men: Legitimizing the Veracity of Lycanthropy in the Scientific Era—A Thesis of Truth*

Lon scanned the living darkness through the coach's window. He'd spent so many nights studying this region by flashlight, hiding under the covers after his stepfucker ordered him to sleep. But nothing prepared him for the aura, the *intensity,* of Transylvania, the legendary haven of the supernatural. These woods were entirely different from any in America. They had a sinister unease, a distrustful stillness. They were the enemy, and they were *watching.*

The brand name for Transylvanian folklore was, of course, Bram Stoker's *Dracula*—one of Lon's very favorite novels. Count Dracula was a new and ambitious vampire who traveled from his remote castle in the Carpathian Mountains of Transylvania to join London society. Looking to spread his thrall, he turned dimwitted socialite Lucy Westenra into a vampire. Her friends enlisted the aid of Dr. Abraham Van Helsing, a well-travelled scholar who had experience with vampires. When the humans fought back, Dracula infected their beloved friend Mina Harker. But Van Helsing hypnotized Mina and used their blood bond against him. Van Helsing looked into Mina's mind to track Dracula back to Transylvania (to a mountain trail not very far from where they were right now!), where they ambushed and finally destroyed him.

But there were so many other tales of this place's mystical powers, some of which even gave Stoker inspiration. Legends of a powerful energy field giving Transylvanians extra-sensory perception. Eyewitness accounts of strange runes written in floating fire. Claims that a hundred thousand ghosts roam the countryside, victims of the notorious tyrant Vlad the Impaler. Gypsy mystics from this region could supposedly curse their enemies with harrowing fates. And, of course, there were these dark woods stalked by werewolves under the light of the moon.

Modern folk were eager to dismiss these tales. Maybe it was the fear in their hearts that kept them from believing. But Lon had faith.

They traveled a narrow, snowy path wandering northward from the mine. The road was illuminated by moonlight, but the pine-and-juniper forest was pitch black except for the shining eyes of nocturnal predators. Lon felt a surge of relief when the thicket broke into meadows of virgin snow.

He was quite familiar with their location. The closest populated area was several miles to the east: the commune of *Comandău*, population: 1,192 (page 196 in Lon's well-worn *Atlas of the World*). They were about 130 miles southeast of the *Tihuța Pass*, the location where Stoker set Dracula's castle. Further to the west was the city of *Sibiu*. That was the location of the Scholomance, the fictional university Dracula attended. Lon's favorite dungeon in *World of WarCraft* was named in its honor. Well, not his favorite, but it held a special place in his heart.

They were deep in the southeastern elbow of the Carpathian Mountains, precisely where Lon believed the werewolf community thrived.

Sweet, sweet validation.

Beethoven, Mantle, Jaguar, and Tildascow were packed with him in the cab of Ilecko's coach. The Romanians had taken off in their helicopter, but Beethoven had arranged for a CIA pick-up when—*if*—they found Valenkov.

Lon had no idea where they were going, or, really, who this man was that they were following. But Tildascow didn't waver when Ilecko told them to get in his coach, and she always seemed sure of herself.

"You married?" Mantle asked Tildascow.

No, she said by shifting her chin a millimeter to the left and back.

"Boyfriend?"

Non-answer said no. Her eyes grew heavy and bored.

"Wheels don't roll that way?"

Jaguar chuckled. Beethoven shut him down with a glare.

"Wheels roll just fine," Tildascow said. "Men are either too stupid or too angry to keep around."

"Not me," laughed Mantle. "I'se just too slick."

"Too stank," said Beethoven.

"Too ornery," said Jaguar. Lon had forgotten what his voice sounded like.

"Too good lookin'," Mantle said with a wide smile.

"I'm gonna go with stupid," said Tildascow. "And I tend to hurt stupid people."

Jaguar and Beethoven laughed. Tildascow winked at Lon, which made him nervous. Should he—

A wolf's howl slinked through the air. The melody beckoned others, and soon there was a chorus. Each voice sounded closer than the last, until the carriage was enveloped in a suffocating threat.

"Jesus fuck!" Mantle whispered.

"Lord's name," Beethoven admonished him.

"You're right. *Christ* fuck."

They waited silently, bracing for… *something.* But the howls faded and their muscles reluctantly released.

Mantle looked down and whispered, "Werewolves."

The coach came to a stop and everyone craned to look out the cab's small windows. On one side of the road was a ditch swallowed by more forest. On the other they saw a modest farm that probably once grew potatoes and grains. Now it was unkempt, dead, and frozen. A footprint path cut through the snow, leading to the shriveled corpse of a log cabin. Even in the bright reflecting moonlight, its entrance was barely visible beneath the porch's sagging awning. The sight of it made Lon realize that he hadn't taken his Lexapro.

This couldn't be Valenkov's home, not if he wore handcrafted clothes and certainly not if he was truly of royal lineage. No, this was Ilecko's place.

The coach quaked as Ilecko climbed down from his driver's seat. Without a word, he set off on the path toward the cabin.

After a moment of uncertainty, Tildascow ushered the others out of the coach. They took cautious steps in the crunchy snow, keeping their rifles trained on the dark woods.

Lon was drawn to the bed of frosted purple flowers running along the perimeter of the farm. They were well-kept, an anachronism amid the decay.

"Wolfsbane," Lon said, taking in the flower's peppery smell.

"That's supposed to scare away werewolves?" asked Jaguar.

"Yep."

"I say we eat that shit up."

"It's poisonous. Paralyzes your respiratory system. They used to put the toxin on arrowheads."

Jaguar backed away, but Tildascow bent down to examine the flowers, breaking and smelling the leaves.

"Fuck on a stick, man, look at these horses!" Mantle pointed to the four emaciated horses driving Ilecko's carriage. He ripped open a Velcro patch on his sleeve and produced an energy bar.

"Mantle," warned Beethoven. He was tired of wrangling the kid.

"It's *my* food." The horses excitedly smacked at the pieces he handed out. "Y'all got any to spare?"

Tildascow handed over two bars with an unenthusiastic glare.

Another wolf bayed from somewhere deep in the forest, causing the horses to neigh.

"Jesus motherfucking porn star Christ," Mantle mumbled.

They moved a few yards up the path, putting distance between themselves and the forest. The Shadow Stalkers crept with rifles at the ready, but Tildascow remained cool, sniffing a sprig of wolfsbane as if it were a rose.

They stopped halfway up the path, when they heard goats bleating from a small barn at the rear of the farm. It was hidden from the road by a snowy patch of willow trees, a cascading of green and white.

Tildascow ushered Lon ahead. "Keep this guy moving."

"Me? Why me?"

"He trusts you. That's why we're here. You trust me, that's why *you're* here. See how that works?"

Lon hesitated, but Tildascow nodded him toward the cabin. And so he found himself approaching this mysterious shithole while the others stayed put midway on the road, well out of saving-his-ass range. From here, he could see that the front door was closed. God knew what Ilecko was doing in there.

When he stepped onto the porch, the necrotic wood creaked like some kind of alarm. He froze and waited for a reaction—it'd be great if Ilecko came out and explained himself—but he got nothing.

With an empty swallow, he rapped on the feeble door. It rattled in the uneven frame.

When the giant emerged, Lon stumbled backward and nearly fell off the porch. As Ilecko hovered over him, he felt like he was looking up at the red monster who'd gotten a manicure from Bugs Bunny in those old Looney Tunes cartoons. Except Ilecko was more fearsome. And smelled. And might kill him.

"*Return to the coach,*" Ilecko said. "*We will leave soon.*"

"*Where are we going?*"

"*To find answers.*"

Ilecko went back inside and the door groaned behind him.

Lon turned back to Tildascow. She mimed pushing him forward.

No! He shook his head. *Fuck no!*

But she gestured more adamantly, with a "don't disappoint me" glare.

He sighed, wondering why the hell he did whatever she—because she's hot, that—but he had Elizabeth, and she—but she's *really* hot—but it's not like he was going to get any—so then why would he—because she's *really, really* hot, and that makes it—but no, it was more like he wanted to prove himself to—

Lon stepped onto the porch again, using the creak like a doorbell. No answer.

"We are in a rush," Lon called out.

No response.

The door was so far off-kilter that he could see movement through the gap in the frame. Balls sweating, he peeked inside.

What he saw might once have been a homey living room; now it was all but abandoned. The centerpiece wood-burning fireplace was empty and ashen. A reading chair sat next to it, draped with an afghan that had practically gone grey. There were assorted stacks of books, ancient hardbacks, but they looked as untouched as the rest of the place.

He shifted left to see the other side of the room, where a cot lay in the corner. It was covered with a shabby cotton blanket and sheets that had been stained brown. The cabin seemed large enough that it would have a bedroom; strange that he'd be displaced in his own home.

But it isn't a home, Lon realized. *It's a crypt.*

The cabin shook as Ilecko returned from a back room. He had a rawhide bag slung over his shoulder, and he'd changed into a proper shirt and coat (black and long, not all that different from Lon's trench).

Lon took cover so Ilecko didn't catch him peeking.

The shaking stopped. Ilecko was still.

Lon took a careful step to his original position on the porch. He'd learned the art of memorizing creaks while trying to avoid his stepfucker's drunken attention. Annnnd mission accomplished.

A moment passed. And then a couple more. What was he doing in there?

Lon tilted his head and squinted. He could see Ilecko standing by the fireplace and leaning against the mantle. He was looking at something.

Lon tilted further, trying to see over Ilecko's shoulder. Or under his elbow. Neither of which was remotely possible.

Ilecko was still for a very long time. What was he doing?

Lon's legs went aquiver. Saliva rushed into his mouth. He *had* to know.

The porch shifted again, far more softly than before as Ilecko took lighter steps. Lon stooped to find that he had moved away from the mantle and left something behind. It was a fuzzy swash of color, probably a photograph.

He turned back to Tildascow. She threw her arms out as a question. He shrugged, since there was no universal sign for *I'm probably about to get myself killed.* But he had to know.

He took the tenuous step back toward the doorframe, avoiding the creak, and peered inside.

It was indeed a photograph—a stunning one, of a beautiful woman twirling in a flowery meadow, her candy-orange curls collecting pools of sunlight, shading her porcelain skin and pale eyes.

And then the door opened and Lon fell backward.

Ilecko's eyes shifted from Lon to the photograph and back again.

"I'm sorry," Lon said in Romanian. In the darkness, he couldn't see his face, couldn't tell if he was seething or sobbing or what. The awful silence made him feel sick and stupid. Finally he fumbled up, *"Was that your wife?"*

Ilecko stepped forward and extended a hand. Lon took it, and his shoulder was nearly ripped from his socket as the giant yanked him to his feet.

Lon followed him back to the stagecoach. He was happy to leave that tomb, but he felt miserable for Ilecko's life and even more so for his own callous intrusion. He wasn't looking forward to the self-flagellation he'd face when he reviewed this moment in the dangerous confines of his own mind.

But how could someone live in that hopeless cave? Lon wondered what Ilecko would think of his relatively palatial dungeon.

Ilecko arrived at his horses, and took note of the crumbs on the ground. The horses were still smacking their lips. Tildascow shot a look of frustration at Mantle, and she stiffened to apologize, but Ilecko nodded modest approval and tossed his rawhide bag onto the drivers' bench.

"He knows we're short on time, right?" asked Tildascow.

Ilecko climbed up onto the cab. He sat pensively, silently waiting for the others to get in the coach.

"I think he understands the situation, yeah."

Tildascow motioned for the Shadow Stalkers to get in, but she stopped Lon. "Ride up front. Find out whatever you can about Valenkov. Make sure we're not wasting our time."

"No, please. *You* ride up front." He tried to push his way past her.

"Ride up front, Lon."

She hopped in the cab and shut the door, leaving him outside. He weakly smiled upward at Ilecko, who nodded him toward the shotgun seat. As he walked around the cab, he glared at Tildascow the whole way.

He reached the passenger side of the driver's bench. And he sighed. The floorboard was *so* high. Lon couldn't even get out of a pool without a ladder.

"Do you need help?" Tildascow asked.

"No," he said, and he waited for Tildascow to disappear into the coach before he tested his footing on the wooden spokes of the wheel. He heaved himself up with a disturbingly feminine grunt, but he didn't have a clue where to step next. Fucking hopeless.

The car shook as Ilecko stepped off. Lon put his head against the wheel and wished he could be anybody but himself. The big guy came around and unceremoniously hoisted him into the carriage by the waist of his pants.

As Lon plucked his underwear from his intestines, Ilecko climbed back into the drivers' seat and took up the reins.

They continued their slow creep through the eerie Transylvanian forest, heading toward the sinister moon on the northeast horizon. The mountains loomed on their right, occasionally blocking the moonlight and shrouding them in darkness. Animals stalked them from the thicket, rattling the trees.

They rode in silence for more than twenty minutes. Lon wanted to open a dialogue, but he couldn't imagine how.

Ilecko's brows cast heavy shadows over his face, making his features shapeshift in the skittering darkness. His smell, though—salty and fruity—that was quite clear. It wafted from every move he made, playing a pivotal role in his "get out of my way" aura. And then there were his hands, so swollen and calloused that Lon wondered if he could feel anything at all.

The wolves still bayed from the forest. Each one would set off a threatening chorus, just in case the travelers forgot they were outnumbered.

Those hills are alive with the sound of music, Lon thought.

Eventually the swaying cab lulled Lon into remembering his exhaustion. The others must have felt it too.

"Anyone got any family in New York?" Mantle asked in the tone of a wake-up call.

Nobody answered.

"I got a bunch of cousins I ain't ever met," he continued. "My father's brother's kids. They all came down south a couple times. Nice folks, but man they're soft. All of them are soft in New York, stuffed in ties and drinking their cocktails, letting other people drive for 'em. No wonder they're fallin' apart right now."

The silence that followed felt too much like a requiem.

"My grandma spent most of her life in Yorkville," said Beethoven, cutting through the morbidity. "My great-grandpa came over from Germany, just as it started to get real bad over there. He had someone sending him fine chocolates, so he opened a candy shop. He sent for his wife and kids, but they were all got by the Nazis. After a while, he re-married and had my grandma. She took over the shop after he died. That was just after the war; she was in her early teens. The importing dried up, so my grandma taught herself how to make chocolate. She once told me she'd worn an apron every day for 40 years."

The others chuckled.

"Good people over there in Yorkville."

"You heard from her since this began?" Tildascow asked.

"She died about two years ago. Tough end, she had Alzheimer's, but it was a good run. She taught me about shuttin' up and doin' hard work. My wife and I are gonna name our daughter after her. Due in May."

A gloomy silence followed. On this road to nowhere, through a forest of monsters, the idea of Beethoven seeing his daughter in May seemed dangerously optimistic.

"My girlfriend is in New York," Lon said, hoping to change the channel.

"That right?" Jaguar asked, shifting to look at Lon through the coach's front window.

"You in it to rescue the princess, flyboy?" Mantle asked.

"Kinda."

"I wish I had me a girl back home," Mantle chortled. "I had two, but they found out about each other. Now I got none."

"Your girl a looker?" Jaguar asked.

"Yeah," Lon answered, hearing the lie in his own voice.

"What color hair's she got?" Jaguar asked.

Great, now how the fuck do you answer this? You lie, right? But what if they ever meet her? But how would they ever—

"She bald?" Tildascow tried to help.

Even Ilecko turned toward him.

"No. She's not bald. She, um…"

"Got like that multicolored hair?" Mantle asked. "Y'know, the blond in the front and the—"

"I don't know," Lon muttered. "I don't know what color her hair is."

And then there was an awful silence.

"How's that work?" Mantle finally asked.

"We…" *Please, God, if one of these werewolves is going to attack, please let it happen now.* "We met over the Internet. In a chat room."

"That's great!" Tildascow said, trying to shut the door on the conversation—

"When?" Mantle asked.

"Um… two years ago."

Another long moment passed.

"Two years and you've never met her? Never seen a picture?"

"I live in Ohio."

"Could drive to New York in six hours," said Jaguar. "I used to make that run for a booty call, girl I met on the Internet too. Didn't know I had to pay her till I got there, but *damn* I went back for more."

The crew laughed. Ilecko turned to him for a long moment. Lon could barely see his face, let alone read it. It probably seemed like the others were laughing at him.

"But Lon," Mantle said, "you ain't like *afraid* to meet her—*ow!*" Someone punched him.

"No," he laughed. "I'm not *afraid*."

They whisper-argued in the cab, everyone against Mantle.

Lon was startled by Ilecko's hand on his shoulder. He finally broke his silence. *"Do not let them intimidate you,"* he said in Romanian. *"They do not understand the way of the chicken."*

Lon's head dropped into his hands.

"Tell them we are close," Ilecko said.

"He says we're close," Lon called back.

Before the others could acknowledge, the wolves howled again. They were close—*very* close—and on every side of the carriage.

Lon's heart was in his throat. He turned to Ilecko, who turned back to him with his typical stoic glare. No reassurance, no surprise, no concern.

Mantle cleared his throat and began to sing about bad moons. His botched melody would've made John Fogerty weep. Tildascow joined in, and they laughed as they fumbled the lyrics.

"You are not like them," Ilecko said quietly.

"I'm not like anybody."

"Why are you here?"

Lon thought for a moment about how to answer. *"I'm an expert."*

"An expert on chickens?"

Lon nodded.

The others laughed as Mantle took a goofy beat-box swing at the guitar solo. Some sort of a slap fight rocked the coach.

Another howl came from the right, practically in Lon's ear. The horses flinched left, breaking the carriage to the very edge of the road. The soldiers went silent.

"Will they attack?" Lon whimpered.

"I do not know. I am not an expert."

Douché, his friends at his *Magic: the Gathering* socials might say. Lon rolled his eyes at himself. *"Why haven't they spread here like they have in America?"*

"It is rare that one survives an attack."

"It seems like most of them survive in New York."

Ilecko contemplated that. It seemed like everything happening in New York came as a surprise to him. *"The mountains are difficult to traverse,"* he added as an afterthought, *"so the creatures do not roam far during the night."*

"Have you killed many of them?"

Ilecko either didn't hear him or chose not to respond.

They rode in silence for a few minutes as the moon continued its game of hide and seek behind the mountains. Nearby branches rustled as something in the darkness matched their pace.

Mantle tried to start up the singing again. No one joined in.

"Ask him about Valenkov's father," said Tildascow.

"We have to find Zaharius Valenkov. His son is blackmailing the United States to find a cure—"

"Zaharius Valenkov is dead."

Lon sputtered. *"Are you sure?"*

"I killed him."

Lon's heart sank. He still hoped the werewolves could be cured, despite the thrashing he'd gotten from the CDC doctors. *"So the bloodline did not end."*

"It did. And then it began anew."

"There was another werewolf?"

Ilecko took a long moment to answer, as if he had to give it some thought. *"It is a curse upon the family. The child inherits from the father."*

"So now Demetrius is the head of the bloodline?"

"He is."

"Why didn't you kill him too?"

"I had no cause. He was…" Ilecko chose his word carefully. *"Different."*

"Different how?"

But Ilecko gave no answer. The man knew how to end a conversation.

The brush on their left waned as the path hugged a tight slope on the mountainside. They could see a village in the valley below, a small community of log cabins and utility buildings.

Ilecko brought the carriage to a stop and gazed thoughtfully into the valley. The village below was dark and eerily still. A ghost town in a haunted countryside. A fanfare of howls erupted through the forest beyond the village, as if the werewolves were staking claim.

"Are we there?" asked Mantle. The others shushed him.

"Something has gone wrong," Ilecko said. *"The creatures should not attack the villages."*

"Why not?" asked Lon.

"It does not suit their master's purpose."

Ilecko whipped the horses, driving them harder than ever. Now he was compelled by something graver than curiosity.

"Master? They have a master?"

No answer.

"The werewolves are controlled by someone?"

No answer.

"Did they kill everyone in that village?"

No answer.

They took a sudden right turn into the forest, climbing the base of the mountain on a small road that could barely stave off the brush.

"Lon," barked Tildascow. "What's going on?"

"I don't know! You ask him!"

"Just relax," she said. "Stay on him."

"You should be on him!"

"He likes you."

Crazy bitch, this guy doesn't like anybody!

The forest closed in on them. Trees swiped the coach, and their branches merged formed a living tunnel, cutting off the light of the moon. The horses slowed their pace until Ilecko lit a gas lantern and held it aloft.

The road curved to the left. The horses labored as their climb steepened. The drop on their left felt infinite, like the trees were ascendant from the netherworld. Lon wished he could write that one down. *Shit!* —

The road began a sudden decline. The coach accelerated and the pull faded until it felt like they were chasing the horses. They took a dramatic swerve, there might have been a moment of freefall, and then they were violently yanked to the right. Lon held tight as his nausea returned.

They broke free of the canopy, and the light of the moon returned. They hugged the subtle curve of the mountainside until it revealed a new structure in the distance. One that took Lon's breath away.

A castle.

A classic Gothic structure, set behind a stone curtain wall. Asymmetrical flying buttresses between the main structure and the two outer towers conjured the spooky silhouette of a cobwebbed candelabrum.

It was perched upon a hill, above the forest but still hidden in a valley between two towering mountains.

And it cut a sharp profile into the moon.

Seventeen
CDC Observation Room
3:15 p.m.

Questions only led to more questions.

First and foremost: What was happening to Melissa Kenzie *aside* from her transformations? She'd undergone an unequivocal metamorphosis, one that had nothing to do with hair and fangs. Post-reverse transformation, she'd displayed an impatient rage that seemed a stark divergence from the God-fearing mouse they'd met, an overgrown child so terrorized that she literally cried for her mommy.

Jessica watched Kenzie through the two-way mirror. Drs. Benrubi and Tsong had taken Richard's place at the monitors. Dr. Rohr stood by the moonlight lamp's switch. Eyeglasses were fogging from the number of staff and security packed into the observation room.

"Melissa," Jessica said over the intercom, "we're going to do another test. Try to relax."

Kenzie's eyes slinked toward Jessica's, as if she could see her through the mirror. "Let me out of here," she purred.

This was *not* the woman they had met yesterday.

"Soon enough. I promise."

"I've lost faith, Doctor Tanner."

Way past you, sister.

She cut the intercom and turned to Rohr at the light switch.

"Let me out of here," Kenzie said again. This time it was a threat.

Jessica nodded. Rohr flipped the switch. The light in the containment room became lavender.

And they gasped at what happened next.

Eighteen
Five Miles East of Covasna
Transylvania
10:15 p.m. EET

The castle loomed above them like some kind of evil kingdom. Just like the village they'd passed, it appeared dark and abandoned. At the outer wall's portcullis, both of the heavy wooden drop gates had been smashed inward.

Tildascow examined the ground by flashlight. It was flat soil, a mound of earth between the stone mountains. The two-inch coat of snow had fallen a week ago, and no one had been here since.

But there were corpses beneath the snow.

Two in the vicinity and maybe more down the road. Facing away from the castle, killed while trying to flee.

"Whose castle is this?" she asked Ilecko.

No response. He was deep in thought, still examining the drop gate.

"Guys…" said Lon. He pulled back a thick growth of lichen to reveal that someone had painted a pentagram on the wall.

Ilecko stepped backward to take it in.

"Whose castle is this?" she asked again.

By now the answer was obvious, but she had to try to open some kind of direct dialogue with Ilecko. He still couldn't bring himself to raise his eyes above her boots. Whether it was her authority, her nationality or (most likely) her gender, she unnerved him to the point where he couldn't even—

"Demetrius must be stopped," he said, in muddled English that surprised the others. And then he looked her directly in the eye.

"That's what we're here for," she said.

"It is not blackmail that he seeks. It is revenge."

"Revenge for what?"

He ignored her question. "Tomorrow is full moon. The werewolves begin blood rage, they become powerful. You will not stop them.'"

"We will not stop them?" Lon stuttered.

"Tomorrow they escape New York."

Nineteen
CDC Containment Room
3:18 p.m.

Kenzie erupted with a bellowing roar. Her neck extended and her jaw exploded into a canine snout. Coarse black hair sprouted everywhere at once. Her ears curled into grey points behind her narrowing yellow eyes. Long fangs grew from her teeth. Her shoulders spread, stretching her back, while her torso tapered into the lean hindquarters of a wolf. Her feet stretched to digitigrade.

This wasn't the werewolf they'd seen. This was a hulking monster.

The cloth restraints disintegrated like paper. The creature ripped free of the gurney.

"Turn it off! Turn it off!" Jessica screamed.

The room went dark except for the light of the monitors. The werewolf threw its tree-trunk arms, laying waste to the equipment.

"What do we do?" someone cried.

"Call security!" another yelled.

The wolf padded back and forth, eyes twinkling in the flames of the ruined machinery.

Howl.

And then it turned toward the mirror. Jessica felt certain it was looking for her. The others backed away. Some fled the room.

The werewolf lunged into the reinforced glass. Jessica fell backward, but the glass held.

The back door flew open. Everyone fled.

The creature took a quickening lap around the gurney, gaining momentum to cannonball into the glass.

Miraculously, it still held.

The werewolf rolled to its feet and shook off the impact. It paced the length of the mirror, visibly contemplating escape.

Someone hit the lockdown switch, sealing the containment room. The light above the door flashed from green to red and alarms rang out.

A guard arrived at the door. "How long until it turns back?"

"An hour," she said.

As soon as she spoke, the werewolf froze.

It was looking directly at her, as if the mirror were clear. The room was soundproof, the mic was off, but it had heard her. Or sensed her.

The werewolf broke their eye contact first. Its gaze tracked upward.

Toward the ventilation system.

The filtered exhaust network contained airtight pipes designed to flush the room of toxic contaminants, and seal them into a containment unit across the hall. It was sterile and secure, but she had no idea if—

The werewolf leaped, raking the vacuum-sealed ceiling with its claws. Debris came down as it landed. It shot up again and tore a gash deep enough to gain a handhold. With one more swipe, it ripped open the airshaft.

The security light flashed back to green. Two guards entered, guns drawn, loaded with silver bullets. They each fired several shots into the ceiling. *Bang Bang Bang.* The creature dropped to the floor.

"Is it dead?" asked one of the—

The monster hurtled onto the wall, loping ahead of the guards' frantic shots, and torpedoed into them, breaking them backward against a countertop.

And the door was still open.

Jessica hit the all-page on the intercom: "All personnel, we have a code red, volatile subject—a werewolf loose in the building. Find a room and lock yourselves in, don't come out until further notice. All security—"

Now crashing, screaming and shattering.

Jessica darted into the hallway, past the blood-streaked walls, a crumpled guard, the swaying containment room door, toward a demolished lab door. Dr. Phil Drake from USC was on the floor, his chest torn open. Harmy Smith, an intern, gurgled through her ripped throat.

The window was shattered.

INTERLUDE

Elizabeth

20 Hours Earlier
New Years' Eve
9:50 p.m.

Elizabeth Anne Golden was having a nightmarish day.

She'd been fired from her job as a barista at Starbucks because the manager said her make-up and tattoos were making customers uncomfortable. But the fucking customers weren't complaining—if anything, she drew in the alt crowd. No, it was the owner's JAP daughter who wanted her gone, because she felt threatened by anyone who didn't kiss her fake-tanned ass.

Elizabeth had a message for that bitch, and it was printed on the tiny rectangle of fabric on the back of her thong: *Fuck Right The Fuck Off.*

Everybody had something to say about how she looked. Her hair was too long, the violet streaks too brash, the pigtails too suggestive. Her mascara hid her eyes, her nose ring was too aggressive, her tattoos ruined her skin.

You'd be so pretty if you'd just let people see your face. Just one of a million little lies people tell an ugly girl.

She *wasn't* pretty. She was bony and pale, with a ridiculous Jewish nose, and at six-foot-two, she stuck out among the desirable girls like a mutant weed.

Fuck, she didn't even have a nice personality.

She missed out on college because it was expensive. Resisted the synagogue because it was closed-minded. Couldn't leave, because her mother couldn't live alone. She had her writing, but how do you get published? No friends—even the other goths were too goddamn emo for her tastes, following manufactured trends and acting out just to get noticed by their daddy. None of them had any truth in their hearts; none of them were artists.

So what if she wanted to sleeve her arm with bleeding roses trapped in spider webs? Who was to say what she could do with her skin? It was beautiful to her, and that's all that should matter.

Yep. Her life was a mess, her options were dwindling, and her resentment had caught fire. Her self-inflicted nickname was oh so appropriate: Elizanthrope.

The only thing she had to live for was Lon. He was her boyfriend, her best friend and her soulmate. And he seemed to have gone AWOL. They'd missed their afternoon date on iChat, which sucked because she needed to unload about Starbucks. She kept her buddy list open all evening, but he never showed. She should've had the nerve to shut it down and let him miss her, but kitten wanted to be stroked.

By nine, Mother had fallen asleep in the living room as usual. Elizabeth checked her oxygen tank and put a blanket over her wheelchair. Then she returned to her eternal sanctuary: her six-by-eight bedroom.

It was barely bigger than a closet, but it was pure Elizanthrope. Overlapping posters of Aleister Crowley, Sisters of Mercy, Nick Cave and his first band, The Boys Next Door. A black tapestry with gold and violet stitching hung from the four corners of the ceiling. Her shelves were overflowing with pewter fantasy miniatures, each of which she'd hand-painted. Most of the lot consisted of she-devils, vampiresses, and succubi. She had a thing for powerful women. In fact, the only phallus on the shelf was her beloved vibrator, which she'd customized with rubber batwings. She left it on display because it was funny that Mom never noticed it.

Funny in Mom's more mobile days, anyway.

Elizabeth curled up on the couch that also served as her bed. She plucked a half-smoked cigarette from her crowded ashtray and lit it with a candle. This was the only room she'd smoke in because of Mom's oxygen tanks.

The thirteen-inch television on the floor was flashing shots of the freezing screwheads in Times Square. It'd be six hours at least before she got tired, so she surfed the Net to some Joy Division while watching the

New Years' show on mute. The chicks in that pop band—the fuck were they called?—kinda turned her on, even if their music made her want to claw off her ears.

The tourists never came past their place on Broome & Orchard, a modest corner in the oh so Jewish Lower East Side. But that didn't stop the locals from getting pissed and making a racket. Even now some douche was kicking on the gate at Guss' Pickles across the street. Never mind that they'd been closed for months. Go back home to your Manischewitz, no pickles for you.

Elizabeth had grown bored with her regular blogstops and chatrooms. Everyone but her was out celebrating. Maybe Lon had found a party. Maybe he'd found a girl.

On that happy note, it was time to scout for some newfangled free porn. Might as well rub one out if she had nothing better to do.

As she opened her folder of dirty bookmarks, the television caught her eye. The camera swung and focused, trying to catch a fracas in the crowd. Looked like a pretty big one.

She took a drag from her cig and turned up the volume, only to hear Ryan Seacrest regurgitating his bloody American Idiot inanity. Right back to mute.

She spent a couple of minutes gazing at goth-fetish.com, and then it was time to get the ol' batwings for some tough love. As she sat up, the TV caught her attention again.

People were scrambling in every direction. It looked like a riot. But they weren't angry, they were scared.

Is this real?

Ryan Seacrest was gone. All channels were showing live, frantic shots from the street.

A helicopter roared past her building, flying way too low, rattling the walls. She dug through her thick black drapes and banged on her craptastic window to loosen the seals. When she finally jerked it open— *FUCK it's cold out*—she heard helicopters. Sirens. Cracks like gunfire.

Could it be a terrorist attack?

After a minute, she could hear the screams approaching. And then they arrived, running south on Orchard. Shrieking in terror.

Now the window wouldn't shut. She banged on the seal until it came free, but then it slammed shut and cracked. A softball-sized shard of glass fell to the carpet and the cold air rushed through the hole.

What the fuck was going on?

Her bedroom shook again, this time on the interior side. Heavy footsteps and banging in the hallway. Muffled voices pleading.

She rushed into the living room to check the locks. They were good. And Mom was blessedly sleeping.

More banging in the hall.

The security in their building was a fucking joke. Goddamn intercom had broken months ago, and since it wasn't getting fixed, someone had disabled the lock on the front door.

Their two deadbolts were no comfort. And their windows were entirely vulnerable. Fuck, they were easily accessible by fire escape.

"Please, please," someone cried. The voice came muffled through her thin walls. "We have to use your phone, we have to find our friend." They were talking to Mister Gross down the hall, through his chain. He must've slammed the door on them, and then they knocked on another door, this one closer. "Please! Please!"

More voices, from the stairwell. *"There's another one right outside!"*

What was outside?

More knocking now. Even closer. Elizabeth covered her ears and stepped away from the door.

She heard a horrible crash from the street, cars into glass. And an alarm—had they broken into a store?

And then the knocking came to her door.

Oh please just go away.

The doorknob rattled.

"Please, please let me in!" a man's voice cried. "Let me in!" The wall shook as he threw his weight against the door. "Please!"

The wall shook again. The deadbolt knobs danced in their sockets.

She had nowhere to go. Even if she could escape through the window, she couldn't leave Mom behind. Her legs were weak, so she sat on the kitchen floor, facing the door.

She covered her ears, closed her eyes and held her breath. *Please go away.*

They didn't bang again.

But the orthodox family upstairs was at it now. Kids crying, mother and father shouting. They were always at each other's throats, but now it was desperate. They'd outright turned on each other.

More footsteps. Screams. Helicopters rattled the building. Gunfire reports bounced off the walls.

She came to her feet and found her phone—but who the fuck to call? Didn't matter. No service.

Light flickered from her room, and she remembered that her TV was on. She returned to more wild footage from Times Square. Streaming text across the bottom told her to stay inside and keep the door locked, and not to call 911 or their local police unless it was an absolute emergency.

The news cut to some new footage, grainy cellphone video in extreme slow motion. It was in the crowd, where a large and dark man, maybe in a policeman's uniform, swung his gigantic hand upward. He ripped into another man's stomach—*oh my God*—and flung him into the air.

Maybe … maybe it wasn't a man. Or was he wearing a mask?

He slashed at the crowd, knocking them down, tossing them aside. People couldn't get out of the way. The crowd went berserk, violence everywhere, and someone smashed into the camera.

***

By 2:30 a.m., the president had come and gone. So had most of the streetwalkers. But the helicopters persisted.

Now the reality of werewolves felt like old news.

Harry Martin kept watch from the anchor's desk at WWOR. They were delivering instructions on how to proceed tomorrow.

Instead of celebrating with a New Year's Day parade, the population of almost two million was supposed to leave the island in an orderly, single-file fashion. A mandatory curfew had been imposed until 9 a.m., and then everyone should remain calm and walk to their designated exit zone… blah blah blah.

What about Mom? The oxygen tanks barely gave them four hours of mobility. How hard would it be to navigate the crowd with her wheelchair?

Elizabeth only had one photograph on her wall. It was the two of them, smiling over hot dogs at Battery Park. Before the cancer. It was a sweet sentiment, one she wanted to believe in. But it was a lie.

The truth was that they hated each other. Or, at least, the hate outstretched the love. But that was the Golden way; they were fighters. They fought each other, they fought JAP Starbucks owners, they fought cancer.

Come werewolves or terrorists or the end of times, Elizabeth wasn't going to leave her mother behind.

***

For a little more than an hour, a squad car had been positioned in the center of the intersection of Broome & Orchard. Huddled in her quilt, she watched them through her broken window. Watched them watch the darkness.

Looking for werewolves.

How many hours had she spent listening to Lon talk about them? He was so sure they were real. And now here was proof for the whole world.

Where could he be? Why couldn't he just—

What was that?

Elizabeth held her breath.

There it was again. *Breathing.*

Deep and heavy. Sniffing. From outside.

And now a scuffle on the wall.

She stumbled from the window, slipping beneath the curtain and landing with her back on the floor.

The wind threw whistling jabs at the curtain.

The breathing returned. Frantic, hungry, like a dog trying to catch a scent.

The curtain stopped moving.

Something was right in front of the window.

She buried herself in her quilt and waited to die. Time passed, but she couldn't track it. She grew impatient and angry, and her chest hurt from crying.

But nothing came through the window before the first rays of the sun.

***

Come morning, Elizabeth had only one thought.

Get the fuck out of this town.

The guys on TV said the moon wouldn't set—and the danger wouldn't pass—until after eight a.m. The curfew was in effect until nine, *"at which point everyone was to proceed in an orderly manner to their designated exit zones and calmly wait in line to be allowed off the island, where temporary housing would be available, along with a wide variety of travel options."*

The government said victims of the werewolves' attacks could be infected and might transform at the very next moonrise. They also promised that all of the wounded would be accounted for. But the cable pundits had the balls to state the obvious.

If everyone who was injured last night was going to transform tonight…

Elizabeth spent the morning packing her black denim backpack. It was—as always—loaded with her iPod, her makeup, and the red velvet deerstalker hat she'd stitched herself.

She prided herself on being the exact opposite of most girls—that is, practical and smart. So she brought socks, underwear, water bottles, and Luna bars. And just two of her pewter figurines.

They had two of Mom's portable oxygen tanks ("portable" meant only 20 pounds), each of which could be stretched to four hours. No choice but to lug both and hope for the best.

The good news began and ended with their location, the southeast corner of the island. According to the radio, their designated exit zone was the Manhattan Bridge to the south. It was farther than the Williamsburg Bridge, but that exit would need to handle traffic from the north.

The Chinatown YMCA would be their checkpoint. Elizabeth knew the place; she used to play in their co-ed basketball league. Sports weren't her thing, but watching the older kids drip sweat? Huzzah.

By six a.m., Mom stirred awake to the smell of bacon, sausage and toast. Elizabeth had prepared a substantial breakfast to sustain them through what would probably be a grueling day. It was the dude on the radio's idea, but it sounded smart.

Elizabeth ate on the move, making sure everything was locked down and switched off. She wondered if she could nail something over the broken window, then decided not to bother.

At nine on the dot, Elizabeth rolled her mother's wheelchair across the threshold of their apartment. With the oxygen and Mom, it weighed over a hundred and fifty pounds. As her memory faded, Mom had become locked into routines. She got frightened when they were broken, and she'd ask questions on a loop.

"Where are we going? What time is it? Where are we going?"

They reached the end of the hall, where Elizabeth locked the wheelchair into the automatic stair lift. It was gracious of the owner to install it (well, gracious and required by law), but the damn thing was aggravating and slow. A Chinese couple carrying small, puffy-jacketed kids passed them on the single flight of stairs. But where was everyone else?

She got her answer when they stepped outside.

Everyone had broken the curfew. The streets were packed. Guards with whistles and bullhorns urged the crowd to keep moving.

So demoralizing.

A cop helped her get Mom down the ramp and over the curb. Then he pointed west and repeated his mantra: "Straight to Roosevelt Park, then left to Hester." And just like that, he lost interest in them.

The five blocks to the park wasn't that bad. In fact, it was kind of comforting to be surrounded by so many people moving in the same direction. It was freezing and she'd worn too many layers, so she was both sweating and shivering. Mom finally stopped asking questions, and eventually she fell asleep beneath her badass old-lady sunglasses.

Trouble began when they reached Forsyth Street Park, a half-block of playground on five feet of raised brick. It was time to turn left and head south for two blocks, past the intersection at Grand to reach the YMCA on Hester. But the crowd on Forsyth was jam-packed and still thickening with budgers from Grand.

Guards scanned the crowd from cherry-picker platforms in the park. Things were surprisingly calm.

Sometimes her ridiculous height was a blessing. From six-two, she could see all the way to the YMCA. They had arranged the checkpoint on an outdoor track behind the building. Only more stagnation down there.

Once they crossed the bridge, Elizabeth figured she could use the Magic Penis to get them onto a train to Florida. "Magic Penis" was her nickname for her credit card because it went in, made magic happen, and then came back out and never had to account for anything. They'd head down to visit her father's shrewish sister, Aunt "anything-but-a" Joy.

Unless she heard from Lon. This would be a great excuse to visit him in Ohio. But cell service was out, which meant no texts. He couldn't get in touch with her even if he tried.

And she hoped he was trying.

***

An hour later, they hadn't moved a dozen feet. In fact, the endless merging of traffic from either side of Grand made it feel as if they were moving backward. The crowd's dueling radios were in a constant argument over volume.

Plus? These assholes were starting to smell. *Bad.*

Elizanthrope wasn't going to talk to anyone if she could avoid it, but she heard others passing the word: Scientists inside the YMCA were going to test people under lamps that re-created moonlight, but they hadn't started yet. Nobody knew why.

They hadn't started yet.

***

Another hour. It was almost two. The last twenty minutes were spent fumbling to replace Mom's oxygen tank. Pushing had gotten bad. Courtesy was failing.

***

A half-hour later, a commotion brewed at the front of the crowd. Waves of screaming and pushing spread backward from the YMCA. Even skyscraper Elizabeth couldn't see what happened.

The radios said every exit was overflowing. People toward the back of the lines should consider returning home and locking down.

No way. They were already here. So close. The authorities *had* to figure this out. How could they not?

***

Three o'clock. The temperature had dropped, and ominous clouds arrived. Mom hadn't said a word in hours. Elizabeth didn't know when the moon was set to rise, but curfew started at five.

She tried to hold onto hope, but they hadn't moved at all for almost a half-hour after that disturbance, and even now it was excruciatingly slow. They hadn't even reached Grand yet.

And the crowd was packed so tight that they had no choice but to relieve themselves in their clothes. That tug in her chest was her hope being drowned.

If they were going to turn back, they couldn't wait long.

***

By three-thirty, authorities began ordering people to return to their homes. The crowd revolted, but police and military unapologetically quashed them. Soon the paddy wagons lining the street were stuffed with troublemakers. Unfortunately, those folks were probably the safest and most comfortable around.

A policeman told her they could stay because of Mom's condition. But moving forward still wasn't happening.

***

At four, police closed off Grand and stemmed the flow coming west on Hester. There were still hundreds of people in front of them, if not thousands, but at least that number wouldn't increase.

The cold had woken Mom up. She asked Elizabeth to take her home, again and again and again.

***

Five o'clock.

Five-twenty.

Less than an hour left in Mom's last oxygen tank.

She was drenched beneath her pink hoodie and leather jacket. A repugnant odor wafted from her armpits.

And it had started snowing. Wonderful.

They were only forty yards north of Hester now, still on Forsyth. She could see onto the YMCA track.

They'd set up a fucking *firing squad*.

Six civilians stepped in front of the guns. A lamp threw purple light on them, and they stood in the rifles' sights for long, nerve-wracking moments. And then the guards escorted them beyond the track as the next group rotated in.

Culling groups of six from this crowd would be like emptying a sandbox six grains at a time. She looked back toward Broome. She wanted so badly to stay. The cops told her to stay. But she was losing faith. And maybe she was crazy, but it seemed like there were fewer cops around. Were they smarter than—

There was a commotion on the track. The group scrambled as a woman contorted under the purple light. The cops had tackled one man, probably her husband. His screams gave way to her howls until the

230

whole miserable thing was silenced by the firing squad.

"We're going home, Mom."

Elizabeth whipped the wheelchair around and hauled ass, pushing her legs to *wake the fuck up.* The crowd was more courteous to make way for them in this direction—less competition, after all. She didn't want to use her mother as a battering ram, but she could at least make threats.

They quickly reached a police barricade blocking late arrivals. There weren't any cops around, so she moved it herself. After so long in the dense crowd, it was refreshing (and a little eerie) to stare down a virtually abandoned Forsyth Street.

She pushed as hard as she could, retracing their path north along the park, all the while cursing herself for never following through on her resolutions to take up jogging. But seriously, who the fuck runs when nobody's chasing them? Her shins caught fire and her lungs went supernova, and she couldn't hear anything but her own—

What was that?

She stopped and held her breath, and then ripped off her hat and shook out her hair to clear her ears.

Howls.

Erupting through the sky, coming from every direction, each one answering the last until they became a chorus.

Howls. Fuck her luck.

Her instinct was to turn back, just so she wouldn't be alone. But they wouldn't offer any protection. The crowd would probably attract the werewolves. Shit, some of them might even transform.

Nowhere to go but home.

She kept up a steady pace, trying to regulate her breathing. That's what joggers did, right? The police posts and cherry-pickers were abandoned; the police had moved forward as the crowd diminished.

Those paddy wagons were still parked on the grass. Five of them, lined up side by side, each filled with handcuffed troublemakers. The last one was quaking. Screams emanated from inside.

Elizabeth watched it curiously, not slowing down but—

The back door blasted open to reveal a man convulsing on the floor, like he was having a seizure. His hands were cuffed behind him. The other prisoners were pulling against their own restraints and trying to kick him to death.

When they saw her, they pleaded for help. *Get the cops! Get us out!* But there were no cops around. The man on the floor threw back his head and howled. Elizabeth ran as fast as she could, forget the fucking breathing.

"What's happening in there?" Mom asked.

Elizabeth didn't waste her breath on an answer. She forged ahead and closed her eyes when those pleas became gurgles.

Everything seemed to be moving. Trash cans, cars, street signs. She couldn't watch it all at once. The trees in the shadowy park were playing tricks with her imagination, so she turned right at the next block.

Grand Avenue's squashed buildings were of little comfort, with their Byzantine fire escapes and confusing signs in Vietnamese or Chinese or Mandarin or whatever the hell it was. As she ran past, a Chinese family was locking the steel security gate of their market with themselves on the inside. They looked at her with detached curiosity, probably the same expression she showed those guys in the paddy wagon.

Make no mistake, their eyes said. *Everyone for themselves.* Desperate as she was, Elizanthrope had spent her life talking that talk, now she had to speedwalk that walk.

A bright orange awning beckoned her toward the intersection at Eldridge. An NYPD cruiser shot past and she ran into the street, waving at their rearview mirrors. They honked at her—whatever that meant— and never turned back.

She continued on, fighting the exhaustion, the urge to just collapse and wait. The street signs had given way to English; now they were advertising furniture stores and electronic repair shops. Lights were off. Gates were down.

The apocalypse is here, Elizabeth. Didn't you know?

In the sky above, something flew from rooftop to rooftop. Was it a bird? Fucksicles, please let it be a bird.

They finally reached the intersection at Allen. Dead trees lined the street's center island. A woman ran past on the far side, squawking lunatic noises. She looked at Elizabeth with wide—

And then it emerged from behind parked cars, a blur of dark hair in pursuit, loping like some kind of canine horse, gaining on the poor woman—

"*Eaaaaaaaaaa!*" she screamed! "*Heeeeeeeeaaaaa!*"

Elizabeth ran harder than ever, praying that thing wouldn't turn back. The woman's screams faded until Elizabeth couldn't tell if they were real or in her imagination.

They're real. They're real. They're real.

"Lizzy, what's happening?" Mom asked. "Have we had dinner yet?"

She forged ahead on Grand, across white street paint declaring "SCHOOL X-ING." An ambulance had crashed into a light pole on the northeast corner of Orchard. The driver was still in the front seat, bleeding from his forehead. He looked at her with the same detached curiosity as the Chinese family. He knew she wasn't going to help him, no point in asking. In one of the high-rise condos farther down the street, a mid-level floor was puffing smoke, nearly obscuring the people gathered on the roof and waving for help.

She turned left onto Orchard, just a block from home. So close now. The wheelchair shimmied on the uneven road, rattling her bones. Her body was burning and aching and screaming, but she was so close now.

They'd reached their intersection, *oh thank God.* Guss' Pickles! The café on the bottom floor of their building waved like a long-lost lover. She could almost feel her quilt's embrace.

A truck had plowed into parked cars across the street and come to a stop over the curb. It was still running and the driver's door was open.

Plank plank, metallic footfalls from its roof.

233

Elizabeth slowed to a creep, trying to go silent.

But it was too late.

A werewolf sidled to the edge of the roof, holding a half-eaten body like a dance partner. It looked at Elizabeth with—*yep*—detached curiosity.

No point in subtlety now.

Racing around the corner onto Broome, she caught a reflection of herself in the glass windows of the café. There she was, lanky and diagonal, pushing her mother's wheelchair while her black and violet hair swirled like a rocket's exhaust. And there was the werewolf diving off the truck, landing mid-stride on all fours and loping—

THE FUCK ARE THE KEYS?

—wait, the fucking lock is broken, how could you forget—

She chanced a look back at the werewolf. It was in the air, descending toward her, claws reaching beneath its hateful yellow eyes.

Everything went dark and peaceful.

And then a tremendous, shattering crash was followed by a whooping alarm. She opened her eyes to find two werewolves locked in combat inside the café, thrashing about in pools of fractured glass.

She yanked the wheelchair through the door. No time to deal with the stair lift, no time to try for the elevator on the other side. She lifted her mother out of her chair and—

The oxygen tank was still attached!

"Is everything okay, Lizzy?"

No time to disconnect! She put Mom back down, locked the chair into the lift and pushed to speed its maddeningly slow ascent. The chair lazily swung around to the second flight.

A single decisive howl came from the werewolf wrecking crew. Somebody had won.

Slam! The front door splintered from the impact, bending the frame inward. The decorative glass plopped to the floor in one piece and the werewolf peered through. Maybe it was looking over the menu?

Then it backed off to reload.

Slam! The door buckled. The wood had already surrendered; now it was just trying to get out of the way.

The lift clicked to a stop. She pulled the release once, twice, three times until it fucking worked. Whipped the chair around. Pounded down the hall. Her gasps ricocheted between the walls.

Smash! The door went down—

Thump thump thump up the stairs—

Keys in hand.

Shaking.

Top lock open.

The bottom—

—wolf coming *fast*—

Door open. Mom in. Deadbolt—

SLAM!

—locked. Second one locked.

SLAM!

Dust exploded from the jambs.

SLAM!

Elizabeth collapsed onto the kitchen floor.

SLAM!

"Go away!" she screamed. "Go away!"

SLAM!

"Lizzy, I think someone is at the door," Mom said. "Do you want me to answer it?"

PART FIVE

One

CDC High-Security Biological Storage Unit
Atlanta, Georgia
January 1
4:12 p.m. EST

Jessica Tanner spent most of her waking hours in a building that also contained over forty biological specimens with the potential to catalyze the extinction of the human race. Call them Mother Nature's greatest hits: a variety of killer influenzas, plagues, and viruses like mutated strains of HIV and Ebola. Each one could wipe us right off the dry erase board of life. If the wind blew in the right direction, it could happen in as little as a month or two.

In fact, extinction-level events have already occurred on our planet. Five times.

Five times the board was wiped clean, and nobody knows precisely why. Floods? Volcanic ash? Meteorite impacts? All theories.

Mankind has reached further and learned more than any of the planet's previous life forms. We've tripled our life span, developed artificial intelligence, glimpsed deep into the history of the universe, and even tinkered with the very building blocks of life. But still, we live on the brink.

New threats appear with frightening frequency, and they'll only come faster as reckless scientists tinker with biological systems we barely understand. Synthetic viruses designed to attack everyday diseases, next-generation vaccines or seemingly benign insecticides could—*oops!*— mutate into apocalyptic ecocides.

Diseases have pushed us to the brink before. In the fourteenth century, 75 million Europeans—up to sixty percent of the population— were killed by a disease thought to be the bubonic plague. And today's technology hardly makes us safe: In 2010, malaria was responsible for the death of one child every thirty seconds and twenty percent of all childhood deaths worldwide.

Mankind's archenemy has to be the smallpox virus, which may have ravaged civilizations dating back to Ancient Greece and the Roman Empire. Smallpox arrived in America with Columbus and killed up to ninety percent of the original Native Americans while also decimating the populations of Mexico and Peru. Up to five hundred million lives were lost to smallpox in the twentieth century before it was finally declared eradicated in 1979, due to the globalization of a vaccine developed in 1796. It took nearly two hundred years to wipe out smallpox, even with the right weapon.

And Jessica and her team couldn't even rest after the fight was won, thanks to the ever-present danger of mutagenesis. What if a strain of smallpox mutated around our vaccine?

The containment unit in the restricted-access Level 4 Biosafety Laboratory deep underneath the CDC Headquarters was one of only two known locations in the world to store living samples of smallpox. Every now and then some media outlet would harrumph about the inherent dangers of keeping the virus alive, but those samples would be vital to developing vaccines if ever a rogue specimen were to fall into the hands of a zealot or a fool.

Besides, there are worse things than smallpox.

Jessica waved her security badge across the scanner at the airlock door. She had already undergone a chemical shower and an ultraviolet examination, and passed through a vacuum to sterilize her hazmat suit. These were standard procedures to enter the most secure laboratory in the world, a self-contained ecosystem that could be entombed from the rest of the world with the press of a button.

The first door sealed behind her and the air cycled before the inner door opened on the data observatory. She stepped into the well-lit room and approached one of the four computer stations custom-designed to accommodate her airtight suit's bulky gloves. This was the last security check, a randomly generated password she had to decrypt from the personalized key she'd memorized. Each keystroke was logged via intranet to a secure offsite mainframe. If she input the wrong code twice, the lab would lock down until an override came from outside.

Once she was in the system, the computer greeted her personally, displaying a customized GUI layout she'd designed on her own PC. The search field query autocompleted her input, and then a strip of glowing LEDs in the floor cordially directed her toward the laboratory's main hub. The BSL-4 had four wings: biochem labs, observational studies, surgery, and living quarters. Jessica was headed for the farthest and heaviest door, which was situated behind yet another airlock.

Finally she entered the specimen library, a cold catacomb of vacuum-metalized drawers with individual climate controls. The outer rim housed odd-sized compartments, while smaller, uniform drawers were arranged in three rows through the center. Many of the library's specimens weren't all that dangerous; in fact, most of them were new, designer agents with antigenic relationships to BSL-4 classified species—enemies of our enemies. But protocol required that they should be handled at this level until they could be properly studied.

The LED indicator led Jessica along the outside corridor to the far wall, where it terminated against a single large incubator.

Before they'd heard of werewolves, Richard and his special pathogens team had spent months studying an anti-personnel biological weapon discovered in an underground laboratory in Sar-e Pol, Afghanistan. The government referred to it by the codename "Sorcerer"; USAMRIID labeled it "Agent M7949"; and the CDC catalogued it as "Staphylococcus unclassified 241." By any name, this thing was immediately recognized as a biological juggernaut and a wicked nemesis of mankind.

Highly virulent and resistant to multiple drug therapies, the S.41 bacteria cause an infection resulting in rapid, lethal necrotizing fasciitis: flesh-eating disease. It's a particularly attractive weapon because it perishes quickly; when its supply of harvestable flesh is exhausted, the bacteria starve to death. A city could be wiped out in a day and safely repopulated a couple of weeks later. The new inhabitants would just have to push aside some bones.

Only one roadblock prevented Sorcerer from being used as an effective weapon: its own efficiency. The bacteria consumed flesh so quickly that it would starve if it weren't kept frozen. A standard transport medium of saline infused with quick-reproducing fetal bovine serum wouldn't last the time it'd take to load a chemical bomb and fly over the enemy. Even if the solution were defrosted just prior to dispersal, Sorcerer could gorge and starve in the air. Dilute the bacteria and we'd be dropping nothing but pig fetuses over our enemies' heads.

Sorcerer needed something that the military didn't have.

Jessica slid open the incubator drawer. She'd spent countless hours poring over Sorcerer research, but she'd never seen the samples in person.

She removed one of the Eppendorf tubes and examined it in her gloved hand. Her body heat began to defrost the frozen liquid inside.

It may not have looked like much, but that pink goo was the last missing ingredient in the most revolutionary weapon in human history.

Two

Valenkov Estate
Five Miles East of Covasna
Transylvania
11:45 p.m. Eastern European Time (4:45 p.m. EST)

Brianna Tildascow believed in patience as a concept. From criminology to psychology to combat, patience rewarded. She liked her read on the Romanian who brought her to Yannic Ilecko, and she liked her read on Ilecko himself.

This was the right place to be. She just wanted to get the fuck on with it.

"Hunt for Demetrius begins here," Ilecko had promised her in his muddled English.

Valenkov's father was dead, Ilecko told them, and his death had cured the previous werewolves. That meant Demetrius Valenkov was the new head of the bloodline. His death would cure the werewolves in New York.

"Your soldiers will not find him," Ilecko said.

He spoke Valenkov's name as if they were estranged but beloved brothers. It was his sincere disquiet that compelled her to follow him, even with Valenkov halfway around the world. When a man does something that tests his emotions, that something is reliably important.

She'd called the Director and conveyed Ilecko's warning about the strength of the werewolves during their full-moon transformation. The clock was set for tomorrow night's moonrise, assuming the military managed to hold the quarantine tonight.

And now they were walking into an ancient, mysterious castle.

Beyond the stone curtain wall, the grounds were pitch black. The moon had set behind the mountains, and the courtyard's tangle of trees blocked the stars.

Her three Shadow Stalker commando escorts, Beethoven, Mantle, and Jaguar, donned their Panoramic Night Vision Goggles and proceeded with silver-loaded 9mm pistols at the ready. She struggled with her own PNVGs, a shit-sucking USAF model, and fell in behind Ilecko's dim lantern.

"Three o'clock," Jaguar whispered, toggling his goggles to throw a directional red dot that appeared only through their lenses. She only caught a glimpse of the dark shape ascending the tree before it disappeared into the network of branches. From above, eyes floated in the darkness.

"Four o'clock," said Beethoven from the rear. "Multiples at seven."

"Ten," reported Mantle. "We're surrounded."

"Guardians," Ilecko whispered. "They will not attack."

"So he controls them?" Lon asked.

Once again, Ilecko left the question as the answer.

They crunched through the pervasive silence until they arrived under the castle. The walls were lined with Byzantine ribbing, ornamental stonework that conveyed the sense of an outer skeleton.

A lone frozen corpse lay at the end of the stone path, a man fallen in mid-stride with his back to the castle as if he'd been caught trying to escape. Black remnants of his decay had seeped into the crust and soil.

The men on point kept moving, but Lon went stiff, staring at the corpse as if it were whispering a secret. Tildascow hesitated in case the kid had found something, but then she realized he'd probably never seen a dead person before. She put a hand on his shoulder and moved him along.

They caught up with the others at the edge of the colonnade and proceeded on to the cloister, a tall outdoor corridor running along the base of the façade. As far as castles went, this guy seemed to know how to do 'em.

The thick cedar door at the main entrance had been demolished in the same manner as the outer gate. Scorched splinters of wood still dangled from the hinges.

Two tall copper statues stood guard on either side of the door. On the left was a crowned king tied to a tree and riddled with arrows. "This is St. Edmund, a Saxon king," Lon explained. "He was captured by Viking raiders, and when he refused to renounce his faith, they did *that.*"

The other statue was of a wolf poised defensively, protecting the king's severed head between his legs. Lon continued, "Then they cut off his head and left it in the woods. When the king's subjects went searching for his head, they heard his voice calling out. And when they found it, it was being protected by this wolf. They took the head back to the kingdom, and when they placed it back on his body, it magically rejoined."

"And then what?" she asked.

Lon shrugged. *How should I know?* Kid had a talent for making you feel stupid for asking any question he didn't have the answer to.

"So what's he mean to Valenkov?" asked Jaguar.

"He's the patron saint of torture victims and wolves," said Lon.

"Of course he is," she muttered.

The statues and walls were smothered in cobwebs, so thick that they could barely see the intricate ribbed vaulting on the roof of the arcade. And a putrid smell was wafting from inside. Rotting corpses, no doubt.

Ilecko stepped over the shattered door, leading with his lantern. The Shadow Stalkers covered them on all sides.

The entrance hall could have fit a tennis court. Tildascow retrieved two flashlights from her vest and took off the night vision goggles to get an honest look.

"Stay close," she warned Lon, handing him the other flashlight.

The castle had been ransacked: Luscious, hand-carved furniture smashed beyond recognition, delicate woodwork scorched by Molotov cocktails, artwork torn from the walls. In the grand fireplace that once served as the great hall's centerpiece, rats had made a nest from the shredded canvas of a Chiaroscuro.

Looking up, her light cast sparkling shadows off an exquisite chandelier. It was cradled by the domed ceiling that had to be fifty feet over their heads—the last untouched relic of the great hall's former glory.

A message had been scrawled on the naked wall over the mantle.

Find a cure.

"He knew we'd come," she said.

Ilecko reached into his bag, retrieving a quirky little shortsword that reminded Tildascow of an Anelace, a European compromise between dagger and sword. The blade was handmade and utilitarian, dented with pockmarks from hammer strikes. He deftly twirled it into a RGEO grip— reverse grip/edge out—the choice of a smarter fighter, since it allowed for either punching or stabbing.

He'd forged his own weapon and understood how to use it. So sexy.

And he knew the castle. They moved toward an alcove left of the entrance hall, where he cut through cobwebs to reveal an arched entrance to a spiral staircase. They took the stairs in single file. Dead lanterns and dusty tapestries marked the walls between shafts of starlight. The air currents moaned, trapped in the spire by the windowless bowmen ports.

She felt a tingle in her left palm, a post-hypnotic reminder from her "prime" training that was triggered to her internal clock. It was time for her DARPA-prescribed pills, a cocktail of unmarked designer drugs.

She'd agreed to the meds on a long jump of faith. She didn't know what most of them did—she didn't even have security clearance for their names. Six months ago, they told her they'd added promoter chemicals to begin preparing her white blood cells for the implementation of nanorobotics. Someday she was going to become the Bionic Bitch.

But she had no reservations about being a test subject. She'd long lost interest in self-preservation. Even in the halfway houses, when she was teaching herself hand-to-hand, it wasn't about self-protection. It was about doling out punishment. Or maybe justice. As long as justice meant punishment.

They did choose to tell her one thing, although she'd never

understood why. Somewhere in Arlington, close enough to DARPA, there was a four-year-old girl in a foster family, a girl with Lucy Tildascow's tender eyes and floral hair: a clone of Brianna the Girl Scout Brownie, before the tragedy and the training.

Someday they were hoping to take her mind and put it into the younger copy of her body. And if they could pull it off, she planned to let them. Why not live a second life and get done all the shit you didn't get done the first time? Take another trip through her sexual prime, watch the rich keep getting richer and the Mets keep losing?

Sometimes she wondered what path her untarnished twin might take. Trophy wife? PR flack? Lawyer? Daddy's daughter the plumber, or Mommy's protégé the singer? Truthfully, she had no idea.

Part of her wished she could see what was going to come of this little Brianna. This girl who was somewhere out there, building a life, unaware that one day she was going to disappear inside herself.

Yeah, the cyclical aspect was nauseating.

She swallowed four unmarked pills as Ilecko turned off the stairs. Crossing through an open door, they left the castle's stale air behind and emerged onto a loggia running across the front of the main structure, perhaps two hundred feet above the ground. Stone columns gave way to a breathtaking view of the snowy mountainscape glowing under bright starlight.

The inner corridor had been retrofitted with modern weatherproof windows. They couldn't see through the heavy drawn curtains, but she felt movement on the other side. Maybe it was the aural tricks thrown by the loggia's columns, making the whistling wind play hide and seek, or maybe it was the Stygian shadows that fell behind the columns, swallowing the stone walkway into whole blackness.

Or maybe she was ready to shit out a horror novel.

Ilecko stepped past a frozen Jaguar and started across the loggia. Tildascow nodded for him to get back on point.

"Stay focused," she said, to herself as much as to Jaguar.

She cued Lon to remain at the cusp of the tower and he went sullen. His excitement must have temporarily surpassed his terror. A dangerous sensation on the battlefield or on prom night.

Weapon drawn, she crept toward the outer edge of the loggia, beside a low parapet designed as a battlement, trying for the best angle on these windows. Goddamn wind was pushing hard enough to wobble the windows, making it impossible to distinguish anything inside. And at the far end of the exposed walkway, one of the windows was either broken or open. The curtains swelled and retracted in an organic rhythm.

Ilecko approached the double-wide door halfway down the inner wall. Beethoven used hand motions to direct Jaguar and Mantle into—

The drapes shifted in the closest window.

Inside that room, someone—or some*thing*—had just moved. She silently alerted the others.

Ilecko put cautious fingers on the door's handle and turned to catch her eye. Try as she might, she couldn't find confidence on his face.

Now you're telling me?

He took a breath and reaffirmed his grip on his shortsword, keeping it tight against the back of his arm.

With no resistance, the door creaked open.

Three
Clifton Road, Northeast of CDC Headquarters
Atlanta, GA
January 1
4:49 p.m.

Jessica Tanner edged through the traffic logjam on Clifton Road, a four-lane highway just north of CDC Headquarters. She was armed with a spritz bottle containing the most lethal biological weapon ever created by man. And onlookers thought she was made up as a clown.

Bacteria, like Sorcerer, are groups of single-celled organisms. Although they're among the simplest life forms on the planet, they have a complex method of communication, called *quorum sensing,* in which they "speak" to one another by sending chemical signals. When they hear enough voices in the roll call, they know they have sufficient numbers to infect their host.

Quorum sensing might be a new exploitable weakness in our war against bacterial infection. Overexposure to antibiotics and the ever-present defense mechanism of mutagenesis might cause bacteria to develop into drug-resistant strains, but if we mute their voices, they'll simply wait forever during roll call.

Vibrio fischeri, a marine bacterium, is one specimen used in QS research. It employs a class of signaling molecules called *N*-Acyl homoserine lactones, which scientists have interrupted with a synthetic compound derived from plants. Either by luck or design—only God or USAMRIID might know—Sorcerer bacteria use *N*-Acyl homoserine lactones to communicate.

In fact, not only would the anti-QS technology shield her from infection, it proved to be the key to weaponizing Sorcerer in the first place. Storing the bacteria in a decaying anti-QS medium would keep it essentially hibernating until it reached its destination. As the anti-

QS medium decomposed, it would take to the wind and distribute the dormant bacteria. When the anti-QS function ceased, Sorcerer would complete its roll call and commence infection.

The decaying process was based on a solution she'd developed herself, in a research paper examining a concern with bacteria used to consume biodegradable elements in sewage waste. Richard liked to remind her that Jessica Munroe was a brilliant scientist before she was buried under administration. Nice as that felt, conceiving the tech to successfully weaponize Sorcerer hardly felt like a noble achievement.

Nevertheless, here she was with the thick, white anti-QS lotion all over her body. If the passers-by mistook her for a clown, she couldn't blame them.

On the far side of the highway, Atlanta PD, EMTs and CDC EIS were on the scene of a fresh car crash. One man was lying on the side of the road with major lacerations; two others were under body bags. She could only pray they'd contained any infections.

The trail of blood led Jessica toward the Emory Hotel across the highway. Police, state troopers, FD, and military were on the scene. They'd barricaded the parking lot, but that was unnecessary: The cats weren't so curious as to peek in on a wild werewolf, not after news reports from New York. Officers and soldiers kept their cover, maintaining cautious aim on the building.

"Ma'am, you can't be over there," a trooper called from behind the cover of his vehicle's door. As if the werewolf might shoot at him.

Several of the hotel's exterior windows had been smashed, including the glass doors to The Emory Lounge, where CDC scientists often went to—

Jessica stopped cold.

—where *Richard* often went to—

The pentagram.

Oh my God no. Please, no.

This was the first place she ever saw him. He was meeting a friend from the Army, who had transferred to the CDC. She'd been reviewing reports with an alcoholic colleague.

The werewolf's roar emanated from inside the darkened shop, followed by a frightful crash of wood and glass.

Jessica's wobbly legs carried her across the lawn, toward the ruined entrance. She had to see.

"Ma'am, please! It's not safe over there!"

"I'm with the CDC," she called absently. "CDC."

They kept yelling for her to stop, come back, but she couldn't hear them. A firefighter came forward, but he backed off upon seeing the strange paste smeared on her face and hands.

She stepped through the tatters of the front door, the same door she had opened when she first saw him. Back then he was sitting at his favorite table, a two-seater by the window, and nursing Cordon Rouge.

And there he was now, sprawled on the floor by the window. His chest had been torn away, his ribcage wrenched open. His heart was gone.

His file on the lycanthropy virus was spread around the burgundy mahogany floor, floating across pools of blood and shattered glass.

There were other bodies strewn about. One had landed in the fireplace, another was draped over the wrecked bar. Something hung from the slow fan above, making a cyclical dragging noise.

Richard's dead eyes stared, asking her *How could it end like this?*

A guttural purr whispered from the far side of the lounge.

Yellow eyes rose from behind the wine bar. The werewolf slinked over the oak surface, blood dripping from its maw. Melissa Kenzie's birdlike frame had disappeared inside this top-heavy beast, whose broad shoulders and thick arms tapered into a canine torso and rear legs.

It sniffed cautiously, maybe pondering the mossy odor of the anti-QS lotion, or wondering why she hadn't fled. Its talons clacked as it approached, keeping time with the skipping fan. Now it was just two feet away.

Questioning Jessica with its eyes, the wolf reared back on its hind legs and roared. Jessica risked one last look at Richard as she tightened her grip on the spray bottle in her trembling hand.

The werewolf was too surprised to react when Jessica lunged forward and sprayed its face. It rolled backward and she backed away, footfalls splashing on the blood-soaked floor.

The wolf shook off the liquid, growling with renewed anger.

Jessica ducked behind an overturned table and the monster lunged. With a thunderous crash, the table buckled and the legs shattered, snaring her within the splinters.

She broke free, but the werewolf had already spun for another attack. Its claws shot out for her—

And then the wolf stumbled, jolted by an itch on its face. Then another.

The werewolf yelped and clawed deep gashes into itself, frantically trying to scratch everywhere at once.

Then Jessica heard the soft pitter-patter of blood, as the creature's flesh began to lose cohesion. Still it thrashed, now throwing off its own skin.

She huddled behind the table, covering her ears from the shrieks and splats of the werewolf's disintegration.

Finally, the monster fell against the bar and slid to the floor, leaving behind a trail of clinging flesh.

She lay there for a long moment as the wolf's remains settled. If the anti-QS solution were going to fail, her flesh should begin to liquify any second now. But she hardly cared.

"Richard?" she called, hoping that maybe he would stand up and come to her, and this all would have been a terrible dream.

"Richard!" she screamed, ordering him to get up.

Moving lights crossed over her head. Distant voices were approaching. An urge flooded her body, telling her to wake him before the others arrived, or else it would all be real. If other people saw him, he couldn't take it back. He'd really be dead.

As the voices grew louder, she forced herself to her knees. Ruffled pages from Richard's lycanthropy file were all around her, bloodstained and pasted to the hardwood floor.

"Richard!"

She crawled toward him, dragging herself on her elbows, but it was too late. Men in hazmat suits stepped through the windows between her and Richard's body. They regarded him and turned elsewhere with their flashlights, finding her.

She collapsed as they approached. Her eyes fell on a page from Richard's lycanthropy file, pasted to the floor a few inches from her cheek.

It was his list of excuses for the pentagram symbol. He'd scratched something at the top while they were on the phone with the kid in Transylvania, and he'd retraced it over and over in the hours since.

THERE IS NO CURSE

Four
Oval Office
The White House
5:50 p.m.

During the last moments before moonrise on New Year's Day, the country's top officials were bracing for the worst.

Deaths from the previous night had soared past three hundred, with injuries into the thousands. And how many unaccounted for? How many undocumented infections?

How many werewolves tonight?

A resupply of silver ammunition was distributed to law enforcement officers as they sealed the perimeter of the island. Streets were cleared. Lockdowns for the infected were established in 26 Federal Plaza, One Police Plaza, One Times Square, and Riker's Island. Several federal and local authorities had been detained for executing the infected, but many such incidents were likely going unreported.

Up to a million citizens were still trapped on the island. Bottlenecking had choked the bridges, and one of the primary exits didn't work at all: Penn Station was kept closed by power outages and damaged tracks, despite the best efforts of AMTRAK and MTA technicians. In their report to the FBI, AMTRAK said they believed the werewolves had specifically targeted key systems.

Above Penn Station, Madison Square Garden held over twenty thousand stranded refugees from the Times Square celebration. They were questioned and inspected, and a dozen snipers were assigned to keep a close watch on the crowd.

It couldn't be contained. Not tonight at least. Authorities' realistic goals were to minimize the spread and buy them more precious hours. Orders were to shoot to kill werewolves on sight.

***

Americans spilling American blood on American soil, President Weston had said to Alan Truesdale, his Chairman of the Joint Chiefs.

He turned us against ourselves, Truesdale had responded.

The administration—and the country, he feared—would never be the same, even if the nightmare ended tonight.

And it clearly was not going to end tonight.

Weston hadn't slept in thirty-six hours. His personal physician checked his blood pressure at his desk in the Oval Office while Weston reviewed the CDC's latest report on the lycanthropy virus. They were still confounded.

His secretary buzzed. "Mr. President, Mr. Harrison is here."

It was 5:51, five minutes before moonrise over New York.

As planned, Weston used Teddy's arrival to escape the doctor's clutches. They walked silently through the West Wing, nodding false reassurance to every scared face along the way.

They were silent in the elevator, and all the way into the Situation Room.

Truesdale and Luft were waiting for them, along with Defense Secretary Ronald Greenberg, Vice President Allison Leslie, and Attorney General Michael Shinick. They all stood as Weston entered.

"Ladies and gentlemen," Weston said, "we need an endgame."

Five

Valenkov Estate
Transylvania
12:01 a.m. Eastern European Time

They'd found the castle's royal bedroom.

The bed was on a raised dais about ten feet from the entrance. Sheer layers of fabric hung from the posts, glistening in the column of starlight falling through the open door. The rest of the room was shrouded in darkness, but Tildascow could sense that it was large.

And there was movement inside.

Rustling drapes in a broken window were playing havoc with the room's ambience. Something shifted on the hardwood floor, but from which direction?

She threw up an arm to stop Ilecko from crossing the double-wide threshold. Crouched beside his waist, she fiddled with her goggles—

Ilecko pushed her aside and entered. She swallowed her instinct to shoulder-throw him back over the balcony.

Beethoven and Jaguar entered behind him, checking the sides first. Her goggles were working, so she followed. Mantle took up cover at the door.

The room was nearly as wide as the loggia, with enough furniture for an entire house. Armoires, chairs, mirrors. And—

Movement behind a wardrobe. Shifting darkness.

"Do not attack," Ilecko said.

And then they saw it: a werewolf, padding amid the ruined furniture. It purred a warning toward Ilecko.

"Do not attack," he said again.

Two more werewolves were positioned around the semi-circular bedroom. They triangulated on Ilecko as he continued toward the dais, matching his every cautious step with their own apprehensive pacing.

Mantle and Jaguar moved inside, prompting Ilecko to warn them again. "Do not attack."

He stepped up onto the dais and Tildascow followed, avoiding the path of dried flower petals. The silk curtain undulated in the wind, just because there weren't enough distractions in this fucking room.

Someone was lying on the bed.

Ilecko stepped slowly. Clearly dreading what he was about to find, he pulled back the curtain, revealing the decayed corpse of a woman in her wedding gown.

She was surrounded by a thick nest of needles and flakes that had once been long-stemmed roses. Her cream lace gown had been stained putrid green by the liquefaction of her flesh. The half-pound diamond dangling from her skeletal finger blazed in the starlight, and her diamond-and-ruby tiara had slipped and gotten tangled in her rotting curly hair.

—just like mom's hair, long and curly and matted down, dripping with her own blood—

"His wife?" she asked, jolting herself from the horrors in her mind.

Ilecko silently assessed the body for several long moments. The shadows covering his face were impenetrable, but Tildascow could feel his sorrow.

All the while, the soldiers tracked the wolves' movement.

Giving Ilecko his time, Tildascow committed the room to memory.

The male dressing area had been arranged along the east wall. A wardrobe, a dresser, and a high-back armchair with wolf heads carved into its handles and claws at its feet. The chair was crooked, and so was the mirror above the table. This room had been ransacked like the others, and set right to create an illusion of peace. It was all part of the shrine.

The west wall held the lady's things: wardrobes, dressers, make-up tables, a jewelry chest, and a privacy shade. Anachronisms everywhere—an antique hairbrush sitting next to an iPod boom dock; retrofit windows in the ancient, stone walls. These were strong-minded people of their own tastes.

Ilecko threw back the silk curtain, now ready to leave.

"Is that his wife?" Tildascow asked him again.

"Ecaterina," he croaked. "The Lady Valenkov."

Ilecko proceeded with a sorrowful gait, ignoring the Shadow Stalkers as they parted to give him a path between their backs.

On her way out, Tildascow noticed a bronze frame peeking out from behind a dresser near the broken window with its angry drapes. As she took a step toward it, the closest werewolf caught her curiosity. She advanced slowly.

"What are you doing?" asked Mantle.

"It's okay."

"Do not touch," said Ilecko from the doorway.

"I got it," she said, keeping her eyes on the werewolf.

"Jesus Christ, Tildascow," whispered Mantle.

The werewolf growled, warning but permissive.

She slid the heavy bronze frame from behind the dresser, trying but failing to keep the edge from scraping the floor. The metal's searing cold cut right through her gloves.

It was a larger-than-life portrait of Demetrius and his wife Ecaterina, a ridiculously beautiful couple. The lady was light-skinned, practically ethereal. She was folded into her husband's chest, peeking out from behind her dark hair like some kind of skulking rogue. The glow of her green eyes *had* to have been exaggerated by the artist, or else Tildascow wanted her money back from the people at the gene pool.

Tildascow felt a rush of cold as she realized that the crown upon Ecaterina's head in the painting was the same one now resting on her corpse. The same rings sparkled on her lovely hands, now mere bones.

Demetrius was barely recognizable without his scruffy beard and long hair. He had light skin, honest brown eyes, and a thick Romanian brow, all on the nimble frame of a dancer. His arms were wrapped around his wife's lower back.

Tildascow lingered on his smile: so calculating, so voracious, and yet spring-loaded with charm.

European elitist fuckwad bastards?

Snide charisma power-brewed from entitlement?

Or… what?

Genuinely happy people?

Fuck happy people.

And the way they were locked together, like their bodies were magnetic but their touch was combustible—Tildascow's scowl grew a scowl—they made her want to puke. Or something else. Something dirty and sweaty.

She slid the painting back into its hiding spot, hoping the werewolves couldn't smell cynicism, and she crossed between the Shadow Stalkers. As she exited the bedroom, the cold air on the loggia hit her like an atomic blast.

Ilecko moved her out of the way—she did *not* like this guy's hands-on shit—and closed the doors on the werewolves' glimmering eyes.

"Why didn't they attack?" Lon asked.

Ilecko rested his head against the seal and closed his eyes in silent prayer.

Sympathy for the Devil, she thought. *Enough already.*

"The werewolves," Lon clarified, "why didn't they—"

"His chosen must listen," Ilecko whispered.

Lon gasped. "Valenkov can *control them?"*

Ilecko nodded.

"Really?" Lon looked around for someone to share his excitement. "So what was in there?"

"His wife," Tildascow said. "Dead."

"Who did this?" Lon asked Ilecko. "The villagers?"

Ilecko nodded, either at Lon, or one last goodbye to Lady Valenkov. Then headed back the way they came.

"Because she was a werewolf?" Lon asked.

"If they thought she was a wolf, they would have removed her head," Ilecko said, never turning back.

"So, what—they just murdered her?"

"And then he killed them all."

Six
Emory Inn
Atlanta

Jessica Tanner was naked and alone.

As faceless workers in yellow hazmat suits soaked the lounge in germicidal decon foam, one man had instructed her to strip. He never looked in her eyes, but he didn't look at her flaccid breasts either. *Of course not. Who could ever find these things interesting, who beside Richard?* He took the clothes to be burned and left her shivering.

Naked and alone.

Her thoughts were like a ride at Disneyland, full of wild and wonderful things to visit. She actually thought that to herself, that her thoughts were exactly like a ride at Disneyland, and then there was the painful chattering of her teeth, what to do with Richard's clothes and mail, her frozen tears, how to tell his parents, the plastic body bag they'd laid over his remains, the growing crowd of hazmat workers, and what time was it—the moon had to be rising soon, could Kenzie have left behind any infected survivors, and were they going to leave her here to freeze to death? And wouldn't that be just fine?

"This way," another man said, escorting her to an inflatable decontamination chamber they'd erected in the parking lot. She suffered the harsh pressure of the pneumatic shower while watching them watch her.

Now she realized why she didn't recognize any of them. They weren't CDC. They were military.

The shower relented, and she was directed through an opaque plastic tunnel, which was sealed to the vacuum-metalized guts of a van. Inside, a flimsy white robe sat on a sterile metal bench.

It was a short ride full of numbing sounds, but at least there was heat. She stared at her hands for the duration, fighting off vertigo.

The van stopped and she listened as they connected the airtight seal to her next destination. When the doors opened, the cloudy plastic tube obscured everything but the night sky. She passed through air transference and yet another shower before taking a long, descending elevator trip to arrive in another airlock and then, finally, a vacuum-sealed metal box with a few breathing holes in the ceiling for air recycling or purging: a cleanroom.

A hard cot covered in plastic was the only furniture. It sat facing the large observation mirror, just like the one Melissa Kenzie looked into as she transformed into a werewolf.

Sitting on that cot, minutes may have been seconds or hours. Several times she felt shocked awake by the sight of Richard's gutted body.

This is not magic, he'd insisted. *This is a virus, a biological entity we can quantify, study and attack.* So damn sure of himself. And now she was left to answer for him.

"Doctor Tanner," a voice blasted through the loudspeakers. She paused, wondering if it'd been in her imagination. "Doctor Tanner, can you hear me?"

"Who are you?"

"It's Rebekkah Luft. You're under quarantine with the Department of Homeland Security. The voice you are about to hear is Dr. Jonathan Drexler, from the DHS Science and Technology Directorate Biochem Division."

The proverbial light bulb popped over her head. "Dr. Jonathan Drexler" was the only name on the leaked SCORN document, the report on the weaponized strain of smallpox. And yet no one among her colleagues had ever met him and he'd never appeared on any of her Google searches or professional inquiries. Richard, of course, had the wittiest turn of phrase, regarding Drexler as "the sasquatch of the scientific community."

"Mrs. Tanner, we're very sorry for your loss," Drexler began. "I worked with your husband briefly and found him to be brilliant and personable."

Jessica rolled her eyes. *Of course* Richard had worked with him.

"I wish we could have this conversation at a more appropriate time, but I'm afraid we're in a dire rush. I'm going to read you the green code as per your security protocol—"

"You want Sorcerer," she interrupted.

There was a moment of silence. They were probably contemplating their psychological scenarios, reviewing their strategies of interrogation. They hardly needed her; they could always storm the CDC's computers or enlist her heads of research to piece together the data, but—

"We need to know if you have a solution for keeping the bacteria alive long enough for effective dispersion."

Jessica was silent for a long moment. *"If* we have it?"

"Yes," Drexler said.

Someday you're going to have to believe in me, Jess.

Richard hadn't given Sorcerer to the military. He hadn't even told them they had it.

He hadn't been using her. He must have…

He must have just foolishly loved her. The big arrogant idiot.

"Dr. Tanner, I'm sure you understand our predicament. We won't be able to find a cure before—"

"You can have it," she blurted. "It's yours."

Seven

Castle Valenkov
Transylvania
1:20 a.m. Eastern European Time

Lon had comprehensively studied Transylvania's castles for profiles on his website, but none of them were quite like this one. Castle Valenkov had a distinct French Gothic influence, a more modern architecture than Bran or Poenari Castle, with far superior masonry. He couldn't wait to cross-reference the stonework. And the deeds, the ownership—where could this place have come from? How could he have missed it in his studies? Sure, they were deep in the mountains, but in this day and age, could something this big go unnoticed?

The world only knows what the Internet tells them. Those words were written by one Magister Lon Toller, and never were they more true. Lon smiled and shook his head.

They retraced their steps by flashlight and crossed through the grand hall, past the main entrance, to enter the eastern tower. The ground floor was dedicated to a hexagonal library lined with giraffe-high satinwood bookcases, each stuffed with rows and rows and rows of books. One fixture had been replaced with a glass case displaying special books and documents. Lon didn't recognize anything, but he took note of a series of bamboo slats with handwritten Chinese text.

More bookshelves divided the floor into private reading nooks with cherry leather seats and handcrafted tables. A reading desk, stacked with a filing pile of books, sat at the base of a spiral staircase.

Ilecko immediately knew which bookcase led to the hidden stairwell.

He pulled a trigger behind a book on a lower row, and then put his shoulder into pushing the invisibly segmented shelves. A section of the bookcase rotated on an axis hidden beneath the floor, revealing a short, narrow tunnel leading to infinite blackness.

Ominous, and yet so deliciously inviting! Lon cracked his knuckles, trying to channel patience as Ilecko crammed into the stairwell and motioned for them to follow.

The descent was slow and, eventually, excruciating. The darkness between Mantle and Jaguar felt like it was closing in on Lon's throat. Time and moisture had made the narrow stairs weak enough to crumble, so they were forced to take slow, vigilant steps. Their breathing grew thick and loud.

"How much farther?" he asked.

"Breathe through your mouth," Tildascow responded, not at all answering his question. And yet, when he did as she said, the knots in his chest loosened. If she ever wanted to give up being an FBI assassin, she could have a great career as a snarky but sage grandmother.

They finally reached the bottom, where Ilecko lit a wall-mounted gas lamp that threw a dim glow over the team. A narrow passage led to a heavy wooden door, which was once locked by a sliding bolt retrofitted with modern steel. Like all of the others in the castle, the lock had been destroyed—but this time someone had broken out, not in. The anchors had been torn from the stone walls.

The cellar was wide and round, matching the diameter of the castle's eastern tower. Lon thought it was probably built as a dungeon, but the Valenkovs had converted it into a workshop, part study and part laboratory. Far more cluttered than the ostentatious library above, this was obviously the place where the Valenkovs rolled up their sleeves and got to work.

Ancient books and sour chemicals mixed with a more pungent version of the estate's native scent to make the air feel gummy. No electricity down here, but the gas lamps on the walls had seen a lot of use.

Every inch of wall space was covered with drawings and notes, and Lon couldn't consume them fast enough.

Breathe, Lon.

His eyes fell first on a section dedicated to theoretical origins of lycanthropy, where Valenkov had compiled accounts from the ancient Greek writings of Petronius, the sixteenth-century Swedish author Olaus Magnus, and the medieval chronicles of Gervase of Tilsbury, along with related lore about Native American Skinwalkers, shapeshifting spells of witchcraft, and demonic tales of the Roman Catholic Church.

All the same research! The same reference materials! Yes!!

The notes were arranged in a thematic cascade and often accompanied by sketches, photographs, flowcharts, or diagrams. Thick stacks of weathered documents were piled on the floor, along with journals and files and books associated with the topics covered on the wall above them. The entire rear section was dedicated to both supernatural- and scientific-based research for potential cures. Exorcism. Surgery. Arcane medicines crafted from nigh-mythical ingredients. Voodoo, black magic, more witchcraft. So many of the same references Lon had used for his own website, "ofwolvesandmen.com."

Lon wondered if Valenkov had ever seen his site.

Could he have read my lycanthropy thesis?

An excited chuckle burst from his throat. Thankfully, nobody noticed.

"He was trying to find his own cure," Tildascow said. She was investigating the chamber's centerpiece, a wooden worktable blanketed with deep piles of handwritten journals, occult references, and science and medical texts. Mostly Romanian, with scatterings of English, Greek, and—*interesting*—Chinese. Her eyes moved in a robotic manner, like they were recording rather than reading.

"Trying hard," Mantle said. He was looking straight up at images on the ceiling: geometric diagrams, mechanically drawn to precision. A spiral divided by right angles, a cone of pentagrams progressing in size, and a variety of triangles divided by smaller triangles with identical ratios.

Wow wow wow! Lon wondered what the diagrams meant to Valenkov. Did the pentagram hold some kind of mathematical or scientific relevance beyond its traditional occult implications? He couldn't wait to research the images.

Deeper into the workshop, the research topics shifted to hard science: sketched studies of werewolves and their evolving forms under the moon's phases; calendars marked with lunar calculations; physical maps of greater Transylvania annotated with landmarks and dates spanning back to the 1400s; and dozens of complex molecular formulae scarred by revision scratchings, including chemical diagrams of silver alloyed with palladium, rhodium, and indium.

Valenkov had also dedicated wall space to advanced mathematics and geometry. Here was the classic pentagram within the pentagon and circle, labeled as the "Golden Pentagram." And the cone of progressive pentagrams, the "Lute of Pythagoras." More geometric formulas and a series of mind-boggling mathematical equations under the title "Golden Ratio." Those notes spilled over to a copy of the logarithmic spiral on the ceiling, the "Golden Spiral." Beneath that, Valenkov had juxtaposed large, colorful photographs of a galaxy, a winter storm, and a seashell, all of which were natural re-creations of the same pattern as the Golden Spiral.

Above all of the mathematical research, Valenkov had posted a quote attributed to Leonardo da Vinci, from *Trattato della Pittura*:

Non sai tu che la nostra anima è composta di armonia, ed armonia non s'ingenera se non in istanti, ne' quali le proporzionalità degliobietti si fan vedere o udire?

It was Italian, not Romanian. Lon had almost flunked ninth grade Italian, but it wasn't a hard translation:

Do you not know that our soul is composed of harmony, and that harmony is only produced when proportions of things are seen or heard simultaneously?

The space on the floor beneath these notes wasn't dedicated to math, but to music. Valenkov had custom-built a wooden soundbox with dozens of strings stretched across its surfboard length. It rested on a frame for adjustable inclination, causing Lon to tilt his head and wonder if you could lie on top of it and play the strings so the box vibrates into your chest. A sketched study of the design lay partially unfurled beneath a nearby desk.

An assortment of recording equipment surrounded the instrument, including a vintage phonograph, a reel-to-reel, and a digital audio tape deck. He even had an iPod and a massive, expensive-looking pair of headphones, both disconnected from a missing laptop. The electronics were plugged into a strip retrofitted into the wall, probably leading to the power cables far above.

"Demetrius studied many years for cure for his father," Ilecko said. He was examining a chemistry set that looked like it'd been stolen from the set of *Frankenstein.* All of the lab equipment looked antique, except for anachronistic touches like a calculator and modern centrifuges and microscopes.

"And the western world wouldn't help," Lon said. "They didn't believe in werewolves. I understand his frustration."

"That don't mean you try to kill the world," Mantle said. "You send a videotape of yourself turnin' into a werewolf. That'd get some attention."

"You think we have the resources to respond to every weird video we get?" Tildascow asked. "We couldn't have found Bin Laden if we'd been looking for Bigfoot."

"Demetrius is smart man," Ilecko said, in a tone both matter-of-fact and threatening. "Very smart man."

"Not questioning that," Tildascow agreed, flipping through the journals at her mechanical pace.

Lon wanted to dive into those diaries, but he also wanted to go back to Valenkov's masterwork sketches, especially the—

He tripped and ate shit into a bookcase thick with hand-labeled journals. He managed to keep himself and the bookcase upright and he held up his hands: *No harm done.* Everyone went back to their investigations.

He'd stumbled over a pair of heavy iron manacles, which were fastened to the wall by thick chains. Werewolf restraints! Valenkov must have used them to imprison himself during moonlight hours.

They'd been broken open.

"What's all this about meditation?" Tildascow asked Ilecko. "Samadhi and Qigong?" She was examining the books on Valenkov's reading table.

"He prepares. For that when his father died, he would be in control," Ilecko said. "He swore there would be no more."

"Something changed his mind."

"The villagers," Lon suggested. "They attacked the castle."

"Maybe they live in fear too long," Ilecko said, still occupied by the flasks. "Maybe they want the werewolf to end forever."

Lon waited for Ilecko to continue, but he didn't. Asking wouldn't help, so he went back to those sketches.

There were precision pencil works on modern manufactured paper, intermingled with charcoals, brushworks and silverpoints on parchment and vellum and other materials Lon didn't recognize. Many of them were ancient, maybe even hundreds of years old. Each one was a masterwork.

The most prominent image was some kind of scraped charcoal on aged parchment. It was placed in a position of honor, perhaps the only thing tacked to the wall that wasn't overlapped by something else. But it would have struck Lon like a snakebite if only one detail was visible from beneath a stack: the eyes.

It was a lifelike drawing of a beautiful woman, probably in her thirties, with mischievous eyebrows and thick black hair loosely pulled beneath a babushka. The textures and tones cast her so vibrantly that Lon could see the wide-eyed child from her past and the crow's feet in her future.

And her eyes! Pale and shallow, with a demonic sparkle that was both enticing and merciless, like she could thrust a shiv into your belly without breaking a long, luxurious kiss.

She was a goddess. A Gypsy goddess.

A *Gypsy*—

Could this be *the* Gypsy? The one who cursed the Valenkovs?

Lon backed away from the drawing… but he couldn't shake the

feeling that she had him harpooned.

Please don't curse me, Gypsy goddess. I didn't mean to stare at you.

He took another step back and bumped into Mantle, who pointed at his feet as if to remind him that they existed.

"This is interesting stuff," Tildascow finally said to Ilecko. "It might be of help the CDC, but how is it going to help us *find him*?"

"It is not here." Ilecko hadn't found what he was looking for in the flasks. "We must go to the mausoleum."

Mantle and Lon spoke at the same time: "The what?"

Eight

Manhattan
January 1
5:56 p.m.
Moonrise

As the moon crested the northeast horizon over Harlem, the season's first snow kissed the streets of Manhattan.

A million citizens were still on the island, half as many as the night before. They barricaded their homes, businesses, or churches; they whispered goodbyes and bargained with their divinities.

Despite the mandatory curfew, up to sixty thousand people still roamed the streets. The biggest crowds were massed at the exits. A few, like Elizabeth Golden, shrewdly abandoned hopes for escape and fled home for safety. But there were plenty of looters and rioters and malcontents, making the streets perilous long before the wolves arrived.

Authorities prepared for the worst. They were too optimistic.

The werewolves in custody were unexpectedly powerful. They snapped handcuffs, shattered reinforced glass, and scaled sheer walls. Escapes were reported at almost every holding facility.

***

The most horrific breakout was in The Tombs.

One of New York's most infamous jails, the Manhattan Detention Complex on the Lower East Side was known as "The Tombs" because its original incarnation was a dank underground complex straight out of Milton.

That morning, rumor spread among the inmates that they would be relocated to Riker's Island for their own safety. Tensions boiled as the

271

prisoners were doubled up rather than transferred, and the lower levels were filled with potentially infected victims from New Year's Eve.

A riot broke out just before sunset. The short-handed staff was quickly overwhelmed, and the electronic cell doors were released, inadvertently freeing the potential werewolves. The moon rose, the fangs came, and the trapped inmates were easy pickings.

When authorities arrived the next morning, they found dismembered limbs floating in pools of blood. Bodies dangling from the balconies. Bones scattered like jigsaw pieces, picked clean of their flesh.

More than a thousand inmates and workers were sealed inside the complex overnight. Fewer than twenty survived.

***

The trees of Central Park were an early draw for the werewolves, a rare stroke of luck for the authorities because most of the human stragglers were at the fringes of the island. But once the park's wildlife was exhausted, the monsters spread out, running in packs of up to ten.

The FDNY were assisted by ground- and air-based military support as they fought to keep up with dozens of fires. Only two firefighters lost their lives, both in the same collision between an ambulance and a fire truck.

Sometime around 1:30 a.m., local power grids began to fail. Sewer fires damaged feeder cables and steam pipes on the Upper East Side. Another fire at the Con Ed substation beneath 7 World Trade Center shut down all of their transformers, blacking out a good portion of Lower Manhattan. Finally, an explosion at 74th Street Station put crushing weight on the grid. The entire island was dark by 3 a.m., with the steam system right behind. Thermostats dipped to six degrees Fahrenheit.

Despite strict warnings, many panicked civilians took to their vehicles. Distraction and snow-slicked streets caused hundreds of accidents, which became pile-ups when the streetlamps and traffic lights went dark. Many ambulances, military vehicles, NYPD, and FDNY were caught in standstills.

Even the skies were hazardous. At the intersection of 43rd and 11th, just north of the Lincoln Tunnel, an NYPD SWAT helicopter attempted an emergency landing to pick up a woman and her child. As they descended, a werewolf leapt from a balcony of the Riverbank West tower and entered the cockpit, causing it to crash into the lower floors of the apartment complex.

***

The Coast Guard and Marines along the island's perimeter had a particularly rough night.

US Coast Guard Petty Officer Third Class Richard Hatem was gunner's mate aboard the 87-foot USCG Cutter *Finback*. He'd been stationed with a Weapons Augmentation Team in Cape May before being called to duty just that afternoon, and now he was on the Hudson River, monitoring the northern section of Riverside Park.

Hatem was manning a 25mm machine gun at the stern of the boat, a second line of defense in case anything got past the soldiers on the shore. Its eight-inch-long bullets weren't silver, but they could liquefy bone. And he was hoping to get plenty of opportunities to do just that.

They expected ground skirmishes, but the assault came by air. Werewolves bounded through the park's trees, catapulting over the sharpshooters and skyrocketing into Hatem's sights. He already had three kills and a great story to tell his kid.

And then a crushing weight fell from the sky. The last thing he felt was his bones snapping flat on the deck.

Two crew members were killed on the *Finback,* and four more were injured before the coxswain shot the werewolf with his silver-loaded sidearm. One of the infected soldiers took his own life two hours later.

Veterans of these battles said the worst part was consoling infected friends. Dozens of suicides were reported; hundreds more weren't.

***

In Madison Square Garden, racial tensions, exhaustion, and fear led to escalating brawls, leaving the guards distracted when a few members of the crowd began to transform. The creatures evaded police and sniper fire, spreading the infection, even as more slipped in through the sewer system. The throng stampeded, broke through the barricaded doors and spilled into the streets. Easy pickings for the predators.

***

The most insulated location on the island was United Nations Headquarters. All resident diplomats and dignitaries had been evacuated by air shortly after the New Year's Eve outbreak, but a formidable UN peacekeeper force was left to defend the plaza. Relentless waves of werewolves assaulted the General Assembly Building, sometimes in packs of twenty or more. By three in the morning, federal coordinators lost touch with the heads of UN security.

Anyone—*everyone*—foolish enough to roam the streets on foot met with a quick end. But meals were sparse until the wolves strayed far from the center of the island. When they reached the bottlenecks at the exits, bloodbaths ensued.

The most crowded portal was the Lincoln Tunnel, where a mob of forty thousand had been testing the military blockade. When the transformations began, Tenth Avenue from 38th to 42nd became a hunter's buffet. Helicopters saw streams of werewolves running toward the tunnel from all directions except the south, where they were feasting on the crowd at the Holland Tunnel.

***

In the basement of the Jacob K. Javits Building at 26 Federal Plaza, Conor Burns and the other guards played cards while they listened to the werewolf prisoners' howls. Cable TV had gone out with the power, but they still had lights thanks to the back-up generators maintaining the government's virtual private network.

Conor was used to tension-filled nights, having done two tours in the first Iraq, but the federal guards and CDC EIS officers were pissing stiff. As the night went on, he took all of their money in Hold 'Em before moving on to IOUs in Gin Rummy.

Around 3 a.m., a fart-ripping crash shook the building.

The guys raced to check the security feeds. Conor's knees weren't all that great anymore, so he trailed the pack. More ruckus came from upstairs, poppin' and clangin' and every kind of alarm. The whooping siren meant the hidden gunports had activated. When he reached the monitor room, Conor had to push through a lot of whinin' and cryin' to get a look.

That's when he realized someone had driven a damned semi into the lobby.

They had a dozen angles on the ground floor and not a one had any good news. Werewolves comin' from every direction, runnin' on four legs or two.

The building shook again. That time it was an explosion. Just about all of the cameras right up and melted.

Conor sent the other guys to the armory. Not that the werewolves could get in, but *just in case* never hurt no one. He watched on the feeds as the guys passed through the door at the top of the stairs.

One camera in the lobby was still working, the one set behind bulletproof glass at the access control door. It'd gone whiteout from the explosion, but the balance was trying to compensate.

When the image clarified, Conor blinked to make sure he wasn't seeing a leprechaun.

There was a guy at the access door. He looked homeless, with scraggly growth and greasy hair, and he was wearin' a tee shirt stretched over a button down. His crazy bright eyes stared right back through the camera, like he could see Conor through the wires.

Freaky motherfucker. And out there with all the werewolves. A fuckin' nut, was what he was.

The guys had reached the armory and they were loading up. Conor reminded himself that it didn't matter, but—

What the fuck!

The creep in the lobby—*there were werewolves with him.* All over the place. But they weren't attacking him.

Why the fuck weren't they attacking him?

Now what was he doing? Fishing something out of his pockets?

An ID card. He had a fucking—

Conor lunged for the override but it was too late. The access light on the console went from red to green and the door was open.

The creep just stood there as the werewolves rushed in.

***

By morning, all of the federal employees at the Jacob K. Javits Federal Building were dead or missing. The government's virtual private network back-up servers had been destroyed, causing interrupts to federal database and email access throughout the tri-state area. And all of the werewolf prisoners escaped, including "patient zero" Holly Cooke.

During the evening of January 1, there were over five thousand deaths in Manhattan and ten times as many injuries. NYPD, Coast Guard, Port Authority, and military stationed at the three tunnels had no choice but to abandon civilian assistance and defend the portals to the mainland at any cost.

Remarkably, almost unbelievably, the quarantine held.

For now.

Nine

Castle Valenkov
Transylvania
1:40 a.m. Eastern European Time

They followed Ilecko through the dead husk of Castle Valenkov.

Back through the ruined foyer, up the grand staircase, and on to the expansive dining room above the common quarters. Various golden utensils were strewn beneath a splintered refectory table.

Gold utensils! Lon hadn't even considered such a thing... a werewolf would have to avoid any kind of silver.

And then they entered the true spectacle: the ballroom.

He could almost see the ghosts of noble society, all gussied up and flirting and dancing as the orchestra's melodies warmed the hardwood. Or maybe it was a masquerade ball, with those fancy Venetian masks, where privileged men and women gathered for a decadent orgy to celebrate the beginning of spring.

Now the rodents were throwing a party for the rotting corpses.

The destruction rippled outward from the center, where the massive chandelier had fallen with the impact of a meteor, launching crystal shards that shattered wood and punctured artwork, hobbled the grand piano, and sliced the giant harp's strings. Lon could still hear the crash. And the screams of the celebrants, now corpses, trapped beneath it.

The ballroom's service door took them back to the ground floor, where they covered their mouths to stave off a stench that emanated from the servants' quarters. Finally, they reached the very back of the castle, where Jaguar torched a bolt to grant them access to the rear courtyard.

Lon took it all in, committing not only the details to his memory, but also his better analogies and metaphors...

A dense wall of pines sealed the grove's perimeter, slicing out a rectangle of bright, starlit sky. Before the trees, strata of diminishing shrubs gave way to an overgrown lawn. A stone path ran from the castle to the back wall, wandering between a series of shoulder-high marble monuments. The landscape was constructed in reverence, as if it were genuflecting toward something at the very back, something shrouded by the shadows of the trees.

Ilecko scooped up a handful of loose soil and considered it thoughtfully before putting it in his pocket. Before Tildascow could ask why, he set off down the path.

"What was that about?" Tildascow whispered.

Lon had no idea. The soil of a man's home plays an important role in many occult tales, including the classic vampire myth. But not werewolves.

The Shadow Stalkers motioned to indicate movement in the trees. Without night-vision goggles, Lon could only sense (or imagine) the branches rustling. They were out there. *They.*

The first monument was engraved with a black bird perched on a miniature tree, stretching upward with an Orthodox Cross in its beak. Lon couldn't remember where he'd seen it before. The monument's counterpart on the other side of the path bore another, similar—

Lon whipped back so fast that he had to right his glasses. Now he remembered!

It was the coat of arms of Wallachia.

From the 1400s to the mid-1800s, this region of Romania was called Wallachia, a kingdom known for grueling power struggles and bloody wars. Could Valenkov's family lineage stretch back to that era?

Lon returned to the other monument. It was also a coat of arms: a simple shield divided in half, the left side cut by horizontal—

Beethoven pushed him to move along.

The next set of monuments displayed carved busts of a man and a woman. Probably Valenkov's antecedents.

More shaking in the trees. The soldiers silently tracked the movement as they crept ever closer toward the back of the courtyard. From here,

Lon could see their destination: a mausoleum, carved in purple-veined Phrygian marble. Its black iron gate was set behind an arched portico resembling teeth.

Geez, man, these people knew how to set a mood.

Even Ilecko was looking toward the trees now. He held his sword tight against the back of his right arm, its crooked tip just reaching his elbow. They were only twenty feet away when they crossed between the final set of monuments. Both of them bore the same shield—

Ohmyfuckingpeterjackson.

Lon's gasp caused everyone to spin.

It was a dragon, curved so that his tail wrapped around his throat, like the *Ouroboros,* the snake eating his own tail. The cross of Saint George was stretched across his back, resting between wings folded across his body.

The seal of the Order of the Dragon!

Lon had never seen this particular version before, but he had drawn his own from a 1408 description by Sigismund, the King of Hungary and later Holy Roman Emperor.

And the mausoleum! Its carvings were clearer now. The features had been softened by time, but those columns *were* teeth, and the façade was—

Breathe, Lon, breathe.

—the façade was sculpted to look like the face of a dragon. It was unmistakable!

But—but—

The Order of the Dragon—*in Romania!*—could only mean one—

Something landed on top of the mausoleum, coming down hard like the crack of a whip. Lon fell over backwards and the Shadow Stalkers converged above him with their rifles trained. All he could see were asses and elbows.

"Twelve o'clock!" someone spat.

"Do not attack!" Ilecko whisper-yelled.

Lon leaned left and right, trying to see between the bodies. Ilecko was the biggest obstacle, until he stepped forward, closer to it.

It was perched on top of the portico, a mass of grey fur soaking up all of the dim light. A growl emanated from somewhere inside its cloaked body, the threatening hum of an idling chainsaw.

"Steady," Tildascow said. "Steady."

As Ilecko approached, the beast's features unfurled from the darkness: bulging shoulders, and then swollen arms quivering with rage as they spread to take ownership of the mausoleum… legs uncoiling from beneath, knees skinning the marble… a tail slinking upward, swaying back and forth. The creature tilted forward, leaning to meet Ilecko, finally revealing a lupine face that could barely disguise the scowl of a man.

A man. A poor, cursed man, whose soul is trapped inside a wolf, Lon thought. And that was the last thing he expected to think, amid the fear and the excitement and the fear and the vindication and the fear. And the fear.

The man was there, you could see him, but he was not present. His body was merely a vessel, which had suffered a mutiny so absolute that you'd think the creature began as a wolf and its form had been twisted to resemble a man.

In that moment, Lon realized that becoming a werewolf was a worse fate than being attacked by one.

Ilecko was unfazed. He kept his left hand up, belaying the soldiers, and he stepped forward to meet the wolf's gaze. It leaned closer in return, dripping saliva in front of the mausoleum's entrance.

More wolves dropped from the sky, landing behind them with soft splats. As they slinked between the monuments, Lon realized these were more lupine than the humanoid werewolf he'd seen in the CDC's video. Ilecko was right; they really did grow stronger in brighter moonlight.

And they had them surrounded.

But Ilecko pressed forward, stepping beneath the guardian werewolf and between the marble columns carved to look like dragon's teeth. He wrenched open the black gate and turned back to them.

Tildascow followed with cautious steps, her pistol raised but not pointing at the wolf. From the safety of the portico, she beckoned Lon with an encouraging nod.

He stood up and tried to walk, but his legs wouldn't work with that werewolf staring at him. *I mean, guys, it's a fucking werewolf. I know this is supposed to be old news, but have you noticed that it's a fucking were—*

"It's okay," Tildascow whispered.

Lon shook his head. It was not the fuck okay.

"Close your eyes."

He did as she said and forced one numb foot in front of the other. It felt like a tightrope in lower orbit. He felt the werewolf's hot breath on the back of his head, and his whole body shuddered, almost causing him to plummet.

A thousand hours later, he reached the portico's recess, where he threw his elbows against the wall next to the gate and took long, heavenly breaths as the Shadow Stalkers arrived behind him.

When he finally found his eyelids, he came across an inscription carved into the cold marble.

O QUAM MISERICORS EST DEUS

JUSTUS ET PACIENS

Lon's excitement rushed back. He knew the translation by heart!

OH HOW MERCIFUL GOD IS

JUSTIFIABLY AND PEACEFULLY

"Casă de Drăculeşti?" Lon breathlessly asked.

Ilecko offered no response, but Lon didn't need one.

Inside the mausoleum, there were three marble statues of knights bearing the Wallachia coat of arms. They were kneeling before a warrior king, whose prideful gaze was locked on the crypt's lid, a marble slab unmarked but for one word carved across its center: *DOMN*, Romanian for *Dominus*, the Latin title for lord or master.

On the base of the king's statue, one word was inscribed: *Întemeietorul.* "The founder."

The founder?

Basarab I of Wallachia! The founder of the House of Basarab!

"You guys," Lon stammered. "You guys—this crypt—this *castle*, you have no idea what this is!"

Ilecko threw a glare at Lon to dampen his enthusiasm.

"Well, what is it?" Tildascow asked, pulling cobwebs from her hair.

"That," he said, referring to the king, "is Basarab I. He's known as 'the founder' because he led a revolution against Hungary and established independent Wallachia, which was basically the beginning of Romania. This was in the 1330s. His family was known as the *House of Basarab.* They ruled Wallachia for a hundred years, but they had all sorts of power struggles until, in 1430-something, the family divided into two rival factions, the *Dănești* and the *Drăculești.*"

Lon hit that last word hard. He paused for a reaction, but all he got was a confused squint from Mantle.

"*Drăculești*," he repeated. "I'm sure that name rings a bell."

He'd lost Tildascow's attention. She had gotten into some kind of cockfight with Ilecko over who was going to lift the crypt's heavy lid. "Too heavy," he muttered when she crouched to help him. Then she hefted it on her own, leaving Ilecko almost too surprised to assist.

"The House of *Drăculești*," Lon urged, "was ruled by Vlad II. Vlad *Dracul.*"

He could hear the steam engines in their brains, just about to go *choo*—

"Dracula?" Mantle trilled.

"Exactly! Vlad was given the surname *Dracul* from the Holy Roman

Emperor Sigismund, the King of Hungary, upon his induction as a knight of the *Order of the Dragon.* The coat of arms on the monument outside represents the Seal of the Order of the Dragon! The original version of it has been lost for centuries, but that fits the description—that *must* be it."

"What is *it?*" Tildascow snapped as she and Ilecko dropped the lid.

"This is the long-lost tomb of the House of Drăculeşti! If what's down there is what I think—"

"We came to Transylvania looking for werewolves and you brought us to the tomb of Dracula?" Tildascow directed her question at Ilecko.

"Not necessarily," Lon said. "Vlad Dracul was actually the *father* of the legendary Vlad III, or Vlad Ţepeş, also known as Vlad the Impaler or Vlad Dracula, the inspiration for the novel. Vlad Dracula's body has been lost for five hundred years, it couldn't possibly…" Lon trailed off, lost in thought.

Mantle filled the silence. "So this is Dracula's *dad's* house?"

"Lon?" Tildascow jarred him.

"Yes," he responded. "*Dracul* means 'dragon' in English and *Dracula* means 'son of the dragon.'"

"*'Devil* in English," Ilecko added pointedly. "'Son of the *devil.*'"

"It means both. It comes from the Latin word *draco.*"

Tildascow looked to Ilecko for a verdict. He shook his head, dismissing the topic as distasteful.

"Are there vampires down there?" Mantle whispered.

Beethoven nudged him to be quiet.

Tildascow was growing impatient. "How does this connect to Demetrius Valenkov?"

"I don't know. But I think I know what this castle is. During Vlad Dracul's reign, Wallachia was immersed in wars and shifting alliances with the Ottomans and Hungary. His marriage to Princess Cneaja of Moldava was a political arrangement. But he also had a concubine, a mysterious woman of legendary beauty known only as *Călţuna.* Some say she was Vlad's true love.

"According to records, Călţuna later became a nun. But, I mean, come on—what sense does that make? How do you go from being the ruler's mistress—and mother of his children—to entering a convent? Right? I mean, these were ruthless warlords; they didn't divorce amicably. When it was time for a change, the women became dead."

"Go on," Tildascow muttered, barely listening. She was crouched at the top of the crypt's stairs, scanning with her flashlight.

Ilecko stepped past her and descended into the chamber. Lon wanted to follow, but Tildascow stopped him with a raised hand.

"Well," Lon continued, collecting his thoughts, "some theorists, including myself, believe that Călţuna was Vlad's true love, and she was spirited away when the family's wars became too dangerous, along with their secret daughter. This would have been Dracula's half-sister. The hope was that one day she would reunite the House of Basarab. In the meantime, Vlad had a secret fortress constructed for her protection."

Lon paused for dramatic effect, but it went unnoticed.

"So this must be it," he exclaimed. *"This* is the secret Drăculeşti fortress!"

"So—so are they vampires?" Mantle squeaked.

"I'm going down," Tildascow said to Beethoven.

"We're behind," he sighed.

Lon was hardly finished. "And there was other evidence to suggest that a secret castle existed. Strange routes taken by Vlad's armies. Children of the House of Drăculeşti disappearing, and later nobles bearing the Basarab coat of arms, but appearing nowhere in the… oh wow."

The vault stretched the entire length of the castle's rear courtyard, far bigger than suggested by the mausoleum above. Something like forty golden sarcophagi were arranged in uneven rows, with their feet pointing toward the *pièce de résistance* at the far end of the chamber: a massive golden statue of a dragon, sculpted with hidden stanchions so that he appeared to be flying. His brilliant wings were spread forward and his claws outstretched.

As the others dillydallied, Lon made a beeline for the dragon.

"Wait," Tildascow may have said.

The dragon was keeping vigilance over a bejeweled paterfamilias tomb. Lon's flashlight found an inscription on the base: *"Mircea cel Bătrân."*

"You guys," he sputtered. "Holy shit, you guys. I was right! This is Mircea the Elder! He was the founder of the House of Drăculeşti. Vlad Dracul's father, Dracula's grandfather." He skulked between the other sarcophagi, whipping his light across their nameplates.

Tildascow dusted off the name on a coffin close to the center of the back row: "Valentina Silviasi," she read aloud. "So this is the entire family—"

"This is it!" Lon shouted, kneeling before the coffin closest to the dragon's left wing. His heart raced as he brushed dust from the marble carving at the base of the casket, choking back excitement and disbelief.

Vlad III.

"It's the long-lost tomb of Vlad the Impaler! It's been missing for five hundred years!" Lon gasped. "Guys. This is the tomb of Dracula."

Tildascow looked to Ilecko for an explanation.

"But he ain't no vampire!" Mantle wailed. "Right?"

"Do not jump to conclusions." Ilecko called from the far side of the chamber, where he was scanning nameplates of the more recently deceased.

Lon had spent countless hours studying Bram Stoker's *Dracula* and its inspirations, especially the legends of the Order of the Dragon and the true Vlad Dracula. And now here he was, kneeling before one of the Holy Grails of occult lore.

"He was inducted into the Order of the Dragon at the age of five, educated by the most brilliant scholars of the day, bred to be a king. Then Wallachia came under the oppression of the Ottomans, and his father willingly donated him as a hostage to ensure their cooperation. Can you imagine that? His father just handed him over to be a slave!

"His teen years were spent as a slave in Turkish dungeons. The fools thought they had brainwashed him. So when Wallachia's royal families rebelled against his father and killed him, the Ottomans invaded and put Vlad on the throne, thinking he would be an ally. But Wallachia was too weak to survive the constant upheavals, so he fled. It took him ten years and several false promises, but he finally amassed his own army and returned to conquer and reclaim his beloved Wallachia.

"On Easter Sunday in 1457, Vlad Dracula invited everyone in the Wallachian upper class to a grand celebration feast in the great hall of Bran Castle in Târgovişte. That's really when the fun began. He took five hundred of the richest, most arrogant socialites and put them on blunt stakes, so they slowly impaled themselves with their own body weight. It was an excruciating death, taking hours, even days. Those he didn't kill, he marched forty miles north and put them to work. There they worked, with no rest, until they died."

"Sheezus," Jaguar muttered.

"Oh, no, he was just warming up. From there, he turned on the Transylvania Saxons, who were in league with the Wallachs. His army took the city of Braşov and he ate dinner while he watched the boyars slowly die on their stakes. And then—then he turned on the Ottomans, and that's where things really got sick. He went to Bulgaria and spent two weeks murdering *twenty-three thousand* men, women, and children.

"So then the Sultan of the Ottoman Empire, Mehmed II, amassed a huge army—we're talking two hundred and fifty thousand men—and set out to destroy Vlad once and for all.

"Vlad's army was outnumbered more than ten to one, and a lot of them were women and children and Gypsy slaves. But Vlad was a brilliant strategist. As the Ottoman army marched, he crept up on them in the middle of the night for sneak attacks, and he poisoned their water and paid diseased men to infiltrate their ranks. It was immaculate, unprecedented psychological warfare, and he totally demoralized them.

"So finally, the Ottoman army arrived outside the capital of Târgovişte, determined to storm the city and put Vlad's head on a stake. And what did they find?"

Lon went into spooky tone. "Twenty. Thousand. Men. *Impaled*. Turkish prisoners. The sultan's own men. The stakes surrounded the whole city. A forest of bodies. Birds picking at their eyes, maggots writhing under their skin, worms falling out of their mouths. Rotting flesh as far as the eye could see, a heinous stench of death… and the only sound was their loose flesh dangling in the wind. So what did the Ottomans do?"

Jaguar muttered, "Threw the fuck up is what they—"

"They turned around. They went home. Even though they way outnumbered Vlad, they couldn't walk through his army of the dead."

"Okay, Lon," Tildascow said. She had crossed the vault to examine the dragon up close. "Enough with the dramatics."

"That's what inspired the legend of Count Dracula, the vampire who could turn the dead against their own." Lon ran his fingers along a golden etching of the Order of the Dragon symbol on the top of Vlad's coffin. "Scholars have wondered for centuries where his remains ended up. They were thought to be in a church, but when it was excavated all they found were animal bones."

Mantle's jittery eyes swept from one person to the next. Even stoic Beethoven had forgotten to swallow.

"Okay, the history lesson is fun," said Tildascow. "But how is this going to help us find Valenkov *now*?"

Ilecko was still examining the sarcophagi toward the back.

Lon continued admiring Vlad Dracula's golden coffin, with its intricate carvings and embedded jewels. He ran his hand around the—

Wait a sec.

"There's no lock," he cried.

"What?" Tildascow snapped, as if she'd just woken up.

"No lock," Lon repeated. "That's… oh man." He turned to the others with a delicious grin. "Do you think they did that because they thought he could come and go?"

"Come and go *what?*" Mantle barked.

The lid was hefty, but he could get it up. It unsealed with a throaty creak.

"JESUS FUCKING CHRIST!" Jaguar shouted. "DON'T OPEN IT!"

All weapons whipped toward Lon. He squinted, waiting for the shots. When they didn't come, he spoke with a quivering voice. "Relax."

"IS HE A VAMPIRE?" Mantle cried.

"Rein it in, fuckchops!" Beethoven yelled at his men.

"No. He's not a vampire." Lon looked inside the coffin. "Well, actually, we'll never know if he was. Vampires die when they're beheaded and Vlad's head was put on a stake in Constantinople. This is just his body. *Was* just his body. Wanna see?"

The box was dusty with grey ash and bone fragments loosely mixed with tatters of moldy fabric. An ancient sword, crusted and brittle, lay in the center of the remains.

"So they're *not* vampires," Mantle reiterated for safety.

"They are not vampires." Ilecko said.

"Are they *werewolves?*" Tildascow demanded.

It was an excellent question, one that sent Lon's mind reeling. The occult scholar within him could only dream of a tangible link between quintessential werewolf and vampire lore, but what did he really have? Vlad's assault on the Ottomans certainly could have inspired Valenkov to take his fight to America, but was there a more concrete connection?

Where did the myths end and reality begin?

Nevertheless… if the Valenkovs, the cursed family of werewolves, were descendants of Vlad Dracula, the preeminent inspiration for vampires…

How could that be a coincidence?

Ilecko had found what he was looking for, a modern coffin near the very back of the vault. He slid its locking bolt and lifted the lid, causing the frayed soldiers to flinch again. Lon closed Vlad Dracula's sarcophagus and hurried to Ilecko's side.

The box let loose a whiff of rotting cheese—a very familiar smell in this castle. This was a much fresher corpse. It had been laid in a ceremonial cape coat of black and burgundy, with a bejeweled golden cross in its clasped hands. Its flesh had putrefied into a thin amber wax, leaving a sunken grin on its face. Little writhing insects had taken up inside the empty eye sockets.

"Who is this?" Tildascow asked.

Lon stepped back and found the nameplate engraving. "Zaharius Valenkov," he read. "Demetrius' father."

Ilecko directed Tildascow to take the lid as he reached into his jacket's pocket. He produced a weathered rawhide pouch, grimy with stains of dirt and blood. From his other pocket, he took the soil he'd scooped from the courtyard, and put it into the pouch.

"What are you doing?" Lon asked. Of course no answer.

Ilecko reached into the coffin and used two fingers to swab the waxy flesh from beneath Valenkov's collar. The soldiers grimaced.

"Oh, what are you *doing?*" Lon cried.

He wiped the pulp into the bag, intermingling it with the soil.

"Why'd you do that?"

He stepped back. Tildascow closed the coffin.

"What's that going to do?"

Ilecko's eyes were heavy with dark contemplation as he pulled the pouch's catgut drawstring. It was a familiar ceremony for him, and a sickening one at that. He held the bag tight, squeezing the contents together.

"Please tell me?"

After a long, pensive moment, he raised his gaze to Lon.

"Your men will provide more of their rations for my horses."

"Uh… um, of course. Sure." Lon looked to Tildascow, who agreed.

"Very well," Ilecko said. "Let's go to America."

PART SIX

One
January 2
Around 3 a.m.

William Charles Weston had bid a lonely goodnight to his wife and kissed the unrecognizable teenagers who were once his baby daughters. And then he had retreated into his office, sat down at his desk, and contemplated killing a million Americans.

In the early days of August, 1945, Harry S. Truman sat here and considered the use of atomic weapons against Japan. On "Black Saturday," October 27th, 1962, John F. Kennedy sat here as the nation crept to the very brink of nuclear war. And on the evening of September 11, 2001, George W. Bush sat here and addressed the terrified people of the United States.

The *Resolute* desk in the Oval Office had been gifted by Queen Victoria in 1880. It was a battery of strength, but whatever wisdom it'd absorbed remained frustratingly silent within its timbers. It was a partner's desk, but it was no partner.

The grandfather clock chimed three times. Weston put down the shot of whiskey he'd been nursing for… well, he couldn't remember how long.

A military action file stared back at him.

(TS—WOLFSBANE) Manhattan Epidemic Cleanse (TS—WOLFSBANE)

Again, he opened the file.

Biological agent M7949, anti-personnel biological weapon also known as "BLUSHBED," *Staphylococcus* unclassified 241, or Sorcerer. Causes rapid infection and lethal flesh-eating disease.

Discovered in 1998 in an underground laboratory seized in the Sar-e Pol province in Afghanistan, likely developed by the Taliban with the help of rogue scientists from Germany and the former Soviet Union.

It will be deployed via CBU-191 cluster missiles, which explode high above the city and release tennis ball-sized sprinklers, AD24 smart bomblets, also called RAPiDS (Robotic Aerosol Pressurized Deployment Systems).

Direct exposure to the weapon will result in almost instantaneous death. Filtration systems will carry the bacteria into buildings, cars, or the subway. Anyone outside of an airtight seal would be infected within 24 hours.

The bacteria will die in the water, so wind distribution will not be an issue. On land, the bacteria will become extinct in two to four weeks. Decay will be monitored by the CDC; cleanup coordinated by USAMRIID. Operatives covered in antibacterial gel will collect the bomblets via GPS guidance.

The victims' clothes and bones will be collected, brought to ad hoc dispensaries, and disposed of in vats of acid. No efforts will be made to identify individual victims. Everyone on the island will be presumed dead.

And then what? Do they just hang a vacancy sign on Manhattan?

Another rap came at the door, so the first wasn't his imagination. He closed the file and stretched his eyes. "Come in."

Teddy Harrison peeked in and assessed. "I can't believe you're still up."

Weston nodded and waved his old friend inside.

"Are we drinking?" Teddy asked.

"We should be."

"Well, then call the Secret Service, because I'm armed." He revealed a bottle of whiskey as he took a seat on the partner's side of the desk. Good ole Teddy, a master of unspoken reassurance. "Thomas H. Handy Rye," he boasted. "Won the World Whiskies Awards for Best American Whiskey in 2009."

"Well shit." Weston leaned past the American flag on his right and tossed his old drink into a planter.

Teddy poured for both of them. "You want the bad news or the bad news?"

"Let's just hear it."

"If we execute Operation Wolfsbane, we'll lose more Americans in one day than we've lost in any war. Ever." Teddy threw back his drink and reloaded. "And if we don't do it by moonrise tomorrow night, odds are the wolves will escape. If they do, the CDC's prognosti—prognosis—prognostica—is it –cate or? Ah fuck it." He took another shot and muttered, "It's across the country in less than a week. Worldwide within a month."

"We have to find him. Today."

Teddy nodded and drew a deep breath. "We have ten hours between the moon's set and rise. Ten hours, to find one man in New York, a man who doesn't want to be found. Amid all that chaos…" Teddy shook his head.

"So that's it? No alternative?"

"Sometimes there *is* no alternative."

"No. I won't accept that."

"This is the hand we were dealt. It wasn't an oversight, Will. There was no mistake on your watch. I'm sure Fox News will uncover that letter from Valenkov and take us to task for not creating a 'Department of Werewolf Defense,' but this is not your fault." He paused for a laugh, but he didn't get one. "History will see that," he said, sputtering. "Just maybe not in our lifetimes."

"Never. They'll never understand killing our own."

Teddy knew he was right. "We'll put Valenkov's face out there, we'll hit them over the head with what you were up against. The CDC prognosi… tigotations… will go public. Your voice will be heard."

"I'll be charged with a million counts of murder."

"The lawyers are already on it." Teddy said, and then he raised his voice to stave off Weston's interruption. "We'll make an executive declaration to classify werewolves as a catastrophic threat to the security of the country."

"They're still American citizens."

"Nope. Not if we can help it. We'll go to Directive 51."

Directive 51 was the National Security and Homeland Security Presidential Directive signed by George W. Bush in 2007. On the surface, it established provisions for the "continuity" of the federal government in times of catastrophic emergency. But there were controversial details of 51 that provided for broad and unilateral executive decisions in regard to military strategy during situations of domestic terrorism.

"We're good on that," Teddy continued. "Liberals will have an epic shit when we're forced to reveal some of the classified details of 51, but we'll give it the spin."

Directive 51 was a perfect symbol of the ideology Weston had been trying to put in the country's rear-view mirror. He hated everything about it. Resorting to it as a defense seemed beyond hypocritical; it'd be a flat-out surrender.

"We'll face a tougher road from the international community," Teddy continued. "They'll throw the BWC at us, as if every goddamn one of them aren't breaking it themselves." He was referring to the 1975 Biological Weapons Convention, an outdated set of rules from a different global landscape. Today it only serves to handcuff legitimate governments, because the enemy—human or monster or whatever between—no longer plays by the rules.

"They'll have to get in line to throw me in jail," Weston muttered.

"You're not alone on this, Will. You'll have the support of everyone in the administration."

"*Publicly* I'll have their support. What about privately?"

"Pussies. They're all pussies. It's too big, that's why they're not sitting at this desk. They can preach all they want if they offer a better alternative. This isn't the best option we came up with, it's the *only* option we came up with."

"Have we tried hard enough?"

"We can't second-guess the team when we're under the gun. Alan is our man."

General Alan Truesdale was the Chairman of the Joint Chiefs of Staff and chief military advisor. His was the most challenging cabinet position to fill as Weston's administration faced the difficult task of revitalizing America's international standing after a decade of international recklessness. The man was born with a gun in his hand, but his judgment was sound. Weston felt confident that he'd done his soul-searching before presenting Operation Wolfsbane.

"Rebekkah's not convinced," Teddy added. "She said, 'If that's the only answer, we have to ask a different question.'"

"And what might that question be?"

"If the clock weren't ticking, I'd sit on the toilet and think of one."

Weston took a deep breath. "Maybe I should go to New York."

"And what? Die with the rest of them?"

"Take the blame. Show my solidarity. Let them paint me as a hero, as a villain, as a madman, whatever they need. The country will move on; the government will continue—"

"No, no, you're a bigger man than that. Martyrdom is a last indignant gasp in a losing fight. You deserve better, and they deserve better. They're going to need you. And look, you're not in this alone. You can push us away, but we won't go. Everybody will sign the declaration."

"No pressure. I'm not going to take them down with me."

"Then they'll shake themselves out."

Weston thought for a moment, imagining which members of his cabinet would turn on him. "Won't matter much in the end."

"Not at all, really."

They were quiet for a moment. The room was so still that the ticking of the grandfather clock became maddening. Weston's arms and legs felt weightless, and then he imagined he could see himself from some third perspective in the room.

When Teddy finally broke the silence, his voice was both quiet and startling. "At some point there will have to be a broad pardon for all of us. Allison's signature will be on the order, so it'll have to go down the chain."

Allison Leslie, the vice president. One of a hundred careers he was about to poison. With her signature on the executive order to carry out Operation Wolfsbane, she wouldn't be able to pardon him for murder.

"We'll need to be smart about who gets the baton when the time comes. We're looking at Rosenbaum." Teddy said.

Weston's eyes erupted.

"He's a good man," Teddy argued, "and an old friend. He'll keep it clean."

"He's the Secretary of Agriculture!"

"Okay—"

"The Secretary of Agriculture is going to become president?"

"Who the hell knows what's going to happen? This is going to punch a gaping hole in the political landscape. Partisanship won't stand aside for long. We need the top name that's not on the order to be a reliable ally, and Ira Rosenbaum is a reliable ally."

As usual, Teddy was right. They were going to need help at the top. Not just him, but the men and women standing by him. "We should sit down with him."

"I spoke with him today. I was vague with details, but the writing is on the wall. He's onboard," Teddy said, pouring himself another shot. "Tomorrow morning, Alan will brief a bipartisan congressional committee on the broad strokes, and then you and Rebekkah will hear them out on the record. Again, the writing is on the wall. I don't think it'll get contentious."

"Not even from Hynds?" Bob Hynds was the Speaker of the House, a notoriously contnentious Republican. It was his job to stand in Weston's way, and the rest of Washington's burden to take a side.

"I already backchanneled with him. Gave him extra time to prepare his *pièce de* condemnation. But he understands our position. He's going to sign."

Weston took some comfort in that. Hynds' reasonableness was one of the best-kept secrets in politics. But it wasn't Hynds that he really dreaded facing.

"Brewer is on the committee?"

Teddy nodded solemnly.

James Brewer was the president pro tempore of the Senate, third in the line of presidential succession and the most senior senator in the Democratic party. He'd overcome a controversial youth in the Ku Klux Klan to serve in the senate for fifty-one years. He was remarkably sharp at 93, and he understood the game better than anyone. And he was born and raised in Manhattan.

"Does he have family in the city?" Weston asked.

"He has a son and a grandson. Lawyers. And they have families."

"Jesus Christ."

"He already called over and offered his support. I'm telling you they're behind you. We'll all be in pain. We'll all grieve. But I'll never apologize for doing my duty to this country. And I don't think you should."

Teddy held his drink aloft, coaxing Weston to meet his toast. The whiskey seared their tired throats.

"Tell me we're doing everything we can to find Valenkov."

"We have all of our best trackers on it. The DHS called in the Shadow Wolves, Native American smuggler trackers. Black ops are in, spooks, FBI. Tildascow is on her way back from Transylvania with some kind of werewolf hunter."

"Good. Good."

"Even if we find him, there's no guarantee this bloodline thing will—"

"I know. I just don't want to give up."

"Nobody's giving up."

Teddy took another shot and threw a coughing fit that almost cost him his last kidney. And then he looked at Weston, who knew he'd run out of reasons to stall what he'd come to say.

"You have to know…" Teddy muttered, "Any troops we send in tomorrow, they won't be coming out. There won't be time for exit checks. Once they hit the ground, they're gone."

"So if we're in, we're all in."

"If we're in, we're all in."

The president ran his hands across the surface of the *Resolute* desk.

"Let's go all in."

Two

Joint Base Andrews
Prince George's County, Maryland
7:04 a.m. EST

Yannic Ilecko had never imagined the texture of America. Foreign lands were irrelevant to a man who had never traveled more than fifty miles from his place of birth. And yet, the country was exactly what he might have expected. They had taken their hard concrete and covered all of the softness of the earth, and then everything else along with it.

Ilecko sat on a cot, gazing across the rows of identical cots in the long, soulless military hangar. Flags adorned the walls, so brash and proud and oozing with the self-ordained superiority of the *Statele Unite ale Americii*.

The chubby American boy—"Lon," they called him—was curled up on a nearby cot, snoring obnoxiously. The plane ride had been taxing, and the boy's weak body was not prepared for such rigors. Ilecko had had no precedent to imagine how his own body would respond to such torture, but an hour later he felt only the fatigue of a hard day's work.

The boy awoke with a start, exclaiming something about a "yo-da." His mannerisms were distinctly American (his first morning's labor was to take a disapproving sniff of his underarm), but he seemed always to be struggling with fear. *"She is not sleeping?"* he asked, mangling *limba română*.

"I slept on the plane."

The boy made a motion to his throat as if to throw up. *"She is not liking the plane. She might toss high."*

"Will you come with us to New York?" Ilecko asked.

Lon was surprised by the question, and again fearful. Not of the thought, but of an answer. *"She is not thinking so. She is not part of the military."*

Ilecko nodded. It was as expected.

The boy thought longer, perhaps from guilt. *"There is many chickens in New York. Will she be safe?"*

"No."

He nodded, first at Ilecko and then at the floor.

"In my home," Ilecko said, *"You asked if my wife was a werewolf."*

"Yes. She is sorry."

"So you know they are not called 'chickens.'"

The boy's cheeks flushed and his eyes watered. His head rolled loosely, causing Ilecko to wonder if he was going to faint. Finally, he let loose a soft, defeated gasp.

"I'm sorry," he muttered. *"I hoped if we appeared helpless, you would… I'm so sorry."*

His Romanian was sharp after all.

"You are a very smart boy," Ilecko said. *"Don't let them make you feel otherwise."*

But the boy couldn't hear the compliment or the advice—he was too soft, raging with self-condemnation. *"I am sorry, though,"* he said, fumbling with his hands, and then he switched to English. "I shouldn't have asked about your wife. I'm—I'm sorry for your loss. I didn't mean to bring up bad… whatever."

"She would have liked you very much. You would have made her laugh."

"Thank you for saying that," he muttered.

Ilecko smiled. The stretch of the muscles felt unfamiliar. And then he surprised himself by telling the boy, *"My wife was not the werewolf. I was."*

The boy looked up, but remained quiet.

"I awoke one morning with her blood on my hands. And my pursuit of Lord Valenkov began."

And then his life had continued, he said; despite lack of purpose, like a record skipping after the music died. He'd fought so hard to purge the memories, but something inside him wanted to tell this boy what he had never told anyone before.

He had awakened naked in the forest, in the grey, damp haze of a spring morning. Sticky blood covered his hands. Dead weeds were pasted to his bare chest. His skin was hard and numb.

The mountains pointed his way home. The sun crested the hills as he walked, but it brought no warmth. He kept to the woods, away from the road. He came across a dead deer, its insides strewn about the shade of a fir tree. It might have been his own work, but he also sensed a bear nearby, watching from the safety of the trees.

Even the most fearsome animals stayed clear of his scent.

There was the farm, where the warm embrace of his wife would ease his terror. The wolfsbane on their land began to throb in his head, slowing his blood, pulling nausea into his chest. He fought through the daze.

The wolfsbane—this much of it—would incapacitate other werewolves. But not Yannic Ilecko. His heart and body were strong from the hard work and honest thoughts taught by his father and grandfather.

He stumbled across the crops, as carefully as possible, to escape the drown of the wolfsbane. When his senses awoke, he turned southeast toward the house.

Only dead wisps of smoke rose from the chimney. That was the first thing he noticed. Violeta should have been cold without a full fire.

Something was wrong.

The front door was open—how could that be?

She must have gone to town?

Please, she went to town, there must have been a reason to go early—

He ran, a naked and bloodstained madman, crushing potato plants as he stumbled across the soil furrows, wrenching both of his ankles, he reached the house and slipped on the porch, smashed his knee into the support beam, knocking down the awning, not knowing until later that he'd fractured his kneecap, he forced the door open, breaking it against the fallen awning and he stooped to limp inside—

He knew the smell. No. The wolf knew it.

Not just blood. *Her* blood.

He found her facedown in a pool of her spilled life.

The back of her head. That was the first he'd ever seen of her. And then she'd spun, and her hair had erupted like a blazing torch, and he'd seen those playful freckles, that sweet smile, and those pale eyes. The color of a winter's dusk. And she smiled, and he wondered how there could be such beauty.

When he didn't return the favor, thinking she could not be beckoning him, Violeta creased her glimmering orange brows and waved. *Get over here, you.* So expressive were her thin hands. So delicate they would burn after only moments in the sun, yet so strong as they caressed his chest.

That right hand that she'd summoned him with, the hand of God, was now gone. It had been stripped of its flesh and severed at the wrist.

She deserved better than him. He insisted upon it. But he could not stand to see her unhappy; he could not let those brows crease again. He could never deny her, no matter how ludicrous the thought of the *floare* Violeta with the *sălbatic* Ilecko.

And in the end, the flower was crushed by the savage.

No other *vârcolac* could have broken through the wolfsbane.

Could she have known her husband was the monster as he was killing her? Did she call out his name, plead with him to fight against the wolf, even as he ate her flesh?

He buried her beneath their willow trees. He tossed dirt on her lovely face, returning the flower to the earth, until he could see her no more. And then she was gone.

He took no comfort in the hunt for Zaharius Valenkov. No joy when he finally lanced the life from Valenkov's heart.

It was just another tragedy for a cursed family. Valenkov had suffered the transformation for twenty years. And he too had loved ones—to deny that would be to succumb to blind rage, and Violeta would never permit such a thing. He would never betray her again, if there was any hope that she might forgive him from her perch in Heaven before he plummeted in the other direction.

Perhaps it was Violeta's silent whisper that made him to come to

America. That might explain what he could not. And yet, here he was, in a strange land, to see to more heartbreak for the Valenkov clan.

After his tale was told, the American boy struggled for words.

Now Ilecko found it easier to look at him. He noticed his red hair and—

Yes. That was it.

With his hair and his fair skin, his eyes… he could have been Violeta's child. Perhaps… perhaps it *was* her whisper, from his lips, that brought him to America.

"I'll go with you," Lon said, breaking his long silence, "to New York."

Ilecko was surprised to realize that that was exactly what he wanted to hear.

Three
Manhattan
January 2
Daybreak

Aircraft swarmed the Manhattan sky like an apocalyptic cloud of locusts.

Nearly nine thousand US helicopters were on active duty, the latest and greatest alongside Vietnam-era Hueys. US Air Force F-22 Raptor and F15E Strike Eagle fighters rocketed above their range, packed with air-to-surface weapons capable of leveling skyscrapers. Air traffic control required circuitous flight patterns, precise lateral, vertical, and longitudinal assignments—and a lot of luck.

The Joint Task Force was comprised of over 170 platoons, deployed primarily by air. Command centers were established on roofs, landing pads, and seaports. Canvass districts overlapped in dangerous areas like Hell's Kitchen and Chelsea in western midtown, where the conflict at the Lincoln Tunnel still raged. Significant civilian resistance was expected in all zones, particularly the island's outer rim.

The haunting surveillance image of Demetrius Valenkov was affixed to every soldier's backpack, pilot's console, and riot officer's shield. Up until six p.m., orders were to capture the HPT (high-priority target) for questioning. After six, shoot to kill upon acquisition.

One hundred thousand leaflets had been dropped over the city during the night. They bore the same image of Valenkov, and the following text:

DEMETRIUS VALENKOV
WANTED ALIVE
FOR QUESTIONING IN REGARD TO
THE WEREWOLF DISEASE
This man should be considered HIGHLY DANGEROUS.

If you see him, alert nearby authorities or assist your fellow citizens in APPREHENDING or TRAPPING him. We will overcome this together. Believe and trust in your fellow Americans.

From six a.m., a cycling broadcast emanated from the skies: *A federal state of emergency has been declared. Clear the streets immediately. Military forces cannot guarantee your safety.*

The moon set at 8:03 a.m. The JTF coordinated to storm the city after a safety window for the reverse transformation.

At 9 o'clock precisely, thousands of paratroopers and rappelling soldiers dropped from the sky. UH-60 Black Hawk helicopters put soldiers down on open intersections. The barricades were moved for armored personnel vehicles. Troops moved against civilian resistance with rapid dominance, establishing swift ground control so the dragnet could begin.

Four

Joint Base Andrews
January 2
7:30 a.m.

Brianna Tildascow was feeling her exhaustion. She'd managed some tormented rest on the return flight from Transylvania, but four hours of sleep in three days wasn't enough. Her fumes were running on fumes.

The kid had pleaded for them to take him into Manhattan. He'd been dug in for a battle, and he was stupefied when she consented without one.

The way she saw it, he'd proved his worth in Transylvania. For some strange reason, he had a place in Ilecko's heart (she'd considered that it might be in another body part, but that didn't seem to be the case). His knowledge was undeniably valuable, and, most importantly, he'd obeyed her orders. She made it clear that this was a do or die mission (in all probability, do *and* die), and also that he'd be left behind if he lagged. He didn't hesitate, so neither did she.

The moon would rise at 7:15 p.m. She wasn't privy to the specifics of the federal government's plan, but the resolution would be decisive. Something had gone badly in Atlanta, something that made them believe Ilecko's warning. They couldn't allow the full moon to rise on the thousands—maybe tens of thousands—of werewolves.

It had to end tonight. If Demetrius Valenkov did not die, everyone left in Manhattan would, her along with them.

Packing was light and easy. She brought a couple of canteens, power bars, a good knife, and two sidearms: her modified .45 Springfield 1911A1 and a USAF-issued Glock 17 loaded with newly-struck 9mm silver ammunition.

The 1911 was all she ever needed in a gun or a boyfriend: a broad-nosed hand cannon with an intimidating metal mouth that would make a seasoned marine wet his diapers. Perfect weight distribution so it felt like it was holding her hand, minimizing blowback and promoting repeat-fire accuracy. It was a SWAT weapon, not standard issue. But she wasn't a standard agent.

The Glock was a far less reliable weapon. Bitchy recoil and a *fucking* plastic handle. Even worse, she couldn't know this particular gun's history. It looked okay when cleaned and inspected, but it'd stay in her belt until she positively needed silver love.

They also gave her a Colt 9mm submachine gun with silver rounds, but she planned on stowing that bulky rifle on the 'copter till sundown.

From a practical standpoint, if they came up against actual werewolves, they'd already be out of time.

She kept the black MOLLE utility vest she'd worn to Transylvania and packed her mother's good looks behind a black baseball cap and polarized sunglasses. They'd be on the move, so the cold wasn't of much concern.

She packed Lon light as well, and she hid a Glock under the power bars in his backpack—no need to tell him about that. Ilecko wouldn't take any provisions or gear other than a new Velcro strap for his Anelace's sheath.

Someone high up was told by someone higher up to give her team whatever they wanted. When she asked Ilecko where they should start searching, his shrugging response didn't exactly inspire a tidal wave of confidence.

"In the middle," he said, with his sticky Romanian d's.

A good ole-fashioned Army-grade SWAG: a scientific wild-ass guess.

Armed with such expert insight, she requested just a couple of high-speed, low-drag troops and constant, redundant air support. Less show, more go.

At 0730 (she was falling back on her armyspeak as she spent more time around these grunts), a wingnut led her, Lon, and Ilecko across the Andrews campus to the helipad, which was the eye in a tornado of noise.

A Black Hawk helicopter awaited them, with its twin engines jutting above the bulky passenger cabin like a boxer's bulging collar. Grunts called it the "Crash Hawk" because of its alarming propensity to crash. Her inner Rambette shrugged as she realized this wasn't the DAP attack variant or even the 60K special ops mod, and it didn't have stub wings attached for weapon stores. A bee without its stinger, purely a transport vehicle.

Mantle and Jaguar were at the helm, a sight she found surprisingly welcome.

"Hooah!" Mantle yelled as Tildascow climbed into the cabin.

They looked like infants beneath their enormous flight helmets, which had lenses mounted on either temple, jutting out like the folds of a king cobra. Tildascow had fooled around with a predecessor of those helmets during her time in Nevada; they were called "TopOwls," and they projected high-resolution images from the aircraft's flight and weapons systems directly onto the pilots' visors, allowing them to guide missiles simply by looking at their targets. It seemed beyond futuristic, but this tech was old hat to pilots trained on videogames.

She led Lon and Ilecko into the forward-facing seats between the empty side cannon stations, got them strapped in, and put on her headset.

"How we doing, boys?" she shouted over the intercom system.

"WETSU!" Mantle hollered, and Jaguar repeated it right on top of him. *We eat this shit up.*

"Hooah!" she responded heartily.

"Hooah!" Lon yelled as he put on his own headset.

Everyone laughed. If you didn't hate this kid, you had to love him.

"Howdy howdy and welcome to your limousine!" said Mantle. "We'll be cruising at 180 miles an hour today on a luxurious flight to lovely New York City, gonna take the apple back from the big bad wolf."

They were off the ground before he got to "apple." Every second counted.

Another chopper lifted alongside them, and when Tildascow saw it she damn near salivated. It was a bulky attack helicopter, dark green, with extended wings loaded with Hellfire missiles and Hydra rocket launchers. A positively impolite 30mm chain cannon was mounted beneath the fuselage, the horse's hard leg that Tildascow wanted from her air support. UNITED STATES ARMY was stenciled in black text, and someone had hastily spray-painted a name across the broad shaft of its tail boom: *"Silver Bullet."*

"I'd like to direct y'all to our escort," Mantle said. "That is the United States Army's preferred delivery method of airborne destruction, the AH-64D *Apache Longbow.* We call that particular one the *Silver Bullet,* I don't know why. Why do we do that, Jaguar?"

"I must confess, I do not know." Jaguar responded with the taint-licking placation of a talk-show sidekick.

"Anyways," Mantle continued, "She ain't quite as pretty as the Black Hawk, but that there 'copter could just about turn a city to mush. I could bore you with all the details, but let's just say when the devil got diarrhea, he put it into a Hellfire missile."

Confidence restored.

Their friend Beethoven saluted from the pilot's position, the raised rear seat in the *Silver Bullet's* tight tandem cockpit. She nodded back as the *Bullet* broke right to escort them northeasterly toward Manhattan.

As Mantle yapped, she wished Beethoven could have been *their* pilot.

"Now we're gonna make this flight extra smooth for the lovely ladies onboard, so you just relax and sun yourself and we'll have you on the ground in no time."

The ride was as smooth as they'd promised, but Mantle and Beethoven's paltry comedy couldn't stave off the nerves wafting off Lon. When the Bay materialized on the horizon some eighty minutes later, she could practically hear his heart stomping. By then, she couldn't blame him.

Apocalyptic plumes of smoke loomed beyond, as if volcanoes had sprouted through open wounds on the Manhattan skyline.

Half a mile from the southern coast, Governor's Island was a hotbed of military activity. Helicopters flowed in organized traffic patterns; the most striking were the *Chinook* cargo 'copters, giant green bananas flying under two horizontal rotors.

Her old CO used to refer to them as "Shithooks." He hated wasting a sentence without slipping in some filth.

A fleet of Coast Guard cutters was in the midst of launching from the southern docks, dwarfing the size of nearby Port Authority and NYPD boats.

And there was the Statue of Liberty on their left. As they crossed through her somber southeastern gaze, it kinda felt like she was crying for help. Tildascow rolled her eyes at the thought.

Can the hyperbole, kill this guy, and let all the biblical consequences eat shit.

Manhattan was so stuffed with clusterfuck that it was almost spilling over the southern tip. A horde of civilians—maybe tens of thousands strong—was massed at the entrance to the Battery Tunnel. It was two after nine, a whopping one hundred twenty seconds after the mandatory curfew lifted. So much for cooperation.

The city proper wasn't as bad as the outlying regions, but it wasn't any good, either. Assorted vehicles littered the streets, skewed in every direction and frequently stashed in Matchbox piles. Tanks and APCs were trying to blaze trails through the metal thicket, but most soldiers were on foot. That didn't bode well for their "start in the middle" plan (which was sure-fire otherwise).

The USAF gave her a Defense Advanced GPS Receiver, which might've been useful if she was trying to pinpoint smartbomb targets in Afghanistan. Here she expected to fare better with her hacked and re-hacked BlackBerry.

Valenkov had been seen at 26 Federal Plaza in the minutes before the government's virtual private network servers were destroyed—right in her own damn building. He could've gone anywhere from there. It was even possible that he'd found a way off the island.

But he didn't want to leave. If he did, he would have slipped out right after Times Square. In fact, he wanted them to know he was still there. The VPN wasn't a valuable target—if Valenkov knew about it, he'd also know they had redundancies. They were back to full speed in a couple of hours. No, he just wanted to be seen, and he knew he'd be seen at 26 Fed.

The military was using Columbus Circle as a staging area and command center. It was located at the southeastern corner of Central Park, as close to "the middle" as they'd get. The dual Time Warner Center towers were rapidly approaching, the skyline landmark for Columbus Circle.

Go time.

Lon's hands trembled. Ilecko had gone stiff. Even Mantle and Jaguar were gazing slack-jawed at the fires and pile-ups and riots. Tildascow kept her eyes on the *Silver Bullet* in front of them.

She kicked the iron divider behind the cockpit. "Got any tunes on this flying coffin?"

A few seconds later, their headsets blasted with an angry trash rock anthem by Kid Rock. Not a bad tune, but she preferred Eminem with her morning meatballs.

She removed her headset and let her ears adjust to the cold. The tinny bangs were still audible above the rotors.

Columbus Circle was surrounded by a mob of civilians, several thousand strong. The five rings of traffic lanes were heavily barricaded in all directions, with riot officers trying to keep the crowd civil. There were two designated landing pads, each wide enough to land Shithooks and off-load vehicles. One was deploying a 6x6 Cougar even now.

Their Black Hawk dropped hard onto the open landing zone, but it touched down gracefully. Her Shadow Stalkers yapped too much for her taste, but the fuckers knew how to fly.

The chaotic frenzy of the city surged into the cabin. Tildascow pulled off Lon's headset and yelled over the din. "You don't have to do this!"

"I know!"

"You've done enough for your country. We can leave you here, and there's nothing to be ashamed of!"

"I know!" he said, shaking his head emphatically. "I want to come!" He leaned around her to nod his reassurance at Ilecko. More than anything, Ilecko seemed deeply offended by the nonsense music.

"Lon, look at me." The kid could never make eye contact and she had to see his pupils dilate to make sure he comprehended what she was about to say: "Within the next ten hours, the United States government is going to level Manhattan. We will not be able to extract. Do you understand?"

He matched her gaze. "I want to go."

The doors swung open. The freeze rushed in.

"Lon," she said into his eyes, "we are going to die."

"No we're not. We're going to find Valenkov. We are going to win this." He seemed to believe it. Maybe more than she did. "So I can come?"

"Go go go!"

Five
Columbus Circle
9:28 a.m.

What a great way to start.

Lon stepped onto the frigid asphalt in Columbus Circle as hundreds of NYPD and military watched, along with thousands of civilians from behind police barriers. Here he was: an important member of the super strike team that represented mankind's best hope against the doomsday threat of the supernatural.

And he tripped.

This was no minor stumble. It was an epic poem of elaborate, prolonged humiliation, a passionate love letter to the very fiber of his self-loathing and a mighty, terrible, and oh-so-ominous symphony of piss-poor coordination.

He'd made valid contact with the ground and he was capably walking away from the helicopter. Maybe he'd entertained the image of a scowling, slo-mo, Nicolas Cage-worthy stride.

And then he tripped the shit fantastic over some kind of flashing strip they'd set down to mark the landing zone.

One, two, three stumbling steps, his balance slipping further from his grasp with each ridiculous lurch until he finally went full-on horizontal, arms spread like Superman. And then, miraculously, he managed to get his leg out—

—only to smash his sternum into his knee before crashing chin-first into the cement. Cherry on top was the blazing explosion of pain that erupted from his tongue as his jaw clamped down.

"Uhhhggghhhuuuhhh…" he groaned as his lungs emptied.

He rolled over, onto that fucking backpack she'd made him wear, thrashing his legs as if they could pump air into his body. His chin throbbed and his tongue was somehow both numb and pounding. Both

315

palms were pocked with bloody holes. And—goddammit—he'd put a scuff on his beloved replica One Ring, which he wore on "the third finger of his right hand," as Master J.R.R. Tolkien wrote in—

Ah, fuck. Never mind.

Tildascow peeked into his sky-filled point of view, holding her baseball cap tight against the helicopter's wind. She yelled something that was probably "Are you okay?" and helped him up.

He nodded a sheepish apology, feeling the fuckingly familiar flush of crimson in his thick cheeks, but he couldn't stand just yet.

Ilecko arrived, squatting to examine two daggers that Tildascow had strapped to her left thigh. She lifted her arm and looked down, wondering if he'd seen a bug or something.

"Silver?" he asked about the dagger.

She shook her head no. Ilecko took one of the knives and examined it.

They both thought that was weird, but Lon was grateful for the extra breaths before she yanked him to his feet—almost *off* his feet. The fuck did they feed her in the FBI?

Lon put his hands on his knees and shook his head at the ground, searching for the shattered pieces of his pride. When he finally mustered the courage to check just how many people would be smirking at him, it wasn't too bad.

Because everything else was so much worse.

A civilian mob had surrounded the camp, and they were on verge of a full-scale riot. Gunshots popped in the distance. Military and cops scurried about like crazed ants at a picnic. Shouting. Arguing. Lon was shoved aside by men carrying a refuel hose for their Black Hawk.

Columbus Circle had been repurposed as a massive bivouac. The flowerbeds surrounding the central monument had been trampled by equipment. The commanders hovered close to a communications rig under a tent. Helicopters rose and fell. APCs and light tanks were on standby. A phalanx of unmanned NYPD motorcycles surrounded the

Trump International Hotel's steel globe. At the perimeters, riot police were trying to keep the civilian mob at bay.

Jaguar removed the last of his flight gear. Mantle checked the magazine on his tan-and-black assault rifle. It had a digital ammo counter, just like in the video games. He winked at Lon, and showed him—

Screams erupted, loud enough to hear over the helicopter.

"Jesus Christ!" Tildascow yelled, drawing her pistol at gunslinger speed.

Lon turned, looking for what could possibly have—

Ilecko had used Tildascow's knife to slice a man's throat.

Six

Columbus Circle
9:49 a.m.

"Civilian down!" one of the soldiers yelled. Countless others raised their rifles at Ilecko.

"No! Wait!" Lon screamed.

Ilecko supported the man's chest over his knee, letting his blood pour onto the pavement. He'd dropped the knife and taken to rubbing his victim's back and whispering into his ear, easing him toward his death.

They were stooped just before the barricade. The man seemed to be a civilian Ilecko had taken from the crowd. Nearby citizens scrambled away from Ilecko and out of the line of fire. Even the riot guards with their heavy shields backed away.

"Blue force! Blue force!" Tildascow yelled, so hard that she spit with each "b" and "f." It probably meant *he's on our side.*

The victim's dirty hands fumbled as he tried to extract himself from Ilecko's odd embrace. His eyes popped as he watched his own blood spill away. He tried to scream, but his throat clicked in gurgling denial, his Adam's apple bobbing above the gaping wound. Lon wanted to do something to stop the man's suffering, but he couldn't move.

Finally, the guy's shock dimmed. His clutch weakened; his arms dropped. Ilecko somberly stroked his back one last time.

The man's body was rife with cuts and bruises. He also was barefoot, and his haggard pants were caked in dirt and old blood. Lon didn't need his Shaman Emeritus title in the International Lycanthropy Studies Association to recognize that this man had been a werewolf last night.

Ilecko glanced up to stave off the officers. His face was grim, and his eyes were wet with sympathy. The look was enough to keep fingers off triggers.

He reached into his pocket and produced his animal skin pouch, the one with the remains from Zaharius Valenkov's coffin. He balanced the corpse on his thigh and used both hands to open its drawstring and hold it under the bloodfall. When he'd collected enough to make the pouch bulge, he carefully laid the man on the ground. They were both soaked in red.

"The fuck are you doing!" Tildascow shouted, stowing her gun.

But Ilecko was focused on his pouch. He cinched the strings tight and rolled it between his palms, just like he mixed the corpse goo with the soil in the Drăculeşti crypt.

"You just cut a man's throat open without saying anything! They almost shot you!"

He continued to ignore her, fueling her flame. Lon felt like Mom and Dad were fighting. Because, y'know, Dad had just sliced someone's throat open.

"Hey, Chewbacca!" she yelled, causing Lon to feel a jolt of attraction to her. "You hear me?"

"How could I not?" Ilecko spat.

"I don't know how they do it in fucking Transylvania, but in America you can't just slit a man's throat—"

Ilecko squatted over a clean, flat stretch of asphalt and turned his bag upside down, squeezing out a few drops of blood.

"The fuck are you doing?" she asked, shrinking from rage to curiosity.

The soldiers and officers leaned forward to get a better look, lowering their guns in the process. Lon tiptoed for an angle. Soon dozens of men were locked on the five drops of blood, waiting for some kind of performance. More soldiers approached, gazing around: *What are we looking at?*

And then the blood began to move.

The droplets rolled ever so subtly against the curve of the street, away from the Trump Hotel's steel globe, southeast toward the center of Columbus Circle. There was nothing natural about it. The blood was seeking the bloodline.

Ilecko stood and nodded toward the southeastern horizon. His powerful brow worked as a natural visor for his thin, inset eyes.

"We go that way!" hollered Tildascow.

The soldiers were still gawking at the creeping blood as commanding officers repeated Tildascow's order: "Start clearing a path, let's go!"

All at once, the soldiers moved with purpose. The southeast exit from Columbus Circle was onto Broadway, but the street was barricaded and packed with civilians. A massive tank creaked forward, its treads—

Ilecko collapsed.

Something had struck him in the head. Lon couldn't see if he was okay; his greasy auburn hair shrouded his face. A baseball-sized stone lay by his side, thrown by a civilian in the park. A torrent followed, as the angry mob went into full-on riot. Rocks twanged off helicopter blades. Gunfire erupted, and everyone hurried to take cover. *Pop-pop-pop* and *plinks* as bullets hit nearby vehicles.

Someone tackled Lon, smacking him down onto his chin again. It was Mantle—Lon could smell beef jerky on his breath as he climbed on top of him. A bit Roman for Lon's taste, but there were real bullets flying overhead.

His cheek was pressed into the freezing blacktop, but he could see under Mantle's armpit as Tildascow flat-crawled to Ilecko, who batted her away when she touched his wound. Good sign that he was okay. He tried to sit up, but she forced him back down.

The wind shear from the Black Hawk diminished as it lifted off. A moment later, a shot hit the ground right next to them and a small bit of concrete hit his forehead, barely missing his eye. Mantle lowered his shoulder, covering Lon's face and leaving him blind.

Scrambling—*bangs* and *plinks*—darkness—Mantle's beef breath—

"Y'alright?"

"Yeah."

"Stay ya's ass *down*."

"Not going any—"

Mantle let out an earsplitting whistle, causing Lon to flinch.

The sound of a powerful spray erupted, dwarfing a whole new wave of screams. They must have been using hoses on the crowd. The rocks rained down and the bullets kept flying.

Of one thing Lon was certain: *They weren't going anywhere soon.*

Seven

Presidential State Car
Pennsylvania Avenue
Washington DC
9:56 a.m.

It had gone better than expected, but that was no consolation.

Truesdale told the selection of congressmen what they intended to do, and how he had reconciled it with his feelings for the country, their careers and their humanity. They kept the men waiting for half an hour, giving them time to ingest the concept—and scream it out, if need be. The delay was Teddy's idea, and it was a good one. By the time Weston arrived, he had a few defenders and a few slack jaws that might have been full of vitriol a couple of minutes earlier.

There had been posturing and pleading, realists and bleeding hearts, sympathies and oppositions. And, of course, a touch of the old die-hard partisanship, which Weston attributed to habit and swallowed gracefully.

It was a closed session with sealed transcripts. It would be someone else's decision whether these recordings were ever released, some special prosecutor whose name would become synonymous with the largest mass murder in American history.

When he entered the Capitol SCIF secure room (he came to their home as a show of humility, and also to get some air), Weston immediately sensed the heavy gaze of James Brewer, the 93-year old president pro tempore of the Senate, whose family was out of touch and presumably still in Manhattan. Brewer's eyes continued to press on his chest as he spoke, and as he answered questions. But Brewer remained silent as the oppositions were noted. The most aggressive dissent came, as expected, from a canned speech by the Republican Speaker of the House, Bob Hynds.

However, when Hynds inevitably put Weston on the ropes, it was

Brewer who intervened on his behalf.

The old man's voice was pained and weak, and so it should have been. He thanked the president for presenting his plan in a respectful manner. He said his heart was with the souls in Manhattan who were risking their lives to prevent this tragic resolution. And then he left the room.

The congressmen were sequestered now. Many of them would likely be preparing statements condemning his decision, hoping to salvage some kind of career in whatever the government would become after today. One of them might unofficially leak details of Operation Wolfsbane, but then the media was already speculating on doomsday scenarios. Wolfsbane would be just one more theory running the tickers on CNN and Fox News.

Traffic was slow-going from the Capitol to the White House. Protesters had jammed the streets. Weston wished he could join them. He would have liked to protest against werewolves too.

Despite September 11, 2001, Weston knew Americans weren't prepared for this kind of hardship. They couldn't comprehend the cruelty, the unfairness of a no-win scenario. Responsibility had become a forgotten myth. They sat back and ignored wars in Iraq and Afghanistan and famines, genocides and human rights atrocities all over the world, fostering international ill will that was becoming increasingly legitimate. Accountability? They'd turned to the government to fix a massive economic crisis borne of their own irresponsibility, and then they complained about the way it was handled. Patriotism? As long as it suited their schedule of Internet porn, rock climbing, Starbucks, video games and romance novels. Sure, the occasional Hurricane Katrina came along, but it was quickly knocked off the front page by the infidelities of a reality television couple.

And it wasn't their fault, not at all. Their grandparents and great-grandparents had fought wars to defend their freedom. Two generations later, it wasn't surprising that they'd become soft and unprepared. How could they brace for such wickedness when they'd never been exposed to it? When war was a channel you could turn off without getting off the couch?

So here they were, protesting. Against whom? Against what? Nature? Supernature? Against the networks for pre-empting their shows?

Any president takes office with the best of intentions and the highest of hopes, but by the end of the day, their legacy is mostly determined by luck. Who was going to be in the hot seat when the reckoning came?

William Weston's luck had run out.

Allison Leslie, Alan Truesdale, and Rebekkah Luft sat beside Weston and Teddy in the presidential limousine. Their motorcade had slowed to a crawl, giving the mob a chance to flex their lungs.

Leslie fought back tears. Truesdale was stoic, his conflict resolved. Luft breathed anxiously—Weston could feel her waiting for an opportunity to talk him out of this. Some part of him was looking forward to that conversation. Maybe she had an alternative they hadn't considered. Or maybe in convincing her that they had no choice, he'd convince himself.

"Did you hear the joke today?" Teddy asked.

Leslie and Luft were aghast at the notion of a joke. Weston hoped for his friend's sake that it was going to be a good one.

Teddy, realizing he'd stepped in something, swallowed before he continued. "They're saying the term 'werewolf' is politically incorrect. They'd now like to be referred to as 'Lupine Americans.'"

Leslie recoiled. Luft gasped. Truesdale resisted.

But Weston lost the fight, and a chuckle slipped out. That broke the dam.

As the limo cleared the mob of protesters, the leaders of the country laughed their asses off.

Eight
Columbus Circle
10:24 a.m.

This city.

An arrogant enemy of nature.

Yannic Ilecko had seen pictures of New York in books at the university in Braşov, but nothing could prepare him for the reality of such a place. Monstrous steel buildings blocked the sky, vulgar concrete smothered the grass and the defiled air smelled of chemicals, body odor, and rot. And, of course, the barbaric American people were a plague unto themselves.

No wonder they were unprepared for the arrival of the beast.

He was hit by something. A crunch sounded as if it had come from inside his ear. And then he was on the ground, his skull ringing.

Perhaps he was rash in taking that man's blood without explaining himself, but he preferred not to speak with these people. He wanted only to help them find Demetrius, let them do to him what they would, and then return home.

The blond woman. Foolish and rash. So very American. She had crawled on top of him as a human shield, but didn't it mean that *she* was even more vulnerable?

The sensation of her closeness was… distracting. Her hair dangled from her cap, wet and cold from collected snowflakes. It was coarser than Violeta's and had a more aggressive smell.

There was an attraction, however conflicted it might be, but it was different from any he'd ever felt. She was more like a *făptură*, an animal. Eager to establish dominance. Even now she lay upon him, her elbows on his shoulders in a manner intended to pin him on his stomach. Of course he could throw her off at any moment. Apparently that moment had not yet come.

"Are you okay?" she asked wetly into his ear.

"Yes."

"We're going to move. It's going to happen very fast. You'll stand up and there will be a transport vehicle to your right. You're going in through the rear. Open door, one step up, half a meter off the ground. Dive in and keep your head down. Do you understand all of that?"

"Yes."

She poked her head up, giving him his first unobstructed air in however long it had been. How was it possible that she wasn't breathing heavily? There was no tension in her muscles, no fear in her voice. Could American training subvert human instincts?

"Go."

She rolled off, and he did exactly as she'd instructed. The vehicle was a hulking behemoth of reinforced metal, a tan rectangular box atop three axles. He threw himself inside and landed on a hatched metal floor that suffered no response to his weight.

The woman was right behind him—he still wasn't sure of her name, the sound of it tumbled in too many directions. The vehicle reversed quickly, inhaling snow, and then it jerked to a sudden stop for Lon and two of the soldiers they'd brought to Romania. The woman slammed the door shut with a heavy metallic thud.

"Let's go!"

The vehicle lurched into a turn and they strapped themselves into the six dark, cushioned chairs. The interior consisted of tan canvas, green metal panels, and thick windows with round gun ports.

"FUBAR out there!" yelled the talkative soldier.

"Can you tell how far he is?" she asked him, yelling over a torrent that sounded like hail hitting the vehicle.

"I can not."

"But you can find him in a few hours?" she asked.

"For nine months I tracked his father."

The soldiers whistled in despair.

"At least you found him," the woman said. "It's only an island, how far can he be? We'll triangulate…" She yelled at the driver: "Take us a few miles southeast!" and continued: "And then we'll run that test again. You caught his father, you can catch him."

"I did not 'catch' his father."

The team fell silent, as they realized…

"What, he *let you* find him?"

The others dropped their heads. But the woman would not show fear. She gazed silently through the portal windows as their vehicle pushed slowly through the mob of wild Americans.

Nine

Broadway and 56th
Two Blocks Southeast of Columbus Circle
12:33 p.m.

"Give it some fucking gas!" Tildascow yelled.

Two hours to go two blocks. The sky had darkened, the snow thickened.

She'd ordered the driver to mow the civilians down. Twice, in fact, because he didn't believe her the first time. Fuck, man, at least try to score some points. It's goddamn *hard* to hit someone if they see you coming. And the Cougar wasn't exactly a speed demon.

Every time they really got moving, they'd hit more abandoned cars. A passenger vehicle was hardly any resistance to this 6x6, 52,000-pound hulk of American piss, but the thick clusters of metal trash were slowing them down. And then the mob would catch up.

One guy was ramming the Cougar with a garbage can. A woman had climbed onto the hood, fallen off, and started back up. Someone was pounding on the window with a brick. Weapons everywhere—guns, knives, baseball bats—one guy was even wielding a sword and shield right out of a gladiator movie.

 She'd hoped they'd have cleared the resistance by now.

"Can you track him from the sky?" she asked Ilecko.

Ilecko shrugged.

Fair enough, it wasn't like he'd stalked the father from a fucking jetpack.

"What's the Crash Hawk's callsign?" she asked Jaguar, taking quick stock of her USAF-issued radio.

"Desperation One."

Of course it is. "Desperation One, this is November Zero Zero One, over."

"This is Desperation, go ahead, over." The pilot's voice came tinny.

"We need an emergency extraction at 56th and Broadway. Can you get down here? Over."

"Negative, November, the street is too narrow. Stand by for alternate PZ."

Fucking driver stopped for another civilian!

"Run them over!"

"November, fall back 30 meters to 57th and Broadway."

That was back the way they came, the previous intersection. She cursed herself for not abandoning this tack an hour ago. "Copy that, Desperation. Wilco. Out."

"Hold on!" called the driver—

Tildascow was thrown against the back door.

A car had rammed them from behind, a black lux Caddy that looked less like an accordion a minute ago. A fifty-year-old grease job in a tracksuit stumbled from behind the airbag and checked his collection of necklaces before reaching back for a pair of .357 S&W Magnums (he must've left his grenade launcher at home). A teenager, probably his son, stepped out of the passenger side with an MP5 submachine gun. It was a serious piece of business, but he was holding it in a ridiculous side-armed manner that would probably break his arm if he fired.

"Alright youse, get the fuck out of there, this is a hijacking," yelled the grease job. The mob cheered as he twirled one of his Magnums, damn near dropping it, then fired a couple of resounding shots into the air.

"Can't go forward!" yelled the driver.

"Then go back!"

"Over them?"

Thought I made that clear, asshole. Fucking reserves knew how to move metal but they couldn't make decisions. She worked the PA mic, her voice booming over the crowd outside: "MOVE AWAY FROM THE VEHICLE OR WE WILL NOT HESITATE TO RUN YOU OVER!"

It just emboldened them. The hoagie shop gunslinger fired his

Magnums at the Cougar. Might as well have been a loud toothpick.

Warnings, posturing, reasoning… none of them were going to work, and all of them would take time they couldn't afford.

She slid the rack on her .45 and unlocked the gunport. She took aim, ignoring heavy gazes from Lon, Ilecko, Jaguar, and Mantle.

And then she shot the grease job through his forehead. A clap of thunder, a nickel-sized hole, a spritz of blood, and he was dead before he hit the ground.

The mob couldn't flee fast enough.

"Now go!" she yelled, and the driver finally took heed. The Cougar flattened the Cadillac like a soda can and reversed toward the pick-up zone.

The grease job's kid stood by as the Cougar crossed between him and his dead father. Tildascow watched his shock ebb into grief until she could see him no more.

"Desperation, this is November. We are on the move to PZ."

She sat down, uninterested in opinions. Including her own.

A few minutes later, they reached the intersection and transferred into the Black Hawk. Civilian resistance had evaporated.

As they lifted off and headed southeast, Tildascow tried to force that kid's image from her mind.

That kid whose father she'd just killed, right in front of him.

Ten

Manhattan
1:29 p.m.

After they had completed their procedures, DARPA's psychologists asked Brianna Tildascow if she felt like she was losing her identity.

When she asked them to elaborate, they explained that there were concerns that she might disassociate her new "enhanced" self from her former identity and come to resent the government for the irrevocable changes they'd made to her body and mind.

And so they asked, "Do you feel like you're losing your identity?"

She laughed at the question. That had terrified them.

Some of DARPA's theophilisophical whatsitwhos feared that the magnetic alterations to her frontotemporal lobe might produce a superior being, one whose enhanced mental capabilities could interpret the world in a way their feeble minds had been unable to predict or imagine. Maybe they thought she'd be able to manipulate matter or control their thoughts. Or bring disco back.

Her laughter wasn't intended to seem condescending or wicked. It was the question itself that she found funny.

Had she lost her identity?

"You're goddamn right I lost my identity," she answered. "When I was sixteen. It's in your records. Now let's go get some bad guys."

When she was finally approved to go and do just that, the results were disappointing. DARPA's mad scientists had enhanced her perception of patterns. She could see the tempo of music, and complex mathematical equations just fell into place. Civilizations, governments, and urban sprawl might fall into patterns, but individual people aren't predictable in the same terms.

And so she went about studying. Her every social exchange became an experiment in behavior patterns.

She began eavesdropping and people watching in common environments. Soon she got involved with her subjects, observing reactions when she broke social mores, like facing people on elevators, standing in movie theaters, or wearing her Sunday best and sitting with homeless people.

Next it was simple suggestion. Tender manipulation. Life coaching. Testing boundaries. Challenging convictions. Finding limits.

Emotional trauma.

Physical torture.

Poker. Lots and lots of poker.

And yet, she still hadn't found reliable patterns in any individual's behavior, particularly if her prey knew they were being watched and especially if she'd never met them. There was no way to truly know what someone was thinking.

But she could *guess* better than anyone on Earth.

Like every FBI agent, she would begin with a profile of her quarry, reviewing all of the available data on a subject and diagnosing broad classifications: Was he organized? Intelligent? Educated? Resolute?

How did he think?

—He was a product of superior education.

The main library in Castle Valenkov, she remembered, spanned the history of the written word, from archaic volumes of history and philosophy to science and medical journals from this decade. Recent selections on his reading table included *Istoria critică a românilor,* a history of Wallachia; *Skazanie o Drakule voevode,* "The Tale of the Warlord Dracula," a fifteenth-century book of folktales about Vlad the Impaler; and, of course, *Harry Potter și Ordinul Phoenix.* In the display cases were Chinese texts inscribed on bamboo slips. The quality of their ink suggested they were less than five hundred years old, but they reminded her of the second-century Yinqueshan Han Slips recently discovered in a Chinese tomb, which included lost sections of *The Art of War*.

In the laboratory below, Valenkov had studied hundreds or maybe even thousands of his ancestors' personal journals. The oldest were inscribed on hand-scraped sheepskin parchment, with iron gall ink treated with eggshells to temper acidity. She placed them in the sixteenth or seventeenth century. Some of them might've been Vlad the Impaler's personal writings.

Most of the journals were concerned with poetic descriptions of the werewolf experience, but Demetrius Valenkov's notes were preoccupied with his experiments.

—He was organized and intelligent.

The long table stretching through the laboratory was covered with stacks of research material. At first glance, the haphazard piles and overlapping open books appeared compulsive and scattered, but in fact their arrangement flowed smoothly through topics and ideologies.

The close end of the table was covered with heaps of twenty-first-century science and medical texts. They'd been left open to subjects like antiviral proteins, gene therapy and lethal mutagenesis. He'd most recently read a dense report from the CDC to the US Department of Health and Human Services, a primer on spontaneous epigenesis. The notes he'd scribbled in the margins suggested that he didn't think much of their theories.

Those materials gave way to studies of mathematics and harmonics. Valenkov seemed taken by Pythagoras' concept of the Harmony of the Spheres, a metaphysical theory proposing that everything in the universe interrelates through vibrations and sounds. He was experimenting with a massive handmade monochord, which he was recording with everything from wax records to reel-to-reel to digital tape. Sadly, all of his samples were gone.

The far side of Valenkov's table was packed with dusty, arcane tomes of the supernatural and the occult. Pages were marked to werewolf encounters, Gypsy folklore, curses, and witchcraft (notably, not a single reference to the fictional Count Dracula or his vampires). Among the titles: *The Book of the Sacred Magic of Abra-malin the Mage,* an ancient French grimoire; *The Picatrix,* an eleventh-century compilation of magical and astrological intersections; a handwritten copy of *Liber Iuratus,* a black magic compendium; *Pseudomonarchia Daemonum,* a sixteenth century encyclopedia of demons; and *Liber Al Vel Legis, "The Book of the Law,"* which Aleister Crowley claimed to have written while he was possessed by a mystical guardian. She also noticed a folded document written in a cipher, which made cryptic reference to something called the "Society of Eight." Cheery reading.

The juxtaposition on Valenkov's table matched the drawings and charts on the chamber's walls, the arrangements of the bookcases, and the placement of his instruments: science versus folklore.

—He was self-aware.

In the center of the table, Valenkov bridged the gap between theorized fact and supposed fiction with a subject that was neither and both: philosophical studies of the body and mind. He'd collected *Tattva-vāicāradī* and Sanskrit Yoga texts, a modern Romanian translation of *Yoga Sutras of Patanjali,* and a dozen books on the Chinese internal martial arts *Nèi jiā* and *Wǔdāngquán.*

This was the gravest revelation in Castle Valenkov. Tildascow was a longtime student of *Nèi jiā* and yoga herself, and well aware of its benefits. If Valenkov was practicing, he probably had a considerable degree of control over his emotions. That meant he'd be far more elusive.

Emotions are what lead people to fall back on habits or comforts: contact with a loved one, attending a sporting event, seeking out their favorite cigar.

Their *patterns.*

Free of emotional distractions, intelligent minds could always chaotically zig or zag, leaving their trail cold. The Unabomber, Ted Kaczynski, lived in a shed in the middle of nowhere and avoided people and technology. He traveled hundreds of miles to send a package, consistently altered his techniques, and waited years between strikes. No patterns. In fact, they only caught Kaczynski because his brother turned him in. It was sheer, dumb luck.

Obviously, it wasn't Valenkov's intention to zig or zag. He wanted to be seen, and he had a message.

Find a cure.

The psych profile on Demetrius Valenkov wouldn't make for a happy read. He'd be a snipe hunt, a case that rotted at the bottom of inboxes until an agent ran into some of that sheer, dumb luck. He certainly couldn't be found on any timetable.

***

Tildascow looked out from the Black Hawk as they flew southeast, following the path set by Ilecko's blood test. New Jersey was on their right, sitting there with front-row seats to Valenkov's morbid game.

How would it end? How *could* it end?

He'd prepared with such patience, executed with such precision. He must have an endgame. He had to know that finding a cure wouldn't take longer than three days, and that they wouldn't be able to cure him before the werewolves spread. Even Ilecko said the army couldn't—

—couldn't—

"Even though the Ottomans outnumbered Vlad five-to-one, they couldn't walk through his army of the dead." Lon's words fluttered through her mind.

Just like Vlad the Impaler, Demetrius Valenkov had been tortured and betrayed. His beloved murdered, his home pillaged.

She knew the sensation. You're goddamn right I lost my identity.

"Twenty. Thousand. Men. Impaled. Turkish prisoners. The sultan's own men. The stakes encircled the town."

Valenkov meant to turn back our army by pitting us against our own. He would occupy Manhattan with his werewolves, his army of the dead, until we found his cure. After all, the werewolves should have escaped by now. It was inconceivable that they hadn't. And they'd contained the spread in Atlanta.

Because spreading wasn't Valenkov's plan.

He'd come to claim his identity.

The Dracula King.

So where does a king put his throne? Where would he go, this man who came from a castle straight out of a fairytale nightmare?

Tildascow's stomach shifted as the helicopter banked. They were passing through a cloud of smoke, their wind shear wiping the sky clean to reveal—

Holy shit.

The Chrysler Building was directly in their path. A 77-story architectural wonder, towering above the rest of the city, topped by a crown—a *crown!*—of overlapping hubcaps, tapering into a spire that reaches the clouds.

Her muscles went tight.

The Empire State Building wasn't too far on their right, and neither was the gigantic *New York Times* Building. But they didn't fit the pattern. It was the Chrysler.

They took a slow bank around the crown, gazing into the blackness of the triangular windows. Mantle whistled from the rear cargo seats behind them. "Ain't she a beaut."

"We're landing here," Tildascow exclaimed. "Right here."

"Say again?" responded their Black Hawk's new pilot, Chief Warrant Officer Paul Kim.

"He's in the Chrysler Building. We're landing right here, right now." Kim turned back to see if she was joking. "Now!"

"We're out of playtime, ma'am," said Kim's co-pilot. "Fuel critical. Same with the *Silver Bullet*. If drop you, your air cover will be gone for up to an hour."

Tildascow didn't hesitate. "Put us down."

"SEC, this is Desperation One," Kim radioed to Southeastern Command. "Be advised, we are putting November down at 8333-3234. Reason to believe HPT is in the Chrysler Building."

The SEC Commander responded over their headsets. "Roger that, November. Negative on landing, that location is very hot. Infected have been rallying there for hours. We have ops in place, we'll advise when it's safe to approach. Proceed to primary LZ, over."

The infected have been rallying there.

"Then we'll go in hot," she said. "No time to waste."

"Negative, November. There is no landing zone. Wait out."

"Roger, SEC. Desperation out," said Kim.

"Where is the primary landing zone?"

"Bellevue Hospital."

Bellevue was just down 26th, already in their sights, and it was a disaster. Plumes of smoke rose from all over the complex. Escapees had taken refuge on the roof. Gurneys were strewn across the helipad.

The streets weren't any better. FDNY fire engines were pinned by vehicle pileups on First Avenue, trying to ram their way through. The firemen were locked in combat with civilians climbing aboard their truck. An overturned ambulance with its doors open lay in the center of First and 26th, looking like a turtle on its back. Gunshot pops, horns, sirens, alarms.

"SEC, Bellevue LZ is hot. Requesting redirect to grid 8333-3234."

"Negative, Desperation, you have no support," the aggravated commander replied. "Proceed to secondary LZ."

"Roger, SEC. I hear you Lima Charlie."

"Secondary LZ? Where is that?" Tildascow demanded.

"Brooklyn Naval Yard."

The Brooklyn Naval Yard was at least five miles south of Bellevue and across the Wallabout Bay. Putting down and refueling, they'd lose at least an hour. Maybe two.

"No, no. Fuck no. We're not leaving the island. Drop us here and we'll go on foot." She turned to Mantle and Jaguar in the seats behind her. "Right?"

"Hooah!" Mantle yelled.

"Drop us."

Eleven
VA Hospital Roof
East 25th & First Avenue
1:49 p.m.

Desperation One and the *Silver Bullet* roared away as Tildascow and her crew readied their gear.

They'd hopped onto the roof of the three-story VA medical building just south of Bellevue, a wide swath of snow-covered gravel. Their view of First Avenue was blocked by a raised façade, not that they could see through the thick smoke from the nearby fires. Tildascow directed Lon to cover his nose and mouth with his elbow. Mantle and Jaguar took a torch to the access door's lock.

Ilecko squeezed some of the dirty blood from his rawhide pouch as Tildascow and Lon watched over his shoulder. The red drowned in the dusty snow as they whisked smoke from their eyes. Soon the top powder collapsed, revealing the blood as it fought its way toward the Chrysler Building.

"He's there," Tildascow said loudly enough for the Shadow Stalkers. "He's fucking there."

Jaguar kicked in the metal door.

"Move fast," she said, readying her 1911. "Heads down, no spectacle."

The Shadow Stalkers led them into a tight stairwell of worn paint on cinderblock. The first landing was at a metal door marked "Third Floor" in godawful 1960's-brown cursive.

Several floors below them, a door slammed open, and a couple entered in mid-argument.

"We can't stay here!" cried a sobbing woman.

"It's safe here! It's safe here, what the fuck do you want from me!" answered a hoarse man. They kept repeating themselves.

Tildascow peered at them over the railing. They'd definitely call attention to her squad and slow them down. Or maybe she was still smarting from having to shoot that grease job from the Cougar. Either way, there had to be another stairwell nearby. She directed the Shadows with hand motions.

She unlatched the door and peeked out onto a long corridor of recovery rooms. No power, so the floor was dark except for murky swaths of sunlight cast from open rooms. No activity other than a few nurses and doctors. A battery-powered exit sign was glowing at the far end of the hall; that'd be the other stairwell.

The argument downstairs grew worse. *"What the fuck do you want from me? The fuck do you want me to do?"*

"Find someone to help us!"

"End of the hallway," she whispered to her team, "to the exit sign."

Lon nodded "affirmative." Ilecko agreed.

"Who's going to help us? Who the fuck is going to help us?"

She slowly, quietly pushed open the—

"Tildascow?"

She froze. That voice wasn't one of theirs. It was dreary, old, and it had come from beyond the door. The others heard it too. Lon's wide eyes wanted an explanation that she didn't have.

She listened carefully, but the idiots downstairs were getting louder. Then it called again. "Tildascow?"

Mantle flipped open a two-part mirror device on the barrel end of his SCAR rifle and eased it through the doorway. Tildascow leaned in for a look.

A ghostly old woman stood in the corridor, backlit by smoky blue light that cast a shadow of her wiry frame onto her loose hospital gown. Gauze crisscrossed her body like scotch tape on a broken vase and her right eye was hidden beneath a patch.

"Brianna Tildascow?" she whispered.

Tildascow pushed Mantle's weapon aside and stepped into the

hallway, leading with her 1911. Jaguar followed to flank, checking behind, and Mantle stayed at the door, watching with Lon and Ilecko.

She squared off, calling across the barrel of her gun. "Who are you?"

"I don't know," the old woman sobbed. Her lips quivered, revealing a few withered, lonely teeth.

"Were you attacked? Are you infected?"

"I don't know," she cried.

"How do you know my name?"

"He told me."

"And who is *he*?" she asked, knowing goddamn well who "he" was.

"I don't know," she sobbed, and her toothpick arms swayed as she shook her head. "I don't know."

All at once, her fear faded, her body went rigid and she raised her good eye in a dead lock with Tildascow's.

Now she sounded rehearsed: "He has a message for you, and for Yannic Ilecko and the United States of America."

"And what is that message?"

She covered her ears and took a deep breath. And then she shrieked, *"Find a cure!"*

It hurt Tildascow to watch. Spittle and blood shot from her throat as she screamed again.

"Find a cure!" And again. *"Find a cure!"*

"Okay, ma'am. Stop!" Tildascow shouted, but the woman couldn't hear her. And she couldn't stop if she tried.

Now a new voice from behind them: *"Find a cure!"*

Tildascow spun to find a wild-haired college student limping from another room. His arm was set in a cast and his face had turned savage purple as he screamed at a throat-ripping volume. *"Find a cure!"*

They overlapped each other, like a tortured version of "Row Your Boat."

More patients filtered into the hall, coming from every direction, joining the disharmony. *"Find a cure!"*

Put-put-put! Jaguar fired his rifle and shouted—

The frail weight of the old woman landed on Tildascow's back, and then she felt something tear at her neck. She whipped her elbow around and felt the woman's brittle jaw and spine snap.

She turned to find the woman on the floor, her head broken from her collar. Chunks of Tildascow's flesh were stuck between her gravestone teeth. Blood trickled from her mouth.

Then Tildascow felt the warm flow seeping down the back of her neck. She touched the wound and came back with fingers coated in blood.

More voices now, rising up from other rooms. The infected stumbled about like zombies, covering their ears and shrieking. They were oblivious to Tildascow or anyone else, but the doctors and nurses and non-infected patients bolted for the exits. Some ran right between them, unimpressed by their weapons.

And then the screams rose from the floors below, echoing up the stairwell. And from the streets outside, diminishing into oblivion. Voices in every direction, of every quality, bellowing mercilessly. Over and over.

"Find a cure!"

Twelve
New York City
2:14 p.m.

It swept across the city like a tidal wave.

They could hear it at the naval yard across Wallabout Bay, a strange din over the helicopters. It reached Rainey Park on the other side of Roosevelt Island, where the media had gathered with telescopes. Snipers protecting the shores even heard it in Edgewater, New Jersey, all the way across the Hudson River.

The rioting in Columbus Circle ceased as the infected covered their ears and began screaming.

Some of the non-infected joined in, trying to discipline the lunacy by turning the cacophony into a chant.

But there would be no discipline.

The message was the chaos.

"Find a cure!"

Thirteen
The Oval Office
2:34 p.m.

President Weston stood to greet USAF Colonel James J. Murdock, Commander of the 28th Bomb Wing out of Ellsworth Air Force Base in South Dakota. Murdock's dossier sat on the president's desk along with the personnel files of four other *Wolfsbane* candidates.

General Alan Truesdale and Chief of Staff Teddy Harrison were also there to greet Murdock as he entered and introduced himself with a salute. Truesdale returned the salute, but Weston greeted him with a measured nod. Some servicemen and women found it distasteful for a civilian, even the CINC, to co-opt the salute. Weston chose to respond with a handshake whenever possible, or a constantly grateful nod. The pundits accused him of grandstanding by breaking a tradition begun by Ronald Reagan, but as far as he was concerned, his tenure was about mending the fences the last guy knocked down. No better place to start than with his own people.

"Colonel James J. Murdock reports as ordered, *sir.*"

"At ease, Colonel," Truesdale said.

"Have a seat." Weston directed him to the hot seat. As an afterthought, he presented an awkward handshake that caught the colonel off guard. "It's nice to meet you."

"It's an honor, sir."

Weston searched the eyes of this man, who had dedicated his life to serving his country, and prepared to ask him to irreparably tarnish his name and his legacy.

Murdock had received his commission from the USAF Academy in the spring of 1989. He'd served in positions from instructor pilot to Wing Weapons Officer to Strategic Warplanner for US Central Command. He had over twenty-five hundred flight hours in the B-1B *Lancer* strategic

344

bomber and the T-38 *Talon* supersonic jet trainer. He'd garnered four major decorations, and President Clinton recognized him as a "Great American" in his 1998 State of the Union Address.

For this job, he stood apart from the other candidates because he had no children.

"You've been briefed on this operation, Colonel?" Weston knew he had, but he wanted to hear the tone of Murdock response.

"Yes sir." Appropriately somber, yet confident.

"And you're prepared to carry it out?"

"Yes sir." And firm.

Murdock was starstruck, but Weston wanted a genuine reaction from the man, not the standard military spiel. Actually, he wasn't sure *what* he wanted. Maybe he wanted to be in the cockpit with him. Maybe he wanted to reassure him that he'd be by his side in the aftermath.

Whatever it was, he just needed this guy to *talk* to him. "James—can I call you James? Or do you prefer Jim?"

"Either, sir."

"Gentlemen, would you excuse us?" Weston asked Truesdale and Teddy.

They nodded at Weston and Murdock on their way out.

"Jim," Weston began, "while we're alone I'd like you to call me Will."

"Yes sir," he said uncomfortably, before forcing out "Will."

"Jim. In 1945, Paul Tibbets and Charles Sweeny dropped atomic bombs on Japan, killing over two hundred thousand people. They faced that reality in the public and in the mirror, every day, for the rest of their lives. Protesters hounded them. Churches cursed them. Some people said they were in league with the devil. They did what their CINC asked of them, and they came home to liberal hypocrites who apologized to the Japanese right under their noses. It never relented, until they died. *After* they died, even."

"I'm familiar with their story, sir."

"Did you know that Tibbets asked not to be buried, because he thought protesters would desecrate his grave?"

The word "grave" hung in the air as Murdock nodded *yes*.

"Are you prepared to drop a weapon of mass destruction over Manhattan?"

"If those are my orders, sir, I will carry out my mission."

Weston frowned and leaned forward. "What if we were to drop all the pretenses, Jim, and we had a man-to-man exchange instead of CINC to soldier? And what if, instead of ordering you to do this, I just asked you?"

Murdock thought for a moment before responding, and in that moment, Weston realized *that* was what he wanted.

"I'd say I appreciate your asking, Will. And I'd say I gladly and proudly serve at your discretion."

Weston cleared his throat and stood. Murdock also stood, although far more rigidly. They exchanged a nod of silent understanding, and then Weston reached beneath his personnel files for an envelope that was unmarked except for his own signature across the seal. "The codes."

Murdock took the envelope. "Thank you sir."

"I appreciate your service, Colonel Murdock. And so does your country."

"Thank you sir."

Murdock saluted. Weston shook his hand.

Fourteen

39ᵗʰ & Lexington

3:07 p.m.

Lon couldn't stop shuddering, and it wasn't because of the cold.

Lexington Avenue looked as though it'd just hosted the most gruesome party ever. Dead bodies lay about like macabre confetti. The older ones had become snow popsicles. Some lay on the ground, staring at him like it was his job to wake them up. And there were dismembered limbs all over the place, little things people had just left behind. Like their arms or their legs.

The Chrysler Building loomed above them on the right side of the street, across from a less-impressive counterpart skyscraper of reflective glass. The two of them reminded Lon of Master Tolkien's *The Two Towers*.

Infected were everywhere, leaning out of buildings, kneeling on the street, standing on cars. Their eyes bulged and their necks contorted as they kept up with their forced screams. Lon's throat was killing him out of sympathy.

He couldn't have predicted Valenkov's ability to enthrall his victims in such a manner; it wasn't in any of his literature. Sure, a pact bond between master and minion was to be expected. Hell, it was practically a religion to the drama mamas writing erotic fan fics. But this sort of overt brainwashing, especially during the human phase, was completely unexpected.

He was writing his doctoral thesis in his head.

His body ached, but he still had energy. Maybe it'd come from Tildascow's pills, or maybe his metabolism had caught up with newfound bravery—or maybe that'd come from the pills, too.

They were power-walking right down the middle of the street, veering between abandoned cars. Tildascow was in the lead, followed by Jaguar. She kept scratching the bandage on her neck.

Lon couldn't shake the image of Mantle peppering that old lady with bullets. Little tiny red explosions all over her chest, punching her backward, but she couldn't be stopped.

The old woman had known Tildascow's name. Valenkov must have targeted her. But why?

"Will it happen tonight?" she'd asked Ilecko.

"Cannot be sure."

And that was all that was said. Mantle disinfected and bandaged the wound. Since then, she'd only barked orders for them to keep moving.

Lon followed their footsteps in the snow, stepping around occasional crimson patches and body parts. Ilecko kept pace next to him, looking at each screamer as if any one of them might have something new or interesting to say. In the VA hospital, in front of Bellevue and in the blocks north, they'd seen hundreds of them. Maybe thousands. And unseen voices came from everywhere. How many were inside these buildings?

Mantle kept up the rear, looking around with a doomsday gaze. When he caught Lon looking, he faked a smiling wink.

Lexington Avenue seemed to grow longer in front of them, an endless stretch of delis beneath four-story brownstones. Somehow Lon's legs kept going.

At 39th Street, an American flag hung above the entrance to a bar. The lower half had been slashed, and its red and white tendrils thrashed in the wind.

At 40th, the buildings grew to six and eight stories, a running jump to the skyscrapers in the blocks ahead. The glut of cars thickened too, so they began climbing over them instead of walking around.

Lon ducked as a low-flying helicopter thundered past. He'd get dizzy trying to count all of the aircraft in the sky. A banana 'copter with two rotors was lowering an armored truck into the next intersection. From here it looked like the truck was sinking in a quicksand of taxis.

The Shadows led them up the last great hill of vehicles before the Chrysler Building. Ilecko lifted Lon into Tildascow's grip on the steeper climbs. She'd pat him on the shoulder after pulling him up, as if that made it better.

They finally reached the military perimeter, half a block from the Chrysler Building at 42nd Street. Special ops soldiers stepped right over screamers to help them climb down the car pile.

Lon couldn't spin fast enough to take in all of the activity.

Armored personnel carriers, Humvees, and two tanks had blocked off Lexington to the north at 43rd. To the west, 42nd was blocked by a three-story dam of abandoned vehicles. An APC headed their way from the east with soldiers clinging to its outside.

Even the street markings were dizzying to this Ohio boy: A frantic crisscross pattern filled the intersection, surrounded on all sides by vertical lines. A woman had fallen in the middle of the street, her tattered clothing soaked in brown slush, her face the color of blood. Everyone went on ignoring her as she bucked and rasped through blown vocal chords, "Find a cure!"

A salty-haired gruff called Major General Jefferson Beach—*great pornstar name,* Lon thought—told them his men were having trouble inside the Chrysler Building because thick groups of infecteds had the stairs blocked. He led them north on Lexington, toward the Chrysler Building's entrance, which looked like a squat coffin lined with black marble (and that wasn't just Lon's goth soul making an observation).

The tower was dizzying and dreary from its base, an endless ladder of gray stretching into the thick smoky sky. Twin twelve-story rectangles hugged the north and south sides of the structure, looking like the legs of—

"A king on his throne," Tildascow said to herself, some kind of profundity known only to her. If there was a king up there, he had a good view of himself in the mirrored Hyatt skyscraper across the street.

On the ground level, a fashion store called Strawberry had been adapted into a makeshift holding pen. Green Berets kept their rifles trained on the growing collection of thrashing, shrieking captives.

Each soldier's backpack was affixed with Valenkov's portrait from the airport security camera. It was a smart move, but it gave Lon the eerie feeling that Valenkov was watching them from everywhere. Hell, maybe he was. Lon found himself diverting his gaze every time it met Valenkov's.

Troops had busted through the window of a drug store called "duane reade." Was that someone's name, and was he morally opposed to capital letters? These drug stores and pizza shops on the ground floors of gigantic buildings—did they, like, pay rent or something? And the people who lived or worked above—weren't they always hungry? And why would folks want to live so crammed together like this?

He'd been trying not to think about his dark goddess Elizabeth, lest he be overcome with worry. But she'd said so many times that she felt lonely here in Manhattan. It seemed impossible to Lon, to be lonely in the most crowded city in America, until he touched the crushing sensation of New York. The gigantism of everything made any one thing—or person—seem pitifully insignificant. In Ohio, his street was *his* street. Nothing truly belonged to anyone here.

Ilecko's blood droplets crept toward the coffin entrance.

"He's in there," Tildascow said, gazing up at the crown.

"It's taken a couple of hours to get to the 20th floor," said Beach. "They got it stopped up good. We're prepping to transport directly to the sixty-first-floor terrace."

"What's holding you up?"

"Nothing," he frowned, not liking her tone. "We're readying the—"

"Desperation One," she abruptly radioed, "this is November, what's your ETA to the Chrysler Building, over?"

"Five minutes, November."

"Roger that, we need pickup on Lexington north of 42nd, plenty of room to get down here. Transport to a terrace on the sixty-first floor. Over."

"Roger, November. Desperation out."

Beach's temper flared over his 'stache. "I want to send a preliminary—"

"All command units this net!" Tildascow interrupted again. "HPT is in the Chrysler Building; all units rally to this location," she said, retrieving coordinates from her loathsome GPS device, "8333-3234. I say again, 8333-3234. Over." Her "threes" sounded like "trees." She stowed her GPS, still with her eyes to the sky, and brushed off Beach. "I apologize, sir, I'm just a bit eager."

"We're *all* eager, Agent Tildascow."

"This is Central Command," the radio blared. "8333-3234. Roger that. Wilco. Over." That was followed by "Southeastern Command. Roger that. Over," and "Southwestern Command. Roger that location. Over."

Tildascow turned to her team. "The Crash Hawk will take us up to the—" She stopped short as a strange sensation swept over the whole crowd.

Thunderous silence. As if someone had hit the mute button on life.

Each person registered the uncanny effect, slowly realizing…

The screams had stopped.

Tildascow turned toward the Strawberry store, where the captives were writhing in pain.

Jaguar and Mantle followed her, rifles trained. Lon went with them, passing Ilecko, who was still gazing up at the sky.

One of the victims was a petite 20 year-old girl. She struggled to her feet, sobbing and wheezing, ignoring the guards' orders to sit back down, and groaned, "Help!"

Tildascow came closer, keeping her hip turned to hide her gun.

"Help," the girl cried. "Please help."

"We're going to help you, miss," Tildascow called. "I promise."

"Help." Now she could only mouth the word. "Help."

"We will."

The woman's face went into sudden shock. Her lids and cheeks were blackened by burst blood vessels, making her bloodshot eyes seem to glow red. For a horrible moment they rolled back and forth between Tildascow and the soldier, teasing some dark secret.

She held her breath, still looking around.

Was she about to pass out? Or die? Did she have a new message?

"Hkkk--" She choked.

"Miss?" Tildascow asked. "Are you okay?"

Her eyes rolled back in her head as she took a deep, sniffling breath...

"Miss?"

And then she howled.

Fifteen
Situation Room
The White House
3:48 p.m.

The madmen at CNN were broadcasting live from their New York studios overlooking Columbus Circle. The shaky, handheld footage they'd shot through their windows offered the best available angle on the central command post.

The heads of state watched along with the rest of the world as the soldiers staved off the rioters to maintain the landing zone for the never-ending traffic of Chinooks.

With the infected screaming themselves silly and the civilians in hiding, the command post had operated unencumbered for a glorious ninety minutes. In fact, their efficiency was so monotonous that most in the Situation Room had stopped watching.

Allison Leslie noticed it first. "Something's happening!" she screamed.

The room fell quiet as an aide turned up the TV's volume. "—screaming stopped just a minute ago, and now the victims seem to be stirring." The unseen CNN correspondents might have been shooting the footage themselves. "Yes, they're definitely conscious now. The soldiers at the edge of Columbus Circle are yelling at them, but we can't hear them."

The soldiers had their perimeter covered. The activity within the circle never slowed as the crowd came to their feet.

"There's so many of them," said another CNN correspondent, panning across the southern end of Central Park. "There must be thousands." As they sprouted like weeds, it became apparent just how decisively they outnumbered the military. "My God."

Quick pans with long-distance lenses made for nauseating viewing. Someone in the control room had the sense to cut to another camera, one with a birdseye shot of a victim who had already gotten to his feet—a teenage boy in tattered clothes, exhausted from his ordeal. The boy ran his hands through his hair and whimpered at the sky.

"What's he doing?" Luft asked, at the same time as the CNN correspondent.

Sixteen

405 Lexington Avenue at the Chrysler Building
3:48 p.m.

"Not yet! Not yet!" Lon's voice cracked through five major scales.

The victims' eyes turned yellow, fur sprouted on their faces, and their lower teeth emerged from swelling underbites. It was only the first stage of the transformation.

And it was three hours early.

Soldiers called out for instructions. Reinforcements raced to the Strawberry, where the pack had begun sizing up their captors.

The werewolves had their own reinforcements en route. A steady stream of wolfmen were traversing the vehicle pile and massing along the military perimeter.

That woman who'd been lying in the intersection slowly rose to her knees. Her soaked, dirty clothes clung to the thin fur covering her body. She panted, her shoulders bobbing, while watching the rifles turn toward her. Yellow hatred glimmered in her eyes.

"What's happening?" Tildascow asked Ilecko.

"It is when moon is bright and sky is thick," Ilecko murmured, drawing his sword in his underhand style. "Wolves come early."

Lon looked up at the "thick" sky. Storm and smoke had created a thick umbrella over the city, reflecting the moonlight from beyond the horizon. Yet another detail that had escaped his research.

"They will transform slowly," Ilecko told him in Romanian. *"We still have time. They will not attack."*

Lon relayed that to—

"This is information we could have used sooner," Tildascow grunted, reaching for her radio: "Desperation, this is November! We need immediate extract, do you read?"

"Roger that, November," the Black Hawk pilot said over the radio.

"We are one minute away. Stand by for evac."

Wolf eyes steadily materialized from corners and shadows, increasing in number and steadily closing in.

The perimeter grew tighter as soldiers backed toward their team, forming a circle of protection.

Lon wanted to believe Ilecko's promise. "You said they wouldn't attack, right?"

Ilecko silently clocked the wolf men skulking in every direction.

He said they wouldn't attack, though. He did say that.

"Switch to silver!" Tildascow yelled.

Amid a chorus of "Hooah," soldiers swapped out their tan SCARs in favor of smaller black rifles.

Tildascow switched her pistol with another in her hip holster. She checked its chamber, flipped its safety, and proffered it to Lon. "Silver bullets."

But they're not going to attack!

"Take it, Lon."

No guns! No guns for him! *Frak!* "I—I don't know what to do."

"Use both hands," she said in a soothing tone, wrapping his fingers around the handle. "Lock your elbows. Point and fire." She removed her cap and glasses and leaned in with bubblegum breath, her pretty blonde curls falling over her face. "Stay with me, kiddo."

"Uhhhkay," he sputtered. He'd never held a gun that didn't shoot water or make laser sounds. The real thing was heavier, as if to voice its serious intent.

Tildascow turned him around and rifled through his backpack, causing his flab to jiggle. She emerged with a gun identical to the one in his hand. He'd been carrying a gun?

"The werewolves are no longer civilians," she yelled to the nearby soldiers. "They are enemy targets!" As if to demonstrate, she slid the rack and aimed at the wolf woman from the intersection, who had come to her feet and begun to approach. "Weapons free!"

Bang! The crash made Lon flinch. The woman crumpled, with no reaction to the new hole in her forehead. Just like the guy outside the Cougar; no ceremony, no time to think about what it meant.

Because that caused the werewolves to attack.

A drumroll of gunfire. Howls and screams. Soldiers down. Shouts! Orders! Locations! *"Reload!" "Fuck!"* and a thousand variations.

Werewolves coming from everywhere, running upright, moving in packs, leaping over vehicles, dropping in the deluge of silver bullets.

Crashing windows, popping metal, exploding tires, shattering cement, splintering marble—everything dusted in blood.

"Desperation, we need you here!" Tildascow radioed.

Lon squeezed one shot off, but he couldn't tell where it went. *And shitballs the handle got hot!*

Ilecko pushed him down and crouched over him. His sword was at the ready, waiting for one of the pack to break through.

A wolf man dropped from the sky, his swollen claws reaching like a bird's talons—

Mantle's rifle swung upward *put-put-put* and the creature landed *splat*, convulsing in reverse transformation.

Tildascow took one of the black rifles from a dead soldier and turned on the incoming wolves with new firepower.

A thunderous vortex drowned out most of the noise as the Black Hawk descended between the Chrysler Building and the Hyatt Tower, blasting them with gun smoke. It hovered just a few feet off the ground, an incredible presence in the middle of a city street.

Tildascow lifted Lon by his belt and midget-tossed him into the cabin. He bounced off the side-facing gunner's seat and almost fell out before his foot found the rudder.

Hairy fingers latched onto the ledge on the far side of the cabin. Then a wrist emerged, extending from a dirty, fuzzy sleeve.

Lon screamed, but he couldn't hear himself over the helicopter's roar.

It was a wolf man dressed as Santa Claus. And it wasn't nearly as funny as it should've been.

The Black Hawk's pilot swung around and fired his gun, hitting weresanta in the chest and slamming it against the side-facing seat. Apparently they weren't silver rounds. Weresanta sprang into the cockpit, and the helicopter rolled toward Lon, spilling him onto the street. He crashed onto his backpack and tumbled backward, pinching his neck and biting his mother*humping* tongue again before ending up on his stomach. He rolled over—

—*blink blink*—

The Black Hawk was above him, rolled laterally so that he could see the sky straight through the cabin. And then the tail shaft whipped over like a gigantic windshield wiper. For half a breath, the Black Hawk was looking straight down at him. The cockpit window was covered in blood.

That… that couldn't be good.

The blades cut into an armored personnel carrier—*ching ching ching*—bombarding soldiers and wolves with shrapnel.

And then it belly-flopped into the Hyatt Tower.

Shattering. A downpour of glass.

Lon curled up on his knees, letting his backpack take the brunt of it. His ass burned *hot*.

More screaming, howling, crashing. Endless gunfire. Liquid flames falling from the sky. Burning corpses in every direction. A gaping wound cut through the Hyatt, spitting flames so bright he could barely see the skeleton of the Black Hawk.

Men and wolves flickered through the curtains of swirling smoke. A werewolf woman emerged from the darkness, on her belly and dragging herself toward Lon. Blackened blood seeped from her broken nose, making her grunts sound like sniffles. She tried to lunge, but her legs had—*oh man*—

Her legs had been torn off at the knees.

Lon's mind screamed, but his muscles froze and his throat misfired.

The werewolf grabbed his wrist—its palm felt like hot gravel—and it pulled him closer to those teeth—

Put-Put-Put!

The creature's chin slammed into the asphalt. Tildascow's black rifle was inches from its head. The sight of her made him want to cry, from relief or love or just because of his scorched ass.

Her eyes looked like flashlights behind her soot-covered face. "Can you move?" she yelled, sounding like she was underwater. "Are you hurt?"

Lon tried, but he couldn't answer.

She pulled him to unsteady feet and put a gun in his hand, maybe the same one she'd given him earlier. He couldn't close his fingers on the grip.

"You're in shock, it's perfectly normal," she said, calmly. *How the fuck could she be calm?* "Breathe deep and—" A rabid wolf man hurtled their way and she fired twice, flipping him backward, never breaking her thought. "Breathe deep and stay with me."

His eyes were heavy. The air was so thick, black and flickering orange.

"This will pass, Lon. You're okay. Hey…" She looked deep into his eyes and repeated his own words. "We are going to win this."

A massive figure surfaced through the smoke: Ilecko, blood-splattered and caked in soot. And then came Jaguar and Mantle, sidestepping toward them, eyes constantly shifting. The band was back together.

A thunderous groan came from the Hyatt, where the upside-down helicopter shell lost its grip and fell to the street.

"Get down!" Tildascow yelled.

She pushed him to the ground, but it made no difference. A blast wave of smoke belched from the crash, blinding Lon and ripping the air from his lungs, leaving him in pure suffocation.

And then he was floating, wondering if he was dead.

No, he was being carried. By his shoulders. The ground was moving fast beneath his floating feet.

A door slammed open and they burst into another world, one with precious cool air. Squeaky boots reminded him of gym class. Warm bodies were pressed close; they were running in a tight pack. Soldiers' voices echoed off marble as their flashlights fenced in the darkness.

"North clear!" "East clear!"

A high, curved ceiling and red marble walls made it feel as though they were running into a living heart. Ceiling murals vomited Art Deco chic onto African colors. Lon found his bearings, and he realized they'd passed through the coffin-shaped entrance. Hideous as it was, they were in the lobby of the Chrysler Building. Mantle and Jaguar were sharing his weight, holding his arms around their necks.

They hugged the right side of the triangular lobby, past an empty reception desk and elevator halls. A phalanx of soldiers barreled through another entrance and their groups merged as they cut right into a triangular stairwell, brass and gold on black marble, wrapping around a golden-piped chandelier.

By Grabthar's Hammer, did *all* of the lobbies in Manhattan look like Roddy McDowall's evil lair?

He floated up the stairs, following Tildascow's very firm ass—*hey now.* No choice but to stare, since it was the only thing he could see.

Pop! Pop! Pop! Gunfire and screams from above.

Tildascow stopped short, slamming her back into Lon's nose. "This way!"

They reached the next floor. More gunfire ahead. Fumbling footsteps and soldiers barking. Some men were backlit by the bright orange glow, kneeling over an injured comrade. "He got me," the guy screamed. "Oh God, he got me!"

"Through here!" Tildascow yelled.

They kept moving, still in their cocoon of faceless soldiers, past a fire door and into a tight stairwell shaft. Helmet lights revealed steel platforms and cement walls. At the first landing, they pushed flat against the wall to let a torrent of soldiers rush past. Their footfalls were steady percussion against the mush of banging, screaming, and gunfire coming through the walls.

Lon tried to wipe the black crud from his face, but his hands and sleeves were so dirty that he just moved it all around. He'd lost his glasses at some point, which would be a serious problem if he had to read the werewolves to death.

Mantle pushed Lon toward the stairs, and they re-entered the flow. He kept steady pressure on his back as they chased Ilecko's heels around the flights.

Soldiers broke off at each floor, covering doors and storming hallways. The ranks thinned behind them and the men ahead gained on them. Soon their small team was isolated between pockets of traffic.

His legs couldn't settle on a method of torture. Hot, then heavy, then numb, then tingly. Each step seemed steeper than the last. Jaguar and Mantle pushed harder, then lifted him outright. But Ilecko had slowed down too, and the Shadows were gasping. Just before the 30th floor, the whole team collapsed at once.

"Okay, take a breath," Tildascow said, as if it were her choice. She dropped to a squat and rifled through her backpack. One deep breath erased any struggle in her lungs.

"Not tired?" Ilecko rasped. Blackened sweat dripped from his nose. She smiled and winked. "*You* okay?"

Ilecko nodded between gasps. Lon wanted that gun back, wherever the hell it was, because he wanted to shoot her.

She removed the bandage on the back of her neck, revealing a clean patch of skin surrounding the red and purple wound from the old woman's bite. According to lore, a werewolf bite might heal at a supernatural pace, but Lon had no way to gauge such a thing. It'd been a couple of hours, and the fist-sized tear was swollen purple, jagged with tooth marks and thick with coagulated blood. Tildascow barely registered any discomfort as she replaced the bandage.

"Long way to go," she said. "Maintain a pace." She held her canteen under Lon's nose. "Sips, not gulps." As the water cut through the paste in his mouth, the stairwell rumbled. There'd been an explosion, maybe a grenade, or something bigger outside.

"Central command," Tildascow called over her radio, "this is November Zero Zero One. Do you read?"

The Shadows' headlamps converged on the radio, waiting for a response that didn't come.

"Fucked *up,* man," Mantle muttered, shaking his head.

"Southeastern Command, this is November Zero Zero One, do you read?" She wiped skin-colored streaks into the soot on her face. "Southwestern Command. Come in."

"Sheezus," Jaguar said, rubbing his head.

"Don't panic," she said. "We may not have reception in here. We'll try again from the terrace."

Another boom echoed through the stairwell.

"May not be able to get up there," Mantle said.

"Guy's been ahead of us every step of the way," Jaguar said between sips from his canteen. "Every fucking step."

"We'll catch him," Tildascow said. "He's up there."

"You really think that?" Jaguar asked. "Or is that just what he wants you to think?"

Seventeen

Chrysler Building

55th Floor

5:08 p.m.

Lon couldn't tell if he was climbing steps or dreaming that he was climbing steps. Also, he thought he saw Mister Spock give him the "Live Long and Prosper" sign back down there, and for some reason Spock had Miley Cyrus on a dog's leash, but Miley had the body of a murloc from *World of WarCraft*.

"Okay…" Tildascow started, and everyone collapsed in response. "Take a break. Five minutes. Eyes open, backs to the wall. And tape up your injuries. They can smell the blood."

How did she know that? And also, why did she have a third eye on the side of her head? And was it staring at him?

Mantle and Jaguar sat on either side of the middle landing, covering them from ahead and behind. But they hadn't seen anyone in forever. Ilecko and Tildascow sat next to Lon, shoulder to shoulder against the wall. Steam rose from Ilecko's sweaty head. The three of them must have looked like *Three Stooges: The Next Generation.* Or, at least, that's what frog-legged Miley said. Except it sounded like *blarrgargahhgargglalrlghr* in murloctongue.

Tildascow poured water into his mouth. "Small sips." It burned.

"Buh—" he struggled to say. "Buh—buh—"

Tildascow leaned in. "Whisper."

"Blarrgarglar," he wheezed, trying to ask Miley for a napkin.

"Lon?" Tildascow yelled, lifting his eyelids. He wanted to tell her he was okay, but his mouth wouldn't work. And also, the blue chick from *Avatar* told him not to. There was that too.

"We can't leave him." Mantle said.

"We're not leaving anybody. We're doing great."

363

"*You're* doing great," Jaguar huffed. "We're broke. The fuck is up with you, lady?"

Tildascow eased more water into Lon's mouth. They sat in silence for a moment, their gasps bouncing off the walls. The blue chick ran around collecting their breath in her purse. Miley tried to bite her ankles. *Get her, Miley!*

"I'm in a special program with DARPA," Tildascow finally answered. "Next-gen anti-terror. Unique training."

"So?" Jaguar asked between gasps.

"And some… designer…" she searched for a word and came up with "alterations."

Mantle hooted. "So what, you're like the Bionic Woman?"

"*No,*" she snapped. Then she whispered, "Not yet."

"I knew it!," Jaguar said. "I fucking knew it! No way a lady could do the shit you do. No offense."

"No way a man could either. Offense intended."

"I'm just glad you're on our side," said Jaguar. "Wouldn't wanna come up against shit like you in AfPak."

"I assure you, you won't," she said, flashing a penlight in Lon's eyes. "Now shut up. I never said anything, and you never heard it."

Lon followed the light, leading him to her baby blues. *Blue eyes. Pretty girl. Pretty Wonder Woman girl. No, blond hair. Supergirl… girl. Lon smiled at the pretty girl. Pretty girl smile back? Yes.*

She began kneading his thigh. "Just relax," she whispered, wriggling out of her vest to reveal a tight black jacket. "I can't have you cramp up."

Well there was no way he was going to relax with her hands *there!* She climbed over his lap into cowgirl position—

Is this real, or is this like Miley the Murloc?

—and pushed her thumbs into his hips. That felt *good.*

This is fucking real. I have no idea why this is happening, but it's real.

She moved in and he braced for impact. He'd never been so close to a girl.

Well, except the *one*.

When Lon was 15, his cousin Seth ("Meth Head Seth") brought him to a strip club where they—*wink wink*—forget to check IDs. He bought a lapdance or four from the hottest girl he'd ever met in his life: a green-eyed brunette with pigtails and draped bangs. She was wearing the hell out of a super-tight *Charlie's Angels* three-quarter-sleeve shirt—Farrah Fawcett vintage of course—and the shortest short shorts in the history of short-ass short shorts. Lon gave her all of his $76—winnings from a *Magic: the Gathering* tournament that were meant to buy a new laser mouse—so she'd gyrate over his lap for the magnificent duration of four songs: "Tempted" by Squeeze, Guns N' Roses' "Paradise City," Lil' Kim's remake of "Heartbreaker," and "Mr. Brightside" by those other guys.

Her name was Mercy. Oh, Mercy.

Boy, she is rubbing hard.

So—anyway—he thought it was really strange that Mercy just kind of went at him while other—

Oboy. Ooooooboy. Really hard.

—other people, um, were watching, as if nothing was going on. Meth Head Seth had his own girl, and there was some girl on girl action at the next—

Think about baseball. Right? That's what you're supposed to do? Baseball. How do they play baseball again?

He thought his heart was going to bust out of his chest like in *Alien*. Then it would screech and attack her, and stop this glorious rubbing.

Oh that Charlie's Angels shirt…

When Mercy kissed him goodbye, his head recoiled into a "Miller Genuine Draft" neon sign. Meth Head Seth's vodka and Red Bull came out of his nose and he spent the rest of the night whining about how bad it hurt and why did Lon have to be so stupid.

Tildascow switched to his other thigh, smiling diabolically. *WHY?*

Fuck how did this happen could the werewolves just come back please—

"It's okay to be scared, Lon," she whispered, leaning in further.

"We're all scared." He could feel the movement of her lips. "I'll bet when you get out of this, you're gonna be able to do anything. Nothing will scare you anymore. Am I right?" At least, that *might* have been what she said.

Her hands kept coming closer and closer to his goodie parts. His brain pounded with fear and desperation. And… other things pounded too.

"Promise me that when we're done with this, you're going to go see your girl face-to-face and give her a crazy *Gone with the Wind* kiss. You know what I mean?"

He forced his head to move a millimeter up and then a millimeter down.

"The kind of kiss that shows her she's safe with you." Her voice dampened the folds of his ear. "Sweep her up, so the world just drifts away."

OhhhhBonerBonerBonerBoner…

"This is what I want you to do, Lon." She lifted his chin, but fear-induced rigor mortis made him unable to comply. Instead, she tilted to meet him. Her hair tickled his cheek, her breath warmed his neck and he felt—

Holyfuckingdouble-bladedlightsabershit!

—wet, rubbery lips gently graze against his—

He snapped backward, but she caught the back of his head with her left hand, cutting off his escape. She held him firm, but she approached slowly, closing in on his lower lip. Her fingers dug into his hair and she shifted forward, her inner thighs creeping toward his waist.

Maybe she thought he was someone else?

She eased away, luring him from his crash position. Then she surged forward again, pushing with her tongue, daring his stiff lips to part.

Why am I thinking? Shouldn't I just be enjoying it? What's wrong with me? Does everybody think this much when they kiss?

Oh my God, I'm kissing somebody!

She squeezed the small of his back, forcing them even closer, and she slid upward, pushing her breasts into his collar. Glorious friction.

Then she attacked from above, mischievously stabbing with her tongue, willing his to come out and play. When they finally met, an electric tickle shot into him, a wild shudder between their locked bodies.

Then she released her grip, letting cold air between their bodies. Her lips pulled away, teasing him, taunting him, escaping—

He gripped her shoulders and took her back in, thinking only in body language, breathing free, tasting her and feeling her and pushing back.

And her hands shifted to his temples. Their tongues said their goodbyes. Their lips softened and unclasped. She pushed one last wet kiss onto his cheek and pulled away.

When he opened his eyes, the beautiful girl with the curly blond hair smiled at him. "That's how you're going to do it. And she'll love it."

Lon squinted, trying to remember what she was talking about.

Oh, right. He had a girlfriend out there. Elizabeth.

Oh, wait! Elizabeth would do *that* with him?

Tildascow sat back on her shins and wiped a streak of skin into the sweaty soot on her forehead. "Ladies and gentleladies, *that* is how you kiss a woman."

Lon smiled, reintroducing his tongue to his own mouth. Mantle was stunned to silence. Jaguar shook his head and chuckled.

Ilecko had no reaction at all. His eyes were locked on the ground.

Tildascow beamed at Lon. For a second he thought she might kiss him again. Then she smacked him on the cheek, hard enough to leave a sting.

"Who's ready for the last twenty floors?"

"I am!" he yelled.

Eighteen

Chrysler Building Stairwell
66th Floor
5:33 p.m.

Hunger.

Explosive ignition in her chest, unstoppable propulsion in her legs.

She couldn't even feel the stairs beneath her feet now. It was like she was climbing the sky, ascending on her prey.

Brianna Tildascow felt more alive than she could ever remember. And *ravenous*. She could almost smell Valenkov now. And not just him, but all of her enemies. Anyone who would threaten her home.

She had gained two flights on the others until they finally stopped at the 64th floor. They called for her to wait, but she couldn't. The ache swelled, torturous starvation.

"I'm going to scout around," she called down the stairs, performing for their concern. "I'll come back for you."

She ignored their protests and left the stairwell at the 66th floor, crossing into a dark room scarcely larger than an average Manhattan apartment. It was empty, dilapidated. Crumbling drywall left wiring and ducts exposed. The exterior windows showed only blackout. Gunfire popped from the upper floors. Her flashlight glowed thick as a sword in the unsettled plaster dust, chasing the taste on her tongue.

At the door to the southwest stairwell, a lone soldier lay facedown in a paste of crimson drywall powder. His blood was sprayed across the wall.

She flipped the body over, no time or need to be delicate. He was Army, a PFC Wissihickon, probably 25. Someone had torn off the right side of his handsome face.

She leaned in for a close look at the wound. Severe bone damage from heavy impact. Fractures of the zygomatic arch, the orbital floor, and the maxilla. The mandible wrenched free of the cranium. Tooth shrapnel had drilled through his intact cheek.

He'd died quickly, not much blood on the floor. And he was still warm. She unzipped his jacket and pulled back his collar, exposing the olive flesh above the thick meat of his pecs. His sweet musk soaked her tongue.

Blood seeped from the innards of his throat. She pulled off her glove to feel its heat. It ran into her palm, lingering in the grooves of her fingerprints.

She couldn't help but bring it to her tongue—*just once*—sticky and thick and tingling of metal.

If only she could—

"You know him or something?"

A light pierced the darkness of the forest and the others scattered.

"No," Tildascow said, confused about everything. It was Mantle, and he wasn't alone behind his light. "He's dead."

Mantle's light swept down to the soldier's ruined face. "Yeah, I reckon he's clear on that fact. You alright?"

"Yeah."

This room—was this where she'd been a moment ago?

She knew this place, or knew *of* it. It was once a posh lounge, the bottom floor of a three-story speakeasy called the Cloud Club.

Yes. Yes—she'd recorded details of the Chrysler Building in her memory, because it was a notable New York landmark, and majority-owned by a United Arab Emirates sovereign wealth fund.

"Nobody owns this space?" Mantle asked. "It's like a ghost town."

"Fuckin' spooky," Jaguar responded, running his light along the walls. "I thought this shit would be posh."

The Chrysler Building had been a symbol of hollow American pride from day one. During its construction, Walter Chrysler was locked in a race to claim the title of the world's tallest building. He secretly erected a larger spire to climb above the Eiffel Tower, and have it become the first building to break one thousand feet. But only days after those rivets were placed, the stock market collapsed and plunged the country into the Great Depression. The elite suits persevered in their Cloud Club, coasting above Prohibition, but eventually even the mightiest fell from the sky. This place, along with most of the Chrysler Building's office space, had gone unoccupied for more than 40 years.

Tildascow clung to those details. There were the elevator banks, opening adjacent to a bronze and marble staircase. There were Mantle and Jaguar and Ilecko and Lon, talking about something. The body. The blood. Her watch: It was 5:42, only 90 minutes till moonrise.

But were there also trees? A swampy forest of green and black. Eyes, glowing through the darkness, watching over them all. Howling.

"You okay?" Lon asked.

She nodded.

There was no forest and there were no goddamned eyes. There was the metal of the rifle in her hand, the burn of the wound on her neck, and the sounds of gunfire above.

She came to her feet and nodded Jaguar toward the stairwell door.

When he took the lead, she realized Ilecko had been standing behind him with his sword at the ready. Her chest caught fire, the same as it had with Lon. She wanted to throw herself at him, to fight and fuck and rip each other—

Goddammit! She shook her head, fighting her way back.

"Your technology cannot save you from this," Ilecko whispered.

"We'll see about that."

He waited for her to go first up the stairs and she did, ceding him the tactical advantage of her back. Lon followed, still gloriously oblivious thanks to the pep hump.

A soldier greeted Jaguar at the next landing. "This floor and the next one are secure," he said. "We still ain't sure about what's at the top."

Bright lanterns revealed the 67th and 68th floors, a two-story gallery that had been converted into a bivouac with heavy military activity. No introductions were necessary; you were human, or you were the enemy.

They were escorted upstairs, to another bi-level space, some kind of office with auburn walls, marble floors, and a high ceiling. They'd reached the triangular windows of the crown, which stretched beyond the ceiling and floor, creating the disconcerting illusion that the walls weren't solid. Outside, they could see a Chinook helicopter descending over a landing zone on the roof of the MetLife Building.

Here was another staircase, spiral with irregular platforms that could have been cut from the sunburst windows. Up they went: Jaguar, Tildascow, Ilecko, Lon, and then Mantle.

At the 71st floor, the building tapered to less than five thousand square feet. This whole level was just one big office, an architectural firm with glass walls.

Beyond the lobby, shapes folded and twisted between the strobing light of gunfire. Howling and screams were punctuated with bangs. Frantic soldiers scurried about, taking cover behind furniture, peering through night-vision goggles.

Tildascow squeezed past Jaguar and the thicket of milling soldiers. They called for her, but there was no time to waste. She entered the forest, creeping between the desks and the chairs and the trees. Through the mist, she saw the wolves.

Her eyes fell on the carpet—or was it soil?

She was crouched, but now she noticed an urge to fall forward onto her hands, to let loose the tension in her legs and run on all fours.

Join us, they howled. *Hunt with us.*

She renewed her grip on her 9mm rifle. *Pop pop*—her shots found the wolves through metal underbrush.

They came in response, rampaging across shattered furniture, some on twos and some on fours, each one reaching with its wicked claws. Their snouts were extended, their limbs now covered in fur. *Tick tock. Tick tock.*

The front line fell under the beasts, but her shots would not miss.

Others fell in beside her, including Jaguar and Mantle.

The wolves filtered down from the access stairs to the tower's spire. Dozens came and fell under their torrent of silver bullets, until all that remained were the death rattles of their reverse transformations.

The soldiers took their tentative steps, but she knew it was clear. She bolted for the stairs, racing over fallen bodies and ruined furniture.

"Where are you going?" called Jaguar.

"It's all clear!"

The stairwell was tight, with brick walls taking arbitrary turns around uneven landings. There was no 72nd floor at all; its passing was marked only by an etching on the wall. The 73rd was a half-story of twenty-seven hundred square feet, surrounded by the triangular windows cut into odd geometry. She crossed between a water tank and the tower elevator's motors to turn and ascend further.

"Valenkov!" she screamed. So close.

"Stati așa!" Ilecko called from below.

Up she went, past a dark room with transformer coffers and an abandoned radio station. The temperature dropped with each step, ten and then twenty below zero.

Finally, the last steps.

Eighteen narrow slabs of concrete, covered in a thick skin of frozen blood.

And then there was the final door. The wind howled from behind it.

"Valenkov!" she yelled again.

She climbed the steps, slipping over the iced blood.

The door had no lock, only a loose handle. Her left hand vibrated as she reached for it; her right tightened on her silver-loaded Glock.

The door opened with no resistance.

Nineteen

Joint Base Andrews

5:55 p.m.

Colonel Murdock took a last walk around his aircraft, a supersonic bomber called the B-1B Lancer. Like all of the airmen, he knew her as the "Bone." He had flown her over Iraq and Kosovo, saying a proper American good morning to the enemy with 2,000-lb JDAMs. Hell, damn near half of the bombs dropped on the Arabs came from Bones.

Murdock was at home in the air, and the Bone was his bachelor pad. From the profile, she looked like a supermodel: long and thin with a bulbous cockpit. With her variable-position swept wings, most folks assumed she was a fighter—but she was even better. Uncle Sam had mothballed their B-52 bombers and F-117 fighters in their rush up to the all-in-one F/A-22 Raptors, but they'd left the Bones running because they were the only bombers that could withstand a defense.

He walked each 150-foot side of the towering bomber as the maintenance crew finished up. The weapons loading team drove off with their trailer, leaving thirty CBU-191 cluster missiles in the three internal bomb bays.

He took a lingering look at the northern horizon. Everything looked fine from here, but somewhere out there Manhattan was burning.

He donned his helmet and climbed the ten-rung ladder on the underside of the aircraft. In the aft crew station, the system officers were running their pre-flight checklists. He slapped their helmets and crossed through the galley to the front cockpit, where his co-pilot was in prep.

Murdock took his seat before the Bone's flight stick and checked his radio. "Command, this is the *Lunar Eclipse.*"

Twenty
The Chrysler Building
75th Floor
5:59 p.m.

There were windows on the 75th floor. It was open like a bell tower, a needle's eye in the wild winds almost a thousand feet off the ground.

Thirty degrees below zero smothered Brianna Tildascow as she stepped into the deafening gyre. Her eyes fought to close, her skin went numb.

It was empty.

Frozen blood nearly covered the floor. Probably gallons of it, no doubt intended to misdirect Ilecko's test. He'd used it to paint his message on beams and crossbar. "Find a cure." Written in his own blood.

"He knows I track him." Ilecko arrived behind her, followed by the Shadows. They took turns peeking into the tower and then retreating to the relative warmth of the brick stairwell.

She stood in the center, the winds pounding her from every side. She tracked the blood streaks, retracing his steps, following his ghost around the room. And even as she did, she could feel his eyes, watching from closer than over her shoulder. Watching her watch him.

"So what now, we're screwed?" Jaguar asked.

"Two more hours 'fore sunset." Mantle said.

Jaguar asked Ilecko: "You got any other ways to track him?"

Ilecko had no reply.

"We can't be done," Lon said. "Right? Tildascow?"

"We're not done."

The last message he wrote was the largest. It was scrawled across the crossbeam facing the door. The blood had frozen almost as quickly as he'd smeared it on the metal. And then he'd poured his containers onto the floor—he'd had three of them. One he poured in the center, another along the edges, and the last down the stairs.

Down the stairs he went.

And she chased him.

"Where ya goin'?"

"After him," she said.

"Hooah," Mantle shouted, falling in line behind her.

"We're going back down?" Lon whined.

She yanked out her radio, resisting the urge to smash it into the wall. "Silver Bullet, this is November Zero Zero One, we need ten-minute evac from the observation terrace of the Chrysler Building at the 61st floor, over."

"This is Silver Bullet, November, roger on your evac. Proceed to the south terrace. Out."

"Where do you go?" she muttered to herself, pounding down the stairs. Her footfalls rattled like a drumroll.

You go all the way down, onto the street. You stand in front of the Chrysler Building, looking up with satisfaction, knowing that's where you'd trap us. And then where do you go?

Manhattan is going to be annihilated. You have to know that.

Where do you go?

You leave, dummy.

"Hold up!" called one of the Shadows.

"I'll meet you there!" she yelled, unable to slow down, uninterested in trying. She navigated the turns through the eccentric upper floors of the crown, watching Valenkov do the same, and returned to the primary stairs.

The Green Berets were hollering on their radios, sending back word that Valenkov wasn't here. She felt their eyes as she passed them, looking like she was on the heels of someone they couldn't see.

And there were the other eyes, glowing in the forest, beckoning her to join them in the hunt. The pressure on her neck returned, pushing her down to all fours. She lifted her head and straightened her back, refusing to succumb.

The wolves were everywhere, empowering her to go faster, to lope and leap. The Green Berets and the walls and the stairs jockeyed against the forest and the call of flesh.

She found herself repeatedly snapping awake in mid-stride, each time groggier, further from her body and the material world.

No. She bit into her hand. Her skin tore easily to her sharpened teeth. *Fight to stay here. Focus on the numbers.*

67. 65.

61.

She blasted from the stairwell and followed the breeze through the hallway, passing through the darkening forest to reach the balcony.

The wind on the 61st floor terrace was downright balmy compared to the observation tower. Her boots crunched in trampled snow, a reminder that she was on concrete, not soil.

She stood at the very edge of the building, atop the southeast eagle gargoyle. Southern Manhattan was sprawled beneath her, jumbled dominoes in uneven stacks. Countless spotlights were playing hide-and-seek between the monolithic buildings and the thick plumes of smoke. The Hyatt Tower still shimmered orange from the flames below, but the ground was lost in blackout.

Tildascow felt a buzz in her palm, her post-hypnotic reminder to take her pills. That meant it was just after six, an hour until moonrise. The government was running out of time. Their last-resort scenario had to be underway.

She took her pills—a speedloader of six unmarked capsules in a gel pack—and shook her head clear. Even if she couldn't see the ground she knew it was there, and she knew Valenkov had stood there, looking up.

And then where do you go?

The wolves were at her side, calling her. Everything in her body and soul screamed to join them on four legs. He was there too, her would-be master.

She pulled off her glove, wincing as it stuck to where she'd just bitten into her flesh. She took a deep breath, steeling herself to bite again, to inflict enough pain to force him from her mind. And then—

—then she realized that if he was inside her mind, she could capture him.

She closed her eyes and took a deep breath, purging her thoughts and abandoning the physical. She reached deep into her subconscious, where she kept her inner truth, and she searched for the intruder.

What she found was sound.

A rushing waterfall of harmony crashed into her, cloaking her in sudden warmth and muting the residual noise in her mind, the buzz she'd never been able to escape. It was glorious music, a concordance of strings, and in the middle of it she found the first true silence she'd ever felt in her life.

So many hours meditating, such rigorous training to align her body and mind, and she'd never even imagined such harmony. And yet it was so breathtakingly simple.

Within the harmony, all concepts were one.

She could feel her own awareness: Wind. Smoke. Sirens.

And she could feel his awareness: Love. Rage. Howling.

The sound changed. It was ever so slight, but anything in comparison was harrowing discordance. The noise returned, the failure and the fear and the pain and the rage. Her heart cried abandonment.

Let me back in. Please. I'll do anything you want.

A hand reached from within. A perfect, powerful hand she knew to be Demetrius Valenkov's.

Come with me, he said. *Come to salvation.*

She took his hand and she wrenched him out.

Come fight me in hell.

The wolf attacked and she fled, naked and defenseless, suddenly unable to navigate the chaos in her own mind. Each refuge was more dangerous than the last. The FBI, the Army, the halfway houses and juvie halls and detention centers, the nights on the streets, the fights and the rapes. The wolf had turned her against herself, and their horrible noise smashed down every door until finally even the walls crumbled. There was no place left to go but home.

But why was the front door open?

Not here. Please. Not here.

All of her conviction failed in a heartbeat. She wouldn't go in, no matter if it cost her everything. She turned and waited for the wolf, standing on the gravel driveway where the limo had dropped her off, naked and dirty and bloody, and she prepared for an unconditional surrender.

But he didn't come. In fact, as her dread subsided, she could hear the harmony again. It was emanating from within the house.

She ran toward the open door—there was Chester, the best dog ever! And the cement path was clean; she couldn't remember them ever not covered in bloody footprints. There were their names!

Mom + Dad + Brianna '82

She barreled through the door. *Mom! Mom!*

And there was Mom. The harmony was her soft lips, her glowing eyes, and her golden curls; so safe and warm. She smiled low and her eyes scrunched, and Brianna knew that meant she was going to tell her she loved her.

But the wolf was with them.

He ripped open her mother's neck and the blood sprayed all the way to the ceiling. The harmony was silenced again.

The agony pushed at the transformation.

Leave the pain behind. Run with us.

No. I won't give up the fight.

Find a cure. It is the only way.

There isn't enough time.

You will not find me.

We don't have to—

They will fail.

No, we—

I know.

She reached out and found his throat.

Clench and she forced him to his knees, crushing his windpipe within her claw. His yellow eyes squinted as he groped, pulling her arms, swiping at her face. But she had him.

She lifted him away from her mother's corpse. The blood dripped from the dining room ceiling, but it fell from vacuum-sealed metal.

She slammed him against the wall, knocking down their family portraits. He kicked off and they stumbled backward, tripping over her father's body and onto the orange couch where she used to hide her extra Oreos.

The wolf crashed into a desk—no, it was a metal console. An ID card and a key ring sat on top of it. They were next to a hazy square of light, maybe a monitor.

She sprang from the couch, hitting hard at the top of his throat, trying to break his neck. His head plowed into clear glass, landing with a solid thunk that said his skull sloshed but didn't break. The glass was a window, smeared by confusion, looking out over a clear, star-filled sky.

Suddenly there was a figure floating above them, a young and beautiful dark-haired woman in a dress of creamy silk. The harmony whispered from within her, as if she breathed it in and out. But she wasn't breathing. Her head rested on her shoulder, her eyes were closed. And she wasn't floating.

It was Ecaterina, his wife. And she was impaled upon a stake.

And then Tildascow was back on the Chrysler Building's gargoyle, back to the freezing, smoky wind, looking out over the city, and not at the starry sky in Valenkov's mind.

"Tildascow?" Lon asked. The others had arrived behind her. "You're not gonna jump, are you?"

"No, I'm just—" Rather than explaining, she reached for her radio. "Silver Bullet, this is November Zero Zero One, we are ready for pickup. What's your ETA?"

"Roger that, November," responded Beethoven. "Be advised, a Black

Hawk is en route."

Weak cheers came from the team, and then weaker laughs at the weakness of their cheers.

"Roger that, Bullet," Mantle responded over his own radio. "Thank you kindly, my brother. November Out."

"See you in the red zone, guys. Bullet out."

Tildascow went back into her mind, re-examining everything she'd just seen. The vacuum-sealed metal on the ceiling, the console with the keys and the ID ring, and Ecaterina—they came from his mind. There were glowing monitors on the console, and he was near a window looking out on a clear night sky.

But Manhattan was choking in glowing smoke. Could he have left the island after all?

No. Still, she was sure. Logic be damned, she could *feel* his closeness, just as she could feel the others surrounding her in the forest. Maybe it wasn't *she* that could feel him; maybe it was the wolf. But it was palpable, and it was real.

"November Zero Zero One," their radios blared, "this is Mongoose Zero Three, coming in for pickup, ETA two minutes."

The console, the ID card, the monitor—what was on that monitor?

Hazy lettering on the screen, white over black.

She closed her eyes, shutting out the wolves and their beckoning howls.

The digits coalesced like a memory rediscovered.

KAM0062 UNGAXXINT 010211 18:12:10

She'd seen that code before.

U. N. G. A.

"United Nations," she blurted. "General Assembly." As her mind caught up to her mouth, she turned to the others. "United Nations. He's at the United Nations."

Of course! That's why he took out the VPN! Killing the network interrupted their eyes on the plaza, giving him a chance to enter the UN without being seen.

"What? Are you sure?" asked Jaguar.

"Oh yeah," she muttered. The pieces rushed together. "I'm sure."

The doomsday shelter. She should have known—*should have known!*

The UN Plaza always drove her bonkers. Major real estate right on the edge of Manhattan that isn't held accountable to the laws or the eyes of the United States government? And it plays home to strangers from all parts of the world, allowing them to go unmonitored because of this ridiculous concept of diplomatic immunity? Who in the World Trade Center had immunity? It infuriated her that the UN was an acceptable liability to the FBI.

A little research made it far scarier.

An architect named Wallace Harrison had spearheaded the plaza's design team. He got the job because he was the personal draftsman of Nelson Rockefeller, whose family donated the lot for the United Nations Headquarters.

The Rockefellers were descendants of the richest man who ever lived. Their influential tendrils reached into oil, industry, banking, and politics—they were the first true global empire. They were also notoriously secretive.

The family was rumored to be involved in any number of secret societies and clandestine activities. More than one legitimate historian believed the Rockefellers were in control of the Illuminati, a secret society that had allegedly manipulated society, politics, and economics for centuries. Some kooks claimed the Rockefellers were in cahoots with the devil.

Whatever nuggets of truth were in those rumors, architect Wallace Harrison was the man who hid them. He came to the Rockefellers' attention in the 1930s when, as a young upstart on the Rockefeller Center design team, he masterminded the underground network throughout the complex. Next he created private homes for the family, sleight-of-hand designs with hidden rooms and secret entrances.

It was clear that Harrison had a talent for hiding things, and the Rockefellers needed things hidden.

It was just after World War II, when the concept of weapons of mass destruction first entered the zeitgeist. The Rockefeller family wouldn't be beholden to the whims of any government that might be stupid enough to get into a cataclysmic barfight. They pulled strings to bring the UN to them, even donated their own real estate for the complex. Once the land became international territory, no longer a part of the United States of America, they were free from the prying eyes of New York's zoning commissions, fire codes, and safety inspectors. Free for Harrison to go wild, conducting his own underground construction as an international team of architects collaborated on the General Assembly, Conference, and Secretariat buildings.

According to legend, what Harrison created was more than just a long-term disaster shelter. It was a massive underground habitat, some kind of self-contained ecosystem that could serve as a new world for the Rockefellers (and maybe the UN's VIPs).

It's a rich madman's secret haven, with no accountability to our government or society, and it's right beneath our feet.

My dearest Baron Dracula Valenkov… if you were in New York and you knew the place was going to be decimated, where else would you go?

Tildascow smiled to herself and kicked snow into the abyss. From the south terrace of the Chrysler Building, she looked out over 42nd Street. The United Nations Plaza was at cusp of the East River, less than half a mile away.

"Makes sense," said Mantle. "Fuck, makes perfect sense."

"Let's go get that motherfucker," said Jaguar.

"All command units this net!" Tildascow called into her radio. "This is November Zero Zero One. HPT is in United Nations Plaza. I repeat, HPT is in United Nations Plaza. He'll be in a bomb shelter underneath the complex. It should be accessible from near the General Assembly Hall. Divert all forces—send everyone!"

She couldn't discern any of the static-filled radio chatter, but at least some of it sounded affirmative. They could only hope there was still someone in charge of this show.

"Here we go!" Jaguar yelled.

Distant lights cut through the sky. Blue on the left, red on the right, with blinkers alternating between the fuselage and tail. Their Crash Hawk was here.

She stepped back onto the terrace proper and dialed her BlackBerry, waiting through the irregular beeps indicating patching connections. Somewhere at the end of it would be the Attorney General and, hopefully, the president.

Slowly, the soothing whup of the Black Hawk rose above the radio chatter.

"Donut Hut!" said a cheerful voice answering the phone.

"This is Special Agent Brianna Tildascow, patch me through to the Attorney General."

No response came, just more beeps. More waiting.

"What the fuck?" Mantle mumbled.

She looked up to find the Black Hawk's lights shaking. At least, it *seemed* like they were shaking—it could've easily been the shifting smoke.

She squinted into the darkness, trying to purge the thought playing the drums in her mind: *Crash Hawk.*

"What's happening?" Lon asked.

The lights stabilized. A moment later, everyone exhaled.

"Call over to them," she ordered, still listening to beeps on her phone.

"Mongoose Zero Three," Mantle radioed, "this is November Zero Zero One, what's your situation, over?"

No response.

"Mongoose—" Mantle went silent as the lights wobbled again.

No question that the helicopter was teetering. Now it was drifting right.

Tildascow's phone went dead. She cursed and redialed.

The Black Hawk veered further and began to sink. The Shadows, Lon, and Ilecko leaned on their hips, like bowlers trying to keep it out of the gutter. It was just a block away now.

But it wasn't going to make it. Tildascow stepped away from the others so she could hear the phone.

"Oh no… no, man… pull up. Pull up…" Jaguar yelled.

"Come on, come on…" Mantle cried. "Mongoose, can you hear me?"

"Donut Hut!"

"This is Tildascow, patch me through to the AG!"

"I did—"

"Do it again!"

More clicks and connections.

The Black Hawk went muffled as it dipped below the terrace. A sickening moment later, the heat and fury of the crash roared upward.

"The fuck is going on?" Mantle screamed.

And her BlackBerry went dead again. *Fuck!*

"Silver Bullet," she radioed, "This is November. Our limo went down, Beethoven, we need you here *now.*"

"Say again, November. What happened?"

"I don't know. 'Crash Hawk' happened. It took a nose dive somewhere on 42nd Street. Lines are down and I can't get through to anybody. I know where he is, man, you've got to come get us."

"He can't pick five of us up in an Apache," Mantle said. Jaguar shook his head to quiet Mantle.

A minute felt like an hour as they watched her radio for a response.

"We are en route, November," Beethoven radioed. "ETA three minutes."

"Roger that. November out."

Tildascow went to dial her shitsucking BlackBerry again.

But the phone faded away, and the ground and the building darkened, and she was in the forest again.

The wolves weren't alongside her anymore.

Now they had her surrounded.

From somewhere in the thicket, Ilecko called out in Romanian.

They'd stopped beckoning.

Now they were growling.

And then she heard Lon. "Tildascow!"

Now she was their enemy.

She felt a tug on her arm, and then Lon was in front of her, pulling her through onrushing snowflakes. They crossed the terrace toward the ledge, where the others were looking down and yelling about something. She reached the rail and looked over the side.

The werewolves were climbing the side of the building, digging their claws into metal and masonry.

Hundreds of them. No—

Thousands.

PART SEVEN

One
Situation Room
6:02 p.m.

The werewolves could have overrun the central command post in Columbus Circle whenever they wanted; that much was clear when they finally did. Their strikes were coordinated from odd directions, giving the soldiers whiplash as their own ranks were thinned.

The final, decisive push came from all sides, laying waste to the men and their machines. If the soldiers had any chance, the shaky CNN footage missed it.

"Reports!" Truesdale yelled over the din.

Everyone was on the phone, but nobody knew anything. They hadn't heard from any of the command posts, and after the assault they'd just witnessed, Weston didn't expect that they would.

"Helicopters are down everywhere," said Shinick, the AG.

"How are they taking out helicopters?" yelled Leslie.

"We lost the MetLife landing zone," an aide called.

"Northeast command is down!" yelled another. And the hits kept coming, on top of one another, as news filtered in from the Watch Center.

"Have all units fall back. Lock down the exits," Truesdale ordered, and his men sent out word. "Get on the line with Andrews, get them in the air."

The jittery CNN camera panned down to Broadway, where countless werewolves ran on all fours, marching with an eerie single-mindedness toward Columbus Circle, like an army in extreme fast-forward.

When the shot panned over, the command post was just a memory. In fact, the werewolf marathon trampled right over the remains and continued southeast down Broadway.

"Looks like they've got somewhere to be," Weston thought out loud.

Two

Chrysler Building 61st Floor Terrace
6:03 p.m.

"Back back back!"

Tildascow grabbed Lon by the collar and dragged him back to a safe distance. As the others fell in beside them, she fished out that silver-loaded Glock and closed his fingers around its handle. "Both hands, elbows locked."

His eyes were fear-struck, but he nodded and firmly grasped the weapon.

She flicked her Colt 9mm SMG's switch from SAFE to SEMI. Ilecko drew his Anelace in reverse grip. Jaguar and Mantle steadied themselves.

"Beethoven, we need you down here right now!" she radioed. "Enemy targets on the side of the building! I repeat—enemy targets on the side of the building!"

The first werewolf caught their spotlights like a rock star. Its human features were completely lost behind its canine snout, swept-back ears, and thick grey fur. It even moved like a wolf, creeping over the ledge and skulking on all fours, head below its hunched shoulders.

Mantle put two shots into its forehead. Three more sets of claws poked up.

"We gotta fall back!" Jaguar yelled.

"They'll trap us in the building," Tildascow said. "Stick to coverage zones." She directionally assigned Mantle, herself, and Jaguar. "Conserve ammo; one silver shot puts them down."

The *put-put-put* of their rifles staggered as they dropped the wolves, but they only came quicker and thicker.

Tildascow emptied her twenty-round magazine in less than a minute. "Reloading!" she yelled, and the others picked up her slack as she slapped in a fresh 32-rounder.

Faster and faster the werewolves came, up to eight across, fearlessly rushing into the firing squad. Mantle's rifle went silent as he reloaded. Lon squeezed off intermittent *bangs* on top of their *put-puts.*

Ilecko crouched with his sword arm at his side, pre-empting the creatures' ability to attack low. Tildascow hoped it wouldn't come to hand-to-hand, but—

"Behind!"

Mantle swung and shot a pair of werewolves rushing through the open door. They tumbled into the snow, screeching from the silver infection. Gunfire lit up the hallway inside; the Green Berets were making a stand against the creatures coming up the stairs.

Tildascow clicked empty and patted herself down for another magazine.

"I need a magazine!" she called, but Mantle and Jaguar were too busy sweeping side-to-side, firing single shots.

And the wolves kept coming, scrambling over their fallen pack mates, reaching ever closer. Tildascow could feel their singular hunger. Valenkov was in their minds; every one of them sensed a pentagram on her palm.

A werewolf soared over the others, hurtling toward Tildascow, claws outstretched—

Ilecko swept upward with his Anelace, rising under the creature and meeting its chest with his blade. He carried its momentum into a backward toss and the werewolf landed in the snow, rolling in a death shriek and reverse transformation. Then Ilecko returned to his crouch, silently waiting for his next victim.

"I'm out!" Jaguar yelled. As he replaced his cartridge, Mantle emptied his own even faster. The pile of bodies at the balcony had grown higher than the guardrail and there was no end in sight.

Mantle's rifle emptied and Lon's last shot went wild. And then there was silence. The emerging wolves padded onto the terrace, stepping over their fallen brethren and spreading out to flank, always watching and snarling.

Jaguar reloaded—"Last mag!"—and sprayed the wolves with quick, precise shots. But each one only delayed the inevitable. One, two, three—

"Silver Bullet, we need you right now!" she yelled into her radio.

—four, five, six—

Another werewolf came galloping from the building behind them. As it cleared the sliding glass door, Ilecko threw his Anelace. The wolf tried to leap out of the way, but it caught him nearly flush with his chest, sending him rolling head over tail to stop right at their feet. Ilecko wiped his sword on the creature's retreating fur.

Jaguar's shots kept coming. Seven, eight, nine, ten, eleven, twelve—

—thirteen, fourteen, fifteen—

She could taste their hunger on her own tongue, so strong that she could easily have bitten into her own flesh.

"That a 32?" Mantle asked.

Jaguar shook his head, his smoky breaths firing from his nose.

Twenty shots. Five more and they were hand-to-hand.

Tildascow dropped her empty rifle and entered fighting stance: left leg back supporting her weight, up on the toes, knees bent, elbows in, arms up, and an icepick-gripped dagger in each hand. She didn't have a cute name for her style, which she'd cobbled together with help from DARPA's combat scientists, the FBI's martial arts experts, and her Modern Army Combatives training. She'd assimilated large chunks of Krav Maga and semper fu, but her primary concern was weight distribution, observant countermoves and appropriated momentum. She didn't beat people up, she kept them moving until they exposed a weak spot in their skeletal or muscular structure. The rest was up to her.

Still, with so many swinging claws, it'd only take one hit to a major artery to end her fight.

—sixteen, seventeen—

Saliva rushed across her tongue. It was so tempting to drop to all fours, to fight with her jaw.

—eighteen, nineteen—

"Last shot!" Jaguar yelled, scanning the ledge, choosing among three targets as they slinked onto the balcony, leading with their bulging forearms.

"Save it!" she yelled. "We go hand-to-hand!"

Jaguar strapped his rifle and drew his own knife. Mantle had already done the same. Ilecko was in his crouched position.

Still more reinforcements cresting the balcony.

They held their breath.

Time stood still.

And then the *Silver Bullet* roared around the Chrysler's crown, yawing into an airborne skid, unleashing hellfire from the 30mm chain gun mounted beneath its nose. *Rat-a-tat-a-tat-a-tat*, ten rounds per second plinking as the armor-piercing rounds tore through the balcony, shattering the werewolves' bones.

As the werewolves that had already reached the balcony turned in surprise, Jaguar and Mantle pounced with their knives.

Beethoven saluted from his rear, higher seat in the Apache's cockpit.

"Let's make this quick, November," Beethoven radioed. "They look hungry." The gunner in the lower front seat shifted the cannon toward the face of the building and opened fire again, picking off climbing werewolves while punching through masonry and glass.

"Be advised, you are going to sit on the EFABs and attach yourselves to the fuselage. I've jettisoned the wing stores to compensate for your weight."

"Five to fly bitch?" Mantle yelled. "Gotta be fucking kidding me."

"What does that mean?" Lon asked, flinching as the chain gun let loose another barrage.

"The outside," Tildascow said. "It's okay."

"The outside? The outside you mean the *outside?*"

"Drop your backpacks," yelled Jaguar. "Any extra weight's gotta go."

"How do you ride on the outside?"

Jaguar yanked Lon free of his backpack and pushed him into Tildascow's back. Using straps from his stores, he linked them together via D-rings in their vests. As he crossed Tildascow's front, he gravely looked into her eyes. "This is going to be a rough ride."

Mantle took over with Ilecko, wrapping buckles around his chest in preparation for attachment to the left side of the bird. Ilecko muttered in Romanian and Mantle hopelessly shook his head.

"Hang in there," Tildascow whispered to Lon.

"Is that supposed to be funny?"

The *Silver Bullet* inched forward and rotated. Beethoven eyed the blades as they crept dangerously close to the tower's edge. The gunner opened his cockpit window and handed fresh rifles to the Shadows, and Mantle immediately opened fire on the next wave of werewolves, now coming at an equal rate from the building and the ledge.

Jaguar directed the linked pair of Tildascow and Lon to sit on the Extended Forward Avionics Bay, a tight jutting panel beneath the right side of the *Silver Bullet's* cockpit. They only had a few inches of perch for their left ass cheeks.

"Are you kidding me?" Lon cried.

Jaguar fastened Tildascow against the fuselage and interlocked her bindings with Lon's. Her right foot could reach the wing for support, but the left would dangle.

Dangle.

"No, no," Lon said as Jaguar strapped him in. "We can't do this."

Jaguar waved an "okay" signal at the pair and threw a circular motion at the cockpit. Tildascow tightened her hold on Lon.

"Close your eyes," she whispered.

And her guts swung free as the helicopter rotated to allow Mantle and Ilecko access to the other side. She and Lon were suspended over infinity, looking up into the sky as Beethoven compensated for their extra weight.

They could feel the chopper buck as Mantle and Ilecko put their weight on the fuselage, as if they'd climbed onto the other end of a seesaw.

She felt a pat on her shoulder and looked up into the wind shear. Beethoven leaned through the side door of the cockpit, passing her a SIG 226 semiauto loaded with silver. She took the weapon with her one free hand. Beethoven gave her a "thumbs up" and closed the door on the cockpit.

Lon screamed as they abruptly swung again, back to where they'd started. Jaguar was the last man on the balcony, and he was still picking off incoming werewolves. When they came to a stop, he dropped his rifle and hastily secured himself in front of Lon, banging on the cockpit just as the last ring locked.

They lurched backward and dropped harshly as the helicopter protested their weight. Tildascow looked down—far down—on East 42nd Street, where toppled military lights illuminated Lexington. A fire burned further east, probably from the second Black Hawk.

"Incoming!" Jaguar shouted.

A werewolf loped across the terrace, fearlessly barreling toward them. Tildascow fought to slide the rack on her pistol with only one free hand.

The wolf raced onto the eagle gargoyle and took a kamikaze leap, hurtling itself across the 60-story chasm. Tildascow and Jaguar both shot at the beast—no way to tell if their aim was true—but there was no stopping the living missile's momentum. Tildascow shielded Lon's body as the monster crashed into them. Her head cracked against the fuselage, but the brunt of the impact missed them.

The Apache bucked hard. Its main and tail rotors battled for control as the bird seesawed on every axis, skidding lopsided through the air. Tildascow clenched Lon tight as their insides were thrown about. The dark monoliths on either side of 42nd shot upward as if they were freefalling. Snow and wind attacked from every direction.

Finally Beethoven regained control of the chopper. Tildascow felt her internal organs settle back into place, and she dared to open her eyes.

Jaguar hung limply from his bindings, his shattered body swaying in a rag-doll fashion. Lon's head popped up from behind his shoulder. His nose was bleeding and he might've thrown up, but he managed to nod that he was okay. He turned to Jaguar, but she squeezed him back to her: *Don't look.*

Scanning for a landmark, she recognized the intersection at Third Avenue. Good news was that they were moving toward the UN Plaza. Bad news was that they were losing altitude.

Not quite dropping… but not quite *not* dropping.

At Third, a vehicle fire illuminated the face of the Mitsubishi Building. Thick packs of werewolves were scaling the tower comprised of irregularly stacked blocks. Many were already perched on the roofs, ready to leap. She could feel their hunger.

She banged on the gunner's window, alerting him to the ambush. The Apache's cannon roared to life, punishing them with heat and volume. Arcing bolts sprayed the Mitsubishi Building, pulverizing werewolves or knocking them loose.

Still dropping, the Apache pitched forward and took up speed, traveling east on 42nd toward the river. Beyond Third, the street was pitch black until it terminated at the United Nations Plaza. They crossed Second Avenue, which Tildascow marked only by the gap between the buildings.

The iconic "Tudor City" sign sat atop the last skyscraper on their left, marking the finish line at First Avenue. A Shithook passed above it, en route to the UN Plaza and carrying some kind of—

A wolf flew in from the darkness, appearing suddenly in the Apache's light. It fell inches short—its claws *just* scraped the wing—and then it plummeted, limbs flailing. Lon was still so clenched that he hadn't even noticed.

They cleared the city cluster and broke left to diagonally cross First Avenue, the quasi-highway between Manhattan and the United Nations.

She sighed with relief when she saw that the Plaza was under a massive siege. Someone had heard her over the radio.

The front lawn was lit up like a baseball stadium as helicopters swarmed overhead, raining rappelling soldiers onto the sloping roof of the General Assembly Building. Rocket-propelled grenades shot from the rooftops, lighting up the ground amid plumes of smoke. The massive rectangular Secretariat Building glowed at its fringes, backlit by a legion of boats in the East River.

The domed turret poking from the top of the GA Building seemed to look back at her, as if it were Valenkov's eyes.

He was close now.

As they closed in, they could see that the amalgam military forces had staged an airhead on the plaza's lawn, a square city block at the northern end of the international territory. Chinooks were jumping from Roosevelt Island, dropping Humvees with roof-mounted M2 ("Ma Deuce") .50 Caliber machine guns that were firing before they hit the ground.

Ma Deuces were earth scorchers, the meanest penises Tildascow ever had the pleasure of stroking in her army days. The trees trembled under their punishment, dropping leaves and branches amid pulverized werewolf bits. The M2's six-inch bullets had no silver, so the enemies kept surging with whatever limbs they had, shambling in the flickering red light cast by flares.

The werewolves had a rally point of their own. They were massing at the fountain dominating the southern end of the campus, hiding in the shadow of the Secretariat Building as they stormed the narrow back entrances to the General Assembly Building.

Man and wolf were going to meet in the middle.

The *Silver Bullet* flew low over the promenade, only a dozen feet above the knotted gun sculpture, *Non-Violence* (damn thing pissed Tildascow off more now than ever). As they spun for clearance and set down on the lawn, Green Berets unlocked the hitchhikers from the helicopter's fuselage. Jaguar's body spilled into their arms.

Tildascow caught Lon with an arm under his chest and brought him to a safe zone on the concrete. Mantle led Ilecko their way and looked back solemnly as they covered Jaguar's body.

She turned toward the marble and glass columns at the main entrance to the United Nations General Assembly Building. The temporary security tent had been razed and the bulletproof doors had met their match. The interior lit up with strobing pops of gunfire. Ringing, buzzing, and whooping alarms made it clear that—*by the way*—something was happening.

The *Silver Bullet's* gunner lifted off to make room for more traffic, but Beethoven had stripped his flight gear to join them. He broke open smelling salts to clear their heads and followed that up with fresh, silver-loaded Colt 9mm SMGs and mag pouches.

"They found the entrance to the shelter, but they don't have the passcode!" Beethoven yelled over the warfare. "They say it's missing from the government servers! They're on the horn with the UN now!"

Tildascow gritted her teeth. Valenkov must've found some way to erase the code from the VPN, even the redundancies. It wouldn't have been easy, but he could've wolfed out a UN security tech or a really talented hacker.

Ilecko passed on the rifle, preferring his sword. His skin was frostbitten and his hair was thick with frozen sweat and dirt. He was sluggish, but steady. And he nodded his readiness, as if he knew he was being assessed.

Lon was another story. He was curled up on the cement, covered in frozen clumps of muck. His eyes were clamped shut and he puckered like a thirsty fish.

Beethoven had a rifle for him, but Tildascow took it and gave him a canteen instead.

"He stays here," she said. "Everyone ready?"

Nods all around.

"Let's go."

Three
White House Situation Room
6:21 p.m.

As everyone kept vigil on the flat-panel screens displaying aerial real-time footage from the UN Plaza, Billy Itz, William Weston's top speechwriter, was furiously scribbling on a legal pad. A White House photographer had his back to the far wall, quietly snapping. Teddy wanted to put people in the room, so it wouldn't be so easy to condemn their choices post-mortem.

Weston's mind kept creeping toward his shirt's breast pocket, where he'd put the laminated card that contained today's Gold Codes, the sequence needed to authorize the launch of a WMD. The codes were provided to him every morning by the National Security Agency, placed in that pocket and forgotten. No president since Reagan had had serious cause to contemplate the Gold Codes; today's political landscape was far more complicated in its simplicity.

Even the president couldn't give authorization to launch WMDs on his own; a second set of Gold Codes was issued each day to his Defense Secretary, Ronald Greenberg. Only together could they issue the command, once both of their code sequences had been authorized.

Greenberg was an older man with thin white hair and a vulture's scowl. A businessman and engineer who had come up bouncing between private weapons R&D firms and federal defense appointments, he hadn't served in the military in almost 40 years. But he had unlimited stamina and resolve, and if the laminated card in his pocket was wearing on his mind, it wasn't showing.

From the far end of the table, General Ryan Jermaine, the Chief of Staff of the United States Air Force, monitored communication with the *Lunar Eclipse.*

Colonel Murdock's voice filtered through the room. *"Lunar Eclipse* post-takeoff routine complete, we are flying high."

"*Eclipse*, this is Home Room, do you copy?" Jermaine responded.

"Roger, Home Room, you are loud and clear. Weapons systems are online, we are proceeding to target zone."

Weston kept his eyes locked on the UN Plaza, praying the men down there would bring him a miracle.

Four

United Nations Plaza

6:26 p.m.

Lon's team was leaving him behind.

"Nnnmeee," he heard himself mumble as he struggled to get up. Of course they couldn't hear him over the war machines. He was too exhausted to shape his thoughts into reason, but he knew he had to keep going. He couldn't let his team down.

He forced himself to his feet. Moving spotlights in the sky cast veering shadows, doing nothing to help his balance.

As his eyes came to focus, he saw a medic hunched over someone in the Shadow Stalkers' uniform. He came closer, looking over the medic's shoulder, to see that it was Jaguar.

His chest was crushed, as if he'd been hit by a wrecking ball. Lon remembered now that a werewolf had hit their helicopter, and Jaguar had taken the impact. The medic startled Lon when he grabbed his kit and raced elsewhere, switching channels and leaving poor, broken Jaguar alone in the grass.

"Come back!" Lon screamed, but the medic paid him no mind. Injured men were being carried in from the other side of the plaza.

Lon knelt down to… well, he didn't know what to do. Jaguar's brown skin had gone blue. Probably there was nothing anyone could do.

He remembered that he had to catch up with the others, but to leave would seem so disrespectful. God, he couldn't even remember Jaguar's real name.

But the others had left. And he couldn't let them down. He started toward the building, turning back once to see if Jaguar had moved. And then he ordered himself not to look back again.

He trundled up the steps (*more fucking steps*) and pushed toward the entrance to the General Assembly Building. Soldiers rushed past with their weapons ready. A couple of them yelled something mean, like "get out of the way," but he couldn't make it out. Fuck them anyways.

A tent of scorched grey canvas was deflated in front of the building, draped over security equipment. Its seal had been dragged away from the front doors, where those soldiers stormed into the lobby.

A moment later, Lon stepped through the twisted doorframe. Glass crunched beneath his feet and the familiar reek of gun smoke enveloped him. Cloudy blue light seeped through the opaque window columns above, combining with the smoke to cast a watery ripple over the dead bodies that lay crumpled in every direction. They were of any age or race, wearing tatters of clothing or nothing at all. One girl—she couldn't have been 30—was sprawled naked in the middle of the floor, her face frozen in a question. *Haven't you heard, lady? The wolves came to town.*

He'd never even seen a naked girl before. What a way to start.

He stepped between the corpses and some ruined artworks and statues. Everything in sight was scorched, bloodstained, or broken. Toppled metal detectors had cut divots into the checkered marble floor. Blood puddles spawned decaying footsteps in all directions. Every wall was riddled with bullet holes.

The latest soldiers were huddled to Lon's left, firing into the darkness of a corridor that extended beneath the main balcony. Howls came in return, bouncing loony echoes. An information kiosk caught in the line of fire sizzled smoke and dust as errant shots hacked it apart. Lon tiptoed toward those men, but Tildascow and the others weren't among them.

A wide, shallow stairwell started to the right before turning around and sweeping over the lobby to the lowest of three white balconies. He found Ilecko in a dark corner beside the stairs, looming a head above everyone else. Beethoven was crouched before him, yelling into his radio.

"Geronimo squad, this is November Zero Zero One. Do you read?" he radioed. "Any element this net, please respond. Over."

"This is UNACOM—", the radio buzzed, but the rest of the message was lost in the din of gunfire.

Ilecko pulled Lon close to him, where Mantle was covering them with one of those big black rifles. They were by an elevator next to a smaller, private flight of stairs descending underneath the big one.

"UNACOM, we need directions to the underground bunker," Beethoven radioed. "Please advise."

"Stand by, November, we are—" Again, the rattle of machinegun fire made it impossible to hear.

"Say again, UNACOM," said Beethoven. "All after 'we are.'" The garbled response would have been unintelligible under the best of circumstances.

Tildascow was behind Ilecko, searching her backpack for a pair of night-vision goggles. As she put them on, Lon could have sworn—

She caught his curious glare, realizing just now that he'd arrived. With the goggles over her face, he couldn't read her expression.

Did she see him notice her yellow eyes?

For a long moment, Lon had no idea what she was going to do. Finally, she went back into her pack and came out with another pistol like the ones Lon had already failed to use. She racked the slide and offered it to him.

When he reached for it, she recoiled sharply. Her mouth hung agape as she stared at his hands.

Startled, Lon looked them over. They were chapped and swollen, each with a thousand little cuts, but he didn't see anything out of the—

Lon's heart dropped as he realized what she must have seen.

A pentagram.

Invisible to him, but to her it would an irrepressible craving. He watched her track every movement of his hands, her head tiling on her neck like a hungry predator.

The others were too focused on the radio to notice. Which was for the best, because they might kill her if they saw it. But Lon knew in his scaredy-cat heart that she could keep herself under control.

"I'll take it," he said, and reached for the gun with a big motion to retrieve her attention. When she snapped to, she put the handle firmly in his palm, right on top of the pentagram.

"You'll use this if you have to," she said over the racket.

"I won't have to."

She gazed at him for a moment, probably deep into his eyes, but he couldn't see through the night-vision goggles. Maybe she was developing romantic feelings? That'd be pretty cool, even though it'd leave him in a bit of a triangle with Elizabeth. And it'd be understandable, because, let's face it, he'd been pulling off some major hero stuff here.

She came toward him, and he thought they might be about to kiss. But then she passed him and went around Ilecko and the Shadows and stepped onto the stairwell leading to the balcony.

"Shelter is accessible from a tunnel behind the GA Hall," called Beethoven, relaying information he'd gotten over the radio. "Straightest route is through the theater."

"Let's move," Tildascow yelled, climbing the stairs.

As they followed, Ilecko gave Lon a stern glare.

"She's okay!" Lon promised.

"It will not be her," he whispered in Romanian. But his eyes said it all: He'd killed the love of his life under the curse. Tildascow wouldn't be able to stop herself.

Ilecko led him up the stairs and stayed between him and Tildascow.

At the top, a squad of soldiers was poised at the doors to the General Assembly Hall. They communicated directions with hand signals, and moved all at once on the squad leader's silent mark. The doors belched smoke and gunfire cracks as they stormed the hall.

"We go straight down the aisle," Tildascow hollered as she took position next to the doors. Her voice was deep and scratchy. Maybe trembling. "There's an exit behind the podium, leading to a hallway. The shelter entrance is straight down on the right-hand side. A team is already in place trying to get it open. Through this door, a few steps to a landing where we wait for clear. Once we move, we do not stop, no matter what you see, no matter if we lose anyone, even me."

After a moment of steeling, Beethoven opened the door and led the way, followed by Tildascow and then Ilecko, who kept a firm grasp on Lon's arm. Mantle came last and moved up to cover Lon's right side. They landed on the steps above one of the rows leading all the way down to the dais of the General Assembly Hall.

Lon could remember the iconic theater in his mind's eye, but now it was a smoky war zone. Furniture was overturned, the podium was wrecked, and one of the large monitors behind it had fallen. The windows in the observation mezzanines were cracked or shattered. A fire in one compartment billowed smoke over melted glass.

The werewolves came from the front, meeting the soldiers in the middle. Machinegun fire sent glowing sparks into their masses, but they still had the upper hand as they advanced up the slope, creeping through the rows, underneath the tables, and between the chairs. They used themselves as live ammunition, dark cannonballs firing at the pinned with crushing velocity.

"Three o'clock," Beethoven yelled.

"*Every* o'clock!" Mantle hollered.

An explosion rocked the ceiling and debris rained down onto the contested zone before them. Shafts of light coming through the breached dome seemed to turn solid in the smoke. Soldiers dropped on rappelling lines, firing all the way.

The werewolves turned on these new targets, opening a window for the teams trapped at the back of the theater.

"Go go go!" Tildascow yelled.

Ilecko grabbed Lon's arm and they raced down the aisle, advancing on the rostrum beneath the golden backdrop. Other soldiers fell in, covering their flanks. Angels with rifles hovered in the dust clouds above.

Shots came from everywhere. Halfway down the aisle, a werewolf slithered from beneath a desk, and Ilecko drove his sword into its head, never breaking his stride.

The walls popped and shattered, the UN emblem fell along with the rest of the backdrop, and the podium collapsed. The soldier on Lon's right faceplanted into the back of a chair. The man behind him went down under a sharp growl. Up ahead, a werewolf launched across the aisle and a soldier disappeared into its grasp.

Each step brought that exit closer. A werewolf soared ten feet over their heads, looking like a hawk with its magnificent arms spread wide before its tapering torso and canine legs. It plowed into a rappelling soldier and they both disappeared into the smog.

Finally, their group narrowed to funnel through the exit.

But the tunnel beyond was hardly salvation. It was so dark in Ilecko's shadow that Lon couldn't tell if his eyes were open or shut. White strobes of gunfire burned moving patterns in the blackness, making footing treacherous even as they were navigating scattered bodies. And the narrow hall trapped sound, turning each shot into an ear-piercing boom. Even their gasps were deafening. Ilecko directed him to put his hand on the wall as a guide.

"November Zero Zero One to UNACOM," Lon heard Beethoven say, "we need those access codes. Over."

He was stopped by Ilecko's hand at his chest. Someone yelled, "Eyes!"

They'd stopped outside of a room no larger than a cloak closet. Something had been torn away to reveal a deeper room inside and another door, one that was round-cornered and thick, like in a submarine. Frantic flashlights converged on a security system between the two doors. The face panel had been removed, exposing a jungle of wires and buttons and lights and circuit boards.

"Should I torch it?" Mantle asked.

"You can't torch that door," Tildascow said.

"UNACOM, we need the access code!" Beethoven radioed.

"Roger that, November, we're working on it. Stand by."

"No time to stand by!"

"Stand by, November!"

"How long we got?" Mantle asked.

"Twenty seven—"

Beethoven's response was interrupted by a growl. Flashlights spun on snapping teeth. Swinging arms. Blinding, deafening gunfire.

Lon fell against the wall, lost behind Ilecko's coat. Someone nearby collapsed amid directionless shouting.

"Fuck! Fuuuuck!"

"Reloading!"

"He's okay!"

"He's *not* okay!"

"We need to fall back!"

"Reloading!"

"No, advance, keep going, take this hall to the end!"

Footsteps all around.

"Go go go!"

"Get this door open!"

From the radio: "November, they're opening the airlock door remotely."

"Copy that, UNACOM!"

"Be advised, they're saying the shelter has been locked down. The inner chamber can only be opened from inside."

Under the radio chatter, the door let loose a depressurizing hiss and a heavenly whiff of fresh air.

"We're in. We're in!" Tildascow yelled, pushing the door open.

Ilecko helped Lon to his feet and they stepped around stacks of bodies and followed Tildascow through the hidden door, held for them by Beethoven.

Now they were in a narrow tube leading to the longest, fastest and steepest escalator Lon had ever seen. It descended beneath a close, curved ceiling with hidden lavender lighting.

"Close the door!" Tildascow yelled.

"Got it!" Beethoven called.

Tildascow led the charge, and Lon followed Ilecko as they tried to keep pace. The escalator was so fast that their hair would've been blowing if they'd just stayed put; skipping downward was like riding a motorcycle. Farther and farther they went as the comforting warm air charmed his eyes closed. He started to wonder if he wasn't sleepwalking. He couldn't see past Ilecko, but how deep could they possibly—

He slammed into Ilecko's back, smacking his nose and *biting his fucking tongue* again.

Ilecko spun, his sword in his hand, all too ready for a fight.

"Well I cad't zee bast you!" Lon yelled, holding his nose.

Ilecko offered to help him up, but Lon made his own way and pushed in front so he could at least see where they were going. The escalator had dumped them at a big metal door, just like the one at the top. It opened into a tight tube, only ten feet long, with a matching pressure door at the far end. Tildascow was inside waiting for them.

Lon hadn't been mistaken; her eyes *had* turned yellow. And it was hard to be sure with all of the dirt and sweat, but her face seemed swollen. Ilecko entered, pushing him toward her. He wished he'd just stayed in the back.

"I'm okay," she said, but the way she was panting through her shoulders made her look like a human wolf. Beethoven entered last and she rasped, "It's an airlock. We have to seal that door."

Beethoven put his shoulder into closing the heavy door, smearing bloody handprints across the shiny metal.

"Mantle!" Lon yelled, realizing they were another man down. "Wait for Mantle!"

But Beethoven didn't wait. He put his back against the door and took deep breaths as it sealed and the air pressure shifted. His uniform was covered in new bloodstains, his face full of turmoil. One glance and Lon understood what had happened to Mantle.

Here the four of them stood, hands on their knees, in stillness for the first time in eons. Lon could have slept on his feet (maybe died on his feet). And yet, as the next door hissed, he found the strength to achieve locomotion again.

The next room was *spectacular.*

They entered a large, circular mission control room, the kind you might find at NASA. It was least 30 feet in diameter, with stations at several elevations, all facing a wall of floor-to-ceiling windows overlooking…

Well, overlooking Central Park.

They were twenty feet above a beautiful garden, where a stone walkway wandered past flower patches, wrought-iron benches, and garbage cans. The trees trembled in a tender breeze. Lon wouldn't have believed they were underground if not for the crisp, clear night sky that he knew to be a lie. It had to be a projection, though it was far more convincing than the planetarium he'd visited in fourth grade.

In sci-fi books, people in space habitats adjusted their lighting for day or night to maintain the illusion of life on Earth, so they didn't go all *Shining.* Lon thought they must've constructed this place with the same philosophy. And it was synchronized to real time; the trees on the horizon were backlit with the glow of the rising moon. Even as he stepped away from the thick curved window, he could barely break the illusion that he was looking outside.

Considering how amazing the shelter looked, the mission control room was hardly high-tech. In fact this stuff was probably outdated before Lon was born. *Black and white* monitors displaying temperature, oxygen rate, and humidity alongside *paper* seismographs and—wow— *corded* phones. He couldn't place the names of some of the instruments; he'd only seen them in flea markets or old movies.

Everything was calm except for the console of mini TVs showing security camera feeds. As if the images weren't dire enough, warning lights were flashing and some sort of automatic typewriter was clicking away.

On the far side of the control room, Tildascow had found the door into the shelter. She slammed it in frustration. "No handle!" she roared. No visible hinges, either. It had a small clear portal, through which you could see that it was at least six inches thick.

"Can we torch it?" Beethoven asked.

"Not enough time," she said despondently, fingering the paper-thin crack between the door and its metal frame. "Try the window."

Beethoven dropped to a knee and produced a torch and goggles from his pack. "Controls?" he asked.

"No," she grunted. "This is just a monitoring station. They wouldn't allow someone to open it from the outside and contaminate the ecosystem."

Beethoven took his torch to the window.

Tildascow collapsed against the door, gasping desperation. Her limbs jerked as she fought the painful transformation. "Fuck," she whispered. "Hurts."

Ilecko leaned against a station within reach of her, staring her down.

"I've got it," she whispered, and he did not answer.

"Not getting anywhere," Beethoven said, blowing on the untarnished glass and starting over.

And then a Godlike voice echoed through the chamber, causing each of them to discover the speakers in the ceiling.

"Yannic Ilecko," it said. It was deep and powerful, with a romantic Romanian accent that was in stark contrast to Ilecko's clunky drubbing. "You promised we would not meet again."

"And you promised there would be no more death, Lord Valenkov," Ilecko responded in Romanian. He was solemn and unsurprised, and looking through the window at the garden below.

Lon followed Ilecko's eyes and saw him, finally, just twenty feet away and looking up at them through the window.

Demetrius Valenkov.

Five

Airspace South of Manhattan
6:49 p.m.

The *Lunar Eclipse* cruised toward Manhattan at five hundred miles per hour. By all accounts, this was an easy run. No need for stealth, no fear of retribution, and a wide margin for deployment. The bomblets were like mini cropdusters, with GPS-controlled navigation systems that would direct them to low-altitude distribution zones and minimize wind dispersion. And since the biological weapon would die in the water, they could paint outside the lines.

Colonel Murdock ripped open the envelope given to him by President Weston and removed a plain sheet of paper with two simple series of random letters and numbers. "Home Room, this is the *Lunar Eclipse.* We are two minutes to Verification Point. Requesting code confirmation."

General Ryan Jermaine, the Chief of Staff of the United States Air Force, responded with the authentication codes matching the first sequence, which would be Defense Secretary Ronald Greenberg's gold code. "—Tango, Delta, Niner, Niner, Charlie, Echo."

Murdock repeated the code back to him, and then a moment passed before he radioed again. Aside from system reports, the flight crew had been quiet for the entire run. "Roger that, Home Room. Verification confirmed."

Next Jermaine radioed Weston's gold code. Both codes would already have been authorized with the United States Strategic Command Headquarters in Nebraska and NORAD in Colorado. The weapons system computer would also confirm the code digitally before allowing launch.

"Roger, Home Room. Verification confirmed."

The B-1B's weapons system officer's voice came through the radio next. "Home Room, we have 136 to VP, requesting permission to deploy."

Six

6:50 p.m.

The White House Situation Room had gone silent.

All eyes were on the president, waiting for his order. But William Weston remained fixed on the grainy overhead footage from the exit zones. Werewolves were massed at the exits, but they hadn't made a serious run at escape. They'd disengaged from conflict everywhere but the UN.

"They're not attacking," Leslie whispered, but even she knew that was irrelevant; they had to act ahead of the wolves, not in response to them. Were it even possible, containing the outbreak on the mainland could cost millions more lives.

But still. They weren't attacking.

"Sir?" Jermaine asked. The *Lunar Eclipse* was waiting for a green light.

"Time is 18:50," Truesdale said quietly, urging him to remember that they'd reached the pre-agreed deployment time.

"Negative," Weston said into his steepled fingers. "Have them loiter."

"*Lunar Eclipse,* light is yellow," Jermaine radioed, pent-up tension rumbling under his voice. "Repeat, light is yellow."

"Roger that, Home Room. Cycle time is 278."

It would take 278 seconds for the bomber to return to its verification point.

"Contingency?" Truesdale asked. They had two contingency bombers behind the *Lunar Eclipse,* but Murdock would be credited with the flight no matter what. The identities of the back-up planes and their pilots would remain top secret forever.

Jermaine read over the shoulder of his flight control tech. "18:56 for number one. 18:59 for number two."

"They're in the bomb shelter?" Weston called, still never looking away from the monitor, as if he could hold off the werewolves himself.

An aide from the Watch Center responded from the doorway. "Yes sir, November team is in the airlock."

"They can't get into the shelter unless it's opened from the inside," Truesdale reminded them. No one had forgotten.

Four and a half minutes for a miracle.

Seven

United Nations Underground Habitat
6:50 p.m.

The shadows of the trees retreated as the false moon crested the horizon.

This show had no effect on the curse, but it was synchronous with the rise of the moon outside. And no walls could stop that light.

No matter where Demetrius Valenkov hid, the moon always found him.

"Of course there is more death," he responded to Ilecko. "As long as the scourge of my family lives, we will always bring more. Death to the Ottomans. And to the Turks and the Saxons and the *Ṭigani* and the Americans. Death to your wife, Yannic, and to mine."

Valenkov felt himself slipping between man and wolf with each draw of breath. The full moon was upon him, the time when even his years of rigorous preparation could not contain the animal. Were he at home, he would have locked himself in his chamber, secured iron shackles to his wrists and ankles, and prayed for morning to come quickly and without incident.

But he was far from home.

"Shoot him," he heard the woman agent growl. She was the perfect American warrior, immune to influence and to compassion, void of conscience.

"Glass is bulletproof," the soldier warned her.

She stepped back and shot her silver at the window. It did not break.

"No longer can you hurt us," said Valenkov.

"My government can't allow the wolves to escape the island," she said. "They're going to kill everyone in Manhattan, infected or not. Hundreds of thousands… of…" She trailed off, distracted by something over his shoulder.

His baby boy had come out from hiding.

Wearing only a diaper, eighteen-month-old Zee teetered forward. His little hands were in his mouth, exploring for new teeth.

Valenkov crouched with outstretched arms, encouraging Zee to stay up on his wobbly legs. It was important to him that his son learn to walk upright.

"And why are any of those lives more important than my own?" he asked the agent. "Than those of my family?" He lifted Zee with his throbbing, distended hands. His yellowing eyes and sharpening teeth looked monstrous, but his boy melted into his arms nonetheless. "Why do you fight so hard to protect them, and yet you ignore our pleas for help? Is it because we are not American? But are we not human?"

The woman agent was too preoccupied to respond. Instead, she blurted out the obvious. "The Cooke child..."

Perhaps, Valenkov calculated, she was not as smart as she thought. Perhaps her scientists were overconfident in their superwoman. For all of her supposed investigative prowess, she assumed he'd chosen Holly Cooke as his first victim because she was high profile, a person whose injury would spark the attention of the government and the media. Indeed, this great American manhunter had forgotten the missing child altogether.

Valenkov had chosen Cooke many months ago, when he learned that she and her diplomat husband were looking to adopt a child from Italy. It took little effort to put his son in their hands; simply a trip to the country and the wolf's influence over one woman in the *Tribunale per i Minorenni*. And thus, his little Zee travelled to America with Holly Cooke.

Distasteful as it was to see another woman mothering his son, Holly Cooke was a fine soul. More innocent blood on his family's crest.

"Perhaps we are only animals to your government," he said. "Wolves. Meant to be hunted. Like you hunt my father, Yannic. And now you come for me."

"You are not a wolf, Demetrius," said Ilecko in *limba română*. *"You are a man. I let you live, because you promised —"*

"I make good on my promise, Yannic!" His fury loosened his grip on the beast. "I make no more wolves! But it does not matter to these men in the village. They live in fear of the past. Moon after moon, there are no wolves. I promise to find the cure. I only ask for time!" His teeth pushed further from his jaw, coursing agony through his chin and interfering with his speech. Hands trembling, he put Zee on the grass. The boy cried in protest.

Ilecko responded and the woman agent spoke over him. But Valenkov did not listen. Instead, he turned inward.

It had become natural to focus on his heartbeat as a tuning mechanism, and organize his brainwaves to the Harmony's vibrations. In this deep meditation, his bodymind became one with the total collective consciousness. Distinctions between himself and his own observations and the universe faded away, and there was only the Harmony. Here he cultivated his body's life energy, his *qi,* and harmonized its movement within his physical body and the universe.

His consciousness was free of the wolf, but his *qi* was locked forever in battle with it, as the curse had latched onto the vital meridians through which the *qi* must travel. It hid between his lungs and his heart, his kidney and his stomach, his liver and his pericardium, and it attacked from everywhere at once under the light of the moon. Here, in the Harmony, the collective consciousness struggled against the invader. Most nights it was kept restrained. Under the full moon, however, the *țigani* curse was too powerful.

Valenkov returned to the ego-consciousness, having stayed the wolf's approach. His gaze fell on the face of his child, the loving boy who was blissfully unaware of the monster lurking within him.

Zee's canine teeth had yet even to break free of his gums.

"The villagers learn we have a son," Valenkov told Ilecko and his Americans. "And they know the curse will continue within him when I die. So they attack. They kill my Ecaterina. My innocent Cat."

He could still hear the mayhem as the villagers ravaged his home.

And there he was, sealed in his dungeon, as they knew he would be on the night of the full moon. The key to his shackles would not be released but for a rudimentary timer constructed by his great-grandfather. And so he pulled helplessly as he listened to the men ram the gate. His beloved Cat was alone and terrified. In his shame, he had hidden the entrance to the dungeon from her. It was the worst mistake of his life.

Still swollen from pregnancy, she hurried to the mausoleum and hid their infant son inside a tomb. She called out to Valenkov, praying that he could hear, that he would know to save the boy come morning. He cried back for her, but the dungeon had been made soundproof to her unsophisticated senses.

She faced the savages alone. They tortured her, demanding to know where her men were hiding.

They thought he had hid from them and left his wife to be their victim.

"And they call *us* monsters," Valenkov said. "Dracula. Sons of the Devil."

For six long years, Demetrius Valenkov had contained the beast by mind or by force. It was a promise to himself, to his father, to Yannic Ilecko, even to the smug ghost of the *ţigani* who had put this curse upon his family. He swore he would thwart their witch and restore honor to their family crest.

He sympathized with the villagers, though, and he tried to still their fears, for they too had been through horror. He promised them he would not have a child until a cure had been found. But Zee had come unplanned, from a feverish and perhaps irresponsible moment of passion. They tried to hide him, but the villagers had spies inside his castle.

When he heard Ecaterina's screams, when he realized they would show no mercy — *God forgive him, he thought they would give him the time he needed* — it was then that he unleashed the monster.

He fueled its strength with his own, working in concert with the wolf only this once, and even still it took too long to break the manacles and the door. Precious minutes, during which his beloved wife was impaled

417

upon a stake. Slowly, agonizingly, her own weight pulled her to her death as the wood tore through her organs.

These men—these cowards—would have thought of her as another of Vlad Dracula's victims. But she was not. Her blood was on *their* hands.

When he was free, Demetrius Valenkov the werewolf caused the villagers *suffering*. The men and their wives were made to watch their children die, and then the men watched their wives die. And then they were wounded, so much more delicately than their loved ones, so that they had time to wallow as their lives slowly escaped from their stomachs.

Only the worst did he let live, the very men who put Ecaterina upon that stake. He put the wolf's curse upon their souls and used his influence to lay waste to their minds. Now they dreamed forever of their loved ones' horrific deaths, waking from slumber only to feel the pain of the transformation. And then, as his *slujitori*, they keep watch over his beloved's body.

This was his revenge. For the anguish had driven him mad.

Had it not?

Only a madman could have eaten the flesh of those women and children. Only a madman could have caused the ruin that had come to New York City, executing such a wicked plan while remaining deaf to the screams of innocents. Innocents like the honorable Mrs. Cooke, whose only crime was to love his son.

Certainly only a madman could have committed the same atrocities, yet again, for which his family was cursed some twenty generations ago.

Alas. If only he *had* gone mad.

"There has been enough death, Demetrius," said Ilecko. *"Too many lives lost. Think of how many more will die. You are too good a man to let this to continue."*

If only he had gone mad, Ilecko's words would not ring true.

"But it must!" he insisted. "It must continue, it always continues as the curse passes down. For all of his life, my son will be punished for crimes he did not commit. You will come for him one day, Yannic, as you came for my father. As you come for me. Or worse, he will be hunted by the likes of *her*. Soldiers stripped of their compassion."

Valenkov attuned himself to the Harmony, where the collective consciousness was one with the minds of his *slujitori*, including the woman who wished to know herself only as Tildascow. He thrust further, calling to her wolf within. Let her try to ignore his plight while suffering the pain of the curse.

Come out. Join us.

Eight

She was a stranger in her own mind, conscious only through the dim light of a keyhole, wriggling from a powerful force that would pull her away. The wolf teased her, daring her to let everything go.

Physical torture, psychological coercion, the temptation of relief. Now, finally, she understood. This was a brainwashing, not a transformation. She wasn't becoming the wolf. She was succumbing to it.

Valenkov's trick, simple yet impossible, was not to succumb.

Ilecko's sword glimmered in the dimming light, seesawing between the blue of the fake moon and the white overheads. He was tired, languid, not realizing his natural sway was letting the blade shift to the easiest angle for her to grab it between her palms.

Even if she could resist the compulsion, the pain might overtake her. The worst of it was in her spreading shoulders and back, but now her hips were constricting. Fireballs swelled in her joints as mutinous tendons pushed her bones apart. And then a sledgehammer came down on her knees, the impact spreading in excruciating slow-motion, breaking her tibia free.

Freefalling through conscious thought, rocketing past distant sensations. Hunger. Cold. Rage. Defiance. Agony.

Now a soothing at the base of her spine: the release of her tail, transcending the pain with an orgasmic wave sweeping her to salvation.

The pentagram in Lon's hand. Deliverance, so close.

And her grip slipped further. The wolf pushed from behind her, desperate to let loose a howl. But it didn't escape.

Not yet.

She closed her eyes and focused. The fleeting thoughts became one: her mother's melodic voice.

She would not be distracted.

Nine

The storm in Valenkov's heart raged dissonance in the Harmony. His *slujitori* felt it too, as their true power dawned with the moon. Never mind their screams as their bones twisted into the canine shape. A madman would not hear them.

The American woman's howl echoed through the speakers. To resist would only intensify the pain. This he knew too well.

"Mister Valenkov!" It was the boy, this child they had brought with them, for what reason he'd never understood. "Please! I'm so sorry for what you've—"

"There is no 'sorry!' You can never be sorry enough!"

"That's certainly true, but—"

"Certainly!" He pointed at Zee, who had been put to hide in a sarcophagus. "Certainly he does not deserve to suffer!"

"We'll look after him, I promise."

"What *promise?*" A fool, this boy.

"I promise, I do promise, we *will* cure him. You have to trust me. You're a good man, Mister Valenkov, you don't want this to continue."

But Valenkov wanted. He wanted to want. Anger seared his tongue.

"You've come as far as you can. Your father would be proud."

"Demetrius—" Ilecko tried to interrupt.

"My father was a coward. He surrendered."

"No, sir, he wasn't a coward. He couldn't have been. He suffered for twenty years. And *this guy* was chasing him. I'd be scared shitless if he was chasing me. Sorry, I didn't mean to curse, but—"

"He was selfish. He held on only for the hope that I could cure him."

"No, Mister Valenkov, he held on for you, to give you time to prepare. Selfish would have been to end it right away, to put himself out of his misery. You should be proud of him. And you should let your son be proud of *his* father."

He could rip this stupid, arrogant American boy's head off.

And yet his words left him heartstruck. He couldn't help but turn to Zee, and he saw himself in his own father's eyes, perhaps for the first time.

Nevertheless, the call pounded in his heart. *Run with the hunt,* it said. *Let the humans suffer if we should feast upon them.* It was the voice of the wolf, and of his mad ancestors.

His emotional disquiet had given the wolf the upper hand. His hands trembled as his fingers stretched into claws. The pain hammered at his resolve.

But Demetrius Valenkov would not now, not *ever*, surrender to the wolf, or the dragon, or the disharmony. He stepped closer into Yannic Ilecko's gaze.

"I promise you we will care for him," Ilecko said.

"You have made me promises before, Yannic."

"I only wish you had let me keep them."

He had looked into this man's soul before, when he implored him to spare his life after Papa died and the curse passed down. Not for his own sake, but for Ecaterina's. Somehow, Ilecko had set aside his sorrow and rage and put his faith in his vow to stop the cycle, to find a cure.

Yet another promise unkept.

And now Ilecko had returned to collect.

Then and now, all he could do was put his trust in the man who killed his father, and who would kill *him.* Ilecko was but a common farm boy, and yet he'd grown into a man of honor and strength, and he had found a reason in his rage that Valenkov, for all of his search and study, could not.

Perhaps if he were he more like Ilecko, there would be less suffering.

He turned to Zee, who had taken to rolling through the fake grass. He reached for him, but his hands had become the same talons that spilled the blood of the villagers' children. They would not touch his son.

"I love you, Zaharius."

He started toward the stairs leading to the control room's door.

"He will not be able to control the transformations, Yannic."

"We will keep him safe. We will teach him from your writings."

At the foot of the stairs, he lost sight of Ilecko in the window.

"He will not remember a time before the wolf. He will not remember me."

"He will know what his father did for him."

Twelve steps to climb, and it would all be over. Twelve steps to climb, and leave his son in the hands of these amoral savages.

"They will want to take their anger out on him, Yannic."

"Upon the souls of our wives, I will not let that happen, Demetrius."

Valenkov's deformed hand fell on the security pad at the airlock door. He entered the code he'd taken from the mind of the United Nations sanitary worker. And then he turned to look upon his son one last time.

"Da-da?"

It was the first time Zee had called his name.

His shoulders dropped and his spine curled and his jaw wrenched and his legs broke and his joints detonated and hatred and hunger—

Ten

White House Situation Room

6:54 p.m.

"They're rushing the exits!" cried a watch officer.

"Mister President, we *have* to deploy—" urged Greenberg.

"28 seconds to cycle," said Jermaine.

"Stand by," Rebekkah Luft said into yet another phone.

Allison Leslie dashed out of the room, fighting off nausea.

Teddy put his hand on Weston's arm. "It's time."

Each one of the aerial views portrayed mass chaos: the wolves catapulting themselves across the river, attacking boats and bringing down low-flying helicopters; flashing gunfire on the Brooklyn Bridge; a massive fire in the Lincoln Tunnel. In the United Nations garden, a werewolf ripped a small tree from its roots and hurled it at a Humvee.

All eyes looked to Weston.

"Deploy."

Eleven
Airspace over Manhattan
6:54 p.m.

"Roger that, Home Room," radioed Murdock. "Green light."

"Green light, roger that," confirmed the Bone's offensive system officer, Lieutenant Colonel Adam Hulse. The launch code had been entered into the SATCOM control panel and the targeting solution was locked. "I have six lights. Repeat, six lights. I have active confirmation. Delivery in 30."

"God bless America," Murdock muttered to himself.

"Bombs away." Hulse deployed the first ten CBU-191 cluster missiles from the intermediate bomb bay. All ten fire-and-forget cruise missiles came online and began seeking their GPS-guided destinations for deployment of the RAPiDs bomblets. "Package is on its way. Repeat, package is on its way."

Twelve
60 Seconds Earlier

They lost sight of Valenkov as he approached the door of the airlock.

Lon held his breath, wishing it could make Valenkov move faster. How much longer could they have until the bomb dropped? How much longer until Tildascow wolfed out and ate him up? How much longer until Valenkov lost control?

Tildascow slid to the ground, leaning against the console closest to the chamber door. She was drenched in sweat, eyes clenched as she fought to contain the transformation. A painful whimper came from her throat, like the earliest warning of a teakettle. Her hands had become claws. Her legs were crossed, but they looked… *wrong.* She'd stopped responding to Ilecko's encouragement. Her snout was slowly but steadily growing.

Her eyes popped open, flicked toward him and then snapped shut. He could practically feel the invisible pentagram in his hand.

Since they'd lost sight of Valenkov beyond the window, Ilecko had kept his gaze on Tildascow, his sword steady in his right hand, the tip pressed against the back of his elbow.

Beethoven was frozen as a one-man firing squad, rifle steadied over a console desk, trigger finger poised, waiting for a glimpse of Valenkov.

"They will want to take their anger out on him, Yannic." Valenkov rumbled, deep and breathy, over the speaker system. His tinny footsteps marked his progress on the stairs toward the chamber door, his march to death.

"I will not let that happen, Demetrius." Ilecko's voice quivered with genuine sadness, even as he tried to wrangle Valenkov up those stairs faster.

Valenkov became visible in the door's window, first looking at Ilecko and then working the keypad lock.

Tildascow's jaw opened wide, revealing fangs. She exhaled a long, threatening purr that grew strained as it escaped her control.

"*Stai*," Ilecko whispered to her. "Think of love. Think of family. End is soon."

An alarm rang and spinning yellow light threw chaos across the observation chamber.

"I love you, Zaharius," Valenkov sobbed.

The door released—

"Da-da?"

They all turned to the little boy, who was sitting on the grass and looking up at his father with wide-eyed concern.

An anguished roar bellowed through the speakers as the door slammed open. Beethoven opened fire, but Valenkov—now the biggest, baddest-ass werewolf they'd ever seen—moved like he'd been swallowed by the shadows.

Ilecko raised his sword, but an uppercut from the werewolf sent him into a wild backflip. His knees crashed into the computer consoles and his face plunged into the floor.

Beethoven kept shooting. From somewhere in the darkness, a chair shot back. The impact brought a clap of thunder, pulverizing the chair and the console and leaving Beethoven motionless beneath twisted metal.

Lon felt certain he'd just seen both men die.

In the darkness, Lon found a pair of yellow eyes trained on him.

The werewolf snarled.

"But no, just wait," he heard himself say.

And then Tildascow let loose a monstrous roar.

She transformed all at once and shot from the floor, tackling Valenkov, intertwining her silvery blond fur with his deep black.

They careened end over end—thrashing talons and snapping teeth, shredded clothing, flying blood. Lon couldn't tell if the werewolves were fighting, or the people within them, or both.

They slammed against a computer console, disengaged, and rolled onto all fours. Both of their bodies quivered with fury and they traded roars.

They charged again.

He thought they might explode on impact, but they crashed and rolled. When they stopped, Valenkov had Tildascow pinned. He reached back with his tremendous arm and hammered a claw into her face.

She fell silent. Her talons dropped from his throat.

He stepped off her body and let loose an anguished roar.

And then his hateful gaze turned Lon's way.

"No wait—"

His eyes dipped down, toward the pistol in Lon's hands, as if—

As if he was asking him to end it.

But Lon's limbs were numb.

He wanted to run. But he couldn't move.

Scream. But he couldn't breathe.

The werewolf barreled toward him, grabbed him by the throat and slammed him against the wall.

"Please don't," Lon croaked.

But Valenkov wasn't there. Only the wolf, leaning in, spreading its teeth…

BAM! BAM!

The wolf's grip loosened immediately. It looked down, dumbstruck, and Lon fired again, the gunshots echoing a thousand times off the consoles and the windows.

BAM! BAM! BAM! BAM!

The werewolf wheezed a muffled, wet yelp and fell to its knees. Blood seeped through its fur, leaking from its collar, chest, and belly. It tried to stand, to attack again, but couldn't muster the strength. Instead it snarled at Lon, trying to kill him with its glare.

"I'm sorry," Lon whimpered. "I'm so sorry."

He locked eyes with the wolf, trying to reach the man. It pitched forward and he stooped, looking for just one knowing glance—*forgive me*—before it was too late...

"I'm sorry," he said again.

But the wolf's eyes lost him. They rolled toward the ceiling— *please, don't die yet*—as the reverse transformation sent the creature into contorting jolts. The fur crept back, the wolf's snout retracted, but still the eyes belonged to the wolf.

"I'm sorry," Lon whispered one last time.

The eyes were still yellow as they lost focus. The wolf exhaled its last breath, and only then did it release Demetrius Valenkov.

Thirteen

From the Lincoln Tunnel to Harlem and right on top of the General Assembly Building, the wolves collapsed all at once.

Soldiers watched in astonishment as their attackers simply went to sleep, no matter if they were in mid-air or locked in combat. Those carrying on despite catastrophic injuries died in their sleep, swiftly and silently.

As the Gatling guns spun their last, only the crazed, irregular chorus of alarms remained. They rang across the island, unwilling to give up the fight even as the men and women of the armed forces cautiously lowered their weapons.

The wolves bucked and shook through their reverse transformations, leaving naked, dirty New Yorkers sleeping in the streets. Cheers erupted among the soldiers, victorious hugs and curses and tears.

Most of them never noticed that they'd been abandoned by their helicopter support. The skies were clear.

Those that happened to be looking up saw light bursts erupt into streaking fireworks. And they realized it was too late.

Fourteen
White House Situation Room

"Can you confirm that?" Truesdale barked into his phone, breaking the horrible silence. "Confirm!"

A duty officer on another phone yelled, "They're down, every one of them!"

Screams came from the Watch Team in the other room. "Down! Down!"

"Can you confirm?" hollered Truesdale. "Quickly!"

Their telephoto images from the safe zones were hazy, but it seemed gunfire on the bridges and the shores had stopped. The CNN footage whipped about haphazardly, until it finally settled on—

"Disarm! Disarm!" Weston yelled.

"Neutralize the weapon, *Lunar Eclipse!*" Jermaine yelled on top of him. "Repeat, neutralize the weapon!"

"Code sent! Code sent!" radioed Hulse, the Bone's offensive system officer.

The room fell deathly silent. Seconds felt like hours.

"Lunar Eclipse, can you confirm?"

"Jesus Christ," Teddy muttered.

"Lunar Eclipse!"

"Can we disarm them remotely?" Luft exclaimed.

Jermaine shook his head. "Not in the next five sec—"

"Package is harmless, Home Room," radioed Hulse. "I repeat, package is harmless."

Cheers erupted through the Situation Room. Truesdale came down on the table with a thundering fist. Shinick fought back tears. Luft dropped her head into her hands. Weston wrapped Teddy in a bear hug.

"Home Room, we are awaiting further orders."

Jermaine responded: "This is Home Room, *Lunar Eclipse.* Disengage and return to the nest. Mission accomplished."

"Mission accomplished," Teddy repeated to Weston as they released their clench. "Mission accomplished."

Weston fell back into his chair, which toppled backward and would've dumped the president ass over teakettle if Teddy hadn't intervened. Relief-fueled laughter tore through the room.

"Can someone get me some aspirin?" Weston warbled. "And some food—I want a fucking cheeseburger. French fries. Onion rings. Big, huge beer—who wants a beer?" Hands went up all around. "Keep the beer coming."

"Yes sir," said one of the duty officers.

Teddy held up a hand. "Whiskey."

"Whiskey, get us some whiskey. A lot of whiskey."

"Yes sir," said the officer on his way out.

"And nobody leaves this room until we fix the debt!"

Fifteen

United Nations Underground Habitat Security Airlock
7:01 p.m.

Lon helped Tildascow pull herself up. She looked frighteningly broken, with a glassy eye and massive swelling. Her tattered clothing hung loosely as she held her head, fighting back nausea.

Beethoven stirred. He strained to speak, but he thought he was okay aside from broken ribs. Tildascow gave Lon a few of her weird pills to put in his mouth.

Ilecko was alive too! Both of his legs seemed to be broken and he was seeing double, but still—he was alive. Relief surged into Lon's chest and he felt the urge to cry. Tildascow caught his gaze with a nod that said it was okay.

So he bawled.

Tildascow lurched over to check Ilecko's legs. He refused her pills, and Lon shook her off before she even asked. Somehow, the exchange transformed his tears into laughter. And then they were all laughing.

"Get in the van, little boy," she rasped. "I have candy—"

A terrible scream ripped through the speaker system.

Valenkov's infant son lay splayed on the grass under the fake moon. His mouth hung agape and his little limbs thrashed as he choked on a helpless wail.

He rolled onto his side, and now they could see the fur sprouting on his back. His legs broke into canine form, his jaw swelled, his ears curled.

He came to all fours, shivered one last time and then howled at the moon. A werewolf in a diaper.

Tildascow racked the slide on her pistol.

She wobbled toward the airlock door, catching the wall to prevent a spill. The injuries to her face masked her emotions—if she had any—as she stepped through the door, steadied herself on the guardrail, and took aim at the child.

The baby werewolf hopped in a circle, yipping with self-discovery.

Lon looked away.

EPILOGUE

Magister Lon "Mythos" Toller

Lon Toller had always suspected that one day he'd discover his destiny, and it would be a momentous and onerous one indeed. He knew that he would be called upon to lead the unenlightened, and tasked with a nigh-impossible challenge of ambiguous moralities. But he also knew that bravery was forged between shades of grey.

—Opening passage from Of Wolves and Men: The Autobiography of Lon Mythos Toller

Lon Toller was an American hero.

The United States government was generous in its gratitude. Officials bestowed upon him their two highest civilian awards: the Presidential Medal of Freedom and the Congressional Gold Medal. They also expanded the scrawny occult section of the National Archives into the Lon Mythos Toller Wing (Lon legally changed his name so that his countless awards and medals weren't besmirched with the loathsome moniker "Boris"). And the president took several opportunities to publically laud Lon and stoke his flourishing celebrity.

He became a symbol for the American spirit, the heroic face of the country's triumph over the "Full Moon Massacre" (a title created by Fox News, which unfortunately stuck).

After a Herculean internal struggle, Lon decided to take just about every offer that came his way. A publishing house advanced him three million bucks *(Three! Million! Bucks!)* to write his account of the Full Moon Massacre. There were also endorsement deals from Nike, Gatorade, Cadillac, and Gillette (they digitally added scruff so it looked like he had something to shave); a lucrative multiplatform partnership with Apple to become the new face of their iPod commercials; and, coolest of all, a marketing deal with Wizards of the Coast, the publishers of *Magic: the*

Gathering, which included a stake in the company and consultation on the game's future expansions.

Hollywood called! Lon created and executive produced a syndicated pop culture show, "Lon Toller's Grimoire Daily," covering videogames, collectible card games, horror, fantasy, and vintage sci-fi. He also began working with a major film producer to develop a trilogy of movies about Demetrius Valenkov, and he presented at the Academy Awards. Best Picture, naturally.

These were but distractions, however.

For Lon had a greater calling, one that he alone could answer. His new resources had to be put to their proper use. He was compelled to learn more about the curse that had befallen the House of Drăculeşti and to prevent such evil from ever rising again. And he was still haunted by that portrait, hanging so prominently in Valenkov's laboratory, of the beautiful Gypsy woman.

Indeed, his work was far from done.

His most intriguing offer of all came from a renowned university in Massachusetts, which offered him a professorship. Just imagine: a class full of students who *wanted* to listen to him lecture on the mysteries of the occult. He needed to brush up on his medieval witchcraft and Book of Revelations lore. Hell, if werewolves were real, what might he uncover next?

And which distinguished organization sent him a personalized invitation, written in deer's blood calligraphy on weathered parchment? None other than the A∴A∴! (*The Arcanum Arcanorum*, thankyouverymuch). He was also consecrated *Magister Templi* in *The Order of the Silver Star*. You might not know what that means, but it's a big-ass deal. His students would refer to him as "Magister Toller." Had a ring to it.

As a signing bonus, Nike bought him a duplex townhouse in Brooklyn. His new home, christened *Solomonari Manor,* served as both living quarters and business offices for his Solomonari Corporation. This all happened before he even went back to visit Ohio for his personal effects (of which his hand-painted pewter miniatures were his primary concern). He created a trust for his mom that stepfucker Frank couldn't touch, and he told her he'd be waiting whenever she was ready to break free. In the meantime, he hired a former Secret Service agent as her personal security guard.

Shockingly, Lon escaped the Full Moon Massacre with no major injuries. Just a couple of cuts and bruises, some minor frostbite and, of course, extreme exhaustion. They kept him in a hospital for a week, but all he needed was some good sleep.

He awoke to a phone call from the president, who was on live television to thank him on behalf of the entire nation.

But Lon only had one person on his mind: Elizabeth.

She was, after all, the love of his life. Sure, Agent Tildascow had tempted him for a moment in the heat of the battle. In another life, they'd probably have made a go of it. But Lon's heart forever belonged to his bitch witch Elizabeth. Love triangles were always messy, but he would let Tildascow down easy.

Cell service was out, and Elizabeth had no landline. Since Lon was a national hero, the president sent an official state car to her home at Broome & Orchard, along with a full-time nurse to look after Mrs. Golden while Elizabeth would be gone.

Lon waited impatiently for word that his dark beauty was safe. He passed hours scanning Nike and Apple catalogs, but still he received no word of his gothic goddess. His mind wandered toward the maudlin; if Elizabeth had perished before they'd had a chance to taste each other's physical pleasures, he would forever be tormented by the tragedy of their doomed love.

And then, late into the evening of January the fourth, a perplexed and grateful Elizabeth Anne arrived at Nassau University Medical Center, escorted by Secret Service and a crew from Entertainment Tonight. Lon struggled from his bed to greet his love in person at last. That she towered more than a foot above him was… discomforting, but their love knew no obstacles. They kissed and held hands while Lon listened to her haunting tale of terror and hope.

When Elizabeth finished her narrative, Lon asked for her hand in marriage.

Then everybody had to leave so they could get busy.

FBI Special Agent Brianna Tildascow

Tildascow's concussion was so severe that she underwent an emergency craniotomy to relieve hemorrhaging in her brain. She was provided the best neurosurgeons in the country, and each of them remarked at her outstanding recuperation, often shooting distrustful glances at her DARPA overseers.

When the time came to return to the field, she passed her psych evals on her first go-round.

But before that, she spent long hours in the hospital considering the state of Brianna Tildascow. The little girl who was turned into a predator. The predator who turned into a monster. The monster she still might become if she couldn't hold on.

Ooo. It was all so… so…

So Vagina Monologues.

Tildascow did a lot of sighing in the hospital, waiting for some cosmic answer. But none ever came. Shouldn't this episode have taught her something? Counterbalanced the loss of her parents? Healed those scars, dulled the pain?

And then *poof*, she'd be a "normal" person.

Right?

They offered her a wig to cover the scars while her hair grew back. She refused at first, but when she saw their judgmental looks (*yep, she's gone crazy*), she decided to go with it. No need to give any trickydick psychologist an excuse to keep her off her feet. She even picked out the curly blond one and said hi to Mom in the mirror.

After her release, she threw on some "normal person" clothes and took the train down to Washington to have lunch with Rebekkah Luft.

They laughed a lot, but their only common ground was the werewolf apocalypse and the time *before*. Not exactly levity in motion. But she managed to hold her tongue every time Luft called her "Brianna."

After lunch, Tildascow made herself personable for a private meet and greet with the brass, where she shook the president's hand and pocketed so many awards that she thought they'd made some of them up on the spot. The president laughed when she asked for his phone number, and, yeah, he might've gotten a bit uncomfortable when she pushed the issue. He finally gave her a line to his secretary, so mission accomplished.

She lied to Rebekkah Luft when she told her they'd do it again soon, and then she caught the last train back to New York. There was a stop less than a mile from her apartment in Hoboken, but she kept going. She felt like sleeping in the office, which had just re-opened after weeks of reconstruction.

Reading still gave her a headache, so she passed the train ride watching the winter's last snow collect on the trees. It reminded her of that trip through Transylvania, with the werewolves howling in the forest. And then her cosmic answer came.

And the answer was Fuck It.

She *had* the life she wanted. Sure, it would've turned out differently under other circumstances, but now she was who she was and she fucking *liked* who she was. She'd wanted the drugs and the training and the procedures and she was looking forward to whatever goofiness DARPA threw at her next.

It'd be (*really*) nice if her next enemy wasn't a supernatural monster, but no matter what came, she wanted to protect her home.

She wanted to get back to the hunt.

Yannic Ilecko

Ilecko awoke in a luxurious hospital, sunk into a warm nook in the most comfortable bed he'd ever laid upon. His first visitor was the Romanian Ambassador to the United States, Gheorghe Bălăceanu, who presented him with a medal.

It was a few weeks before he was released from the hospital, with a brace on his left knee and a cast on his right ankle. He went to physical therapy, during which a doctor asked him to do things that he normally did a hundred times within the course of a day. And for this he had to fill out endless amounts of paperwork. If only his hand had been broken, all of this writing would serve as therapy for that too.

There were more awards to come, many of which he was forced to accept over ridiculous dinners with politicians. Thankfully, Lon attended each of them by his side, working the media with a professional verve far removed from the self-defeating child he'd first met.

Lon would often ask what Violeta would think of people they met. He would have expected it to feel intrusive, but instead it was comforting. Lon came to know her so well that they could both speak her thoughts.

Slowly, his memories were cleansed of her death. In a manner of speaking, Violeta was blessedly returned to him.

He had money now, and new opportunities in America. There was no reason to return to his cold grave in Romania, so he donated his farm to a charity and sent money to ensure proper care for his animals. They sent a few things from his home, and then his old life was but a memory.

Every damn one of the Americans felt they were entitled to his time. Unfortunately, they did not speak the language of physical intimidation. They did not speak any language at all, in fact. They simply yelled at each other in English, without ever listening in return. Perhaps they learned this from their television programs, which were incapable of focusing on one image or conversation for a single considered moment.

He learned to appreciate the television for the electronic golf on his Nintendo Wii, a gift from Lon. The technology was beyond anything he'd ever seen—how they could put this money and effort into a time-wasting device was enough to make him grieve again for Zaharius and Demetrius Valenkov and their ignored plight.

And yet he could not deny the pleasure of watching the squat digital representation of himself cheer when his ball sank in the cup.

Lon helped him purchase a home in Brooklyn so they could be close to one another. Ilecko didn't understand the legal details of such a transaction; the mortgage and insurance and taxes seemed unnecessarily complicated. Would they not be content to agree that the house cost a certain amount, and that amount was less than the government had awarded him? It should have been a simple issue of subtraction.

Often while Lon was busy, Ilecko would walk through the city of Brooklyn. One day he spotted a man giving rides on a horse-drawn carriage. It felt nice to see this reminder of his life in Romania. And so he asked the driver for information—it was interesting that Americans did not feel as though *he* was entitled to *their* time—and soon he took a job with the company. They paid him a modest amount of money—less than it cost for his monthly electricity, which was only important for his golf— but it gave him something to do. Lon convinced him to buy the company, which became another complicated legal matter and resulted still in less money than it cost for his monthly electricity.

Ilecko spent a great deal of time with the American woman while she recovered from her injuries. He still could not pronounce her last name, but she permitted him to call her "Brianna." He appeared to be the only one with such a privilege. He did not know what was growing between them, but he wasn't prepared to replace Violeta in his heart.

When he broached this subject with Brianna, her response was quite surprising, and not altogether unpleasant.

"That's fine," she said. "It's not like I'm gonna *love* the shit out of you."

President William Weston and America

Only hours after giving the command to murder a million souls, William Weston was branded as the country's savior. He won the hearts and minds of the people with his frank talk about the losses in New York, verbalizing the peoples' survivor's guilt even as they silently basked in relief that the werewolves hadn't reached their doorsteps. Soon his official portrait was commonly found in American homes, next to the vacation pictures, family portraits—and wolfsbane.

The Weston administration hardly emerged scot-free, however. There were questions about Valenkov's visa and suspicions about his ulterior motives. The press demanded the opening of the sealed White House records while scrutinizing the official timeline, the involvement of each staff member and, particularly, the government's potentially morbid contingency plans.

Teddy Harrison decreed the company line: While the United States government evaluated the werewolf threat, every option was considered. That phrase, "Every Option Was Considered," made worldwide headlines as pundits speculated upon its meaning. Officials refused to elaborate.

Documentarians discovered grainy video, supposedly taken on the evening of January 2, which depicted a plane that may have been a B-1B bomber dropping dozens of small objects over the city. But how could it be that none were ever located?

In fact, the AD24 smart bomblets with the Sorcerer payload were tracked by GPS and recovered in mere hours by special ops strike teams, including some from the Shadow Stalker division. In recovery mode, the bomblets emitted a nausea-inducing sonic blast when lifted by unauthorized users. Refraction coating made them appear like rainbow blurs in photographs. Even in this surveillance age, no convincing evidence of their existence emerged.

The so-called Full Moon Massacre fascinated the world. Werewolf-related books flew off shelves as new ones arrived every day. Personal accounts were in abundance, and the public found each one more captivating than the last. Journals dedicated to the occult rose to outsell celebrity lifestyle tabloids. Conspiracy-driven headlines burst from supermarket racks: HITLER WAS A WEREWOLF! MARILYN MONROE'S KINKY WOLFMAN LOVER! JFK'S "MAGIC BULLET" MADE OF SILVER?

Werewolves took their place in the pantheon of conspiracy theories, alongside aliens, superflus, cure-alls, and other things that go *kaboom* in the night. The most disturbing rumor, and also the most persistent, was that the government had a secret underground laboratory in which they were running experiments on captured werewolves: "Area 52."

Recovery efforts in New York were arduous. Real estate and tourism tanked, insurance companies buckled, and the struggling unions pressed harder than organized crime. Paranoia grew to dangerous levels and there were just too many guns in the city. The economic fallout reached well into the trillions. Globalizing technology allowed more companies to leave the metropolis, diminishing the city's necessity. Such repercussions kept the wound from healing. The psychology industry flourished and state governments established programs to send counselors to offices and schools.

Nevertheless, Weston's administration enjoyed unprecedented political opportunities while he had the attention of the American people. He seized the moment, tackling previously gridlocked issues like election reform, corporate taxation, and gun control loopholes, while squelching the special interest groups that had held them hostage. Science and defense technology were also newly important to Americans, so federal standards to foster cooperation among researchers were easily passed. Congressmen who dared vote against Weston faced outrage among their constituency.

William Weston, the man, had nightmares about that pivotal moment in the Situation Room for the rest of his life. In his dreams, the members of his security council transform into werewolves as he pleads with them to disarm the weapon. His team of doctors and psychologists has recommended that he not run for a second term, but he and his family remain undecided.

Dr. Jessica Tanner

The days following the werewolf crisis were hard for Jessica Tanner, and an outright nightmare for the CDC.

Their decision to extract an infected werewolf from the New York quarantine ignited a firestorm of outrage. When a traffic camera revealed that a creature had been on the loose in Atlanta, the media called for their heads.

Headlines renamed the organization "Set Disease Free."

President Weston lauded the efforts of the entire team, but Jessica stepped down from her position as Director of the CDC. It was the right choice for her regardless of public sentiment; she would be happiest where she belonged: in a laboratory. She quickly decided that relinquishing the administrative duties was the best decision she'd ever made.

It was funny, she supposed, how life can dump you in the most unexpected places. After countless hours on the opposite side of the table, Jessica joined the Department of Homeland Security's Science and Technology Directorate, putting her in bed with USAMRIID's Select Agents Division as the joint head of the lycanthropy virus team.

There were long hours and too many dead ends, but they kept her from dwelling on her empty bed. And moving across the country helped her gain distance from her sorrows.

And no, she wasn't hopeless without Richard. As the scientific community banded together, Jessica found inspiring new colleagues—and friends.

She wished Richard could have experienced this new collaborative mindset. And the new, independent Jessica. But a part of him would be with her forever: Miraculously, the IVF treatment took. She was pregnant.

Parenting would be daunting, especially as a single mother with so many responsibilities. But she'd gotten a head start.

In an unnamed laboratory hidden deep beneath the wildlife refuge on Protection Island, five miles off the coast of Washington State, Jessica was working on a top-secret project.

She was raising Zaharius Valenkov IV.

GRATITUDES

A wide variety of wonderful people were generous with their time and talent to help me bring this novel to fruition. One of the best things about having finished is that I finally get a chance to rave about them.

(And if I got something wrong, I'll betcha it's my fault and not theirs.)

ON INSPIRATION

Curt Siodmak wrote the 1941 film *The Wolf Man*, in which he created the lore of the werewolf's connection to the pentagram and the wolf man poem. **Lon Chaney, Jr.** played the cursed Lawrence Talbot and the wolf man. **George Waggner** produced and directed.

Monster makeup guru **Jack Pierce** defined the look of the werewolf in *The Wolf Man* and **Rick Baker** revolutionized it in *An American Werewolf in London* (1981).

John Landis wrote and directed *An American Werewolf in London*, the movie that ruined my childhood and began my fascination with werewolves.

Bram Stoker wrote the 1897 novel *Dracula*.

Bela Lugosi played Bela, the cursed Gypsy who infected Lawrence Talbot in *The Wolf Man*. In the 1931 film *Dracula*, he defined the role of Count Dracula.

Gerry Conway wrote many of the best issues of *the Amazing Spider-Man*, including issue #124, "The Mark of the Man-Wolf!" (art by **Gil Kane**). A Book & Record set of that story fueled so many of my nightmares that I finally made my father break the record. Spider-Man was created by two of my favorite influences, **Steve Ditko** and **Stan Lee**.

Stephen King wrote the most terrifying novel I've ever read,

Pet Sematary. His book about the craft, *On Writing,* has served as my inspiration and my crutch on many occasions.

I've also been inspired and educated by the works of **Shane Black, James Cameron, Wes Craven, Cameron Crowe, Michael Crichton, Frank Darabont, Richard Donner, William Goldman, Lawrence Kasdan, George Lucas, Aaron Sorkin, Steven Spielberg,** and **Joss Whedon.**

Judy Burns taught me how to take an idea and make it a story.

ON SCIENCE & TECHNOLOGY

Dr. Paula Cannon, an associate professor of molecular microbiology and immunology at USC, took the time to assist me with the intricacies of the lycanthropy virus and the Sorcerer bacteria, as well as the politics of government and private scientists. She gave me a tour of her laboratory and shared her fascinating research into a cure for AIDS.

Diana Colleluori, PhD in Biochemsitry, reviewed my jargon.

Demetrius Valenkov's meditation techniques are an amalgam of the practices he and I researched. **Dr. James Hopkins** directed me toward Pythagoras' concept of the Harmony of the Souls and inspired Valenkov's harmonic therapy. Dr. Hopkins is an old friend, and he has enlightened me with his astounding talent and wisdom in so many ways. Please visit him at harmonixhealing.com.

I created Brianna Tildascow's artificial savant syndrome from research and imagination. Forecasts of her physical augmentations were born from my studies for another project, which was inspired by the work of **Ray Kurzweil** and his book *The Singularity is Near: When Humans Transcend Biology* (Viking Press, 2005). Learn more at kurzweilai.net.

Rick Loverd and **Jennifer Ouellette** from the Science & Entertainment Exchange put me in touch with a number of brilliant scientists, including Dr. Cannon and Mr. Reed. Their website is scienceandentertainmentexchange.org.

Anna Murdock, RN, helped with medical terminology.

My dear friends **Jay** and **Lisa Orlandi** shared their experiences with In-Vitro Fertilization, helping me describe Jessica Tanner's physical trauma.

Timothy Reed lent me his expertise in the realm of optical physics. We had great fun discussing theoretical spectral catalysts and inhibitors for the lycanthropy virus.

I pieced together Jessica Tanner's anti-quorum-sensing technology from an article in *Discover Magazine* ("Field Notes," September 2010). The article, by **Dava Sobel,** explored the research of chemist **Helen Blackwell** into QS-resistant compounds. Graduate student **Margie Mattman** and biochemist **Andrew Palmer** are also credited in the article.

Ira Sterbakov, best father in the universe (and crackerjack/crackpot physicist and mathematician), introduced me to the subject of heuristics as I designed Tildascow's problem-solving methodology.

The sunrise/set and moonrise/set times presented are accurate to the corresponding dates from 2009/10.

ON LAW ENFORCEMENT & MILITARY

Attorney **Jason Alderman** proposed legal ramifications for President Weston.

Ian Anderson was invaluable in helping me understand every aspect of Brianna Tildascow's life in the FBI. We discussed a wide variety of topics, including her relationships, her job structure, her interrogation techniques and FBI culture in general. Mr. Anderson also provided advice about firearms and tactical combat. **Matt Senreich** put me in touch with him.

Sergeant Christopher Angelone, USMC Scout Sniper (Ret.) talked me through sniper technology and assisted with dialogue in the attack on New Year's Eve. **Jerry** and **Chris Scarmuffa** put me in touch with Sgt.

Angelone.

Dwight 'Cpt Awesome' Cenac and **Moe Suliman** also provided firearms advice.

Chief Warrant Officer Jonathan Hulse of the 1-82nd Armed Recon Battalion (Attack) (Airborne) was my guide through the world of the US Army and their helicopters. In his downtime between flying combat missions in Iraq, CW3 Hulse E-mailed long, detailed descriptions of the Apache and Black Hawk helicopters, Army society, and the pilots' dialogue. **Mel Cherney** put me in touch with CW3 Hulse.

Colonel Tim Wray, US Army (Ret.) provided legal and military advice in regard to Operation Wolfsbane and the fallout for President Weston. Col. Wray's son, **John Wray**, put me in touch with him.

My research suggested that the government might consider detonating a nuclear weapon over New York in order to thoroughly eliminate the werewolf threat. I chose to pursue the biological weapon simply because it was a more palatable scenario for entertainment purposes.

ON ROMANIA

The accounts of Vlad II Dracul and Vlad III Dracula's military achievements are accurate according to historical records. My description of their fictional secret castle was drawn from other Romanian castles linked to the Basarab lineage: Bran, Poienari, and Hunyad.

Claudiu Trandafir contributed all of the Romanian translations in the novel. He also undertook tireless research on topics from Romanian history that aren't readily available in English, particularly in regard to Vlad II Dracul's wives and the history of the Order of the Dragon. My great friend **Paul Kim** put me in touch with Mr. Trandafir, and **Garrett Frawley** also offered assistance with Romanian translations.

ON THE BOOK

Bob Boardman, my tireless editor, had a deft touch that cleaned the whole house without moving any of the furniture. You can find him at RobWrite.com.

Rob Prior created the cover art, as well as concept images.

Manny Galan, an all-star supporter, finessed the cover design.

Katrin Auch solidified the book and cover design, tolerated my nitpicking of fonts and wording, and assisted with marketing materials. See more of her work at KatrinAuch.com.

MISCELLANEA

Mike Fasolo, Renae Geerlings, Fred McFarland, Robert Taylor, Robin Taylor and **Brian Turner** provided feedback on early drafts.

Christa Starr was a spectacular proofreader, nitpicker, supporter, and advisor. She also authenticated Lon's goth playlist.

Sandra Rohr, my second mother, gave me a grammar lesson.

Dan Amrich educated me on Lon's taste in Bach.

Kevin Weinstock supplied architectural lingo and partnered in several of my crimes during a frantic research trip to New York.

Rebecca Brooks, Rich Hatem, Brad Meltzer, and **Josh Ortega** also took the time to give me much-appreciated advice.

Zoa Keith always kicks ass on my behalf.

The City Under the Moon website was created by **Craig Fisk,** with assistance from **Jonathan Coates** and **Matt Hancock.**

Allison Binder is my rockstar entertainment lawyer. The best thing about having her on your side is that you'll never have to come up against her. Thanks also to my agent, **David Saunders,** who—despite what they say—always takes my calls.

"Bawk Bawk" to my friends and family at Robot Chicken.
"Oh, bye there" to my friends at the One of Swords podcast.
And a very special thanks to my loyal and devoted Freshmen fans.

My home team, supporters and advisors:
Amy Freese, Amy Neely, Anna Murdock, Brian Turner, Caroleigh Deneen,
Christa Starr, Clare Green, Dan Amrich, Dan Milano, David Freese, Fred
McFarland, Jay Orlandi, Katrin Auch, Kevin Weinstock, Lyman Massey,
Mack Culkin, Matt Senreich, Mila Kunis, Momma Rohr, Rich Hatem, Zoa
Keith, and my co-pilots and cheerleaders, Bill Itzstein and Seth Green.

"Think where man's glory most begins and ends,
And say my glory was I had such friends."
-William Butler Yeats

For
Ben and Derek, who taught me how to be a friend and a man.
Poppa Sterb, who saved me, supported me, and believed in me.
Lisa, the best wife I could never have imagined.
And our glorious children, Sophie Pie and Sammie D.

March 2012

ABOUT THE AUTHOR

Emmy-nominated writer Hugh Sterbakov was born and raised in Philadelphia. He attended Ithaca College in New York for his BFA in Cinema and Photography, and then moved to Los Angeles, where he earned an MFA in screenwriting from UCLA

He has sold TV and feature scripts to AMC, Paramount, Urban Entertainment, G4, Fox, SyFy and Disney, and developed projects with industry icons including Donald De Line, Gale Anne Hurd, Don Murphy, and Ben Stiller. He has twice been nominated for Emmys, for Robot Chicken: Star Wars and Robot Chicken: Star Wars: Episode III. For the latter, he won an Annie Award for Best Writing in a Television Series.

Hugh wrote the critically acclaimed comic book Freshmen, which he co-created with Seth Green. Freshmen and Freshmen II are available in graphic novel form. Hell & Back, a stop-motion feature film written by Hugh, is currently in production at Shadowmachine Films, featuring the voice talents of Nick Swardson, T.J. Miller, Mila Kunis and Danny McBride.

He lives in Los Angeles with his wife and two daughters.

To order additional or autographed copies of

CITY UNDER THE MOON

please visit

www.cityunderthemoon.com

Also visit

www.facebook.com/CityUnderTheMoon

On Twitter: #CityUnderTheMoon

Made in the USA
Lexington, KY
12 May 2012